Praise for *The Sound Between tl*

"In her second novel, Barbara Linn Probst delivers yet another powerful story, balancing lyrical language with a skillfully paced plot to build a sensory-rich world that will delight those who loved *Queen of the Owls* and win countless new readers. Offering a deep exploration of the search for identity and connection, *The Sound Between the Notes* reminds us to embrace everything we are—and everything that's made us who we are."

—**Julie Cantrell**, *New York Times* and *USA TODAY* best-selling author of *Perennials*

"Beautifully told, *The Sound Between the Notes* is a story of tragedy and triumph, of the push and pull of family, of the responsibility we feel to ourselves and those we love. Once I started the book, I couldn't put it down until I reached the last gorgeously written note."

—**Loretta Nyhan**, author of *The Other Family* and Amazon charts bestseller *Digging In*

"Family ties can bind or blind us—even with relatives we've never met. In *The Sound Between the Notes*, trails of music connect generations separated by adoption—while the same notes threaten a family believed sewn with steel threads. In this spellbinding novel, Barbara Linn Probst examines how the truth of love transcends genetics even as strands of biology grip us. Once you begin this story, suffused with the majesty of music and the reveries of creation, the 'gotta know' will carry you all the way to the final note."

—**Randy Susan Meyers**, international best-selling author of *Waisted, The Comfort of Lies*, and *Accidents of Marriage*

"As soaring as the music it so lovingly describes, poignantly human, and relatable to anyone who's ever wondered if it's too late for their dream, *The Sound Between the Notes* is an exploration of our vulnerability to life's timing and chance occurrences that influence our decisions, for better or worse. Probst creates her trademark intelligent suspense as Susannah, an adoptee trying for a mid-life resurrection of an abandoned music career, confronts lifelong questions of who she is. A story that speaks to our universal need to have someone who believes in us unequivocally, and how that person had better be ourselves."

—**Ellen Notbohm**, award-winning author of *The River by Starlight*

"Probst writes very well and convincingly. The characters are well drawn and the tight plot is just one agonizing twist after another. . . . The climax, on the night of her performance, is a tour de force steeped in suspense, and Susannah's subsequent revelations are satisfying and authentic. A sensitive, astute exploration of artistic passion, family, and perseverance."

—*Kirkus Reviews*

"A great story that had me turning the pages nonstop, a tale of passion, identity, and art . . . *The Sound Between the Notes* is so beautiful, so lyrical, so musical that it was hard to put down. It is a story that will not only appeal to fans of music but to mothers and anyone looking for a good read. This is a wonderful story from a skillful writer, one that appeals strongly to the heart. It features awesome characters, a twisty plot, and gorgeous writing."

—*Readers' Favorite*

Praise for *Queen of the Owls*

"A nuanced, insightful, culturally relevant investigation of one woman's personal and artistic awakening, *Queen of the Owls* limns the distance between artist and muse, creator and critic, concealment and exposure, exploring no less than the meaning and the nature of art."
— **Christina Baker Kline**, #1 New York Times bestselling author of *A Piece of the World, Orphan Train*, and *The Exiles*

"This is a stunner about the true cost of creativity, and about what it means to be really seen. Gorgeously written and so, so smart (and how can you resist any novel that has Georgia O'Keeffe in it?), Probst's novel is a work of art in itself."
— **Caroline Leavitt**, best-selling author of *Pictures of You, Cruel Beautiful World*, and *With You or Without You*

"*Queen of the Owls* is a powerful novel about a woman's relation to her body, diving into contemporary controversies about privacy and consent. A 'must-read' for fans of Georgia O'Keeffe and any woman who struggles to find her true self hidden under the roles of sister, mother, wife, and colleague."
— **Barbara Claypole White**, best-selling author of *The Perfect Son* and *The Promise Between Us*

"Probst's well-written and engaging debut asks a question every woman can relate to: what would you risk to be truly seen and understood? The lush descriptions of O'Keeffe's work and life enhance the story, and help frame the enduring feminist issues at its center."
— **Sonja Yoerg**, best-selling author of *True Places* and *Stories We Never Told*

The Sound
Between
the Notes

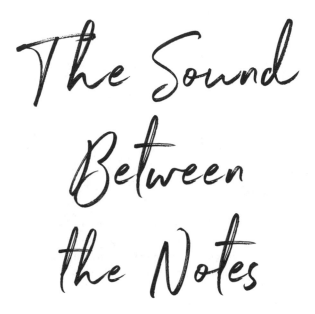

The Sound Between the Notes

A Novel

Barbara Linn Probst

SHE WRITES PRESS

Published 2021
Printed in the United States of America
Print ISBN: 978-1-64742-012-3
E-ISBN: 978-1-64742-013-0
Library of Congress Control Number: 2020913973

For information, address:
She Writes Press
1569 Solano Ave #546
Berkeley, CA 94707

She Writes Press is a division of SparkPoint Studio, LLC.

this isn't
a contest but the doorway

into thanks, and a silence in which
another voice may speak

Mary Oliver, from *Praying*

Part One

The Audition

Do not take up music unless you would rather die than not do so.
Nadia Boulanger, renowned composer and piano teacher

Chapter One

now

S usannah looked at her watch. Seven minutes to go.

Really, there was no reason to be so nervous; she'd done this plenty of times over the years. It was like pulling on a pair of familiar boots or diving into a pool—muscle memory, they called it. It had been a long time since she'd sat like this, waiting on a folding chair for someone to open a studio door and beckon her inside, but her body remembered. And her emotions. They definitely remembered.

Fifteen years, Susannah thought, since she had auditioned for something this important. But the music world didn't change, even if the musician had. Auditions were rituals, stylized to maximize their gravity. She'd been to enough, before she walked away, to know what was on the other side of that studio door. A big windowless room, where a Steinway grand piano would greet her, its lid raised like an ebony sail. A panel of judges with their clipboards and cool professional smiles. A clock on the wall. Only the details varied: the color of the judges' clothing, the piece she had picked to play.

Fifteen years was a long time. So was seven minutes.

She raised her eyes to scan the hallway. A Styrofoam cup, abandoned next to a wastebasket, cast a shadow like a misshapen halo on the blackened planks of the hardwood floor. She couldn't help wincing. What pianist would bring coffee to an audition? You needed to be quiet inside, not revved up. She was already revved up enough, with an excitement bordering on panic.

An elevator pinged in the distance. There was the clang of a radiator, and then the hallway was silent. She looked at her hands again. The ridge of her knuckles, the thin gold band. The blue veins just below the surface, like a road to somewhere.

Or nowhere. That was always a possibility. Vera had been confident that the solo was hers if she wanted it, but Vera was like that, arrogant and imperious. Susannah knew—and she knew Vera did, too—that there weren't any guarantees in the music world, no matter who you were or what famous teacher had recommended you.

"Susannah Lewis?" A tall man with a neatly trimmed beard opened the door and squinted at her over the top of his glasses.

She sprang to her feet. "Yes. Here." Her voice caught, eager and high-pitched. Good lord, she sounded like a schoolgirl instead of a woman nearing forty.

"You're on in five minutes," he told her.

"Yes. Thank you."

The man gave a quick nod and slipped inside the studio, pulling the door shut behind him. Susannah dropped back into the chair. Five minutes to relax, clear her mind, let the music find its way into her hands. She squared her feet, heels aligned with the edge of the floorboard, and tried to ignore the sounds filtering through the oak door. Arpeggios and chromatic sevenths. Rachmaninoff, that showy part of the *allegro agitato*. Not her style. Even though they had been given strict instructions to avoid overlapping, she had arrived early and glimpsed the young man who was auditioning before her. His youth had shocked and dismayed her.

She bit her lip, willing herself not to think about the young man or what she had been like at that age or how long it had really been since she'd offered her music—and herself—to a panel of strangers. She couldn't help wondering what Aaron would think if he knew what she was up to. There were no secrets in their marriage, yet she hadn't dared to tell him about the audition. If she didn't get picked, it wouldn't matter. And if she did? Well, she'd deal with that later.

If. So much weight and yearning in those two letters, that tiny syllable.

The elevator pinged again. Susannah looked at her watch: four minutes to go. She wiped her palms along the side of her skirt. Then she realized that the hallway was silent, no more Rachmaninoff coming from the other side of the oak door. Had the other pianist finished early? The silence could only mean one thing. He'd been dismissed.

Her pulse shot skyward. The committee was only listening to three people, four at most; that was what Vera had told her. They had to make it look like an actual selection based on merit, not convenience driven by desperation. Three or four pianists, each willing to step in and replace the Chilean virtuoso who'd been whisked off to rehab. And she was one of them, thanks to Vera—the renowned piano teacher who had shocked the music world by leaving the concert circuit at the height of her fame and devoting herself to her pupils. Susannah had become one of those pupils when her feet could barely reach the pedals.

She had told herself, getting dressed and heading into Manhattan, that this was simply a job, a nice return to the professional stage after fifteen years of safe little programs at churches and schools. But there was something else, and that *something else* was the reason her heart was beating such a crazy staccato.

The rapture. She'd lost it, somewhere between teaching and giving workshops and making sure that everyone's life was running smoothly. It wasn't Aaron's fault, maybe not even her own fault. But the magic was gone, and she wanted it back.

She had known and not-known, avoiding what she knew—until she sat down at the piano, right after Vera's call, to run through what she thought of as her reliable repertoire. Late Brahms, those show-stopping Chopin mazurkas, the Pathetique—like flipping through a wardrobe of familiar clothes in case she decided to audition, as Vera had insisted. She was halfway through Brahms' Opus 118 when a strange sensation made her stop in in the middle of a measure.

I'm not here. I'm not hearing the music.

Hear, here. They were the same thing, listening and knowing she existed. They had always been the same, their union so intrinsic to who she was that she'd never questioned it—until, suddenly, its absence assaulted her.

The door swung open. "We're ready for you."

Susannah rose, more slowly this time, and followed the bearded man into the studio. The first thing she saw was the Steinway: a concert grand, splinters of light glinting on the mahogany surface. There was no sign of the young man. She noticed a door on the far wall, below a red exit sign. He must have left that way.

"Mrs. Lewis? Or is it Ms. Lewis?"

A woman held a notebook in one hand, a sharpened pencil in the other. Red hair was heaped on her head; a necklace of big amber beads, roped twice, dropped to her waist in descending arcs. Libby Kaufmann, the organizer and publicist. Not a musician, but this wasn't a piano competition. It was a fundraising gala, and Libby was in charge. Next to Libby was an older woman with short gray hair. On her other side, a man in a blue turtleneck uncapped a water bottle.

"Ms. Lewis," Susannah said. The person facing the trio of judges was someone who had existed long before she became Mrs. Lewis. Someone who could exist again.

"I have you down for a Schubert sonata," Libby said, turning a page in her notebook. "D-960. Is that still correct?"

"Yes, that's right." Susannah took the book of sonatas from her bag. "Here, I've got the score. Did you want to follow along?" She didn't know if Libby could read music, but she extended the book anyway.

"Not especially. You keep it." Libby closed the notebook. "Do you need to warm up?"

Susannah met her eyes. For a wild instant, everything rose up in her: the hunger, the longing—then the doubt and the fear. Libby dipped her head, as if she'd seen.

"Just for a minute."

She walked to the piano, the book of sonatas under her arm. Every piano was different: the touch, the response, the feel of the keys. She flexed the pedal, tried a few arpeggios and chords. Yes, good. The keys had a nice weight, a warmth to the tones. Then she opened the book and creased the page with her thumb. She didn't really need it—she'd memorized the piece long ago—yet it felt good to see the notes, like a gathering of old friends.

If this had been a competition, she would probably have chosen one of those virtuoso pieces like the Rachmaninoff. A Chopin etude, maybe, or La Campanella; everyone played Liszt at the big competitions. But this wasn't a competition, and she didn't want to do that. She wanted to play a piece she loved.

Schubert's B-flat major sonata. His final sonata, full of majesty and radiance and the exquisite longing of a man knowing he was about to die.

Each person was supposed to play for twelve minutes, no longer— that's what Vera had explained—but Susannah couldn't do that to the B-flat major sonata. It would mean stopping right in the middle of the first movement. Maybe she should have chosen another piece, one that fit into the time she was allowed, but she'd decided: no, let them hear the piece she intended to play at the concert. Vera had agreed.

Susannah looked at the three people sitting across from her, pencils poised, ready to note her mistakes. Then she thought of Schubert, dying at thirty-one, ugly, isolated, in pain, pouring all of his yearning and ecstasy into the music. No one had the right to play his sonata without the same commitment, the same passion.

She centered herself on the padded bench and readied her hands for the opening theme—the glorious B-flat and the steps up to D, stately and inevitable, and then the C octaves that weren't repetitions at all but a widening, a preparation for the slow return. Her long spidery fingers had always made it easy to play chord after chord, octave after octave, with a purity that lifted the melody right off the keys. For that clean true sound, the hand had to be loose, free, the little finger landing just so on the top notes. It wasn't something she thought about any more than she thought about how to breathe.

Until now, when the finger didn't land, didn't sing.

A jerk, like a hiccup. Then a thud, the sound of wood instead of crystal, as her finger found the key a fraction too late, a fraction too heavily.

Had the panel noticed? It was a small misstep, obvious to her but perhaps not to anyone else. The next measures were fine—then, there it was again, when she used her fifth finger for the B-flat. She could barely reach the top note. And, worse, she couldn't voice the upper line the way she needed to. The sound was coarse, wrong. Tears of frustration stung her lashes. If the top notes didn't soar, the whole thing was ruined.

An instant, that was all she had. Susannah stretched her hand and took the note with her fourth finger. The gesture was awkward—bizarre, really—but the sound was there, just the way it was meant to be. The way it used to be.

She kept going. There was no time to think about what had happened or to register her relief. She kept playing as the music shifted to a new section.

The end of minute thirteen was a logical place to stop, the slow release into silence before the long repeat. Even that was a minute past her allotted time. But the first movement wasn't over. Schubert had wanted the music played twice for a reason, and it was up to the pianist to search for that reason.

If she hesitated, the return to the opening theme would be ruined. You had to do it or not do it—play the whole movement, the way Schubert wanted, or let it go.

Her eyes darted to Libby's face. Libby gave the merest nod, like the flicker of a sixteenth note, so quick that Susannah couldn't be sure.

She kept playing. The first movement was twenty minutes long. She sounded the final chord, held it for the whole five beats, and then looked up, trying to read the faces of the three people across from her. Were they outraged by her presumption, the way she had helped herself to those extra minutes? Nothing. No one moved. No one said, "What do you think you're doing?" or even "Thank you, Ms. Lewis" or "You can go now." She reached up to turn the page. She felt her hand moving through space, touching the corner of the paper.

Their faces were fixed on her, attentive, alert. No one was telling her to stop. Did that mean she could go on?

Susannah could feel the weight of the silence, filling the auditorium.

Vera's call urging her to audition—ordering her, really—had ripped away the veneer of her complacency. In a single fierce instant, Susannah felt the pain of what she had lost. And with the pain came a swell of longing. That longing had brought her all the way to the cracked stone steps of the music school where the auditions were being held, up to the black door with its brass hinges and a doorknocker like a lion's jaw. She had gone inside, waited on a metal chair—needing this, daring to need it.

She pulled in her breath. One more glance at the panel. Then she pinched the corner of the page with her thumb and forefinger. Waited. Nothing.

The hell with it.

She flipped the page with a quick snap of her wrist. One more glance, just to be sure no one was jumping up to yank her off the bench, and then she began the second movement, the andante sostenuto. The deep C-sharp, and the perfect bell-like answer. Angelic, celestial. Music that could break your heart.

She played the whole piece, all the way to the astounding, triumphant presto.

There was a throat-catching moment when she thought her little finger was going to fail her again. It was in the scherzo, those eighth notes right before the trio. The slip was almost imperceptible but she knew she was off, missing the connection, the clarity. Somehow, again, she switched fingers right in the middle of the measure. Another intelligence stepped in, carried her forward—all the way to the crystalline quarter notes in the last movement, all the way to the glorious B-flat and the final measure of the piece, a measure made entirely of silence.

She waited the three empty beats, then dropped her hands into her lap. She didn't dare to look up until she heard Libby say, "Thank you."

For the third time that afternoon, she met Libby's eyes.

"We'll let you know," Libby said. Then she repeated, "Thank you."

Susannah closed the book of sonatas and slid off the bench. Her heart flapped against her ribs. Should she call Aaron and tell him what had happened?

No. Not until she knew if Vera's intervention—and her own bravado—had worked. If it hadn't, she'd rather mourn in private.

—

The trip from Manhattan to Abner's Landing took an hour under the best of conditions and these were the worst, right at the peak of rush hour. Her audition had been scheduled for 4:00, but by the time Susannah left the studio and got her car out of the parking garage, it was well past 5:00.

She stretched her neck, but there was no way to tell how far the line of cars extended in front of her, not with that eighteen-wheeler blocking her view. All she could see was the back of the truck and the words, in bold red script: *How's my driving?*

How's my playing? That was the question. She'd searched Libby Kaufmann's face before she left the studio but Libby, inscrutable, had given nothing away.

Sighing, Susannah inched the car forward. She dreaded the thought of arriving home later than Aaron or James and having them pelt her with questions. She pictured herself insisting, like a child, *It's all because of Vera.* James had never met Vera, but he had heard about her. Vera Evangelista, his mother's famous piano teacher.

Vera had been her teacher since early childhood, the person who'd grabbed her chin one afternoon when she was pouting because she hadn't been invited to Kimberly Morgan's birthday party. "Don't you understand who you are?" Vera had hissed, her face so close that Susannah could see the two stray hairs that poked out of her eyebrows, dark and stiff, like porcupine quills. "You aren't like those other girls. You're a pianist. An artist. Don't you ever forget that."

And she hadn't. All through elementary school, high school, college, she'd done what you had to do if you dreamed of entering the elite echelon of concert-level pianists. It wasn't just the hours and hours at the keyboard. It was the ferocity of your commitment, the willingness to drop everything if an opportunity came your way. You didn't reject a chance to perform because it was inconvenient. You said *great, thank you, I'll be there,* and you went. No matter what, you went.

You couldn't do that with an infant, though. At least, Susannah couldn't. She'd thought *Vera knows my story, she'll understand.* But Vera hadn't understood. She had made that clear.

Susannah twisted her neck again, trying to see around the eighteen-wheeler. There was a whole car-length ahead of him, for heaven's sakes. Why wasn't he moving? As if the driver sensed her annoyance, the brake lights dimmed and the truck inched forward. Instantly, a blue Toyota tried to edge into the space that had just opened. Susannah pounced on the accelerator, claiming the yards that belonged to her.

Vera's phone call, after years of silence, had come at the perfect moment. James, a teenager now, didn't need mothering the way he had when he was small. Susannah had tried, with only partial success, not to feel hurt. And then Vera called.

Vera got right to the point. Her great-niece, publicist for a major women's organization, was in charge of a fundraising extravaganza, a cocktails-and-concert gala to raise money for the organization's five-city expansion. The niece, Libby Kaufmann, had gotten a renowned performing arts center to donate its 1500-seat hall and a well-connected ex-mayor to be the evening's host. With the famous Chilean pianist as their soloist and an admission price usually reserved for high-profile political banquets, the event had become the season's must-be-seen-at gathering of the rich and powerful. Then, when the Chilean pianist had to be escorted—discreetly, of course—to a secluded detox facility, Libby had to come up with a quick replacement. She'd called her great-aunt, knowing how well-connected Vera was to the music world. And Vera called Susannah.

"Do it," Vera had ordered. "I'm getting old, waiting for you to prove I haven't wasted my time."

"This is pretty sudden, Vera. I have to think about it."

"There's nothing to think. It's yes or no. Libby wants to hear a few people—tomorrow. She's saving the 4:00 slot for you. Take it or leave it."

Tomorrow? Vera had to be joking. But Vera never joked, not about music.

"How many more chances like this are you going to have?" Vera had snapped, her voice sharp as a javelin. "None, that's how many."

"It's just a referral. Not a guarantee."

"Don't be naive. Libby needs you more than you need her. I've sold her on your brilliance. The solo's yours—unless, of course, you don't think you're up to it."

Of course she was up to it. The suggestion that she might not be made Susannah angry, as if Vera had offered her a gift and then snatched it away. Well, that was Vera. Praising and insulting in a single phrase.

A flash of taillights jolted Susannah back to the present—the highway, the line of cars. Damn. She'd been lost in her reverie and let the eighteen-wheeler creep forward again without filling the space between them. Before she could react, the blue Toyota cut in front of her.

The hell with it. The same words that had thrust her past the twelve-minute limit at the audition. Tired of waiting for the traffic to clear, she yanked the steering wheel and cut across two lanes of traffic into the right-hand lane that, improbably, was moving ahead at a steady clip.

At last, there was Exit 21. Susannah shot down the ramp and sped the last few miles to the house. She angled the car up the driveway and pulled into the carport. Nearly seven o'clock, but the house was dark. It wasn't unusual for Aaron to get home late, but James—where *was* James? She scrambled for her phone.

There were two texts. One was from James, letting her know he was at Andrew's house working on their civics report. *Back 4 dinner.* The other was from Aaron. *Leaving the lab now. Home soonest. XX.*

Susannah's lips curved in a soft smile. Her two men. She sent James a thumbs-up emoji and dropped the phone back into her purse. Then, on impulse, she turned her hand and looked at her palm. There was a tiny bump right in the center, like a blister about to push through the surface. Was that why she had faltered? She prodded the bump, gingerly at first, then more firmly, but it wasn't painful.

She'd had blisters before. Pianists got used to the cramped muscles and the small sores, the inevitable effect of long hours at the keyboard. You played through it, and it went away. It wasn't like the lumps and moles that doctors warned about, changes that were dangerous to ignore. Her mother had done that—too busy and confident to worry that anything might be amiss—and the cancer had gone undiagnosed until it was too late. Susannah didn't think this was the same thing. Whoever heard of cancer of the palm? Besides, whatever traitorous cells had invaded Dana's bloodstream weren't likely to be lurking in hers; nothing linked their DNA.

No, that wasn't what was making her feel so vulnerable. It wasn't even the audition. It was the unexpected yearning that had bloomed in her chest. The ache for something she'd lost when she wasn't paying attention, and had forgotten to want.

Chapter Two

now

S usannah heard the metallic rolling of the garage door, which meant that Aaron was home. She sprinkled a fistful of grated cheese onto the pasta and wiped her hands on a dishtowel. She hated rushing like this—cooking needed time and care, not the slapdash flinging of basil and mozzarella into a bowl—but was glad she'd managed to put a reasonable meal together before Aaron got home.

She folded a sheet of foil over the dish as Aaron strode into the kitchen, dropping his briefcase against the door. He eased out of his jacket and tossed it onto the back of a chair.

Susannah turned to him. "Long day for you?"

"It was. But a good one. The new lab assistant turned out to be great."

She stepped away from the counter and wound her arms around his waist. "Better than the assistant you had before?"

"A standard deviation better."

"Math snob."

"I prefer research nerd." She lifted her chin for his kiss. "What about your day?"

"Me? Oh, I worked on the sonata. You know, the Schubert?"

It wasn't a lie; in fact, she'd come up with a brand-new fingering right in the middle of a passage. But it wasn't the whole truth. The whole truth was that she had driven into Manhattan to audition for a concert he knew nothing about, and then taken a second risk—more audacious than the first—by playing the entire sonata straight through to the end.

She wanted to tell him, and almost did, but she wasn't prepared for the questions that would follow—or the harder question of why she hadn't told him yesterday, when Vera called, or this morning. Still, there was no real urgency, especially if nothing came of it. That was the most likely outcome, no matter what Vera thought.

Suppressing a sigh, Susannah spread her fingers and grazed them lightly along Aaron's back. The joints felt all right. Loose, the way they were supposed to. No need, then, to mention the stumble on the B-flat or the blister that had probably caused it. Besides, it was impossible to explain the difference in sensation to someone who wasn't a musician.

Aaron wasn't particularly interested in music—except hers. That was what had drawn him to her when they met. He would stand behind her, entranced, while she played Chopin, Brahms, Schumann, the most gorgeous pieces she knew. It had been strangely intimate, as if the intensity of his listening went right through her skin, all the way into the keyboard. As if he were playing it with her.

That was years ago. Maybe he'd missed it, too.

Aaron glanced over her shoulder. "James isn't home yet?"

"He's on his way back from Andrew's. Some civics project. He should be here soon."

"A glass of wine while we wait?"

"Good idea." Susannah stepped out of his embrace and went to open a bottle of Chardonnay. Holding it aloft, she followed him onto the deck.

The house was cantilevered on a rocky crest. Its wide rectangular deck—the first thing she and Aaron added when they bought the place a dozen years ago, exchanging their urban life for the rustic charm of Abner's Landing—offered a sweeping view of the slate-gray Hudson. Susannah lifted her face to peer at the sky. A copper sun, hovering at the horizon, was surprisingly vivid after an overcast day. "Aha," she said. "The sun's coming out from behind the clouds."

"The sun isn't coming out from behind anything," Aaron corrected her. "It's the cloud that's moving, getting out of the way." He gave her an amused smile. "But you know that."

She did know, he had told her that before, but what did it matter? Spikes of gold were spreading across the water, zigzagging from the shallow marshes to the channel that sliced the river's midline. It was the result that mattered, the unexpected illumination.

"I suppose I do," she said. Aaron was a research scientist; he hated inaccuracy. She had been annoyed by his insistence on precision until she realized that sloppy explanations offended him the same way that sentimental music offended her. If you loved something, you wanted others to treat it with respect.

She met his smile, then returned her gaze to the river. A pair of kayakers in red boats cut parallel lines across the channel, their paddles dipping soundlessly into the water. A heron gave a harsh squeal. The plaintive meow of Oscar, their cat, from the other side of the screen door meant that he'd heard the heron too. He swiped at the screen, claws catching on the mesh.

"Either way, it's a beautiful evening," Aaron said. He wrapped an arm around her, gesturing at the bands of topaz and mauve that stretched across the sky. "Did you know there's a scientific basis for the old saying 'red sky at night, sailor's delight'?"

"If you had your way, there'd be a scientific basis for everything."

"Indeed there would."

"Phooey. Where's the fun in that?"

"I'm full of fun." He turned to look at her, and Susannah felt the wordless thrill that was, amazingly, still there between them.

She remembered how it had been, in their early days together. Music had made her feel lush and sensual. She had let Aaron see that, feel that—playing for him in the dim light of her apartment, draped in a loose blue kimono, her arms lifting like birds beneath the gauzy folds.

Suddenly the notion of keeping the day's events from him seemed absurd. Aaron was her husband. She wanted him to be part of this.

"Aaron," she said. He raised an eyebrow, an Aaron-expression that was both ardent and wry. "Seriously. I have to talk to you."

His face shifted at once. "What's wrong?"

"Nothing's wrong. It's the opposite of wrong. Or it might be."

She told him about Vera's call, the audition, Libby's odd response. But not about the experience that had prompted her to accept Vera's offer—the shocking instant in the middle of the F-major Romanze when she realized that her playing had grown dull, ordinary, without the glory she assumed would always be hers.

Another thing that was too hard to explain to a non-musician. Aaron thought her playing was beautiful. Better that he still thought so, even if it wasn't quite true.

"They let me play the whole sonata," she said, "even though they weren't supposed to. I was only supposed to have twelve minutes."

"That's great, honey. They must have really liked you."

"I don't know." She shook her head. "It was weird. No one said a word."

"Well, actions are more important than words. Did they let anyone else play that long?"

Susannah considered the question. There was no way to know if the panel had kept to its strict instructions, although she was pretty sure the young man with his Rachmaninoff had been sent away before twelve minutes were up. Supposedly, there had only been one or two others. According to Vera, who seemed to know everything, the other pianists had played before her. She'd been the last one the committee heard.

"I don't know," she repeated. "Vera was so sure that Libby would pick me. Libby doesn't know anything about music but she trusts Vera's judgment."

"Sounds like you have every reason to be hopeful, then. This could be a real step up for you. A new beginning."

The very possibility she had scarcely let herself name. Susannah's breath caught in her throat the way Oscar's nails had caught on the screen. "It could be."

Aaron gave her a penetrating look. "This isn't like your other gigs."

No, not like her other gigs. Not like teaching at a summer institute or playing for the university centennial. Vera's words echoed in the cavern of her skull. *How many more chances like this are you going to have?*

Vera had answered her own question. *None.*

Susannah searched Aaron's eyes, not sure how to explain. "The concert's turned into a big society thing," she said, finally. "It's going to have major visibility. I could get noticed, reviewed." Her pulse quickened. "It's not Carnegie Hall, but that's not the only way to get noticed."

A flicker of concern dimmed the pleasure on Aaron's face. Susannah knew him, so she understood: he was jumping ahead, his logical scientist's mind flipping through the possible equations. *If x plus q, then y. If x plus p, then z.* Being reviewed could mean praise, attention, offers to perform, a leap to the next level of status and acclaim. Or it could mean humiliation. Aaron was already there, weighing the risk, wondering if it was worth it, trying to protect her from getting hurt.

Yet his calculations were wrong. It wasn't the outer glory she wanted, but its interior cousin, the sense of being a pathway for the music and, through that, of being most fully herself. It was the best thing she'd ever known, and she wanted it back.

In itself, the public setting was nothing; you could play in a giant auditorium and be awful. But without it, you couldn't take flight.

It was something she'd learned long ago, during her very first performance. If you kept the music to yourself, it stayed small. If you played for others, the surrender was deeper, freer, more generous. *Here, I give this to you.* It made the music—and the musician—more real.

That was why the concert mattered. She had drifted so far that only a huge wave could carry her back to shore.

"Are you ready for all that?" Aaron asked.

"Getting noticed?" Susannah couldn't help laughing. "First I have to get picked." Then she grew serious. "If they pick me, I need to do it right. Someone to record the concert, for one thing—a really good recording—and that costs money. Maybe my own publicist, since I don't have a manager. It could add up."

"Yes, understood."

She studied his face. "You're on board? Truly?"

"If it's what you want, sweetheart."

Oh, yes. It was what she wanted.

She saw the leapfrog of emotions cross Aaron's features: approval of the chance that had come her way, anxiety about its unknown cost, and then a bright gleam of desire—as if her new passion had made her into that woman again, the musician with the regal presence and rapt expression, the woman he'd fallen in love with.

"Anything else you want?" He put his hands on her wrists and pushed her sweater up along her arms.

Susannah could feel his eagerness and her own response, the choreography familiar and exciting. Yet another part of her was already clicking through the folders in her brain. Things she needed to do, to prepare for the concert. Things she would have to postpone or reschedule.

She made herself return to the present, to her husband beside her on the deck. "James," she murmured.

"James is at Andrew's house."

"He's going to walk in at any minute. Starving." She put a palm on Aaron's chest, refusal softened by reassurance. The trill of her cell phone sounded from the kitchen.

Vera, she thought, wanting to know how the audition had gone. She'd been too intent on pulling together a passable dinner to call with a report.

No, not Vera. Vera's ring was the aria from the Goldberg Variations. The opening bars of *Für Elise* meant the call was from her father. Susannah cast a concerned look at the screen door. It could be nothing, just Tyler being lonely. Or it could be something. She was never sure, these days.

"I'd better get it." Gently, she removed Aaron's hands and crossed the deck. Oscar stared at her through the screen. "Shoo," she said. She pulled the door open and scanned the countertop for her phone.

"Suzie?"

"Hey, Dad." She signaled to Aaron, miming the lift of a wine glass.

"I'm not disturbing you?"

A plea for permission instead of a greeting; that was how he'd been since her mother's death, nine months earlier. Susannah kept hoping for the return of his puckish humor but it hadn't happened, not yet. Holding the phone to her ear, she pulled out a kitchen chair and sat down. "Of course not. How are you doing?"

Aaron opened the screen door and handed her a glass. She nodded her thanks and set it on the table. Absently, she began to collect the crumbs, still there from breakfast, into a little pile.

"Not so good, but I will be." It was the phrase Tyler had taken to using whenever someone asked. It had been clever at first, then comforting, but now it was simply a placeholder, a way to soften his dejection with an optimism that Susannah wasn't sure he really felt.

"Onward and upward," she replied.

"If the fates decree."

Oh Dad, she wanted to tell him. *You* decree. You have a say in what happens next.

She missed her mother too, but not the way he did. Without Dana, her father was unmoored, adrift. Dana had been the family sextant, calibrating and recalibrating the distance between each of the pairs in their triad, the third point that gave stability to the other two. When Susannah was small, she had longed for the *real mother* whose absence had loomed so large—the birth mother she'd never known—yet the hole left by someone who had actually been there was a different kind of emptiness.

"So. What've you been up to?"

Tyler cleared his throat. "I was thinking I might order that new biography of John Adams. It got excellent reviews."

"Sounds good." Susannah raised her shoulder to squeeze the phone in place while she collected the crumbs. Aaron arched his eyebrow in a question. She motioned him away. *It's okay.*

"I finished the one about Franklin," he said. "I can loan it to you if you want."

"Sure. I'll get it next time I see you." Then she added, before he could ask, "Soon. I promise. We'll find a day next week."

"That'd be great, honey." His voice brightened. "Something to look forward to."

Susannah sighed, wishing her visit wasn't the only thing her father looked forward to. It hadn't always been like that. "Hang in there, Dad," she said. "I love you. And thanks for calling. I appreciate it."

"Love you too, Suzie."

She tapped the *end* icon and stood, dropping the crumbs into the garbage can. She did love her father, but speaking with him was like being pulled underwater, the way James used to grab her around the neck when he couldn't feel the bottom of the pool. It hadn't been that way when her mother was alive. Dana had kept everyone afloat, pointing out the rocks and seaweed, telling them which way to swim.

Oscar, reappearing, rubbed against her shin. Susannah jerked away. Cats were supposed to be aloof but Oscar's demand for attention seemed insatiable. He'd follow her from room to room, sliding along her leg with a mewling sound that was, somehow, both needy and arrogant. She hadn't even wanted a cat, only agreed because James begged and begged, and who could refuse James anything?

Her gaze drifted to the debris from her high-speed dinner preparation, the pine nuts and basil stems and confetti of grated cheese that littered the counter. Aaron had gone upstairs; James wasn't back yet. She could clean up the kitchen or she could go over the scherzo, the third movement of the sonata, while they waited for James. The scherzo was short, less than five minutes.

She wiped her hands, flicking off the remaining crumbs. Her fingers were already twitching. They could feel the music before she reached the keyboard.

Chapter Three

now

Newborn James had been the reason for halting her career. Nearly sixteen years later, teenage James was the reason for resuming it, or hoping to.

James was like a firefly these days, dropping in to bestow his quick beautiful light, then darting away again, off to a world that didn't include his parents. It was what teenagers did, what Susannah herself had done. Yet there were times when she couldn't help yearning for a younger James, the one who'd sat next to her on the piano bench, chubby hands on top of hers, pretending that he too was playing. The sort of thing that present-day James, with hands that were bigger than hers, would be mortified to hear her recall.

Of course, it was his very independence that was allowing her to think *maybe it's time.* A wider radius. A real career.

The two feelings collided in her chest. Nostalgia for a vanished past, a spike of greed for a possible future.

Susannah let out her breath, pushing the thoughts away. Determined to focus on the present, on Saturday breakfast with her family, she reached across Aaron for the pitcher of orange juice. Above them, she heard the clomp of teenage feet pounding down the stairs.

"The prince has arisen." Aaron raised his coffee cup in a mock salute.

James swung through the doorway into the kitchen. "Hey-hey-hey. Are those blueberry pancakes I see before me?" He leaned across the table to pluck a pancake from the stack.

"Take a plate," Susannah told him. "Don't use your fingers."

James plopped into a chair. "Funny advice from a piano-playing mom, but okay." The cat jumped onto his lap. James wriggled a blueberry from the dough and popped it into Oscar's mouth.

"Do *not* do that," Susannah said. "You know better."

"You are exiled," James declared, setting the cat on the floor. Oscar gave Susannah a deadpan stare, then stretched and curled into a ball under the chair.

"You know the rule about the cat at the table."

Aaron touched her arm, code for *relax, honey.* Was she tense? Maybe. Fragments of the audition darted across her mind. The finger that wouldn't respond. The indecipherable expression on Libby's face.

Aaron edged his chair closer to James as he reached for the creamer. "You have a game today?"

"Just practice."

He tipped cream into his coffee cup. "The new coach seems good."

"He's tough. No mercy."

"That's what I meant by good."

James gave an appreciative snort. Then he devoured the pancake in three swift bites and pushed away from the table. "Anyway, I have to go. Patrick's picking me up."

Susannah stiffened. She hated entrusting James to the teenage driving of his friends, but there seemed no way around it. They were all getting their licenses, one after another; James would be next. Patrick, a senior on the basketball team, was eighteen and allowed to have passengers. Forbidding James to ride with him led to unhappy battles that she never won. "It's broad daylight," he'd assure her. Or, "It's just to the gym."

She rearranged her expression into what she hoped could pass for benign acceptance. "Off with you, then."

James grabbed another pancake, pulling out his phone with the other hand. "See you." Head bent, he was already swiping and tapping in that one-handed way Susannah had never been able to master. She hated the constant texting almost as much as she hated letting him drive around with his friends; still, if she complained, she knew he would tell her, "Hey, you have your keyboard, I have mine."

She looked at Aaron. "You going to the lab today?" She didn't say *on a Saturday*. Aaron was in charge of an important grant, with a deadline ahead. Saturday was just another day.

"I have to," he said. "I'm so sorry."

Susannah shrugged. They'd been through these deadlines before.

"I'll get back as early as I can. Weekend evenings are sacrosanct, grant or not." He picked up her hand and gave it a gentle squeeze. Then he frowned. "What's this?" He turned her hand palm-up. The spot was impossible to miss, an ugly lump at the intersection of the crisscrossing lines.

Susannah pulled away, closing her fist. "It's nothing. A blister, probably."

"Let me see." Carefully, he opened her fingers. "Does it hurt?"

She shook her head. *I told you it was nothing.* But she waited while he traced the rounded edge. It had seemed small in the carport. Now it was huge, a mountain instead of a bump. Aaron was quiet, his lips pursed.

"I almost wish it did," she said, finally. "If it hurt, I'd figure, oh well, I've been overdoing it. Every musician knows what it is to play through pain. You just do."

She hadn't wanted to talk about the spot on her hand, as if talking would make it real. But she'd told him about the concert and this was part of it. "It's not that. It's just—I couldn't hit the top notes the way I needed to, during the audition. I was off."

Aaron eyed her thoughtfully. "Maybe you were anxious. You know, overthinking it."

"You mean, it was all in my mind? I was imagining it?"

"I didn't say that. Not imagining. Over-sensitive, maybe."

"No, I can hear it, and I can feel it too. I can't make that clean landing, that separation, so the melody sings."

"You think it's because of the blister?"

"I don't know what to think."

Aaron studied her palm again. It seemed funny for a moment, as if he were reading her fortune. "It's actually two little ones. See? There's a smaller one, next to the spot in the center." Then he took her hand and held it between both of his. "I think you should let Leo Mathieson have a look."

Leo, their family doctor, had seen them through a dozen years of ailments and injuries. Susannah lifted a shoulder. "I have a busy day. Anyway, Leo doesn't work on weekends."

"No one does. Except me, unfortunately." Aaron placed her hand back on the table. "Seriously, honey. Go see Mathieson on Monday, see what he has to say. He can probably give you a cream or something."

Susannah resigned herself. She knew Aaron. He'd pester her until she went. "Fine."

"Really. Call him first thing. He can prescribe something better than that over-the-counter stuff."

Aaron wanted her to agree with him, so she did. But Monday was two days away and the little bump might be gone by then, like a mosquito bite or a patch of poison ivy that got better if you left it alone. She just had to wait it out.

—

The phone rang while Susannah was sorting through the day's mail. Flyers from the supermarket and the discount tire place. The newsletter from James's school, a bill from the tree service.

Her eyes flew to the caller ID. Slowly, she wrapped her fingers around the black rectangle. "Hello?"

"Susannah?" Libby sounded cheerful, almost flirtatious. "Glad I caught you."

Susannah's heart leapt into her throat. She tried to stay calm. Libby was probably being courteous and calling each of them personally, since there weren't many contenders. *Thank you for your time. These decisions are always so difficult.*

"I'm sure you know why I'm calling," Libby said. She gave a sly chuckle. "If you want the job, it's yours."

Susannah barely trusted herself to exhale. Elation. Relief. A giddy happiness. "That's great," she managed to say. "I mean, I'm thrilled."

"So are we." Libby's voice turned brisk. "Come by my office on Monday—say, at two? We'll iron out the details."

Susannah wanted to punch the air in triumph. Then, before the triumph had a chance to take root, doubt crimped the edges of her joy. She opened her fingers. The bump was still there, hiding under a cap of skin. She pressed her left index finger against the traitorous spot—hard, as if she could push it out of her hand, out of her life.

Libby wanted her to come by on Monday.

Aaron was right. She'd better call Mathieson.

They had known Leo Mathieson for years—ever since the day, right after they moved to Abner's Landing, when Aaron needed an emergency tetanus shot. They'd been ripping up the old deck, board by board, when Aaron gouged his arm on a rusty nail. Susannah had driven them straight to the nearest clinic, where they'd met Leo. She had liked him at once.

She didn't like him now, though. Leo was supposed to give her a cream and assure her that the bump was nothing to worry about. Instead, he was regarding her with a troubled expression. "I think you're at the beginning stage of Dupuytren's contracture."

Susannah frowned. "Contracture? What's that, some kind of muscle thing? From playing too much?"

"No," Leo said. "It's not from playing too much."

Her scowl deepened. Of course it was. Pianists strained their hands all the time. It was those repetitive movements you had to make, hour after hour, day after day, if you wanted to master a difficult piece. But you rested, did some exercises, and it got better.

She leaned forward, eager to explain. "I've been playing a lot lately. That's probably what did it."

Leo's face was grim. "I'm afraid this isn't an injury."

Remembering her mother, Susannah blanched. "Is it cancer?"

"No, nothing like that. I'm sorry, I didn't mean to scare you."

"So what is it—this thing I supposedly have?" Her gaze dropped to her palm. The delicate lines, crisscrossing the center. The long fingers that could always span nine notes. The white bumps that were like eggs under her skin, waiting to hatch.

"Dupuytren's contracture." Susannah raised her eyes, and Leo continued. "It's a progressive hereditary disease—fairly common, actually—that causes the fingers, over time, to become bent and unresponsive."

"Unresponsive?" A chill crawled into her limbs. Icy fingers, pushing into her own. "What does that mean?"

Leo opened his hands and placed them on the desk, palms up. "Dupuytren's begins in the palm and spreads, gradually, into the digits. The connective tissue in the palm starts to thicken, creating nodules under the skin, like the little bumps you have. Then the nodules bind together to form cords that extend from the palm into one or more of the fingers, usually the fourth or fifth." He squeezed his left palm with two fingers of the other hand to demonstrate. "Over time, the cords contract, drawing the fingers into the palm. The contraction, or shortening, makes the fingers bend, stiffen, lose flexibility. Eventually, though it can take years, they can't be straightened."

Susannah watched as Leo's fingers arched into a claw. Her stomach mimicked the movement. *They can't be straightened.*

For a wild instant, she wanted to lunge across the desk and grab Leo by the ugly white collar of his lab coat. *You don't have to terrorize me into getting this taken care of. That's why I'm here.*

She willed herself not to move. Seconds passed, thick with everything Leo hadn't said—because surely he understood what his words implied?

Finally he relaxed his hand. "Dupuytren's is rather common, as I indicated, although it's unusual in a woman your age."

Susannah's face brightened. "Meaning I might not actually have it?"

"Meaning it's unusual. That's all."

"Oh." She looked away. The window behind Leo's desk faced the street. Two men in sweatshirts were pointing at their cars and arguing. A woman with a poodle on a red leash stepped off the curb, swishing past them. "I guess I have to take it easy for a little while."

Leo shook his head. "We don't know Dupuytren's exact cause, but we do know it has nothing to do with overuse. Taking it easy won't make any difference. It's genetic, not behavioral." He reached for a notepad. "Early onset and generational patterns are high risk factors. Did anyone in your family have it?"

At first Susannah was confused. She thought of Aaron and James. That wasn't what Leo meant, of course. Then she thought of Dana and Tyler. But they weren't the family he meant either. He'd said genetic.

She stared at him. "I have no idea."

Leo knew she was adopted—that was part of the history he'd collected when she first went to see him—but she'd told him she didn't have any medical information. It wasn't quite true. There was a file Dana had given her when she was pregnant with James, information the agency had gathered from her birthmother. "You should probably have this," Dana had told her. "In case any medical questions come up."

Dumont, Corinne. Susannah had never opened the folder. She knew everything she needed to know about Dumont, Corinne. She'd locked all that away, years ago.

"I don't know," she repeated. A cascade of emotions swept over her—helplessness, resentment, regret. She blinked, then swiped her cheek. To her surprise, it was wet.

Misunderstanding her distress, Leo told her, "It's nothing you did wrong, Susannah. Nothing about the way you practiced." He seemed intent on reassuring her. "You can't blame yourself. It's the genetic lottery, that's all."

Genetic lottery. The irony was hard to miss. She had gotten her musical talent and the disease that threatened it from the same source: two legacies, one that could undo the other.

"Who should I blame, then? My genetic donors?" Then she thought: Oh, what did it matter? She still had the damn disease. "Let's cut to the chase. How can I get rid of this?"

Leo looked tired and old. Susannah saw the bags under his eyes, the deep grooves that framed his mouth, the beginning of an ugly chicken neck. Then it struck her. He didn't know how to get rid of her disease.

Over time, he'd said. How much time? A year, a week, a decade? Six months, like her mother had? What about the concert, and the possibilities that might follow? Was this Dupuytren's thing going to screw that up?

She gave Leo a piercing look. "I can't let anything happen to my hand. Playing the piano is the only thing I know how to do." Her voice dropped. "It's who I am."

Vera had told her that, long ago. Her whole life, the one thing she'd known for certain was that she was a pianist. She wasn't about to let some pimple take that away from her.

"Let's see how it goes," he said. "Dupuytren's progresses quite gradually. It's much too soon to be alarmed."

He was wrong. It was never too soon to be alarmed. The collision of past and future that she'd tried to prevent—only two days earlier, at the breakfast table—slammed into her like a fist.

Part Two

Yellow Rose of Texas

To achieve great things, two things are needed: a plan,
and not quite enough time.
Leonard Bernstein

Chapter Four
then

Fog drifted in from the ocean and left a thin cold glaze on the Adirondack chairs and wooden railing where Susannah had propped her feet. She was slumped against the damp green slats, ankles splayed, hands dangling off the armrests. Normally she'd worry about the fog ruining her hair, but the only people who were going to see were her parents, and who cared how she looked around them?

Her parents rented the same place on the Cape every summer, a big square house with cranberry-colored shutters and a tire swing in the front yard. They loved the place, but Susannah didn't. Maybe she'd loved it when she was little, but she didn't now. For one thing, there was no one remotely near her age in any of the houses that lined their strip of beach. And for another, the clunky old upright in the living room was totally out of tune. How was she supposed to play on something with a dead E-flat and an upper register that sounded like pebbles clattering on tin? There was only so much time she could spend collecting seashells, scouting for beach glass, or holding the platter for her father while he lifted burgers off the grill and announced, the way he always did, "Looks good enough to eat."

She slid lower in the chair, her fingers tapping an idle two-against-three on the wood. From the corner of her vision, she could see her father framed in the orange light of the window, engrossed in his beloved History Channel. Whatever he was watching was making him happy. Her mother, on the other hand, sitting in the Adirondack chair next to hers, seemed distant and distracted.

As if sensing Susannah's scrutiny, Dana adjusted her posture and turned to the ocean. Susannah followed her mother's gaze. The tide was coming in, big dark splotches spreading across the rocks and sand. Wisps of fog settled over the water. A few seabirds hopped from boulder to boulder along the jetty.

"You know," Dana said, pointing at the slope of beach that slanted from the deck to the shoreline, "you learned to walk on that very spot."

Susannah could barely suppress a groan.

You were so tiny and precious, now you're so big.

"You'd take these great big excited steps," Dana went on, ignoring the groan or maybe not hearing it. Her eyes were faraway, as if they were watching a tiny Susannah take those very steps. "It was like you couldn't believe you were really walking—and then *plop!* You'd look so surprised to discover that you weren't upright any more. But up you'd go again, a moment later."

Susannah had heard the story a million times. Part of her wanted to roll her eyes, though another part didn't really mind. It made her sound determined, which was good. You had to be determined if you were going to be a famous pianist.

She twisted onto one hip, tugging at the edge of her bathing suit. The wood was starting to feel slimy against her bare legs; she really should have changed out of her wet suit like her mother told her to, but she hadn't wanted her mother to win. She pulled at the fabric, wincing at the thwack of wet nylon on her skin, and wondered if she could get up and do it now, without an *I told you so* look from her mother.

But Dana was still looking at the beach, not at her, and still talking. "You were barely ten months old. Only ten months, and there you were, walking on the beach. Ten short months since we flew to Texas."

To bring you home.

The rest of the sentence, and her mother's favorite story.

Susannah had liked that story too, even better than the one about how she learned to walk. She'd imagined a big silver airplane, and her parents coming down the ramp like a king and queen, and a beautiful woman in a long white gown handing them a baby. Her. Like a prize they'd won.

Her mother would tell the story while she brushed Susannah's hair. The phone call that came right when she was scrambling eggs for breakfast. *So I could be your mommy.*

A pretty story when Susannah was six. She was sixteen now, and knew better. The phone call was just adoption talk for *your order is ready for pick-up.*

She loosened a patch of skin that was starting to peel, then flicked it away with her nail. She could hear the ocean slapping at the seawall. The fog had thickened, a dense gray wetness that settled on the boulders and the jagged posts of the old abandoned pier. The only thing she could really see in the mist was her mother, tall and straight-backed in the Adirondack chair, her face smooth and silver as a moon.

"I still remember how it felt to hold you, that very first time." Susannah waited for the rest of her mother's story, how she looked right into the baby's eyes—her eyes—and promised to be the best mother there ever was. Instead, Dana's voice grew quiet. It wasn't her regular voice, the one that told Susannah to come in for dinner or hang up her towel, but another voice, low and intimate, like a girl-friend whispering a secret.

"You weren't even two days old, and you had those astonishing blue eyes. The nurse put you in my arms—well, I never thought I'd get to experience that."

"You never thought you'd hold a baby?" Susannah wasn't sure if her mother meant her own baby, a baby she'd given birth to, or a general baby. Any baby.

"Oh, I always assumed I would," Dana said. "I imagine most girls do. But when I didn't, or couldn't, it seemed so unfair, like I was cheated out of something every other woman took for granted."

Susannah didn't know why her mother was talking like this, telling her things she didn't want to know. Maybe it was the fog, the way it shrouded everything, as if they weren't really there.

Dana brushed a strand of hair from her cheek. "No one ever thinks they're going to be—I suppose the word is barren. A terrible word, really. That's why it was so extraordinary to hold you. It was like I'd been redeemed, told I could be a mother after all." She reached across the space between the chairs and took Susannah's hand. "I only wish I could have been the one to grow you, bring you into the world."

Her mother's words were soft, they didn't weigh anything at all, but they sucked the oxygen right out of the air.

Dana laughed, half apology and half joke. "Of course, then you would have been tone deaf, like me. And what a shame that would have been, if you'd gotten my impossible tin ear."

But I didn't, Susannah thought. I got perfect pitch.

From someone else. It wasn't a joke.

She pictured that *someone else* adjusting a music stand, tuning a violin, replacing the reed on an oboe. A shiver raced up her arms. She wondered if Dana could feel it through the fingers she had laced through hers.

A girl in her chemistry class, Darcie, had a cousin who had given a baby up for adoption, but the only reason she didn't have an abortion was because she was too stupid. The cousin hadn't wanted to admit she was pregnant and then, when she did, the clinic wouldn't do it because she was too far along. She'd been mad about that and shut herself in the house till she could get it over with. Someone had gotten the baby, Darcie didn't know who, even the cousin didn't know. It was just someone on a list. It was their turn, and that was the baby they got.

When Susannah heard about Darcie's cousin, it hadn't felt like it had anything to do with her, even though she knew perfectly well that she was adopted. Now, with her mother blabbing away, it was like someone had punched her in the stomach.

She pulled her hand away from Dana's. The fog clung to her skin like lace.

Her mother was always saying how lucky she was to have such an amazing daughter, how special Susannah was. The white organdy dress with a pink ribbon that she'd worn for her first recital. The trip to Boston to meet Vera Evangelista, the famous piano teacher. But Dana had no idea what it was like to make a perfect two-note slur, the way a note passed from one finger to the next and then floated off the key. She only pretended that she did.

Was there someone who would understand?

Of course there was. The very person who had thrown her away.

"Mom." A single flat syllable, like a stone flung into the gauzy air, landing at Dana's feet with a toneless thud. Susannah heard the water slapping at the rocks, the shriek of a gull, and Dana's silence, as if she already knew what Susannah was about to say.

"I want to meet her." She didn't need to explain who *her* was. Raising her eyes, she met Dana's. Two beats passed. Three.

Dana tucked the strand of hair behind her ear. "There's plenty of time for that, sweetheart. When you're eighteen, you can ask to see the adoption papers and put in a request for contact. We've told you that."

Susannah could see her mother's eyelid twitch. It was the way she looked when she was trying really hard to say the right thing. But the right thing had changed.

"You mean I have to wait."

"That's the law."

"But you can ask." Susannah jerked upright, amazed that she hadn't thought of it before. "You can ask the lawyer, the one you used. You're the client, so they have to show you."

Her mother's face grew stern. "It's not like asking to see the deed to a house. You can't barge into people's lives."

"No one's barging. We're asking." Susannah's voice rose with excitement. They could do this; her mother could do this for her. A sliver of fear crept into her elation—or maybe it was guilt, making her want to snatch back her eagerness.

"We're just asking," she repeated. The guilt gave way to defiance. "There's no rule that says you can't ask."

She shouldn't have to beg for something that was hers to begin with. "Just *ask*. She can always say she'd rather wait till I'm eighteen."

She. Her birth mother.

But she wouldn't. Her birth mother wouldn't want to wait a second longer than she had to. Susannah was sure of it. She locked eyes with Dana, refusing to look away.

After an endless moment Dana dropped her shoulders. "All right. We'll look into it when we get home. I'll contact the lawyer who handled things."

Things. Why not say *your adoption*? But Susannah knew enough to keep quiet. She had gotten her way; that was what mattered.

The law firm's office was on the seventeenth floor of a glass building with a two-story lobby, bare except for a Ficus plant in a stone pot and a glossy reception desk across from the elevator. The guard behind the desk checked their IDs and gave them stick-on passes with *Curtis and O'Hanlon* and the number seventeen in dark green letters. Susannah followed Dana into the elevator. She could hear the strains of piped-in music, Mozart's Concerto in C-major, the Elvira Madigan one. She tightened her lips. It was too beautiful for elevator music; they really shouldn't waste Mozart like that.

The Curtis and O'Hanlon receptionist greeted them with a benevolent smile and indicated a triangular arrangement of couches. "Please. Ms. Warren will be right with you."

"Thank you." Dana took a seat in the center of the nearest couch, motioning Susannah to join her. She gave an encouraging nod, and Susannah's heart plummeted. She knew that nod. *See? I'm fine with this. Some adoptive mothers might feel threatened, but not me.*

Susannah could hear the whir and chug of a copy machine, the roar of her own blood. The seconds ticked past, loud as a metronome. She stood by the couch, hands clenched in her pockets—knowing she looked like she didn't want to be there, when she was the one who had begged for the appointment—until, mercifully, the attorney pushed open a glass door and strode into the reception area.

The attorney was sleek and stylish, with a dramatic slant of chestnut hair that brushed the collar of her perfectly tailored suit. "Penelope Warren," she said, extending a hand.

Dana rose. "I'm Dana Richardson. And this is Susannah."

"My pleasure." The attorney motioned to a hallway. "My office is around the corner. And do call me Nell."

Then why didn't you *say* Nell? Susannah thought, annoyed. What was the point of introducing yourself one way, and then changing it?

She bit back the remark and followed the attorney into her office. She didn't want to sound bratty, like someone you wouldn't want to help.

Nell waited until they were settled on the leather couch—sleek and modern, like her haircut—and had declined her offer of coffee or soda. "Here's the situation," she said, steepling her fingertips under her chin. "Our office handled your adoption sixteen years ago, Susannah. That was before I joined the firm, and the person who oversaw the case has retired, off in Florida, I think. So I'm coming into this cold, as it were. All I have to go by is what's in the file."

Susannah strained forward, as if inching closer to Nell would bring her closer to the secret Nell was about to reveal. From the edge of her vision, she could see her mother's wrist and a corner of her navy-blue skirt. *Like I'd been redeemed, told I could be a mother after all.*

Nell's expression was kinder than Susannah had expected. "As you know, when you're eighteen you can search for yourself. But for now—" She paused to glance at Dana. "—for now, the best option is for me to send a request to the Texas agency that arranged the placement, and they can pass it along to the birth mother. She can say yes or no, or she can simply choose not to answer."

Susannah frowned. That didn't make sense. "If they don't get an answer, maybe it means she never got the letter."

Nell's eyes flashed approval of her acuity. "They'll send it certified, signature required, so we'll know she got it. That's the best we can do."

Susannah saw Dana meet the attorney's gaze. A private message seemed to pass between them.

She caught the look, and it made her angry. This was her life, not some little strategy the two of them were cooking up to placate her. She pointed to the file on Nell's desk. "Does it say her name, in those papers?"

"I'm afraid that's confidential."

Nell's fingers edged toward the open folder, and Susannah's voice dropped to a hiss. "Tell me her name." She felt Dana tense beside her on the couch. A spear of remorse shot through her. *I'm sorry, Mom. But I have to do this.*

She wanted to throw her arms around Dana, bury her face in her mother's calm familiar shape. Then she wanted to push them all aside, snatch the folder from Nell's ugly claw, and run screaming down seventeen flights of stairs, to freedom.

"Susannah," Nell began, and Susannah thought: my birth mother's name is Susannah too? Then she realized that Nell was addressing her. "It's not information I can disclose without her consent."

Stealing a glance at Dana, Susannah gathered her breath. "Just tell me this one thing." She hated how needy she sounded, and she knew this was probably hurting her mother. She could almost hear Dana's unspoken question. *Haven't I always been the best mother ever?*

Maybe. But not her first mother.

Somehow she got the words out. "Does it say if she saw me before she gave me away?"

A glint of compassion softened Nell's features. "It's all pretty factual. Notarized signatures, affidavits, things like that."

Dana touched Susannah's hand. "Let's wait to hear from her and you can ask her yourself."

There was a knock on the door. Nell raised an eyebrow, clearly startled by the interruption. "Will you excuse me, please?" She stood and crossed the office, her spike heels soundless on the thick carpet. She opened the door. "Yes?"

Susannah couldn't hear what she was saying, only a blur of words. Nell's back was to her. *Now.* With a swift look at Dana, she leaned across the desk, twisting so she could see the open file. Dana furrowed her brow, about to reprimand her, but Susannah flung her a warning. *Don't you dare.*

She could hear the back-and-forth of voices in the doorway. Quickly, she angled the paper and scanned the jumble of words. Petitioners. The child named herein. Vested with all rights and responsibilities. She spotted her parents' names. Below them, there it was.

Corinne Dumont.

What a strange name. It didn't sound like anyone she would ever know.

She straightened the folder and sank back onto the couch. Nell closed the door and returned to her desk. Susannah saw Nell's eyes dart to the open folder, a concerned look creasing her forehead. She could almost read Nell's thoughts: Oh damn, I didn't close this before I got up?

Susannah glanced at her mother and saw the warring emotions flicker across her polite expression: displeasure, embarrassment, concern. *She doesn't know if I saw anything.* She sat on her hands, itching with what only she knew.

"Please forgive the interruption," Nell said. "My secretary isn't supposed to do that, but there was a call from my son's school."

"Is everything all right?" Dana asked.

"Yes, thank you. They just needed my permission to give him some Tylenol." Dana nodded again, mother to mother. "Getting back to the matter at hand, I'll contact the agency this afternoon and let you know when I hear from them."

"Very good," Dana replied. "We'll stand by."

Susannah said nothing. *Corinne Dumont.*

The person who made her.

The person who could tell her who she was.

She could see the concert program, so clear in her mind. Embossed letters on cream-colored paper. Corinne Dumont, soloist with the Dallas Symphony Orchestra. Corinne Dumont, in concert at Carnegie Hall. She could almost feel the raised script beneath her fingertips.

When a reply came, it was from the director of the Children's Home Agency in a Texas town Susannah had never heard of. Nell Warren summoned them back to her office so she could tell them what the letter said.

Nell folded her hands and studied the paper in front of her. Then she looked at Dana and Susannah, side-by-side on the white leather couch where they'd sat for their first visit. "I'll share the substance of the letter with you," she told them, "since, technically, it's addressed to me."

"Why is it addressed to you?" Susannah interrupted. "I'm the one who wants contact."

Nell peered at her over the top of the paper. "At this point, the agency can only communicate with me." Susannah sat forward, ready to protest, but Nell put up a hand to stop her. "That's the rule, given your age. Would you like me to go on?"

Susannah didn't want to look like a toddler having a tantrum. "Fine."

The Children's Home Agency had reached their former client through her mother, Nell explained, who still lived at the address on file. "They went to her house, since no one answered their letter. The mother was home, and she told them that her daughter—your birth mother—didn't live there anymore, but she gave them the new address."

"They wrote to her?" Susannah said. "Or they went to see her?"

"They wrote," Nell replied. "But the letter came back, unopened. Actually, it was inside a fresh envelope, with a piece of paper." She wet her lip. "It was a handwritten note. Do not contact me about this again. That's all it said."

Susannah glared at the attorney. No way her birthmother would have said that. Not after she'd written to her, and asked so nicely.

Besides, anyone could have written that note. Her birthmother hadn't even signed it. It didn't prove shit.

"How do you know she even *wrote* that stupid note?" She thrust her chin at Nell. "Did any of you people do, I don't know, a handwriting analysis? Were her fingerprints on it?" She crossed her arms. "This is total crap."

Nell regarded her evenly. "I know it's not what you were hoping, Susannah, but your birth mother has the right to give whatever response she wants."

"You have no idea what she *wants*." She wanted to slap Nell's smug little face. "She didn't even *read* the letter, so you don't know what she wants." Her birthmother was probably too busy rehearsing for a concert to read the letter. Someone else had answered it, not her.

"Susannah." The single quiet word, a warning.

Susannah. She wanted to throw her name back at her mother. She didn't care about her manners or her language or what some prune-faced lawyer thought of her.

"It's the response we received," Nell said. "Our letter was sent to the address provided."

"But she never read it." Tears filled Susannah's eyes. This wasn't supposed to happen. If adoption meant you did what was best for the baby and that baby wanted to meet you, then what was best for the baby would be to say yes, I'd love to.

Which was worse, not wanting to meet your own child when you had a chance, or not wanting that child in the first place? Unless there was something really, really wrong with the child. Then, duh, of course you wouldn't want it.

"I'm sorry," Nell said. "But it's her right to say no."

"But *why*?" The words burst from Susannah's lips. "Why would she say no? What's so bad about me that she wouldn't want to meet me?"

"Oh sweetheart." Dana blinked back tears of her own.

"We don't know why," Nell said. "It could be so many reasons, especially if she's kept that part of her life a secret. You shouldn't assume it has anything to do with you, personally."

"Oh, really? Yeah, well, it has *everything* to do with me. It's one hundred percent personal."

Nell gave Dana a quick look. *Over to you, please.*

Dana put her hand on Susannah's. "Susannah dear, you have every right to be hurt. But try to put yourself in her shoes. It was probably a total shock, out of the blue like that. She wasn't prepared."

Susannah wanted to shove her fists into her ears. Dana was right that it hurt, but wrong about putting herself in Corinne's shoes. How could she even *say* that—like that was something a person could do, or ought to do? No one was that noble. It wasn't fair to expect that of her. Dana was always doing that, making her feel like a failure for being selfish and small.

"Your mother's right," Nell said. "It's best to set it aside for now. You can try again in two years."

Susannah slumped against the leather couch. "Forget it."

Nell studied her carefully, as if weighing whether Susannah would listen. "You know," she said. "You were born at the end of what was called the Baby Scoop era. Abortion wasn't legal, and girls who got pregnant 'out of wedlock,' as they called it, were hidden away and pressured into giving their babies to agencies that could place them with couples who desperately wanted them, like your parents. I'm guessing that your birth mother had no real options. Being reminded of you, after all these years, must have been—like your mom said—quite a shock."

Nell gave a soft shrug. "Not long after you were born, it all changed. The women's movement, access to birth control, Title IX that ended the ban on pregnant girls going to regular high schools. There wasn't the same stigma about raising a baby on your own, and adoption rates went way down."

"Lucky me," Susannah sniffed. "Born too soon." Then she looked at Dana and felt terrible because it wasn't her mother's fault, and it had to be awful for her too. Her mother tried so hard. The books. The talks. There had even been a support group for adopted adolescents that her mother had made her join, but they were mostly kids from Korea and China.

She tried to keep the tears from spilling down her cheeks. "No offense, Mom. I meant, like, historically."

"It's okay," Dana said. "None taken." She put out her arms and, without really meaning to, Susannah melted into them. One part of her wanted to lash out and tell them how little their stupid history lessons mattered to her. The other part wanted to curl up in Dana's arms and let Dana tell her how wonderful she was, how beautifully she played the piano.

Any parent would want a child who played the way she did, right?

Only her real parent hadn't.

The only reason her parents got to *fly to Texas to bring you home* was because someone else had left her there, like a package dropped in a trash can. The rest was bullshit.

Chapter Five
then

Even though Corinne Dumont had told her, "Do not contact me about this again," Susannah still assumed that she would try to find her, on her own, the moment she turned eighteen. But she didn't. She'd been admitted to a prestigious music conservatory, where life was busy and complicated. There were papers, performances, competitions. Everything was oriented toward an urgent and demanding future that would pass you by if your attention strayed.

Then she assumed that she would search when she graduated, but she didn't do that either. Life was still too complicated, requiring absolute focus if you wanted to succeed as a professional musician. There no room for the vulnerability that a search for someone who hadn't wanted you the first—or second—time would surely bring. Corinne Dumont had already said no. Susannah had nothing to gain from hearing her say it again.

She moved to New York, eager to launch her career. There were plenty of opportunities to play, but most were just ways to get exposure, not jobs that paid. Even the ones that did pay—accompanying a ballet class, providing background music for a corporate reception—didn't pay very much, and they were hardly the kind of music Susannah had trained for and imagined herself playing. Still, you couldn't be a purist if you wanted to eat.

The only musical events that really mattered were the special evenings that Vera arranged—in Boston, four hours each way by train, and always on short notice. Under Vera's merciless supervision, her best pupils would gather and play for each other in round-robin master classes that always made Susannah feel nourished and renewed. She found herself counting on the inspiration from those evenings as much as she counted on the income from the ballet classes and anniversary dinners.

Part of it was the re-affirmation of her place as Vera's star pupil. She'd held that place for so long that she never questioned her right to it—until Vera pulled her aside one evening and snapped, "You're repeating yourself. We've all heard that damn prelude, exactly the way you just played it. No one wants to listen to you do the same thing, over and over and over again. If you're not developing, it means you're going in the other direction." As if to make sure Susannah understood, she added, "Going stale. Decaying."

Susannah stared at her. "How can you say that? You always tell us to go back to pieces we've worked on before, start again."

"I said start again. I didn't say repeat." Vera threw her a scornful look. "Don't quote me back to myself so it sounds the way you'd like it to sound." With a Vera-like sniff, she went to join the others.

Susannah's heart slammed into her ribs. What was Vera telling her? That her talent could wither? That someone else might supplant her as Vera's favorite? No one had ever believed in her the way Vera did. The only place she had ever belonged was on the piano bench.

She ran after Vera. "Let me try one more time. Please."

Vera was already deep in conversation with another student,

peering over his shoulder at the open score. She looked up and frowned. "You had a turn tonight. There are other people here who'd like to play."

"Just the first page, so I can—"

"You can try next month." Vera's voice was curt. "If you wish."

Susannah shrank back, chastened.

Vera gave her a penetrating look. "Go back to your core. The root of your music. That's my advice."

She had no idea what Vera meant by core. All she knew was that a rift was unthinkable. "All right. I will." She'd toss everything aside, learn a brand-new piece—because Vera was right, her music had gotten lifeless and stale. Vera was always right.

It was all the time she'd been spending on simplistic pieces. Those sing-song ballet exercises, the sentimental show tunes that people wanted for their wedding anniversaries and retirement parties. That was where the money was, but it was making her sloppy, ruining her touch. She had to find a different job, one that paid well enough so she could eliminate the freelance work that was distracting her from her real music.

She got lucky. There was an ad the next week for a position teaching piano at a girls' school in Brooklyn Heights. The previous instructor had left abruptly in the middle of the term. "No scandal, nothing like that," the director assured her. "It was a personal matter, a situation with one of her children."

Susannah didn't care why the instructor had left. The job paid decently; that was the point.

She had only been there for a few weeks when the director asked if she'd be interested in giving private lessons to the more motivated students. "After school. Your own hours, your own price. The parents appreciate getting referrals from us because they know the person's been vetted, but once you make the contact, it's between you and them."

Susannah agreed, grateful for the extra work. Her first referral came a few days later: Charlotte Silverman, seventh grade.

When she arrived at the Silverman apartment, she was surprised to see that Charlotte was Chinese. Her parents were not. Charlotte's mother took Susannah aside to whisper—in that half-smug, half-awed way that reminded her of Dana—that they were eager to nurture their daughter's mysterious talent. "She's been like that from day one," Wendy Silverman confided. "It's obviously in her genes."

Susannah nodded politely, but pinpricks of alertness were dancing across her flesh. "Do you know anything about her biological parents? If they were musical?"

Wendy Silverman shook her head. "All we have are medical records."

"It doesn't matter," she said quickly. "I was just curious."

It was more than curiosity. A new idea bloomed in her mind.

She'd been desperate for answers when she was Charlotte's age, and then hurt when Corinne Dumont refused to read her letter. But maybe Corinne had a reason that nobody knew. Maybe Corinne had been afraid to meet her—maybe she thought Susannah wouldn't like her, or would be disappointed in her—but maybe that had changed and she'd be overjoyed to have another chance.

Susannah had thought, over the years, of trying again. But whenever she thought about it, she'd punted the notion down the road called *later*. If Corinne rejected her a third time, it would make her feel awful, and she couldn't afford that. Nothing screwed up your playing like misery.

Well, according to Vera, her playing had gotten screwed up anyway. "Go back to your roots," Vera had said. What did that mean—the place she came from? *We jumped on a plane to Texas to bring you home.*

Maybe there were people who could tell her who she was. Maybe they were in Texas, waiting for her to find them.

A lot of maybes, but what did she have to lose?

Dana and Tyler had given her a generous check when she graduated from the conservatory. "For something special," Tyler had insisted, "something you really want to do." When Susannah protested that there wasn't anything she wanted, Tyler told her to save the money until there was. She was glad, now, that she had, although it seemed ironic: her adoptive parents funding her journey to find their biological counterparts.

The girls' school had a four-day weekend for Presidents' Day. Susannah bought a round-trip plane ticket to Houston, rented a car, and drove to La Posada, Texas, where the trail had ended seven years earlier.

She had her birth certificate with the date, time, and place—Sisters of Mercy Hospital, La Posada, Texas—although, oddly, it gave her parents' names, Tyler and Dana Richardson, as if the woman who had given birth to her had never existed.

She tried the adoption agency first, as Nell Warren's successor at the law firm recommended, but the Children's Home Agency had gone out of business. Not enough demand to keep it going, she supposed. Girls didn't need agencies to place their babies. They had abortions or they kept them—ever since Murphy Brown did, on TV—or else they wanted to pick the adoptive parents themselves, from newspaper ads and websites. Anyway, no one knew where the records were. The attorney suggested trying the hospital and gave her a note on the firm's letterhead.

Susannah showed the letter, along with her adoption papers, to the clerk in the Sisters of Mercy medical records office. "You're not the first girl to come by like this," the clerk remarked, wetting her fingertip as she searched through a stack of folders. "It's all on computers now, you know. And not near as many, like there used to be."

She gave Susannah a quick glance. "Back in the day, there were a lot of babies got put up for adoption. Girls had their babies and then— whoosh, whisked 'em right off with a social worker."

"Made an adoption *plan*," Susannah said. "Not *put up* for adoption, like cattle." Dana had drilled the language into her.

The woman dropped her eyes. "Right. Sorry."

Susannah waited while the woman searched through the files. "Yep, here it is." She wrote an address on a slip of paper, tore it off the notepad, and handed it to Susannah. "Good luck, honey."

Corinne Dumont. 1274 Mill Creek Road. Lynette, Texas.

A name that was impossible to forget, even though she had half-dreaded, half-expected that someone would tell her: No, she wasn't your birth mother. You wrote to the wrong person, back then. No wonder she wouldn't write back.

Mill Creek Road. Who knew if anyone named Dumont still lived there, after all these years? But it was a beginning. The only beginning she had.

Susannah folded the paper into careful halves, tucked it into her wallet, and pushed through the hospital's revolving door. The Texas heat was thick, solid as a mattress. She gripped her purse as she walked to the rental car, as if the paper might escape.

She checked into the Super Seven Motel in La Posada, threw her suitcase onto the bed, and kicked off her sandals. There was a telephone on the desk next to a laminated folder describing the nearby restaurants and church services. The air conditioner rattled behind her. Susannah dug her toes into the shag carpet and looked at the phone. Then she picked up the receiver and punched two for an outside line. "Information? Do you have a number for Dumont at 1274 Mill Creek Road in Lynette?"

"I have a Beryl Dumont," the operator said.

"At that address?"

"Yes, ma'am. Would you like the number?"

Yes, she would like the number, and no, not yet. She hung up the phone.

Who was Beryl? The mother?

It didn't matter. Whoever she was, she'd know how to find Corinne.

Despite the bright blonde of her bouffant, the woman who answered the door was clearly in her sixties. She stood in the doorframe of the yellow house, big hair framing a weathered face. "Morning," she drawled. "But y'all better not be selling anything."

Surely this wasn't Corinne? No, the woman was too old. "I'm looking for Corinne Dumont."

The woman snickered. "Cah-*rynne* Dew-*mon*," she mimicked. "You mean Coh-reen?"

Susannah turned white, then pink. "Yes. Okay."

The woman dug into the waistband of her stirrup pants and pulled out a pack of Marlboros. "Uh huh," she said. "And you might be?"

I might be. "I might be her daughter. That is, I am."

"Her daughter." The woman's eyes narrowed, and Susannah felt a jolt of panic. Did she really think it would be that easy?

She tried not to move. If she moved, the woman with the stirrup pants would find a reason to tell her to go away. But if she stayed quiet, small, the woman might let her cross the threshold and come inside.

"And you know that how?" the woman said.

"I've been to Sisters of Mercy." Susannah opened her purse and rummaged inside for the envelope. "I have the adoption papers."

"Sure you do, honey." The woman tapped out a cigarette.

"Look." Susannah extended the papers. "This is my birth certificate. La Posada, Texas. And this is the adoption decree with my parents' names and Corinne's signature." She was careful to say Coh-reen.

The woman took the papers from Susannah's outstretched hand. She read slowly, head to one side, unlit cigarette hanging from the corner of her mouth. "If you're Corinne's daughter, why does it have other people's names on the birth certificate?" She arched a penciled eyebrow, as if to say: You think I'm stupid?

"It's just what they do. It's called an amended birth certificate. But the adoption papers are clear. See? Her name is above the notary stamp." She pointed to a place on the page.

The woman reached across Susannah and plucked a lighter from its resting place on the window ledge. Squinting, she placed the cigarette between the third and fourth fingers of her right hand, clamping it in place. "That so?" She snapped the lighter. Smoke pooled around her face.

"It is."

The woman looked at Susannah, as if taking her measure, then shot a suspicious glance up and down the street. It was empty, only a butter-colored dog nosing at a patch of grass. "Guess you'd better come in."

Susannah stepped into the house. The woman pulled the door shut, waving her into a square living room. Patches of sunlight dappled a floral rug. Two couches, facing each other, were covered in plastic. A credenza, curio cabinet, and TV lined one wall. A soap opera was on, a close-up of a stern-looking doctor and a woman with long dark hair who was sobbing into her gloves.

"Have a seat," the woman said, indicating one of the couches. "Go on, now. It won't bite." She picked up the remote and lowered the sound of the TV. Susannah sat down carefully, the plastic crinkling beneath her.

"So." The woman settled onto the opposite couch. She took a slow, thoughtful drag on her cigarette.

"You're not Corinne," Susannah said.

"Ha. I'm Beryl. Her mother." The cigarette jiggled. "And your grannie, if you are who you say you are."

Her grannie. No, her grandmother was Nana Sophie, maker of chocolate sponge cake and devotee of Cathay Crimson nail polish.

Nana Sophie would never approve of the way Beryl's cigarette was dropping ashes onto the rug.

Beryl narrowed her eyes again. "You sure these papers ain't fake?"

"They're not. It's me." Then she remembered. "I tried to get in touch about six years ago. The law firm sent a letter to the agency. They said they contacted you, and you gave them Corinne's new address." She sat up straight. "She said no. But that was me."

Beryl met her gaze. "I might remember that." Then, as if coming to a decision, she craned her neck and yelled, "Jimmy Ray! You'll never guess who's here."

"Who's Jimmy Ray?"

Beryl gave a mischievous grin. "Jimmy Ray Calhoun, number three. I kept my own name after the first one went bad. Too much trouble changing my driver's license every time someone hung his jeans on the bedpost."

"He's not Corinne's father?"

"No, ma'am. Corinne's daddy was Boyd. Number two was Whitey. I finally got it right with Jimmy Ray."

A tall man in a Hawaiian shirt walked into the room. He had thick white hair that came to a deep widow's peak and dark eyebrows, like bird's wings. "What's up, Beryl?"

Beryl made a wide gesture. "Jimmy Ray, meet my granddaughter." She turned back to Susannah. "What did you say your name was, honey?"

Susannah wanted to burst into tears. Who were these people? They weren't the people she'd come here to see. "Susannah," she said, her voice cracking. "Susannah Richardson."

Beryl peered at her closely. "You know, I think I can see it." She motioned to Jimmy Ray. "Around the eyes and nose? See?" She sat back, smiling in satisfaction. "She's one of us."

Jimmy Ray looked at Susannah. His eyes were kind. "Would you like some water? A Coke or a 7UP?"

She didn't want a 7UP. She wanted her mother. "Where's Corinne?" she asked.

Beryl and Jimmy Ray exchanged glances. "You'd better get her that water," Beryl said. She patted the plastic covering of the cushion next to her, motioning for Susannah to change couches and sit beside her. Jimmy Ray disappeared into the other room. Susannah could hear the thump of a refrigerator door, ice cubes tumbling into a glass.

"Here you go, honey," he said, handing her a heavy amber goblet. The surface was slick and cold. She set it on the coffee table.

Jimmy Ray sat on the opposite couch and nodded at Beryl. *Go on now.* Beryl set the cigarette in a nearby ashtray and covered Susannah's hand with hers. Beryl's hand was tan, freckled, with big glass rings that made Susannah think of her real grandmother, only Nana Sophie's rings were made of amethysts and pearls.

"I'm awful sorry, sugar," Beryl said. "I know you come all this way, and I can only imagine."

Dread filled her chest, sharp and thick at the same time, like razors and cotton.

"Tell me," she whispered.

Beryl let out a sigh. "Corinne's dead, honey. Three years, next month."

"No." She grabbed Beryl's wrist. She wanted to squeeze all the way to the bone, pinch back the impossible words. "She can't be." Why hadn't someone called, told her to hurry? "But *why*?"

"Why?" Beryl gave a bitter sniff. "Because she shot up one too many times, that's why. I warned her and warned her, for all the good it did."

Jimmy Ray reached across the table and picked up the water glass. "You drink this, now."

Numbly, Susannah took the glass from him. She brought it to her mouth but didn't drink. "Shot up *why*?" she managed to ask. "Why would she do such a thing?"

"I don't think she meant to OD," Beryl said. "It was a stupid mistake." She stubbed out her cigarette. "She was always stubborn, didn't like anyone telling her what to do. I'd tell her, when she was small, you better not keep eating that peanut brittle, it'll split your teeth by the time you're thirty. She'd just laugh and say, 'Oh Ma, I can't worry about being thirty.'"

Susannah's head began to spin. Why were they talking about peanut brittle? The room swirled; she was dizzy, parched. She drank the glass of water in big greedy gulps.

Beryl tapped another cigarette out of her pack. "Must be a shock for you. Coming here, and now this."

Susannah set the glass on the table. "I never dreamed she wouldn't be here, once I came."

"I'm real sorry," Beryl said. "But you did come, and I for one am pleased." Then she regarded her keenly. "I always wondered, you know."

"I wondered too." Susannah looked around, her gaze moving from the TV to the floral rug. "I have so many questions."

She'd never imagined sitting in a room like this, talking to people like Beryl and Jimmy Ray. Whatever picture she'd had in her mind had been distant and vague, a blurry vision of a mother in a hospital gown opening her arms to a pink-cheeked baby. It never occurred to her that Corinne might be a junkie. Or dead.

"We'll try to answer 'em," Jimmy Ray said, but Beryl gave him an annoyed look.

"This ain't your business, Jimmy Ray. It was before your time."

"Don't mean I don't have something to say." He patted Susannah's arm. "We'll try to fill you in. Me, your grannie, Hollis."

"Hollis?"

"My other daughter," Beryl said. "She knew Corinne good as anyone."

Susannah looked at Jimmy Ray. "Is Hollis your child?"

Beryl gave a snort. "I wish. Nope, that was Whitey's little present. We called him the UPS man. Dropped off his package and left."

"What about *my* father?"

"Oh, *him*. Don't worry about that lot."

What did that mean? There were too many people. Grandmothers, husbands, aunts. She hadn't come looking for all these people, only for the one person who wasn't here.

"You stay for dinner," Beryl said firmly. "I'll call Hollis. It's ribs."

Susannah fought another wave of dizziness, then forced herself to smile. "Yes, thank you. That would be nice."

"You know," Beryl said, "I tried to talk her out of it." She flicked the lighter and bent her head to light the cigarette. The tip glowed as it caught the flame, a crimson flash the color of Nana Sophie's nails.

Susannah thought she was talking about the overdose, the drugs. But then, when Beryl continued, she realized that Beryl was talking about the adoption.

"I knew she didn't have any way to support a baby, but I would've helped. It was my grandbaby, after all. But no, she had her own ideas." Beryl shook her head. "I told her, 'hey, you're giving away my grandbaby.' But she said, 'Mama, it's the right thing to do.' Like I said, the girl had a mind of her own." She lifted her chin and blew a perfect smoke ring. It hovered in the air like a halo. "Anyway, here we are. Go figure."

Go figure. Beryl was no more like her Nana than the mysterious Corinne was like Dana. And that meant she, Susannah, was like—who?

Susannah remembered her childhood dream of a birth mother who played the piano, just like her—only better, more famous. A virtuoso, who yearned to play a four-handed Brahms waltz with her long-lost daughter.

She looked at Beryl. "Was she musical? Corinne."

"Musical?" Beryl echoed. "Well, she sure could pick out a tune.

Even when she was a tiny little thing, Boyd had this guitar, it was nothing much, but little Corinne, she'd climb on his lap and pick out the melody all by herself." She gave a quick laugh. "Oh my. I'd forgotten that."

"She could sing," Jimmy Ray said.

"She could," Beryl agreed. "'You Are My Sunshine'. That was her favorite. 'Course, she'd insist it was you make me happy when eyes are blue, instead of *skies* are blue. She knew perfectly well that it was *skies*, but what did she care? Her eyes *were* blue, you know. Real bright blue, like yours." She tapped her cigarette against the ashtray. "Yup, that girl could sing."

Brahms receded, replaced by a girl who could sure pick out a tune. A girl with a mind of her own who'd decided that a different life was best for her child.

"I'd like to meet Hollis," Susannah said. "You said they were close, Hollis and my mother?"

Maybe Hollis would know the real story. What Corinne had been like. Why Corinne hadn't kept her.

Beryl blew another smoke ring. "You'll meet her soon enough, sugar."

Suddenly, Susannah couldn't take one more minute of the conversation. "I need to settle a few things back at the motel." She rose quickly, desperate to leave—back to the Super Seven Motel, back to New York.

"You come back when you're settled," Beryl told her. "We eat at five."

"Five. Yes." Susannah managed another smile.

"Don't you run back to New York now," Jimmy Ray said.

Susannah turned and met his eyes. They were warm and full of understanding. He knew she'd been about to do exactly that.

Chapter Six
then

Susannah brought yellow roses as her hostess gift, handing them to Beryl when she returned for dinner. "No need to do that," Beryl said. "You're family, not company." She held the door, then followed Susannah into the house. "Sweet of you, though. Guess someone raised you right."

Susannah tried not to flinch. *Someone* meant her parents, Dana and Tyler. The compliment felt strange and sly—unless Beryl was being clever, calling her family, as if Dana were some kind of governess, carrying out her duties before returning Susannah, properly raised, to her true home?

She turned to Beryl, but the woman's face was cheerfully neutral. No, it was just her own confused loyalty. She wished, again, that she had told her parents she was going to Texas, yet she had been afraid. What if it led nowhere, or ended badly? She would hurt them for nothing.

And if it led somewhere? *We jumped on a plane to Texas to bring you home.* That would hurt them even more. Her mother had been gentle and understanding when Corinne refused to know her, but it might be harder to be magnanimous if she knew her daughter had taken a plane in the other direction. Hurried across town for dinner with her birth family. Brought them flowers.

"Anyway, let's get these things in water," Beryl said. She strode across the living room, pulled a vase from the top of the credenza, and removed the plastic tulips. Susannah followed her into the kitchen. A woman with a blonde braid stood at the sink, peeling carrots. "Scoot over now," Beryl told her. "We need water."

The woman turned from the sink and looked into Susannah's eyes. Hers, too, were a deep cornflower blue. "Well, my gosh," she declared. Wiping her palms on her jeans, she said, "I'm Hollis. And you're Susannah."

"I am."

"Well, how about that?"

"Better get those things in water," Beryl repeated. Hollis stepped aside, and Susannah filled the vase at the sink. Loud footsteps pounded behind her. "Ma! Ma!" Two boys in shorts and tee-shirts raced into the kitchen.

"Randall and Robert Junior," Beryl said. "We call 'em R and R. A joke. No rest and relaxation with them two around. Two little hellions, ain't ya?" She smacked the younger one on the rear.

"Quit it, Grannie."

"Mine," Hollis told Susannah. "No daddy to bother us, thank you very much."

"Another loser," Beryl said. Hollis shrugged.

"Big Robert," Beryl explained. She raised her chin, tossing a nod in Susannah's direction. "Didn't last long. Had a perfectly good job as a guard over at the prison, but got way too full of himself. Warden said he'd better leave town if he knew what was good for him, so that was that. Sends her a little money once in a while." She gestured at Hollis, who had resumed peeling the carrots. "But he ain't no father, if you ask me."

"No one asked you," Hollis said.

"Jimmy Ray's the only good one ever come along, but that's because he don't have any responsibility."

Susannah's mind was reeling. They were telling her too much, too fast, but not what she needed to know. She set the vase on the kitchen table. The roses, with their shock of yellow, looked showy and wrong next to the basket of bills, receipts, and supermarket coupons.

She remembered that the two boys were still in the kitchen, hearing every word. "Hi there," she said, offering what she hoped was an encouraging expression.

"Please to meet you, ma'am," the older one said.

"Who's she?" his brother asked.

Who was she, indeed? She looked at Beryl. "She's your cousin," Beryl said. "From up north. That's why she talks funny."

The younger one flicked his eyes at her, as if deciding whether she was worth any further questions. "Can I have some chips?"

"You'll ruin your dinner," Hollis told him.

"A few chips never hurt anyone," Beryl said. "Here you go." She handed him the bag. "Say 'thank you, Grannie'."

"Thank you, Grannie." He grabbed the bag and ran out of the kitchen. His brother ran after him, yelling, "Hey, give me some!" Beryl reached for her lighter.

Hollis shrugged again. "Want to help?"

"Yes, of course." Glad to have something to do, Susannah took a potato and a nylon brush from Hollis. She felt oddly disappointed. Weren't they going to ask her questions, find out who she was? Instead, they had simply let her in.

She had a million questions for them, though. Swiping at the potatoes with quick determined strokes, she ventured, "It was lucky for me that you were at the same address."

"You bet I'm at the same address." Beryl leaned against the counter and watched Susannah work. "You can dig the spots out with a knife, you know." Then she bent her head, snapped the lighter, and inhaled swiftly. "Thirty-year mortgage, and I paid the whole thing off, one damn month after another. Not many people can say *that*." She blew two overlapping smoke rings, then wedged the cigarette in the curve of her fingers. "Them husbands came and went, but it was my house and I stayed."

Susannah set the peeler on the counter and looked around the room. She saw the faded linoleum, the café curtains with their tasseled hems, the red Formica table. She turned to Hollis. "You grew up here?" She really wanted to ask: And what about my mother, growing up beside you? What was it like to be sisters, here in this house? Did you share a room? Did you whisper about your dreams, throw pillows at each other, lie in the dark listening to the radio?

I never had a sister. Tell me.

"Sure did." Hollis drew the peeler along the length of a carrot. A curl dropped into the sink, revealing the deeper color below. "Only house I knew, till I went out on my own."

"And what about Corinne?" Susannah corrected herself. "Cohreen. I guess she moved out, after I was born? There was a different address when the agency tried to contact her."

Hollis and Beryl exchanged looks. "She did," Hollis replied. "A year or so later." Susannah waited, but Hollis didn't continue. Why weren't they telling her the whole story? They must know how much she wanted to hear it.

Tossing the peeler onto the counter, Hollis sank into a kitchen chair and crossed her legs with a sigh that was both weary and flippant. She motioned for Susannah to sit too. "Vegetables ain't gonna peel themselves," Beryl said.

Hollis gave her a dry look. "We're almost done." Then she eyed Susannah again. "Yep, sure was lonely without her. I'm twelve years younger, you know, so I thought she was *it*. But then she took off. It's hard to be a groupie when the rock star's gone."

"Why did she leave?" Susannah asked. "I mean, why *then*?"

"Oh well." Hollis lifted a shoulder. "You know how it is."

No, she didn't know.

Hollis gave another shrug. "Why do any of us want out of our parents' noses? Freedom. Independence. Some guy."

"What guy? Was it my birth father?"

Beryl cut in again. "Forget about him. Nothing to talk about."

Susannah looked from one woman to the other. There were two conversations taking place, one that she was part of and one that she wasn't. The second conversation was a silent exchange between Beryl and Hollis made up of looks and secrets and little dismissive flips of the wrist. There were things they weren't telling her. The very things she needed to know.

Maybe they didn't trust her—though why should they? Did she trust them?

Jimmy Ray ambled into the kitchen, wearing a different Hawaiian shirt, yellow and black flowers on a lime-green background, and holding a can of Budweiser. "You girls want me to fire up the grill?" Seeing Susannah, he bent and wrapped his arm around her in a firm hug. "I'm glad you came back, honey. Beryl wasn't sure you would, but I told her she was wrong."

Beryl gave him a playful slap. "Hush." Then she told Susannah, "Don't listen to him. You're very welcome here."

Then why wouldn't they tell her anything? They knew why she'd come.

"I'll start up the coals," Jimmy Ray said, "seeing as how we're all here." He grinned. "We do real grill. Texas style."

Susannah smiled back; it was impossible not to. Then she felt Hollis studying her. "You look a little bit like her," Hollis said.

"Around the eyes and nose, right?" Beryl pointed at Susannah's face. "Am I right or am I right?"

"Maybe," Hollis said. "I can't put my finger on it."

They were talking about her like she was on display. Yet they were talking about Corinne, too, so she wanted to hear. When she was young, she'd pictured a birthmother who looked exactly like her, only bigger: an elegant woman in a long black dress, bowing beside a nine-foot concert grand, looking out into the audience for her missing daughter. She knew the image wasn't real, but she didn't know what to put in its place.

Susannah gathered her courage. "Was she pretty?"

"Sure was," Hollis said. "Pretty as anything."

"Before all the drugs," Beryl put in.

"Fine, Ma. You know what she meant."

"You want to see a picture?"

Without waiting for a reply, Beryl stubbed out her cigarette and went into the living room. Susannah heard the opening and closing of a drawer, a whooshing sound as the wood slid along its track. She shivered, realizing what was about to happen. Beryl would come back with a photo. A face.

"Here you go," Beryl said.

The picture in the gilt frame was a high school graduation portrait: draped background, V-necked dress, airbrushed features. The girl who smiled at Susannah from the center of the rectangle had glossy brown hair that rose from her forehead and arced out on both sides in a cheerful flip. Her blue eyes were heavily outlined and there was a dimple on the left side of her mouth. "See?" Beryl said proudly. "She looks exactly like the girl who won Miss Texas. She was runner-up for Miss America, you know. Corinne was the splitting image."

Susannah's eyes were riveted on the picture. "It's the white lipstick," Hollis explained. "Looks weird, right? But it was the style. All the girls wore it."

Susannah didn't care about the lipstick. It was Corinne's expression, sassy and pleased with herself. Corinne had no idea, when that picture was taken, of what lay ahead. No one ever did. There was something about her expression that Susannah recognized.

Below her collarbone was a necklace with a blue stone. "Sapphire," Beryl said. "Corinne's birthstone. She liked the way it favored her eyes. Bought it with the money she made at the Frosty Freeze."

Susannah kept staring. She didn't know this person, this high school girl from Lynette, Texas. Not a person she could connect with the word *mother*.

"She looks good, I'll say that much," Beryl declared. She regarded the picture for another moment. Then, with a terse *hunh*, she went to return it to its place in the drawer.

"It's hard for her, you know," Hollis whispered. "She pretends like it's all fine, but it still hurts, even now." She put a finger to her lips as Beryl re-entered the kitchen.

Susannah flushed. It hadn't occurred to her that talking about Corinne would be hard on Beryl, but of course Hollis was right. She'd burst into their lives without stopping to wonder if she might be reviving an old pain. Amazing, really, that they'd welcomed her so openly.

She wouldn't push them too hard for information. Not yet.

But she would, when it was time. It was her life, after all. She had a right to know.

Susannah returned for a second visit during the next school break, at the beginning of April. Vera's soiree—the event she had intended to use to regain Vera's favor—was scheduled for the same weekend, but she didn't have another vacation until June and that was too long to wait.

When she arrived in La Posada, Beryl took her suitcase and rolled it into the back bedroom, proclaiming the motel a waste of money. Susannah hurried after her. "No, really," she said. "You don't have to."

She was glad to save the cost of the Super Seven, but the idea of staying in a room—maybe even a bed—that Corinne might have slept in filled her with horror.

Beryl hoisted the suitcase onto the bed and gave Susannah a swift knowing look. "Never had a real guest room till last year, but I figured it was time." She folded her arms, pointing her chin at the bureau with its double line of drawers and gilt-edged mirror. "Did up the whole thing brand new, every last bit, right down to the doorknob."

Susannah managed a nod. Beryl had said *every last bit*. Surely that included the bed. That meant it wasn't really the room Corinne had slept in when she was growing up, dreaming about movie stars and music and clothes, feeling a baby—herself—moving inside.

Beryl plucked a pack of cigarettes from the waistband of her stretch pants. "Hollis didn't want me to change it, naturally, but it's my place. She's got her own." She tapped a cigarette from the pack and wedged it between her third and fourth fingers. "Not that you'd know it."

It didn't take long for Susannah to understand what Beryl meant. Hollis had her own apartment but seemed to spend most of her time at Beryl's house—clipping out coupons at the kitchen table, chopping onions, or sprawled on the couch with a magazine. Sometimes she'd yell, "Hey, Ma, listen to this," and read something aloud. Sometimes she'd call to the boys, "Y'all behave now," even though nothing in particular had happened.

Hollis knew something about Corinne; Susannah was sure of it. She was just as sure that Hollis didn't want to tell her. But that was the reason she had come, and Hollis knew it too.

She had a feeling that Hollis might be willing to talk if they were away from Beryl, so she waylaid Hollis as she was pulling a bottle of Windex from the cabinet below the sink. "Hey, let's take a walk. You and me. You can show me the sights."

She had expected Hollis to resist, but to her surprise Hollis let out a merry laugh. "Okay, ladybug, why not? Can't go back north without a tour of good old Lynette, Texas." Hollis set the Windex on the counter and lifted the keys to her pickup from the basket of coupons and receipts. "We can drive over to the bayou. You might not think we have bayous in Texas but we do."

Susannah followed Hollis to the pickup and climbed into the passenger seat. She sat obediently, elbow pointing out the open window, while Hollis rattled off the names of streets and buildings. After a while Hollis pulled into a dirt lot and turned off the engine. She pointed to a clearing in the brush that surrounded the lot. "We can cut through here."

Hollis jumped out of the truck and began to walk quickly, and Susannah hurried to catch up. Before long, the dry grass and cypress gave way to an expanse of wetland. They had to walk single file along the narrow path, pushing away the tangle of branches and vines. Then Hollis stopped as they came to a high rock. "Let's rest a bit."

Susannah scrambled after her. Hollis was more than seven years older but surer, more agile. It was odd to think of Hollis as her aunt. They belonged to overlapping generations, with little in common except the color of their eyes.

Hollis patted the flat surface of the ledge. "Hop up. Just watch out for the rougarou."

"What's a rougarou?"

She let out another peal of laughter. "Oh, it's just an old superstition. The werewolf of the bayou. You know, to scare the kids? You'd be smarter to watch out for snakes."

Grimacing, Susannah settled onto the ledge. The whole place was surreal: the jumble of plants, the shrieking of the birds. She pulled in her breath and faced Hollis. "Tell me about my mother."

"I knew that's why you wanted to get me alone." Hollis gave a satisfied smirk and stretched out her legs. "Yep, there's a lot your grannie won't talk about. She'd rather remember Corinne like she was in that pretty little high school picture. Wouldn't we all."

Susannah held still, hoping for more, but Hollis was quiet. Was Hollis going to make her work for each piece of the story?

Tired of waiting, she asked, "How did Corinne get pregnant?" She blushed. "I mean, I know *how*. Duh. But why? Who was he?"

"The sperm donor. Good ole Wayne." Hollis bent over the side of the rock and spat. "That's what I think of *him*."

"Why? Was he that awful?"

"Selfish and mean."

"How was he selfish? How was he mean?" She was bursting to know everything now.

As if tired of all the questions, Hollis snapped, "Because he took Simone, that's why. And then we had no one."

Simone? Who was Simone?

Susannah felt cold all over. The Texas heat disappeared.

"Here's the thing," Hollis said, sliding off the rock. "We're glad to know you, but you came looking for us. We didn't go looking for you."

Susannah waited, desperate to hear what Hollis had to say, and dreading it too. "Now you come here," Hollis went on, dusting off her jeans, "and ask a lot of questions. Okay. But you got no clue what you're stirring up." She made a face. "Let's go. It's too buggy here."

Abruptly, she headed down the path. Again, Susannah tried to keep up. She tripped on a root, and Hollis turned around. "You okay?"

"I guess." She rubbed her ankle.

"Let me see." Hollis squatted and held the ankle, turning it right and left. "Yep, it's fine. Good thing, too. I'm not carrying some damn Yankee all the way back to New York." Seeing Susannah's confused look, she made a goofy face. "It's a joke."

"Hollis," Susannah said. "Who's Simone?"

The marsh was quiet. Even the birds were silent.

"Your sister," Hollis said.

"My sister."

"Oh yes." Hollis straightened and began walking again, flicking the tree bark with her fingertips. Susannah ran after her and grabbed her arm. "You have to tell me."

Hollis sighed. "Fine. But you have to shut up and stop asking questions and let me tell it my way." Susannah nodded. She let her hand fall to the side.

"First of all," Hollis said, "I was only seven when you were born. I was a kid. I saw what I saw, and I didn't see what I didn't see." She paused, looked around to survey their surroundings, and led Susannah through a clearing on the left. "We can take a short cut. There's a boardwalk someone built, the town, I guess." She slowed her strides so Susannah could follow. They stepped up onto a wooden walkway, elevated above the marsh.

"So," Hollis went on. "Like I told you, Corinne was so, so glamorous to me, and she didn't take shit from anyone. Ma never could stand Wayne, but of course I thought he was the coolest ever. He'd tease me and do these dumb magic tricks, like pretending to pull a quarter out of your ear? But when Corinne got pregnant, he had a giant fit. He was too young to be tied down, he had big plans, blah-blah-blah. So they broke up and she ended up giving you away. I was Miss Nosy Pants, so I put two-and-two together that Corinne was having a baby—of course I didn't exactly know how you got a baby, except for watching the dogs—and then suddenly there wasn't any baby. So okay."

"And then?"

Hollis stopped and pointed at the water. "See that? We call 'em water puppies. They're salamanders, really big ones." Susannah leaned against the railing to watch the creatures glide between the tangle of roots and vines. "That's a live oak, and that there's a black gum."

Shut up about the trees. Tell me about Simone.

"And *then*," Hollis said, "she got pregnant again. She had Simone nineteen months after she had you. I was eight and a half. She sat me down on my bed and looked me square in the face. 'I'm keeping this one,' she said, 'I don't care what anyone says.' And she did."

"She did," Susannah repeated.

"Yep." A bird trilled overhead. Another answered. "Yep," Hollis repeated. "We sure loved that baby. She was like a little doll."

She couldn't believe that Hollis could be so cruel, talking so happily about that second baby, but Hollis didn't seem to notice the impact of her words. Susannah dug her fingers into the rotting wood of the railing. The wet strips came loose and peeled away.

"Even Wayne had to admit she was one cutie pie." Hollis glanced at her. "He was the father, of course. They got back together. Guess he couldn't stay away. Well, Corinne was a charmer, back in the day. I'll give her that."

It took all Susannah had to form the words. "Did he ever see me?"

"You? No, like I said, they'd broken up. Only ones who saw you before Social Services came were Ma and Corinne. They wouldn't let me into the hospital. They had a rule you had to be twelve. I didn't even get to see Simone till she came home."

Susannah could hardly breathe now. Hollis's blithe tone was more hurtful than anything she could have imagined. "What happened when Simone was born?"

Hollis gave a dismissive wave. "Oh, it was sweet for a while."

"She kept her, like she said she would?"

She couldn't say their names. Corinne. Simone.

Dana had insisted that her birth mother *couldn't keep any baby*, and that's why she *made the very best plan she could*. But Dana had lied. Corinne could keep a baby, and she did.

"She kept her," Hollis echoed. "But then Corinne and Wayne started fighting and broke up, and then Corinne started doing her drugs—you got that from what Ma said, right? Wayne and his mama didn't like that one iota. So they went to court, and they took Simone."

"Were they married, Wayne and Corinne?"

"Nah. But the judge gave Simone to Wayne anyway. Everyone knew he was the daddy; he even did that paternity thing. Plus, no way Corinne could take care of her."

Susannah gripped the railing and tried to place everything Hollis was saying into the crazy history that was getting harder and harder to understand. "When?"

"When they took her? Oh, she was five, maybe. I was in junior high. I pretended she was my little sister." Hollis flicked back her hair and sighed. "It was awful for Corinne. She loved that little girl to bits. But they were right, you know. It was better for Simone."

Breathe, Susannah told herself. Just breathe.

She had to hear the whole story. "Did you ever see her again?"

"Well, of course." Hollis looked at her like she was an idiot. "We had her every other holiday." She picked up a fallen branch and poked at the water. "It's not like Corinne didn't try to get her back. She tried and tried. But Wayne and his mother had some big lawyer, and they always won. Corinne kept figuring that when Simone was fourteen and could pick where she lived, she'd pick her." She flicked a leaf aside. "Well, she didn't. She didn't want to leave her girlfriends and her school and her room. Anyway, by then Wayne had got married, so she had a brother and sister and a whole regular family, not some single mama who was broke and stoned half the time."

Susannah watched the circles the branch was stirring up in the water. Slow rings, expanding but going nowhere.

"From what I figure, that was about the time your letter came. I'd guess it was like salt on a sore, hearing about some other child instead of the one she'd lost. Or maybe she thought it was some kind of mean trick, who knows? Plus she hated lawyers. We all did. I'm surprised Ma even gave out her address, though I think it was the social service people who knocked on the door and told her she had to, I don't really remember. I had other things on my mind. I had Robert Junior by then."

"And after that?"

"After that? Oh, Wayne got promoted. Simone went to high school. Corinne pretty much gave up, got into drugs big time, and next thing we hear she's OD'd. Fast forward, and here we are, you and me."

"And that's it?"

Hollis gave a shrug. "That's it, ladybug. What else do you want?"

I want my mother.

Susannah fought to keep from crying. She kept the other one, and she tried everything she could to get her back. *But she didn't want me, even when I asked so nicely.*

She could have had one of her daughters, at least.

But I was the wrong one.

Part Three

The Sonata

The music is not in the notes, but in the silence between.
Wolfgang Amadeus Mozart

Chapter Seven

now

Susannah settled herself at the desk in the alcove between the pantry and refrigerator. When James was younger, he would do his homework there while she cooked dinner. Times tables, spelling words divided into syllables. Once he got older and insisted on doing—or not doing—his homework upstairs, in his bedroom, she had appropriated the desk for herself. It was small, hardly more than child-sized, but there was something cozy and comforting about the warm yellow pine, the dropped ceiling, the blue-and-white Delft tiles that framed the back wall.

She flipped open her laptop and waited while it booted up, drumming her fingers on the edge of the desk. Those fingers were the reason she was going online. She needed to find out about this Dupuytren business, the legacy of her birth family. It was ironic, really. If they'd considered all the possible diseases to bequeath to her, they couldn't have picked a more damning one. Susannah supposed she should be grateful that it wasn't some sort of life-threatening illness, yet the thought of being unable to play did feel like a kind of death.

Her hands connected her to the world. Without them, her music would be locked in her mind.

She looked at her hands—the arch of her knuckles, the fingertips that couldn't help making a rhythm of her impatience as they tapped on the wood. There were so many things her hands knew, a precise knowledge deep in her flesh. A way of striking a key that was like plucking a single crystal and tossing it into the air. And another way, when one note passed to the next, inevitably, yet with a fraction of uncertainty and longing, until it dropped into place.

They were completely different movements. She needed hands that knew the difference and could be trusted to do what they knew.

The screensaver popped into focus. It was a photo, taken by NASA, of a black hole in the Perseus galaxy cluster. Aaron had told her about the black hole when she made a remark, years ago, about how many wonderful pieces of music were written in B-flat. "That's the sound of the universe," he had answered. She'd given him a skeptical look, but he said it was true.

There was a massive black hole 300 million light-years away that emitted a tone, 57 octaves below middle C, that corresponded to a B-flat. Not a B-flat the human ear could discern. The lowest sound a person could hear had a frequency of one-twentieth of a second; she'd learned that in music school. The sound coming from the black hole in Perseus had a frequency of ten million years. Yet it was the same note, B-flat, like her sonata. And the black hole had been singing that note for two and a half billion years.

She remembered how happy Aaron had been to offer a gift from his storehouse of scientific knowledge that had meaning to her as a musician. She had made the photo her screensaver.

She hadn't expected to end up with a scientist. Most of the people she'd dated had been musicians. There was a common language, an instant ease, yet there was always an undertow of competition or else a familiarity that made them feel more like brothers than lovers.

When she met Aaron—at the college where they were both new-ly-hired adjuncts, teaching evening courses that none of the full-time faculty wanted—she was struck at once by how grounded he seemed. His square solid body and deep voice, his dark eyebrows and the fine black hair along his arms. He was like a bass note, a sustaining tone, present and true. His solidness had aroused her, made her want to win him. And she had. He'd fallen in love with her music, and with her.

After three months, they talked about moving in together. They found a loft near Fourth Avenue and Tenth Street that had a big open space for her Steinway. There was a crazy little kitchen in the corner, hardly more than a hot plate and a toaster oven, and a huge tiled bathroom that used to be a sauna, with spigots coming out of the walls. "There's no sink," Susannah said, turning in a circle to survey the bare sun-filled space. "We'll have to take our clothes off to do the dishes."

Aaron grabbed her waist, laughing. "Hey, works for me."

They signed the lease and explored the neighborhood, marveling at its faded elegance and offbeat charm. Two delis side-by-side and a tiny basement shop that boasted: *We alter anything.* Above the shop, an even tinier restaurant that offered cheap takeout Thai. The smells of cumin and coriander and lime as Aaron opened the bag in their new home. An unopened carton of books for a table, a single candle with its spikey blue flame.

Susannah let the memory linger, then launched the browser and typed *Dupuytren's pianist* into the search bar.

To her amazement, a link appeared at once. Misha Dichter. She knew his work; what pianist didn't? The Liszt Hungarian Rhapsodies, his acclaimed recordings of Beethoven and Brahms. But she hadn't known that Dichter had Dupuytren's.

Dichter, apparently, had spent years compensating for the fail-ing fifth finger of his right hand—altering the obvious fingering or taking some of the treble notes with his left hand, the same strategies she had used during the audition. Eventually, though, compensation wasn't enough. One day, without warning, he couldn't even stretch to a major sixth. That meant he couldn't play. But he found a doctor who told him, "We can beat this." He had some kind of surgery, made a miraculous recovery, and played in a concert two months later.

Dichter had put off treatment because he'd seen what two botched surgeries did to his father, who suffered from the same condition—the *family history* that Leo Mathieson, her own doctor, had asked about. Family history might be nice to know, Susannah thought, but it didn't keep you from getting the damn disease.

She needed to be cured now, not when her finger was so bent that she couldn't even reach a major sixth. If you were famous, like Dichter, the world would grant you a hiatus while you healed. If you were nobody special, like her, you couldn't do that. With a progressive disease, her career—if she was lucky enough to launch it—would be short-lived.

She erased the word *pianist* and wrote *treatment*. There were pages of links—articles, reports, testimonials. People posted before-and-after photos of distorted and miraculously restored hands; others warned of swelling and bleeding, contracture that reappeared later, or in the other hand. One person told of fingers that were curled more than ninety degrees, a magic injection, and twelve years later no one could tell that he'd ever had a problem. Another person had an ugly cord running from finger joint to palm that had thickened grotesquely overnight, even after treatment had supposedly cured it.

"There are treatments for the hand deformities caused by Dupuytren's contracture," Susannah read, "but no treatment for the underlying process of the disease itself." She didn't care about some underlying process. She just needed to keep her fingers from bending.

She scrolled through the websites. The actual treatments—slicing the cord with a needle, softening it with an enzyme injection and then breaking it manually—were as terrifying as the disease. A pianist spent her life protecting her fingers, not breaking them.

She still hadn't told Aaron about her diagnosis. When he asked what Leo Mathieson had to say, she'd given a vague reply. "Oh, you know doctors. *Keep an eye on it.*"

"Did he give you a cream?" Aaron asked. "A prescription?"

"No. He didn't think it was a cream sort of thing."

Another half-lie, after years of telling him everything. She'd been wary of telling Aaron about the audition—she hadn't wanted to see the bright gleam of hope in his eyes, and then watch it fade when she wasn't picked. Yet she had told him, and he'd been happy for her. And then she'd been picked, and the gleam had spread, blazed, the way it used to.

Her music was the reason Aaron fell in love with her. "Do you have any idea how gorgeous you are?" he had told her, the first time she played for him. Chopin, the E-minor nocturne, in a music room at the university. The low E, ascending. The exquisite unfinished perfection of the D-sharp, and the glorious crescendo.

She hadn't played like that in a long time, with so much rapture and abandon. But she would do it again, at the concert. And when she did, Aaron would be enchanted again.

There was no place for a degenerative disease in that plan. That was why she had to stop it. Until she had, there was no reason to tell Aaron. No reason to make him doubt her.

"I need to nip this thing in the bud," she told Leo. What was the phrase Aaron always used? Evidence-based protocol. She sat back, pleased that she'd remembered. "The most evidence-based protocol. That's what I want."

But Leo shook his head. "There's no preventive treatment, Susannah. Not when we're dealing with a genetically based condition. Maybe one day we'll know how to stop a gene from expressing itself, but we're not there now."

"I'm not saying to keep it from starting. It's already started, that's what you told me. I'm saying to keep it from getting worse."

"It doesn't work like that," Leo said. "One of the challenges of a progressive disease is that it varies so much from person to person— the extent of its effect, the speed at which that happens. It's impossible to predict until the fingers actually begin to contract. Once they do, we can chart the progression of the contracture, and that can give us a reasonable indication." He shrugged. "Even then, not always. Sometimes people stabilize at a certain point."

"You mean, I have to wait till my fingers get useless and distorted, and *then* maybe you can tell me something?"

"It's too variable," he repeated. "Some people never progress beyond the stage you're at right now. In other cases, there's a rapid deterioration." He gave another shrug. "You're at the very beginning. It's too soon to know how it will go."

"So you're saying, just wait and see?"

"There's not much else we can do, especially without knowing your family history. All we can do is keep an eye on it."

Keep an eye on it. What kind of non-plan was that?

Susannah crossed her arms. "That can't be true. They treat other diseases at the beginning. Cancer. High blood pressure. Gum disease, for god's sakes."

"That may be. But with Dupuytren's, the available treatments address the contracture itself. They break up the cord that's making the finger contract."

For an instant she was confused. If you broke up a chord, you had a bunch of separate notes. No, he meant cord. Obviously. Not chord.

"There's no treatment to prevent the cord from forming in the first place," Leo went on. "Your nodule is the first stage. We can't treat Dupuytren's until stage three. And like I said, some people never get there."

"No disrespect, Leo, but how much do you really know about this? You're not a hand expert."

"True, I'm not. I think you should see one, in fact, when the time is right."

How about now? Now would be a good time.

"The problem is that I really can't wait." She offered her most winsome smile. "I'm a pianist. My hands are everything. I can't wait till they've stopped working."

"I can understand your impatience—"

"Just give me a referral. It can't hurt to have a conversation with a specialist."

"It's far too premature—"

"All I want is an appointment. Now, not later." She abandoned the smile. "I have a big concert coming up. I need to know what to expect."

"I'm trying to explain," Leo said. "There are several treatments, but none of them can be administered until your fingers have started to bend. Every specialist will tell you the same thing. You're going to have to be patient."

No, she did *not* have to be patient. There had to be someone who would help her now, not in some nebulous future when her fingers were deformed.

"Like you said, you're not a hand expert." Then, afraid that sounded too harsh, she added, "I mean, you said so yourself."

They locked eyes. Her heart began to beat wildly.

I can outstare you. Just do what I want and I'll go away.

Leo sighed. He placed his palms on the desk, preparing to rise. "All right, I'll give Evan Chu a ring later today."

"Give him a ring now. While I'm here."

He turned crimson. Susannah was sure her face was as red as

Leo's. She clenched her fists, fighting the urge to rescind her imperious demand.

To her relief, Leo reached for the phone. "Very well." She waited while he made the call, agonizing because she couldn't hear what Chu was saying. After a brief exchange, Leo hung up and told her, "He'll see you on Thursday at eleven."

Susannah released her breath. "Thank you so, so much." She relaxed her hands. Then she turned her right hand and wiggled her fingers, seeing if she could make the nodule stretch and collapse.

Leo watched her, and she dropped the hand into her lap.

"Go see Evan Chu," he said. "But I doubt he'll say anything I haven't already told you. I don't want you to get your hopes up."

Why not? Susannah thought. Why was everyone so worried that she might feel a glimmer of hope? Hope was the reason she'd auditioned—hope of restoring the magic she seemed to have lost. She'd done it once before, when she was in her early twenties and Vera shamed her by saying that her playing had gotten shallow and predictable. She'd done what Vera ordered and looked for the source of her music, the same *family history* that Leo kept pestering her about. The journey hadn't ended the way she had imagined, but it had restored her music. She had returned from Texas with a richer sound, more vibrant and true. Suddenly she was tackling pieces that had always eluded her. Invitations opened up, chances to perform and compete.

Then James was born. Vera thought she was being an idiot, a martyr, when she stopped performing to care for him. Vera had withdrawn too—years ago, preferring to guide the next generation of performers—so she'd been certain that Vera would understand. Vera understood so much, but not this. When Susannah felt James emerge from her own body—not *we jumped on a plane to Texas*, but flesh from flesh, life from life—everything changed.

Her music was for James now, and for Aaron. The *Rondo Alla Turca*, so three-year-old James could race around the room, jumping from cushion to cushion. Schubert's G-flat major Impromptu, after she and Aaron made love. Her gifts to them, the best of herself. Yet James had never seen who she really was—had never seen her at a gleaming Steinway in a hall full of people, her long black dress falling in a graceful arc as she bent to accept wave after wave of applause.

I will give him that memory, she thought. A memory he'll have for his whole life, of who his mother truly is.

Leo pushed to his feet, signaling that their time was up. Susannah rose too. "I'll let you know how it goes with Dr. Chu," she said. "I'm sure there's something I can do, even at this stage."

"I've told you my view, but I'll let Evan take it from here."

"Meaning: let him deal with me."

"You want to be thorough. There's nothing wrong with that."

"My mother used to say I was determined. I think she was being polite. She really meant stubborn."

Leo took her hand. "None of us knows what lies ahead, Susannah. Our genes have their secrets, to be revealed in due course. No sense fretting too much."

"Easy for you to say. You aren't playing the B-flat major sonata for fifteen hundred people."

"Luckily for those people."

Susannah laughed. "Thanks for getting Evan Chu to see me. I'll keep you posted." Then her voice dropped. "And I definitely intend to get my hopes up, no matter what you say. Someone has to be at the good end of the bell curve. Why not me?"

"Diseases like this are odd, aren't they?" Leo tilted his head as he regarded her hand in his. "Their origins are long ago, in our ancestors. And their futures are already set, even though we can't see them."

"In other words, live in the present."

"Never a bad idea."

Yes and no, she thought. The future mattered.

After all these years, the past did too.

Chapter Eight

now

Susannah turned the page of her novel, pretending to read. Aaron was settled into the tan leather chair across from hers, glasses low on his nose, engrossed in a scientific journal. She studied him for a moment, admiring his profile, before returning to the page.

The banker's light next to her chair wasn't strong enough for reading; then again, she wasn't actually reading. She was fretting, Leo's word. And not just about the nodule on her palm. Even without the specter of Dupuytren's, the notion of a renewed professional career seemed like a fantasy. Did she really think she could leap into the music world at her age?

It wasn't age *per se*, because there were world-class pianists more than twice her age, but they had been famous for decades. Prodigies and old men, that was what people liked. Mozart, composing at five years old; Glenn Gould, reading music before he could read words. Or else Horowitz, giving concerts at eighty-three; Rubenstein, when he was nearly eighty-nine. An almost-forty-year-old woman was an oddity, a fluke—an impressive surprise if she made a splash, an embarrassment if she didn't. And there would be no gradual ascent, as there was for someone in her twenties. No learning curve, no second chance.

This was it, this one performance. This one sonata.

Susannah laid her book face-down on the coffee table. With a quick glance at Aaron, she stood and crossed the L-shaped room to the corner where her Steinway was waiting. She opened the book of sonatas, the map that Schubert had left for her.

It was an extraordinary piece, completed only months before his death at the age of thirty-one. Everything was there. Sound and silence, suspension and resolution, ecstasy and despair. The whole of life, written by a man on the brink of death. The doom of that dark trill in the first movement, and the return of the melody with its surge of hope. Then, in the second movement, an unbearable yearning—and the knowledge, the acceptance, that the yearning would never be fulfilled. Not a reluctant resignation, but a calm and lucid letting-go. And then, at last, the chaotic joy of the last two movements.

She began to play. The music filled her with the hope that everyone told her not to have. She could do this. Find that special kind of listening, when listening and playing were the same act, taking place in the same instant.

She remembered. Felt it again.

Then, like the flutter of an eyelash, her hand slipped and missed the top note. Trying not to panic, she went back to the beginning of the measure. She reached the note this time, but it didn't soar. No rope-like thickening in her palm, but the note didn't soar. She made herself keep going until she finished the passage. Each time she tried to voice a top note, there was the same dull thud.

She away pushed from the keyboard and went to look under the lid, checking to see if there was a culprit on the strings, a fallen pencil or another mysterious object that would explain the flattened sound. No, nothing. She knew that already. It wasn't a hammer or string. It was her.

"Aaron," she called. "Can you listen for a minute?"

He set the journal aside. "Listen to something you want to tell me, or listen to you play?"

"Play." Susannah fought to keep her voice from quavering. "I need to know if it sounds wrong. Thin, maybe. Or dead. Unmusical. I don't know."

"Sure." He rested an arm on the back of the chair, dipping his chin to signal that he was ready. She played the opening theme. Tears stung her eyes. There was no way to pretend that it lifted the soul, as Schubert had intended.

"Sounds fine to me," Aaron said.

Susannah shook her head. "It doesn't."

"It does, honey. Really."

"Please don't humor me."

Aaron eyed her over the top of his glasses. "If I say it sounds fine, it's because it *does* sound fine."

"I wish you wouldn't patronize me." She knew it wasn't Aaron's fault that the passage was leaden. But it was, and his denial only made it worse—made her angry, instead of simply afraid. "I hate when you do that."

"Susannah." He took off his glasses. "What's going on?"

Nothing. Everything.

Aaron waited, and then he gave a tired sigh. "I might not have your developed ear, but it really doesn't sound any different than usual."

That was the problem. Her usual had become mediocre.

A new thought flickered across her awareness, a question that hadn't occurred to her before. If she was so mediocre, why had Libby Kaufmann picked her?

Libby had let her play the entire sonata. Susannah hadn't known the reason, but secretly she'd assumed it was because she was so amazing and Libby had been too entranced to tell her to stop. She hadn't been amazing, though. The only amazing thing was the way she had pushed through the refusal of her finger to voice the top notes. But Libby hadn't known about that. Even if she had, it wouldn't have mattered to her. If anything, it would have made her wary of hiring an unreliable performer.

Doubt inched its way into the elation of being chosen. Maybe she hadn't been picked for herself, because of what she could offer. Maybe Libby was just doing what Vera, her famous aunt, had suggested, and everything else—the pride and possibility, the secret satisfaction that the magic was returning—was her own wishful thinking.

She looked at Aaron. "That's how I always sound?"

"I guess. To be honest, I don't listen that closely anymore."

She flinched, stung by his words and the casual way he had uttered them. Her music used to draw him from the other side of a room. "That's a shitty remark. It's like saying you don't listen to anything I say."

"Come on, Susannah. You can't expect me to give your playing my rapt attention, after all these years."

Yes, I can.

"Well, I'm asking you to do that now. There's something wrong, and I need you to tell me what it is."

"I already told you. I don't hear anything—"

"Because you're not listening! You're not paying attention. Just like you said."

"I can only hear what I can hear. I'm not some super-sensitive music aficionado. If that's what you want me to be, I'm sorry."

"I just want you to listen."

"I did. In my brutish, non-musical way."

Oh, she wanted to jump up and grab him. "Why are you acting like such a prick?"

"Why are *you* acting like such a diva?"

Now she really was livid. Calling her a diva—when he was the one who was being difficult, as if she was making an unreasonable demand, as if there wasn't a *bona fide* medical reason for her to—

She froze. He didn't know about her diagnosis, because she hadn't told him. No wonder he thought she was being a prima donna, fretting over imaginary flaws, fishing for compliments, and then rejecting them when they were offered.

She wasn't. They were real flaws.

A bolt of fear shot up her spine, like the needle that doctor had told her about, the one that sliced through the palmar cord. She turned to Aaron, ready to explain why she was so concerned, but his face was shuttered, locked.

She'd offended him, challenged his sincerity. She had to fix this—now—yet no words seemed right or even possible. She started to say, "Aaron," but all that came out was a strangled *aah* as his name dissolved into silence.

She wanted to start over, but she could already hear his answer. *Stop manipulating me.*

This wasn't how they were with each other. Her heart raced as seconds passed and neither of them said a word. Finally, after a long terrible moment, she closed the piano and pivoted on the bench.

James was standing in the doorway, a bag of pretzels dangling at his side. Susannah tried to speak, but he signaled *no.* Then he swirled around and disappeared.

Her hand flew to her throat. She wanted to run after him, assure him that his parents were fine, his life was fine, the nasty little scene he'd witnessed was nothing, nothing.

Aaron couldn't have seen James from where he was sitting, but he must have sensed her dismay. "Susannah?"

She pushed off the bench and slowly, woodenly, crossed the room. Then, as if an invisible string had been snipped, she collapsed into the vacant armchair. "I'm sorry," she whispered. "It's just that I'm so worried."

Concern darkened his features. "What is it? What's wrong?"

She couldn't remember why she had kept it from him. The bump that wasn't nothing. The diagnosis. Leo's infuriating *wait-and-see*. The words tumbled out, like pebbles bouncing down a staircase.

"I want to be worse, so someone will help me. But I'm scared of being worse."

"Jesus. Of course you're worried."

"Leo refuses to give me a timetable. 'Oh, it can take years.' Then again, 'Sometimes things shift dramatically.' Apparently, the *progression is quite individual.*"

"Aren't there any indicators?"

"Family history, supposedly."

"Shouldn't you look into that?"

She felt her shoulders stiffen. Aaron knew she had been adopted, but it wasn't a subject they ever talked about. "I can't. Anyway, it doesn't matter."

"It could be important," he insisted. "There must be records."

"It's not, and there aren't. And even if there were, it's only an indication. Every case is different."

"Well, what are the treatment options?"

"Besides breaking my finger?"

"Besides breaking your finger."

She winced, and he pulled his chair closer to hers. "Let me see what I can find out. Maybe there's a clinical trial, a new treatment in the pipeline."

"Another treatment?"

"There could be. An emergent protocol, something the average practitioner wouldn't be aware of." He gave a wry shrug. "You know how researchers are. They won't say anything till the data's been analyzed. But they might tell a fellow researcher."

Susannah knew Aaron was right—he might be able to find

information that hadn't been released to practicing doctors—yet she felt a familiar wariness, like a nearly-forgotten melody.

She knew her husband. Once he made up his mind to solve a problem, it became his problem, his enemy to defeat. The mildew in the basement, the way their CD player kept jumping tracks. Aaron bounded into action, taking for granted that it was a solo mission, leaving her out. She remembered how he had insisted on looking into childcare options when James was an infant, even though she'd told him that she wanted to take a leave from performing. Finally she had gotten angry, and he'd stopped sending her links to daycare websites.

"—keep going, meanwhile," Aaron was saying.

His voice jolted her into awareness. Her gaze jumped to the piano.

"Exactly," she said. "Which means back to my practicing." She gave him a quick smile, assurance that she was grateful for his support. "Maybe I can figure out a solution." Aaron looked startled, so she added, "To the musical part of the problem. Not the medical part. That's your area."

Another reassuring smile, and then she returned to the piano. She thumbed through the score to the place where she'd stumbled during the audition. Maybe shift from the fifth finger to the fourth in the measures where she had to hold the top note? *Yes.* With the new fingering, there was a shade of expression she hadn't noticed before, a subtle shift in emphasis that revealed another aspect of the musical phrase. An understanding that she never would have found, or even looked for, if she'd stayed with the fingering she was used to—if Dupuytren's hadn't made her keep searching.

Excited, she thought: What if I finger the next section differently too?

Pencil behind her ear, lips pursed in concentration, Susannah bent over the score to see what other secrets it might yield. Engrossed in discovery, she barely registered James's reappearance. He crossed the

L-shaped room and hovered by her shoulder, trying to get her attention. It was only when he said, "Mom—" that she raised her head.

"Can't it wait?"

Horrified, Susannah caught herself. She, of all people, should know that a mother had to be there for her child, never making him feel that his presence was unwanted.

She wheeled around. But for the second time that evening, her son had already left.

The generic marimba of her ringing phone meant that it wasn't her father or James or Vera, with their special melodies. The call was from Evan Chu's office.

"Mrs. Lewis? You have an appointment with Dr. Chu at eleven o'clock on Thursday?" The receptionist made it sound like a question.

"I do," Susannah said.

"Yes, well, I'm terribly sorry but Dr. Chu has had to go out of town rather unexpectedly. He asked me to call and apologize."

Out of town? She'd been counting on that appointment. "Well, when can I reschedule?"

"I'm afraid I can't say. He isn't rescheduling anything at present, not until he knows when he'll be back." The receptionist lowered her voice. "It's a family matter. That's why it's open-ended."

"Can't we just put down a time and then change it, if we have to?"

"As I said, he's not rescheduling anything at present." Her pleasant tone was beginning to fray. "The best thing is for you to check back in a couple of weeks."

Susannah's impatience grew. "I can't wait a couple of weeks."

"Is this an emergency?"

It depended on how you defined emergency. But no, it wasn't.

The receptionist's voice was polite, but the intimacy was gone. "I should be candid. Our first priority will have to be Dr. Chu's regular patients, the ones he's already working with. You're down for an initial consultation, yes?"

This was getting worse and worse. Susannah shut her eyes. "Fine. I'll call you next week."

What rotten luck. For Chu himself—although she didn't know him and had no idea what family matter meant. It could be anything, a honeymoon or an ailing relative.

She tried not to let her frustration slide into despair. Dupuytren's was slow to progress—supposedly—but how did she know where she fit on the spectrum? If you were a pianist, your biggest fear was having something wrong with your hands. Gradual or acute, it almost didn't matter.

She ended the call and sank into the chair. Every musician knew stories about pianists whose hands had failed them. Leon Fleisher and Gary Graffman, rising stars, with right hands that no longer worked. The same fingers, the fourth and fifth, curling inward, stiff and unresponsive. Doctors told Fleisher it was all in his mind, but years later they discovered that he had a treatable disorder called focal dystonia. Byron Janis, getting cortisone shots between his fingers so he could continue to play, even with crippling arthritis. Other pianists, stricken with tendonitis or repetitive stress injury, told that they had to stop playing for a year, two years, forever. That had happened to people Susannah knew. She had felt shock, pity, a secret gratitude that it would never happen to her, a secret fear that it would.

This Dupuytren's thing was different. It wasn't from abusing her fingers. It was a curse, waiting in her genes.

A legacy from people she hadn't thought about in years, and didn't want to think about now.

Chapter Nine
then

Learning that Corinne was dead was bad enough, but learning about Simone was worse. There wasn't supposed to be a Simone, that's what Dana had told her. *Your birthmother couldn't take care of any baby.* The fact of Simone meant that Dana was wrong. There *was* a chosen baby, but it wasn't her.

Why had everyone wanted Simone so much? Not just Corinne, but Wayne too. When Susannah set out for the hospital in La Posada, she hadn't thought about searching for a birth father, only for the elusive Corinne Dumont. But Corinne was dead, and her secrets were buried with her. Wayne, on the other hand, was alive. Knowable.

Who was he, after all these years? Hollis had mentioned a family and a promotion. Clearly, he wasn't the person he had been at nineteen, reluctant to be tied down. He was settled, mature. Surely he would embrace her, the way he'd embraced his other children. Want her, the way he'd wanted Simone.

First, though, she would have to find him. Hollis would know where he was. Hollis knew everything.

There was no time to ease into it. She had to corner Hollis again and ask for his address.

She found Hollis the next morning, sitting at Beryl's kitchen table, drying her nails. "What do you think?" Hollis asked, holding out her arm and peering at the turquoise ovals. "I got tired of the pink."

Susannah pulled out the opposite chair and sat down. "It's pretty."

Hollis wrinkled her nose. "Maybe not."

"I like it," Susannah said, even though she didn't. She had no idea which answer Hollis wanted.

She watched as Hollis dipped a brush into the jar and started on the second coat. "Hollis," she said. There was no point pretending to be interested in nail polish or bayous. "You need to tell me where to find Wayne."

"Wayne." Hollis blew out a puff of air.

"I have to talk to him."

"Whatever for?"

Susannah couldn't believe that Hollis was so obtuse, or would have the nerve to pretend that she was. She glared at her, daring Hollis to make her explain.

After a long minute Hollis sat back, spreading her fingers in a tur-quoise-tipped fan. "Done and done with that one. No point stirring up trouble."

"You're the one who told me about him," Susannah said. "You had to know I'd want to meet him."

"I told you because you kept pestering me. To put an end to it, not jump-start a whole new bunch of demands."

"If you know where to find him, you have no right to withhold that information from me."

"I can do what I like." Hollis blew on her fingernails again. "What's he ever done for me, except steal that little girl and break my sister's heart?"

"You're not doing it for him. You're doing it for me."

Like that would be a big motivator, Susannah thought. But it was all she had.

"Lord, you know how to carry on." Hollis flicked her eyes skyward. Then she gave a pained sigh. "Fine, I'll tell you, but don't you go saying it came from me. And do *not* let on that you know about Simone. In fact, forget about Simone." When Susannah tried to ask why, Hollis cut her off. "I know what I'm talking about. So promise." Susannah nodded. "Out loud."

"Okay, I promise."

"I mean it. There's no way you'd know about Simone except from me or Ma, and Wayne would figure that out in two seconds flat."

"All I want is a chance to meet him face-to-face. I've got no reason to bring you into it."

"You better mean that, ladybug." Hollis threw her a sideways look. "Well, it's Wayne Russell, if you must know. Lives in La Posada." She gestured at the counter. "Grab that notepad so you can write down the address. My nails aren't dry."

Susannah found the notepad that Beryl kept by the phone. Wayne Russell. She would have been Susannah Russell, then. Or maybe they would have named her something else. Probably they would have, since Dana and Tyler were the ones who named her Susannah. Maybe she would have been named Simone. Funny to think like that: herself, in the same body, but with someone else's name.

"Thank you, Hollis," she said. "I really appreciate it."

"Thanks don't pay for the coffee. Just do like I said."

"I will." Then she repeated, "I promise."

Tucking the paper into her pocket, Susannah pushed open the screen door and stepped into the backyard. Randall's toy truck lay on its side in the dirt, missing a wheel. A row of shirts and pillowcases flapped on the line.

She turned her face to the Texas sun. Would she be glad she'd insisted, or would she wish she'd taken Hollis's advice and left Wayne alone?

She thought of calling first, giving him a chance to prepare, but decided it would be better to just go to his house, as she'd done with Beryl. She told Beryl she had some errands to run, borrowed her car, and drove to La Posada.

She found the house easily, a ranch-style building on a treeless cul-de-sac with a red Camaro in the driveway and basketball hoop over the garage. A flagstone path zigzagged to a covered entrance with Doric-style columns and a big double door.

When she knocked on Beryl's door that first time, Susannah had no idea what she might find, but now she knew enough of the story to be nervous. Steeling herself, she pressed the doorbell. She heard someone yell, "I'll get it!" The front door was flung open. A girl with a flaxen ponytail stood in the doorway. She looked about ten or eleven. Her face fell when she saw Susannah. "Oh," she said. "I thought you were Lorelei."

"Nope. Sorry about that."

"Well, who *are* you?"

Another sister. "My name's Susannah. Is your Daddy home, by any chance? Wayne Russell?"

"Da-ad!" she hollered. "Someone at the door for you."

The voice was baritone, with a deep drawl. "Don't tell me it's one of them Jehovah's Witnesses."

"I don't think so," the girl yelled back. Then, as if remembering her manners, she told Susannah, "Won't you come in?" Susannah stepped inside. She saw a coat tree and a brass umbrella stand, a light fixture styled to look like a candelabra with flame-shaped bulbs. She heard a footstep, loud on the tiled floor, and there he was.

Tan, slim. Another pair of cornflower eyes. "Yes?"

She realized that she'd forgotten the adoption papers, the ones she had showed Beryl to prove who she was. Without them, why would he believe her? Was his name even on the papers? Why hadn't she checked, prepared better? She was crazy, showing up like this.

"Yes?" he repeated. There was no recognition on his face. She had thought, somehow, that he would just know. That was why she hadn't needed any papers. But he didn't.

Her mind raced, desperate for a story that would explain her appearance on his doorstep. Normal, not suspicious, not demented. What connection could she possibly have to this family?

An answer came to her at once, the only one that seemed believable.

"I'm a friend of Simone's," she said. "From last summer." Surely Simone had done something last summer. A job? A summer class? They were close enough in age to know each other. "She told me to look her up if I was in the area."

Then why did she ask for Wayne and not Simone? *Shit.* Why not point a neon arrow at her deception? But Wayne didn't seem to notice. Maybe he wasn't sharp like that.

"Simone's at college," he said. He leaned against the doorjamb. "She'll be home in a few days for her Spring break."

"Oh, too bad. I must've got the dates mixed up." Sweat poured down her back. The very thing Hollis had told her not to do, and she had done it in the first minute. But Wayne had bought her story. That was the main thing. He didn't suspect her of—what? What was the terrible act she didn't want to be discovered committing?

"Course, you could run up and see her now, if you're in a rush," Wayne said. "Hardly more than a three-beer drive."

"No, it's okay."

"You're a friend of Simone's?" the girl piped. She was still in the foyer, watching them. She squinted at Susannah. "You kind of look like her."

Susannah's heart jumped. "That's the college style."

Wayne frowned. "Hush, Ruth Ann. Mind your manners." Then he peered at Susannah, his eyes narrowing. "You want me to give Simone a message?"

"No, it's fine. I'll catch her later." Susannah brushed back her hair. "I just figured it was worth a shot, being in the neighborhood and all."

The girl gave a prim, queenly smile. "Who may I say is calling?"

A wildness reared up in her. She raised her eyes to Wayne's. Blue, like hers.

"Susannah," she said. She searched his face for a sign. "Susannah Dumont."

He stepped back, as if he'd been slapped.

Good Lord. What had possessed her? Then she thought: why not? That was why she had come.

The message seemed clear: yes, Corinne's daughter, and your daughter too. Fear and hope collided in her chest. But Wayne drew a different conclusion.

His face grew dark. "You some relation of that crazy Beryl Dumont? I told her to leave Simone alone. It's over. Let the girl be." His eyes were blue slits. "You give your relations a message from me, missy. Leave. Us. The. Fuck. Alone. You got that?"

"Daddy, you said the F word!"

"You bet I did." He kicked the front door open. "You need to leave," he told Susannah.

She gazed at him for a moment that felt like a lifetime. Then, lowering her head, she turned and fled down the flagstone walkway. Her heart was thundering, cracking open.

Wayne's letter arrived by special delivery the next day. It was the last day of Susannah's visit, and she wondered if she was lucky or unlucky that she was there when it came.

The letter was addressed to Mrs. Beryl Dumont. "This business was settled years ago," he'd written. Anger seeped through the typed lines. "The court decided, and Simone decided, so do not get some new relative of yours to come trespassing on my property pretending to be her friend. This is called harassment, and I got a lawyer for that."

"What the H is this?" Beryl demanded.

Susannah took the letter, turning pale as she read. "Well?" Beryl repeated. "I smell your meddling all over this." She grabbed her Marlboros from the table. "I told you to leave that snake alone. Now see what you done." She lit a cigarette, shaking out the match with a snap of her wrist.

"I just wanted to meet him."

"Nobody ever listens to me." Beryl dropped into a kitchen chair. "You think I said all that about him 'cause I felt like being ornery?" She peered up at Susannah. "Hollis know about this?"

"No." Susannah shook her head. "She gave me his name and address because I wouldn't leave her alone, but she made me promise not to say anything about Simone."

"But you did anyway."

"I panicked. Made up a stupid story to explain why I was there." She felt worse and worse. "I didn't know what else to do."

Beryl gave her a disgusted look. "There's always something else to do. Might be to do nothing."

"You're right. I just—"

"Just what? You stir things up, and then you go back north. Who's supposed to clean this up now? Not you. You're gone."

"I'm so sorry."

"You should be." Beryl stabbed the cigarette into the ashtray. "You know, we welcomed you into our family, no problem, but if I say *no* about something, it's for a good reason. I don't need no more lawsuits from that man. Lawyers ain't free, case you haven't heard."

Susannah nodded miserably. This had gone so wrong. Wayne

would never want to know her now. Beryl was angry. And Hollis would be furious.

Then, all at once, she had an idea. It was so obvious that it almost made her laugh. "You're right, I was crazy to make up a story. But I can fix it. All I have to do is tell him the truth." Her voice rose, eager now. "He'll understand why I showed up at his house, and he'll see that it had nothing to do with you harassing him."

Beryl's gaze was sharp. "He might see that I didn't put you up to anything, but that don't mean he'll be thrilled to meet some long-lost love child." She tucked the cigarette between her fingers. "So tell him the *truth* if you want, but don't expect nothing from it. Save yourself another disappointment, is all I'm saying."

Susannah's excitement faded, doubt taking its place. Beryl watched her keenly. Then her face softened, and she said, "Come with me."

She beckoned Susannah to a bedroom at the far end of the house, across from the guest room where Susannah had been staying. Her own bedroom, and Jimmy Ray's. There was a four-poster bed with a pink-and-gold spread and an oversized bureau. A line of porcelain dolls, arranged from smallest to largest, were aligned along the top. Balancing her cigarette on the edge of the bureau, Beryl pulled out a drawer and removed a velvet box. "This was hers. Corinne's."

Susannah took the box and opened the lid. A gold chain rested on lavender padding, pulled into a V by a tiny sapphire pendant. "Might be little," Beryl said, "but it's real." Susannah touched the stone. It was surprisingly warm.

Beryl tossed her head. "I figured, no sense *it* going into the ground. She wore it all the time, you know, but I said heck, take it off and let me have it. I figured—well, who knows what I figured." She put a hand on her hip, watching Susannah. "I thought of giving it to Simone, but we weren't having much contact at that point, to tell you the truth, so I just put it in a drawer. I never imagined there'd be someone else come along to give it to."

Susannah picked up the gold chain and slipped it over her neck. "Pretty, ain't it?" Beryl said. "Well, you ought to get something for your trouble, coming all this way. Makes me glad I never gave it to Simone."

The chain was light. Susannah could hardly feel it. She adjusted the pendant and turned to Beryl, suddenly curious. "Were you angry at Simone?" she asked. "For picking him?"

"Oh, I suppose. But you couldn't really blame her."

She thought of the ranch house on the cul-de-sac, the flame-shaped bulbs and the well-tended yard. "I suppose not." Then she looked at Beryl. For the first time, it struck her: Beryl had buried a daughter and lost a granddaughter. People she had known and cared about, not just people she imagined. "You missed her."

"Well, of course." Beryl stroked the lavender velvet. "We just loved Simone. She had the sweetest voice, you know, and she played that autoharp good as June Carter."

"Autoharp." Not piano.

"Yes, ma'am. Haven't heard her in years, though." Beryl's expression grew wistful. "Never heard her play in that band she's in. Lorraine—that's Jimmy Ray's sister—went to hear 'em. Said they weren't half bad."

Another musician, Susannah thought. "Maybe I could go to hear her some time."

She kept her eyes on the velvet box. *And see what's so great about her.*

Beryl seemed to read her mind. "It ain't personal, you know. Never was. Corinne let you go 'cause she thought it was the best thing for you. She cried plenty over it, but in her own way she knew she did right by you. With Simone, it was different. She had that little girl for five whole years. Felt bad that she'd failed her, which she had, of course. She was a lousy mother, and that's why Wayne got Simone."

She reached out to touch Susannah's cheek. "It's just chance that

you were born first and Simone was born second. Just the way it happened, sugar."

Even so, Susannah thought. *I need to meet her.*

Her. The one who looked like her, and was kept.

Chapter Ten
then

Susannah made her third trip to Texas on a humid Wednesday at the end of August. Her job at the private school wouldn't resume until September, but the colleges in Texas were already in session. Simone was at one of those colleges, and Susannah intended to find her.

This time, she didn't tell anyone, not even Beryl. She needed to be on her own, free to follow the trail wherever it led.

She had enough to get started. Name. Age. In college, somewhere in Texas. Wayne had described the campus as a *three-beer drive* from La Posada. Susannah had no idea what that meant—how fast did a person drink beer?—but it didn't sound far. And Simone was in some kind of band, playing the autoharp. A bluegrass or country group, good enough to play for audiences.

She booked a motel room in Houston, figuring that Houston would be a good base. It had a big library, with microfilm and bound copies of the local newspapers. If Simone was in a band that performed publicly, there had to be a notice, maybe even a photo. There were music festivals, a calendar of events. Jimmy Ray's sister had heard them play somewhere.

She had five days. Surely someone smart and resourceful could find a missing sister in five days.

Susannah began with the main library in the Jesse H. Jones Building. The young woman at the front desk directed her to the reading room where they kept the periodicals. It didn't take long to find the prior year's bound copies of the *Houston Chronicle, Texas Observer, Austin Chronicle,* and *Austin-American Statesman.* She spent a whole day poring over the newspapers but there was nothing remotely related to what she was looking for. The papers covered first-run movies and concerts by famous singers, not amateur bands.

Next, she tried researching the Country Music Association and their annual music festival. There was a list of performing groups but no photos or captions, so there was no way to tell if any of them was Simone's. Anyway, it looked like only the most famous people performed there.

Local clubs? She tried the yellow pages. The number of venues was endless. She tried calling a few to ask if they had a list of groups that had performed in recent months. They didn't, though they all said she could come down and take a flyer for their upcoming shows. She tried that, trekking from club to club, but the only photos on the flyers were of male guitarists in cowboy hats. If Simone's group was mentioned—and there was no way to know, not without knowing the name of the band—it would probably be as a second or third act, in small print, without a photo.

This was useless, Susannah decided. A list of bands wouldn't help, not without already knowing which one Simone was in. She went to bed the second night, no closer to finding Simone than she had been when she arrived in Houston.

She awoke the third day with a fresh idea. Simone's college. Maybe her band had played on campus. There couldn't be that many colleges in the area. She went back to the library and found the Peterson directory of colleges and universities. There was the University of Houston, Sam Houston State, and the Lone Star College, a network of community colleges. She ruled out the historically black institutions, religious colleges, and medical schools; Simone was twenty-one, too young for graduate school, not black, and probably not religious enough for a Bible college. The University of Houston had the *Daily Cougar* and Sam Houston had *The Houstonian*. Susannah read the campus newspapers with mounting excitement but found nothing. Then she thought: maybe Simone went to school in Austin? It made sense. Houston was too close to La Posada to be a *three-beer drive* and Austin seemed like a hipper town, more like a place a girl her age would want to be.

She went back to the Peterson directory and looked up Austin. The University of Texas at Austin was a whole tier above the University of Houston. Was Simone that good a student? She tried Austin Community College first, figuring—coming from her background— that Simone was more likely to be at a small community college. But its student newspaper, the *Accent*, had nothing about a band with an autoharp player. Her disappointment was keen. She'd really thought that this was the answer. Then she realized: no, Simone was too old to be at a two-year college. She went back to the Reading Room and found *The Daily Texan*, UT-Austin's campus paper. Nothing there either, though it did mention a few local venues where student groups performed. She skimmed the listings. Apparently, Austin called itself the live music capital of the world; that was why there were so many clubs. Maybe she should just go there, check around. Well, why not? She didn't have any better ideas.

On the fourth morning Susannah drove to Austin. The trip took less than three hours. Was that what he meant by a three-beer drive? She located the UT campus, found a place to park, and followed the campus map to the Student Activity Center. There had to be a bulletin board with information about student performers. She wandered from room to room, from wall to wall. This was starting to feel ridiculous. Why didn't she just ask Beryl? Or forget the whole thing? No, she'd come this far. She was going to find Simone, no matter what she had to do. If she didn't find her on this trip, she'd come back.

She spent the afternoon wandering around the UT campus, studying the papers tacked to kiosks and bulletin boards, scanning the faces of passing students. She was tired. Her feet were sore, and her whole body felt gritty and soiled.

It was late in the afternoon when she found it. A wrinkled flyer, tacked to a cork bulletin board by the bookstore, advertising *The All-Girl Lone Star Mother Plucking Band*. There was a picture of four laughing young women in cowboy hats: one on the standing bass, one on guitar, one on what looked like a banjo or mandolin, and one on the autoharp. The caption read: Friday through Sunday at 8:00. The Red Rooster, Congress & Sixth.

The girl with the autoharp stared back at her, like a face in the mirror.

The Red Rooster was a small club with a garish wooden rooster over the bar and round tables around a raised stage. The host seated her at a table with three other women. Susannah apologized for intruding, but they brushed her apologies aside and resumed their conversation. A waitress came and asked what she'd like to drink. "Do you have Merlot?" she asked.

"No ma'am. Just house red and house white." Susannah ordered a glass of red wine before realizing that everyone else was drinking beer.

The lights dimmed, and a stocky man in a tan cowboy hat walked across the stage, dragging a microphone. Susannah held the edge of the table, her fingers so tight she thought they might snap, like piano strings that had been stretched too far. The waitress brought her wine. She nodded thank-you but didn't touch it.

"Evening, y'all!" the man boomed. "Everyone ready to have a good time?" The crowd cheered. "Before we bring on Tommy Lee and his amazing twelve-string, we have an opening act I know you're gonna love. Give it up for four of the prettiest and most talented UT coeds you'll ever meet." He clapped loudly as four young women ran onstage, carrying their instruments and waving. They wore white fringed jackets and bright green neckerchiefs. All four had big hair, teased high and falling in curls to their shoulders.

Susannah watched, transfixed. The tallest girl adjusted the microphone, shook out her long auburn hair, and gave the audience a wide grin. "Hi there, y'all. Glad to be here. We're the All-Girl Lone Star Mother Plucking Band." She paused for the laughter. "We do a bluegrass-country fusion with a bunch of rock-and-roll thrown in. We hope you'll like our sound." She pointed to her fellow musicians. "This here is Maggie Rose on the steel-string, and Noelle on the mandolin and fiddle. Simone does the honors on the autoharp, plus our lead vocals. And I'm Ava on the stand-up bass."

It really was her, then.

The women took their places. "We'll lead off with a Carter Family favorite," Ava said. "I think y'all know *Wildwood Flower.*" She signaled to the others, and the opening notes filled the room. The music was joyous, irresistible, like a game of catch between the mandolin and the autoharp. Then the other instruments stepped in as the four women passed the music back and forth, joinig voices in a jubilant ending.

The audience applauded loudly, and the band went straight into a playful mixture of *You Ain't Woman Enough to Take my Man* and *Stand by Your Man.* Simone's voice was clear and strong. After two verses she backed away from the microphone as first Noelle and then

Maggie Rose did instrumental solos. Then she raised the autoharp and joined back in. The applause was even louder.

Susannah reached for her drink, her hand shaking. Part of her longed to jump up and grab the fiddle that was lying in its case. Right, she thought. I'll just add my sound to the mix. Maybe a little riff from Bach's Partita Number Two?

She set the glass down, without drinking, as Simone stepped to the front of the stage. The spotlight caught Simone's thoughtful gaze, and the crowd grew quiet. A plaintive line arose from the bass, followed by the guitar, and then her tremolo. *I'll only be in your way.*

Susannah squeezed her eyes shut. Simone sang the ballad country style, pure and painful: the quavering notes, the heartbreaking ascent. *I Will Always Love You.*

She'd always thought the song was about a woman walking away from the man she loved, but now she heard it differently. It was about a woman leaving her child. Or maybe it was the child leaving its mother. Either way, they were being ripped apart. She could almost hear the screech of the fabric.

Your birth mother loved you very much, and that's why she made the very best plan she could. That was what Dana always told her. But Dana didn't really know that; it was a story she'd made up and liked to tell. No one knew what her birth mother had felt. All they knew was that she had given her child away. One of her children.

You have a special gift. That was the other thing Dana liked to say. The way Susannah could make the music rise up out of the piano. Mind, hands, heart—together, the harmony of herself, transforming the hieroglyph on the page into something glorious and alive.

Susannah's pulse beat against her temples. Special gift. Chosen baby. Were the two things connected? Dana always made it seem like they were. But Simone had a gift too.

Slowly, she opened her eyes. There was a beat of silence as the song ended, and then a riot of applause. The women at the little wooden table jumped to their feet. Behind her, someone shouted, "You go, girls!"

The man in the tan cowboy hat strode back onto the stage. "What'd I tell ya about these gals? Ain't they sweethearts? They've got one more number, and then we'll give 'em a rest."

The other three members of the All-Girl Lone Star Mother Plucking Band joined Simone at the front of the stage. Simone picked up her autoharp. Noelle gave the opening notes on the mandolin, and the band burst into a joyous, rock-and-roll rendition of *Ring of Fire*. The audience loved it, shouting and clapping. Susannah wanted to applaud too, but she couldn't move, couldn't even lift her hands. The musicians ran offstage, waving happily. Susannah excused herself as she stumbled between the tables.

She thought, for an insane instant, that she might push past the bartender and rush into the dressing room or wherever the band had gone. And do what? Throw herself at their mercy? Instead, she ran out into the street. She took great gulping breaths, as if her lungs couldn't fill quickly enough.

When she was halfway down the block, she stopped. Why was she running away, after coming so far? Maybe she ought to turn around and go back, introduce herself? She sagged against a building and brushed back her hair. The strands were damp with sweat. A few people glanced at her as they passed. "You okay?" a man asked.

Susannah managed a faint smile. "I'm fine. Thank you."

She wasn't fine. She was weak, ill. She'd wanted to see Simone for herself. If she saw her, maybe she'd understand the difference between them—why Simone had been kept and cherished and fought over, and she had been given away.

It ain't personal, Beryl had said. The same thing that lawyer had told her, back when she was in high school. *Don't assume it has anything to do with you personally.* Susannah gave a bitter laugh. Of course it was personal. That was like saying your life wasn't personal.

She'd seen Simone but she still didn't understand. Simone was pretty, with a lovely voice, but it wasn't that. It wasn't something you could see just by looking at her. It was some secret essential thing that no one would tell her.

Susannah squeezed her hands into hard little fists. The wall she was leaning against, peach-colored stucco, was scraping her skin right through her shirt. A million tiny stings, burning their pattern into her flesh.

Passers-by were looking at her strangely. This wasn't like New York, where people leaned against buildings muttering to themselves and no one cared. She needed to get off the street, away from Austin. With a jerk, she pushed away from the wall and started walking, back to the side street where she'd parked the rental car.

Shivering, even though the night was hot and humid, Susannah bent to unlock the car door. She didn't know what to do. All she knew was that she had to get out of there.

Chapter Eleven

now

To Susannah's surprise, Libby Kaufmann had been effusive and generous, insisting that a photo of her at the piano would be the central image on the publicity material and program notes. Across the top of the program, Libby told her, they would have the name of the concert hall, the date and time. Then Susannah's name and—in big bold letters—Schubert's B-flat Major Sonata. Then a color photo and, below that, the name of the organization: *The Isis Project*, after the Egyptian goddess of healing and transformation. "Because it's to help women recover," Libby explained. "Trauma, abuse. You know, things like that."

"Don't you want to feature the organization, rather than me or the music?" Susannah asked. "I mean, since it's a fundraiser?"

But Libby was sure of her vision and Susannah didn't want to argue, especially about being the featured image. "You should look like you're playing," Libby added. "And smiling, of course."

It was a ridiculous instruction. People didn't smile for the camera while they played the piano. But Susannah knew better than to act like a purist. Libby was a publicist, and she was in charge.

Libby wanted to meet at the concert hall to block out the photo shoot. "I need to see you in the actual space, with the actual lighting. I want something fresh, with flair. Not some dreary old cliché."

It seemed excessive to Susannah, but refusing wasn't an option. She canceled her Tuesday pupils and drove into Manhattan. She arrived first, and the building manager let her into the hall to wait for Libby. It was a beautiful structure, built in the same beaux-arts style as Grand Central Terminal and the Metropolitan Museum of Art, with ornate moldings and carved bannisters, an arched ceiling, and a graceful curve of polished steps that led to the stage. Susannah tilted her head to study the pattern of acoustic tiles on the ceiling. Everything mattered when you performed: the shape of the room, the temperature, the way the sound traveled from wall to wall.

"Dang, you beat me here."

Wheeling around, she saw Libby stride into the auditorium. "I meant to be early," Libby said, "but traffic was an absolute bear." She crossed the room and gave Susannah air kisses on both cheeks. "Are you excited or are you excited?"

"About the photo shoot or the concert?"

"Hey, be excited about both." Libby drew back and tapped a manicured finger against her lips. "Much better. The piano they had in here was unbelievably ugly, hardly photogenic at all. This one is much more attractive, don't you think?"

Susannah turned to the stage. She hadn't really noticed the piano when she came in; the architecture had captured her attention. What she saw stunned her. This wasn't the instrument she had played when she came to meet with Libby after they signed the contract, when Libby showed her the concert hall and the room where they would hold the reception. "Get a nice dress," Libby had told her. "You know, long and black. People like that."

This piano was white, with a red velvet bench. Susannah recoiled at the shock of color, like a child's Valentine. How could she have missed it? She'd been looking at the carvings, the tiles on the ceiling—it seemed impossible that she hadn't taken a moment to look at the piano.

It was because she'd assumed. No one would switch pianos like that, not without consulting the performer.

She turned back to Libby. "You mean, for the photo shoot, right? You wanted a white piano for the photo?"

Maybe she was over-reacting and her heart was pounding for no reason. She wouldn't have to play for the photo shoot, only look like she was playing.

Libby waved a hand. "Oh, for whatever."

Susannah's heartbeat grew louder. "What does that mean?"

Libby opened her purse, rummaging through it while she answered. "The evening's black tie, you know, with a great big price tag. People will expect something striking. So will the media."

"You mean, this is the piano for the *concert*?"

"It's fabulous, isn't it?" Libby pulled out her cell phone, squinting at a text.

"I don't know." Susannah tried to stay calm. The piano might be fine. "I can't tell you till I try it."

She didn't want to make Libby angry, but what Libby had done was wrong. This wasn't a stage set for a play called *The Concert*. You didn't switch instruments because one was more photogenic.

Slowly, Susannah climbed the steps and crossed the stage to the piano. As soon as her fingers touched the keys, she knew. She made herself play for a minute so Libby wouldn't think she was making a snap judgment, but there was no doubt: it was all wrong, the action, the voicing, the regulation. She couldn't possibly play the second movement of the sonata on this thing.

She drew in her breath. She had to make Libby understand without making her angry. There were other pianists who would be glad to take her place, no matter what instrument they had to play on.

"I was okay with the piano you had before," she said, "but truthfully, this one is pretty awful. We need to get the other one back. If you want to wait till after the photographer comes, okay, but right after that, please."

Libby's tone was airy, unconcerned. "Oh goodness, is it really all that different?"

"Yes. It really is all that different." Susannah wet her lip. "Each part of the sonata has its own quality. You have to have an instrument that's sensitive and responsive. Otherwise—" Her words trailed off.

Libby walked to the piano. "Once we put the lid up—" she began, but Susannah shook her head. "Well," Libby said, "I don't really see how we can switch them back at this point. They needed the other one somewhere else, and I told the facilities person this one was just fine."

Then she sat down next to Susannah and put an arm around her waist. "Actually," she said, lowering her voice, a girlfriend eager to share a secret. "I have some news for you that's much more exciting than whether we've got ourselves piano number one or piano number two. You wouldn't mind a little special attention, would you?"

Susannah stiffened. She'd been talking about the tone and touch, not about a publicity stunt.

Libby gave a conspiratorial wink. "You are going to *love* me for this, Susannah dear." Sliding closer, she whispered, "You are never going to guess who's coming to the concert. Specifically to hear you play, thank you very much."

"Who?"

"Carlo Perez-Smith, that's who."

Susannah's eyes widened. "Perez-Smith?"

"Mr. Important Music Producer." Libby sat back, clearly pleased with herself. "Apparently he heard the late Brahms program you did last fall, in that church? Anyway, he's absolutely dying to meet you. I told him you were our soloist, and he asked me to save him a front row seat. So there."

Carlo Perez-Smith. Everyone in the music world knew who he was. A king-maker. Or queen-maker. "He heard me play last fall? He remembered, and he wants to hear me again?"

Libby gave a smug, cat-like smile. "I think you're about to be discovered, my friend. Like I said, who really cares which piano it is?"

Susannah stared at her in disbelief. Libby might be a terrific publicist but she understood nothing about music. Having the right piano was more important now, not less.

Libby gave her another quick squeeze. "You're the one, Suzie-girl, with your B-flat whatever. I knew it, the minute you started to play."

No, Susannah wanted to cry. It wasn't her B-flat whatever. It was Schubert's final gift, demanding the best a pianist could offer. You couldn't play it any old way, on any old instrument. Your piano and your hands: those were your tools.

"So we're good to go?" Libby asked. It wasn't really a question.

Susannah met her eyes. "No," she said. "I need a better piano."

Libby's face hardened. "This is one fine piano."

"It's not, Libby."

Libby removed her hand from Susannah's waist. "Here's the thing," she said, her voice turning cool and businesslike. "I got you star treatment, I got you a perfectly good piano, and I got you Perez-Smith. If you want to bring in a different piano, be my guest." She rose, smoothing her skirt. "It's fine, whatever you want to do. But I'm sure you'll appreciate that we can't pay a lot of extra labor charges to move a bunch of pianos around for you. This *is* a fundraiser, after all."

Susannah got the message. She'd find another piano on her own, then, without Libby. She'd go to Steinway Hall, rent a concert grand. People did that; she remembered Vera telling her stories about finding just the right piano for a specific performance.

She'd figure it out. Whatever it took.

—

James stormed in, banging the door behind him. The sound of wood on wood was harsh and angry. "Where the fuck were you?"

Susannah looked up from the keyboard as he stormed into the room and planted himself in front of her, his face dark with fury. "*James*. You are not permitted to–"

"Not permitted to what? Be embarrassed and pissed off that I had to call Andrew's mom because you never showed?"

"Never showed? What on earth are you talking about?"

Then she remembered. Oh my god. She was supposed to drive James and his friends home after their basketball game. Her eyes flew to the clock above the bookcase. Five-thirty, when she'd promised to be there, had come and gone an hour ago. She'd been so upset about Libby, so keyed up about Perez-Smith, that she had gone straight to the piano when she got home, escaping into the most restorative music she knew. Bach's transcendent cantata, *Gottes Zeit ist die aller-beste Zeit*. The aria from the Goldbergs.

She'd lost track of the time. And now it was six thirty-eight, and her son was livid.

"Oh James," she breathed. "I am so, so sorry. Why didn't you call me?"

He gave a disgusted snort. "I did. Twice. You never answered." He gestured toward the other end of the house. "You probably have your phone buried somewhere or on mute, so it won't *disturb your practicing*."

Susannah turned ashen, because of course he was right. She hated the phone's incessant demand, like a hungry infant clamoring to be picked up. "I didn't realize—no, never mind. You're right. I let you down terribly. How in the world did you get home?"

"We had to call Andrew's mom. She left work to get us."

Susannah winced, grateful for Andrew's reliable and reachable mother, and aghast that she'd forgotten. "Thank goodness she came through for you. And I am so very sorry, James. I can't tell you how mortified I am."

She assumed he would be the kindly James she had always known, the boy with the big sunny grin that seemed to say *Hey world, don't you just love me?* The James who knew she meant well and would tell her that everything was fine. She'd done that for him, over the years. Consoled him when he dropped the little clay bird he made for Mother's Day, shattering it and leaving her without a gift. Assured him that she wasn't angry when he announced that Zev's mother made the best chocolate chip cookies in the world. In turn, he had accepted her shortcomings. The way she tuned out when he talked about sports. The time she burned the lasagna because she was absorbed in working with a student, another boy, not him. But this was a different James, huge and unforgiving.

He glared at her, his eyebrows meeting in an angry slash. "No one cares if you're mortified. Feeling mortified isn't like an overdue fine at the library." He mimed wiping his hands. "I admit I suck. Fine paid. Good as new."

Susannah's mouth dropped open. This couldn't be James, no matter how upset he was. But it *was* James, bright with rage, as if he could hardly believe she was sitting there, the piano score open in front of her, telling him how sorry she felt—as if the woman facing him across the piano was just as much a stranger to him as this furious man-child was to her.

He bent to scoop up Oscar, who had sidled into the room mewing and looking for attention. "Forget it," he said, burying his face in the cat's fur. "I'll get my license in a couple of months and you won't have to interrupt your precious schedule to pick me up."

Susannah inhaled, torn between anger at the way James had spoken to her and shame at having let him down. She didn't know if she wanted to ground him for his rudeness or apologize for her own. Her role as a mother had always been her safe harbor, the job she did well. Of course, she'd never forgotten to pick up her child before. If she hadn't forgotten, he wouldn't have sworn at her.

She let out a sigh. She was still his mother, even if she had screwed up.

"Look," she said. "I respect how you're feeling, and you have every right to feel that way. But cursing at someone, without even stopping to ask what might have happened—it's nasty and arrogant and well, just plain wrong. You can't do it, James."

"Fine," he muttered. "Just show up and I won't curse."

Susannah gritted her teeth. He wasn't making it easy. "I know I've been preoccupied lately," she began, "and I can see how that would make you feel neglected." She almost said, "Of course, you're never home anymore, so you've been neglecting me too." But that wouldn't be fair. A child could venture into the world precisely because he knew his parents would be there when he returned. That was the whole point of the life she'd built for him.

Lifting his face from Oscar's fur, James eyed her coolly. "Sorry, Mom. *Preoccupied* doesn't give you a free pass for fucking up."

"My messing up doesn't give you a free pass either."

"Free pass for what?" His voice rose, cracking with righteousness. The cat wriggled free and jumped down.

For being so disrespectful, she wanted to cry. *Not even trying to see my side, not even wondering if I had a side.*

The James she knew would never talk to her like that. But he wasn't that James any more. He was fifteen, not five. Nearly as old as she'd been when she reached out for the mother who told her to go away.

With a swift piercing ache, she longed for the younger James, the cherub who climbed on her lap and put his dimpled hands on top of hers while she played. When he got too big for her lap, he'd sit close to her on the bench, brow knitted in concentration as he pretended to read the score. That James had morphed into a sullen teenager, full of secrets and scorn.

She moved her legs out of the way as Oscar slithered past. "Free pass for cursing," she said, finally.

"I don't need a pass. I didn't leave anyone stranded."

"I'm sorry. I don't know what else to say."

I'm sorry I forgot about you. Went on, busy with my music, as if you didn't exist.

I'm sorry I didn't want you. Went on. As if you didn't exist.

When James was born, with his spikey lashes and rosebud mouth, she had wept with gratitude—not just because he was there, real, safe, but for herself too. Because she was truly connected, in a way she had never known.

James had grabbed her finger in his fierce little fist. Her heart had opened, letting in the terrible, vulnerable love.

She tried to catch his eye, hoping for a glimmer of forgiveness. "Anyway, I made that casserole you like, the one with the bacon that you're always—"

"I'm getting pizza with some of the guys," he said. "Patrick, Zev. Maybe Andrew if his mom isn't too pissed."

"Patrick? Is Patrick driving you around? I don't like the idea of—"

James laughed, but there was no joy in the sound. "Really, Mom? You don't like the idea of someone else driving me?"

Susannah recoiled. "All right. I get it." She forced a smile. "Okay. Have fun."

"Always." He gave a mock salute, breezing out again, leaving her sitting at the piano.

She closed the lid. She didn't feel like playing any more.

Chapter Twelve

now

Susannah ripped a sheet of yellow lined paper from the pad, uncapped her pen, and started a list of things she had to do. Talk to Vera about renting a concert grand; Vera would know how to do it. Put James's basketball schedule into her iCal. Call the hot water people.

She underlined the last item. The shower had sputtered again that morning, angry plops of tepid water, then a hiss and a strangled throb before the hot water finally kicked in. "Can you get someone to come and have a look?" Aaron had asked. "Let's be smart about it, instead of waiting till the thing dies on us." Susannah assured him that she would.

She added three more items. Check with Chu's office, just in case. Find a publicist. Visit her father.

She wrote *basketball* and *water* on a post-it and left a message for Vera, who didn't answer. Then she thought about her father, and how lonely he had sounded on the phone. She had promised to visit him again. Better to do it now, before the frenzy of last-minute tasks as the concert date approached.

—

Tyler was still living in the elegant apartment complex that he and Dana had moved into when they retired. It featured a nine-hole golf course, on-site hair salon, and Wednesday night movies. The day's offerings were posted in the lobby: bus trips, themed dinners, Bingo. Susannah's parents had prided themselves on being the only residents to never once attend a Bingo game. Determined to keep their brains from turning to risotto, as she put it, Dana had organized a book club—picking the books she thought everyone should read, planning the discussion questions, writing reviews for the community newsletter. When she got too sick to get out of bed, the book club members came to their apartment. After a few weeks, she told Tyler to send them away. That was when Susannah understood that her mother was really dying.

The receptionist at The Oaks knew her by sight, so Susannah gave a quick wave and strode down the hall to her father's apartment. She rapped on the door, two brisk taps of the brass ring against the wood. She could hear Tyler fumbling with the lock, and then he pulled open the door.

"It's you." He beamed. "My date." Kissing Susannah on the cheek, he ushered her inside.

"I really wanted to come sooner," she told him. "It's just that I've been so busy preparing for my concert."

"A concert? I'm sorry I missed it, honey. You'll have to tell me all about it."

"No, no. I've been *preparing*. It hasn't happened yet." She eased out of her jacket and looked around. Several days' worth of newspapers were piled in a corner, still in their plastic wrappers. For as long as she could remember, her father had read the *Times*, the *Globe*, and the *Post* every morning.

Tyler caught her eying the newspapers. "Guess I'm a little behind."

"Hey, no one's obliged to read all those papers." She hung her jacket on the coat tree. "Why don't you join the current events group instead?"

Tyler drew back in mock horror. "Please. I *taught* current events."

"Don't be a snob. It's a way to socialize."

"Bah, humbug. No one in this place grasps what's happening in the world. Or is capable of grasping it."

"Not everyone is as smart as Mom was."

"Are you telling me to lower my standards?"

"I'm telling you not to be such a hermit."

"I repeat. Bah, humbug."

Susannah let out a sigh. "Come on, Dad. I don't want to fight. I just want you to be happy."

"You know what I tell everyone. I'm not happy yet, but I will be."

"Promise?"

"No one can promise that." Then he squinted at her, surprising Susannah with the acuteness of his gaze. "And what about you, Suzie? Are you happy?"

"Of course I am."

"I worry, you know. If you're not happy, we failed."

"Don't fish, Dad."

"I'm serious."

"And so am I. Anyway, no one's happy all the time."

"It's a simple question. Yes or no."

"You're wrong. It's not simple."

"It is," he insisted. "You look around at your life, and you know."

"I'm happy, okay? You and Mom did a good job."

"We did the best we could."

"Of course you did. If your child feels loved, it means you did a good job."

Susannah bent to adjust his collar. It was half inside, half out-side the V of his sweater. There were patches of stubble on his cheeks, spots he must have missed while he was shaving. Did he need a new razor, new glasses? "Come on," she said, "let's go to the dining room for lunch. I hear this place does a mean Jello mold."

Tyler placed a hand across his chest. "Be still, my heart."

They made their way to the dining hall, past the crafts room and the Internet Café. "I'll have a small Internet with cream and sugar," Tyler joked, as he always did.

"Hello, Mr. Richardson." Miguel, the head of food service, stepped forward to greet them. "Two for lunch?"

Susannah surveyed the dining room. Gold drapes framed the tall windows. The well-dressed residents, mostly women, sat at round tables covered in white linen. "There aren't any vacant tables for two," Miguel said. "May I seat you with Mr. and Mrs. Paxton?"

"That's fine," Tyler answered. They followed Miguel to a table in the far corner that was already occupied by an older couple and a man about Susannah's age. "Arthur," Tyler said, inclining his head. "I hope we're not intruding."

"No, no. Please." The older man, Arthur, made a welcoming gesture.

"This is my daughter, Susannah," Tyler said. "She's come to make sure I'm not becoming senile. So far, so good."

Arthur dipped his chin. "This is Grace, my wife, and Gordon, our son."

The younger man looked remarkably like his father, with the same square jaw and unusual eyebrows, one flatter than the other. "Pleasure," he said, half-rising.

"Gordon is visiting from Illinois," Arthur said proudly.

"How nice," Susannah replied.

"Sit, sit," Grace said.

The server took their orders. As soon as he left, Grace clasped her hands and said brightly, "Arthur, show them the pictures." She gave Tyler a regal nod. "Our grandchildren."

Susannah peered over her father's shoulder. Three more clones. "Adorable," she murmured.

"Marissa made the honor roll and the swim team," Grace announced, raising her voice so the people at the next table wouldn't miss the report. "Conrad plays trumpet in the school band. Henry's a National Merit semi-finalist."

Tyler reached for his water glass. "You must be very proud."

Susannah thought of James and how, despite her own history, she hadn't been able to stop herself from thinking: Ah yes, he has Aaron's eyes, Aaron's temperament, my nose. It anchored her, made her feel normal. Her father didn't have that. Did it bother him when other people's families were so obviously cut from the same genetic cloth?

She told herself she was being ridiculous. It was a question for an adolescent, not for a woman her age. Besides, she'd had endless conversations with her parents about adoption. What more was there to say?

Yet there *was* more. Her parents' story, never included in the tale that began with *the phone rang and we hopped on a plane to bring your home.* Whole chapters had taken place before the phone call that made them a family. Her parents had never talked about that, and she'd never asked.

The Paxton family finished their desserts while Susannah and her father were still eating their broiled salmon. They excused themselves, explaining that Gordon had to catch a plane, and Susannah and Tyler were alone at the table.

Ask, Susannah told herself. Now. Her father loved her; he wouldn't be offended if she wanted to know.

She pushed her plate aside and raised her eyes to his. "Tell me the truth, Dad. Did you ever feel bad, not having biological kids?" Seeing his startled look, she added, "You can be honest. We never really talked about it, you and me. It was always Mom, giving me one of her *chosen baby* pep talks. But we can talk about it. I'm a big girl."

Tyler removed his glasses, inspected them for spots, and put them on again. "Did I ever feel bad? Oh, a bit when I was young, I suppose. You know, the swaggering male out to sow his seed, prove his virility."

It was hard to imagine her father as a swaggering male, but yes, that made sense.

"But then," he continued, "when your mother and I decided to adopt, the whole thing went away. I knew how much she wanted to be a mother, and that mattered far more than my precious DNA." He lifted his chin. "And, of course, there was you. Love at first sight."

Susannah blinked back the tears she hadn't expected.

"It's funny you should ask, though," Tyler said. "Lately—maybe it's getting closer to death, realizing that we're all going to die, who knows?—but there's this wish that I could have left a trace behind, a part of me that would continue, down the generations." He sighed. "Probably just some atavistic superstition, like that would mean I wasn't really going to die after all. But there it is, for whatever it's worth. It started a while ago. Or maybe it was always there and I brushed it aside."

Susannah tried not to feel hurt. It wasn't the answer she wanted to hear. But how could she object? She'd been the one to ask.

Tyler touched her wrist. "Please don't misunderstand. I couldn't possibly love you more than I already do. Chalk it up to an old man's fear of disappearing."

Eyes moist, she nodded. She wanted to tell him: *Don't you dare disappear.* Not you too. Not yet.

Yet the question was still there. "Even so," she said, "it makes sense that a person would want to look at their child and say: Hey, I know you. We're from the same tribe."

"There's something to that," her father agreed, plucking the napkin from his lap. "Then again, every tribe has its quirks and limitations. Mine's always had too many damn intellectuals. If you'd gotten my genes, you'd have just been one more egghead in the carton, and I never would've gotten to hear all that beautiful music."

"Mom used to say that, too."

Tyler's voice was firm. "I love you, Suzie. And your mother loved you. You've been a great joy to both of us. Never doubt that." He wiped his mouth and laid the napkin on his plate. Then he studied the napkin, as if weighing what to say next.

Susannah was certain he was about to say something more, but Miguel returned to their table and said, "Would you like some dessert? We have berry pie, lemon custard, layer cake, ice cream."

Tyler looked up. "Jello mold?" he asked, his expression deadpan.

"Yes, we can do that for you, sir."

Tyler pretended to give the idea serious consideration. Then he declared, "Chocolate ice cream for me."

Miguel looked at Susannah. "Make that two," she said.

"So," Tyler continued, when Miguel had left. "Now tell me about this big concert of yours. It sounds important."

"My concert. I thought you'd never ask."

Susannah placed her hands on the tablecloth, spreading her fingers. They looked the same as always; it was hard to believe that anything was wrong.

She let out her breath, not sure how to begin or how much to share. "Playing the piano was always the truest part of me," she said, after a moment. "You and Mom were great about that. Always supporting me, even though you weren't musical yourselves."

"It was your mother, mostly. She wasn't musical—well, that's an understatement, as she'd be the first to admit—but she knew it when she saw it. Me, I went along with whatever she thought. If it made you happy, and it made her happy, then it was fine with me."

"Still," Susannah said, "not everyone would have been that generous. Music camp. My own Steinway, for heaven's sake."

"We never saw it that way. It was just who you were. Are."

And who am I? She looked at her father, his thinning hair and sad little smile. How proud he'd always been of the way she played. What if she couldn't do that anymore? What would he have to be proud of?

Images flashed through her mind. Ugly distorted fingers, like chicken feet. Leo had told her that the contracture often returned, even after treatment.

Stop it, she told herself. Instead, she told him about Libby and the Isis Project, Vera's recommendation, the audition. "So you're giving it a go again?" he said. "Now that James is ready to leave the nest? Good for you, honey."

"We'll see. Getting picked by Libby was one thing, but it all depends on what happens at the concert, and then afterward. It might be too late, you know. I might have lost my spark."

"It's never too late. Not for a girl like you, with your beautiful talent."

Susannah was touched by his faith in her, though she knew better. *Never too late* was a nice sentiment and she was sure her father thought it was true, but the music world didn't operate like that. Common wisdom was that if you hadn't made it by the time you were thirty, you wouldn't, and generally that was right. There were exceptions, of course. Alicia de Larrocha was relatively unknown in her thirties; her best decades came later. But de Larrocha had fingers that worked.

"There's something else." Then she hesitated. Was it selfish to tell her father about her diagnosis? It might spoil his pleasure in her good fortune; he'd worry. Yet if James had a progressive disease, she'd want to know. That was part of being a parent.

She tried to keep her voice light. "It's kind of ironic, actually. Right after I aced the audition, I found out that I have this condition called Dupuytren's contracture. It's where your fingers curve in toward the palm and you can't straighten them."

Tyler's face grew pale. Yes, he understood. "Dear girl." He reached across the table and covered her hand with his.

She looked at her father's hand. No Dupuytren's, but the skin was wrinkled and old. She really should get up here more often. And she would. After the concert.

"Isn't there some sort of treatment?" he asked. "Doesn't make sense that there wouldn't be a treatment."

"Well, it's still at the early stage."

He nodded, then picked up his water glass. "Tell you the truth, honey, I'm relieved. I was expecting something worse. What you have is pretty awful, but it's not like the news your mother got."

Susannah watched her father take a careful sip and replace the glass on the tablecloth. His hand quivered. There were dark blotches just below the knuckles, liver spots, that's what they were called. She hadn't noticed them before. They had that in common now: their hands were changing, whether they liked it or not.

"You're right," she said. "It's not like the news Mom got."

"Here you go, folks." It was Miguel, with their ice cream. "Will there be anything else? Coffee, tea?"

"No, nothing, thank you." Tyler inclined his head. "Looks good enough to eat, as they say. As I say, in fact." He picked up a spoon and dipped it into the ice cream. "So. How exactly did you get this contracture thing, Suzie? Too much practicing?"

The irony of the disease's origin struck her anew. "It's hereditary."

Susannah could feel her father sifting through the implications. "Oh." He carved a spoonful of ice cream from the mound in the silver cup. When he spoke again, his voice was quiet. "You never think of things like that when you decide to adopt, but I guess every gene pool has one thing or another."

"I guess."

Her gene pool, with its hidden waters. The undertow tugged at her feet, loosening the mud around her toes.

Susannah looked at her father. Again, she thought: ask him.

No, how could she possibly ask such a personal question, at this point in their lives? *Hey, Dad. Why couldn't you and Mom have children?*

A strange expression crossed his face. "Dad?" she said. His mouth was slack, stupid looking. "Dad?"

Tyler gave a start. He gazed around in confusion. Slowly, his eyes regained their focus. "Sorry. We were talking about your mother?"

"Kind of—"

"You know," he interrupted, "I forget, sometimes, that she's not here. I'll see a bit on the news, and I'll think—" His voice faded, the rest of the sentence trailing away.

Susannah's heart was banging a crazy staccato against her ribs. If she didn't ask now, she never would. "Why did you and Mom decide to adopt?"

His brow furrowed. "It was the only way. She knew it made sense."

The lines in his forehead were sharp, like cuts. Susannah felt a dart of alarm.

The frown softened, disappearing as quickly as it had come. His expression turned baffled and sad. "What do you remember?" he asked. "When you think about her?"

"Mom?" Susannah remembered her mother wasting away. The sores on her mouth, her labored breathing, her hair brittle and thin. That wasn't what her father meant, of course. He meant Dana as she had been, before the cancer.

Her well-groomed presence at every recital. Her purposeful walk, and her staunch defense of Harry Truman—a shamefully under-rated president, in her estimation. Her fierce concentration when she helped with school projects—a pioneer village made of tongue depressors, a paper mâché map of New England—and the way she made Susannah brush her teeth for sixty seconds, until the sand in the pink hourglass had trickled to the bottom. She'd try to fool her mother by sloshing the toothbrush under running water, but Dana always knew and would make her do it again, not like Tyler, who was easy to trick.

"Oh gosh, so many things. You know, Mom things." Her father's eager look sent a flash of pain through her chest. "Halloween, when she made that mermaid costume I absolutely had to have? With that wire thing, so I could pick up the tail? And how she went on that Girl Scout camping trip and brought a *book* with her." Susannah shook her head. "I don't know if I can pick just one. What about you, Dad?"

"Ah." He smiled gently. "That's easy. I remember your mother when I first met her."

"In grad school." Susannah thought of the photo on the bureau, a black-and-white portrait of an impossibly young Dana in a sweater set and dark lipstick, looking straight into the camera. "A good way to remember her."

"It's how I see her. How I've always seen her."

The words slipped out. "And how do you see me?"

Tyler seemed surprised by the question. "Why, playing the piano, of course." His smile widened. "I wouldn't trade my piano playing Suzie for a dozen Richardson clones."

Susannah's eyes grew moist. That was the only answer that mattered.

She touched her father's sleeve. "There's a piano in the lounge, right? Come on, I'll play for you."

The old mahogany upright was wedged between two bookcases filled with board games and a scattering of paperback novels. The casing had been polished, although Susannah doubted that the instrument had been tuned in years. She motioned for Tyler to sit beside her on the bench. "Requests?"

"Anything you like, Suzie. Whatever you play will be beautiful." He settled next to her, palms on his knees.

She thought quickly. What might he like to hear? Maybe a Bach chorale? The only music on the rack was a volume of old show tunes, but she didn't need the score. Her mind and her hands: they were all she needed. She inhaled, readied herself, and touched the keys. The ascendant purity of *Jesu, Joy of Man's Desiring* filled the room.

When she finished, she put an arm around her father. "I have an idea. Let's play a duet." Before he could object, she said, "Really. You can do it."

She flipped through the mental roster of pieces she had taught James when he was small. The Anna Magdalena Book, the little minuet in F-major—Tyler could do that. Susannah put her hand on top of his. "Put your left hand on the keyboard. See? Right here." She positioned his fingers. D-E-F-G-A. "They go in order. Two beats for the D, one beat for the E. Like that, and then down to the A an octave below."

Carefully, he raised and lowered each finger. Then Susannah joined in with the right-hand melody. Tyler grinned. "We did it."

"We did indeed, maestro. Here, let me teach you the rest."

Susannah counted aloud as Tyler repeated the left-hand notes until he could play them smoothly. "You've got it, Dad. Let's put it all together."

She moved closer, leaning against his shoulder the way James used to lean against hers. The minuet was bright and clear. When they finished, she looked up and saw that a crowd of residents had gathered to listen. "Who knew you had it in you, Richardson?" one of them laughed, applauding.

Tyler looked happily embarrassed. "I have a good teacher. The best." He beamed at Susannah. "I'll practice while you're gone. We can do our duet the next time you visit."

"That'd be great." They stood, and Tyler motioned the crowd away. Susannah linked her arm through his as they made their way back to his apartment. "I wish it could be sooner. But like I explained, I can't come very often, not till after the concert."

"Ah yes." He nodded sagely. "Your mother will be sorry to miss it." Susannah gave him a quizzical look. It seemed like an odd way to put it. Tyler nodded again, as if to explain. "She never missed any of your concerts, you know."

"Nor you, Dad."

"Well, neither of us will be at this one, I'm afraid. It's too far for me to drive, especially at night. Truth be told, I don't drive that much anymore."

Susannah stopped walking. "Dad. You don't drive at all." He'd sold the car and let his license expire months ago. Didn't he remember?

She had thought he would protest when she urged him to give up driving, but he hadn't, admitting that his eyesight was failing and his hands were starting to shake. She had been relieved.

"But never fear," he said. "I'll be cheering from my cell here at The Oaks." His expression turned dry, puckish. "Me and my fellow inmates, even if they can't tell an arpeggio from an archipelago."

Susannah released her breath. He was all right, then.

"You come when you can," he assured her. "I know it's a long drive for you. You come when the concert is over."

When the concert is over. So much seemed to hinge on those words.

Chapter Thirteen

now

When Susannah told Vera how Libby had switched pianos, Vera was furious. "The woman's a philistine," Vera snapped. Susannah could feel the phone crackle with her teacher's displeasure.

"You think I can make her switch them back?"

"You can't make that type do anything," Vera said. "Forget her. Get your own piano."

"At Steinway?"

"Of course at Steinway. Call Harry Quinn. He's in charge of their concert rentals." Vera let out a short barking sound. Susannah wasn't sure if it was a laugh or a cough, but Vera cleared her throat quickly and continued. "Harry used to study with me, back in the Pleistocene. That boy could stretch to nine notes without even trying. But in the end he liked the technical part more than the performing part, quit his lessons and went to work for Steinway. Well, that was years ago, but he stays in touch. So call Harry and tell him Vera Evangelista says hello."

"I will. Thank you." Susannah switched the phone to her other ear and squinted at the window over the sink. She could see the rain through the glass, big silvery beads, each on its own downward trail, disappearing, replaced by another.

"Make sure you talk to Harry. Not some underling."

Susannah watched as two raindrops collided, altering each other's paths. "They let you try the pianos, right? You can pick the one you want?"

"That's the fun part," Vera said. "You can try a lot of different instruments, see what they feel like. I remember the old days, going down to the basement of Steinway Hall on Fifty-Seventh Street—that's where they kept the concert rentals. It was like a secret underground world. People up in the showroom, right over your head, had no idea it was even there. Now you have to go to some god-awful place in Astoria."

"Astoria? You mean, in Queens?"

"In Queens."

Susannah groaned. Not only was she going to have to pay heaven-knows-how-much money, since Steinway didn't loan nine-foot grands to people like her at no charge, but she was going to have to take a whole day to do it.

The fun part, she reminded herself. She'd get to pick her own piano. That was what mattered.

When she called, Harry Quinn told her that she didn't have to come in person if she didn't want to. "A lot of performers just tell us what they want, and then trust us to pick the instrument. They tell us what the venue is—since we know most of them—and what pieces they're going to play, and our technician figures out which would be the best piano to meet their needs."

"People don't pick their own pianos? They let you do it?"

Quinn sounded amused. "We do have a reputation for knowing what we're doing."

"Yes, of course." Still, it didn't feel right to her. This was too important, too personal. It wasn't just a matter of what suited the space and the program; it was what suited her. The Steinway people didn't know her. If she had to find a piano herself—well, that was exactly what she had to do. No one else could do this for her.

"Of course," she repeated. "Nonetheless, I'd like to come out and make my own selection."

"Whatever you prefer. When did you want the piano?"

"The concert's in three weeks. Is that going to be a problem?"

"Not at all," Quinn assured her. "That's plenty of time."

To arrange a rental, Susannah thought. Not for everything else. Some of the things she needed to do might not be possible in three weeks. Or at all.

Harry Quinn ushered her into an enormous room where a dozen nine-foot concert grands were lined up, lids open, facing a wall of windows framed by red-and-white striped curtains. The same candy-cane color scheme, Susannah thought, as the piano she was here to replace. The opposite wall was bright red, punctuated by couches covered in a black-and-white zigzag pattern. Quinn settled onto one of the couches. "Take your time," he told her. "Any questions, just ask."

Her first question was the price. It almost didn't matter, because whatever it cost, she'd pay it. "It's mostly the cartage," Quinn explained. "The transport, there and back. Plus the tunings. We recommend at least two. One after it's installed, and another right before the performance."

"Yes, definitely."

"We do require that you use our tuners. And you might want to rent it for two days so you can practice on it the day before. People often prefer that. Otherwise, it can be a pretty tight turnaround."

Another *yes, definitely.* She could almost hear the *ka-ching* as the expenses mounted. Well, what choice did she have?

Besides the piano rental, she needed to hire her own publicist; she'd already decided that it would be foolish not to. And a dress. She hadn't worn a long black dress, which was what the audience expected, since she was a size six. Before James.

When she added everything up, it would be thousands of dollars. The cash would have to come from somewhere, since she couldn't put a publicist or a Steinway rental on a credit card—well, she probably could, but she didn't want Aaron to see the charges, not yet. Better to borrow the money from their savings account and pay it back later, after she—what? Lined up a tour, got a recording contract? Susannah tightened her jaw. She couldn't think about that right now.

"Yes, two days," she agreed. She turned to regard the row of nine-foot pianos. They did look magnificent, lined up like that, dark and gleaming and full of possibility. It wasn't the same as playing her own piano, the one she was used to, but it would be unrealistic—and far more expensive—to arrange for private cartage and insurance. Horowitz was famous for doing just that, shipping his own piano to whatever city or country he was playing in, but he was Horowitz.

Susannah filled her lungs with air, felt the warmth and life and purpose descend into her body, all the way to her fingertips. One of these beautiful Steinways would speak to her, and together they would find the rapture again.

She sat down at the first piano and tried the opening measures of the sonata. Then she grimaced. The sound was too bright.

Well, every Steinway was different. Different trees provided the wood for the sounding board; different hands put together the 12,000 parts that made up the instrument. "Plenty of others," Quinn said. "Take as long as you need." Susannah moved to the second piano, but that one wasn't right either. She began to worry. Was she being too picky? These were Steinway Model D's, for heaven sakes, not like the silly prop Libby had offered.

The sixth one was exactly right. She knew it at once. The response, the clarity of the tones. The rumble of that trill in the bass and the crystal of the top notes—the instrument had both, exactly what the sonata demanded.

She made the arrangements with Harry Quinn, remembering at the last minute to tell him *Vera Evangelista says hello.* When she got back in the car and checked her phone, there was a message from Evan Chu's office. "Dr. Chu has been able to return sooner than expected. Are you available to come in on Friday?"

Of course she was. She would make herself available.

Susannah felt a surge of optimism, the first she'd felt since her meeting with Leo Mathieson. She had solved the piano problem, and now she would solve the hand problem. Everything was going to work out after all.

Evan Chu was tall and thin, formal, yet the bright purple shirt—collar and cuffs visible beneath his white lab coat—made Susannah hope for an unconventional streak, a rebel she could talk into breaking the rules and beginning early treatment.

"There's a simple diagnostic test for Dupuytren's," Chu told her. He asked her to place her hand flat on the desk. "We call it the Table Top Test. If you can flatten your hand, you pass." He paused for emphasis. "Which you do."

"And passing means—?"

"That you're not ready to see me."

"But I *am* seeing you." Susannah tried her most beseeching smile. "I'm here, so what can we do?"

Chu reached across the desk and took her hands. She thought, at first, that he meant it as a gesture of comfort, but he turned them over and felt each joint, one at a time. "I wanted to be sure, but no, you don't have any cords."

Releasing her hands, he regarded her matter-of-factly. "You're not even at what we call Stage One, because your fingers haven't started to bend. We delineate the stages by the degree of distortion. Degrees, like in geometry."

She didn't care about geometry. "I have these spots in my palm, and they're messing up my playing. So I'm obviously at stage *something*."

"You have two nodules at the base of your little finger," Chu agreed, "and I don't doubt that as a pianist you're sensitive to small changes that the average person wouldn't notice. But there's no bending. Without bending, there's no treatment."

Not that again. She'd thought Chu would have a better answer. "And when is this bending supposed to happen?"

"There's no way to know," he said. "Progression of the disease is just too idiosyncratic, as I believe Dr. Mathieson told you. It can be slow and gradual, and years can go by without anything more than the palmar nodules. In other cases, the change can be quite swift and dramatic."

"Well then, how do you know which group you're in?"

"The fingers bend, or they don't."

This was crazy. He was no better than Leo. "So I have to wait and hope I get worse, and *then* you can cure me? Oncologists don't do that. Dentists don't do that."

Chu looked unhappy. He was probably sorry he had agreed to see her. "There isn't a cure *per se*, if you mean reversing the progression." He pulled on the sleeves of his lab coat, covering the purple cuffs. "Once again, we can only correct the bending once it's occurred."

"That's it?" Then she remembered Misha Dichter. "Why can't you do whatever Misha Dichter's doctor did? Dichter had Dupuytren's, and they fixed it."

"Everyone's story is different, Mrs. Lewis. I don't know anything about Misha Dichter's medical history or how, specifically, he was able to come back so fully after surgery."

"But he did."

"Yes, but that's not relevant to your current situation. As I've explained."

Susannah wanted to argue, or stamp her foot, or cry. What good had it done to bully Leo into setting her up with a specialist, if that was all he had to say?

There were other specialists, though. Evan Chu wasn't the only game in town.

As if reading her mind, he added, "Every reputable physician will tell you the same thing, Mrs. Lewis. I know this is frustrating, but you really have to take it day by day."

He pushed out his chair and stood, the ubiquitous signal for *time's up*.

She shouldn't have expected him to understand. He hadn't been given a now-or-never chance to prove he was a great doctor. Trying to be polite, she said, "Well, thank you for your time. For fitting me in."

"No problem."

Lord, she hated that expression. There was as a problem all right. Her problem, still unsolved. She should have known that conventional doctors would have nothing to offer. Even if there was a new treatment—in the pipeline, as Aaron had put it—they weren't about to give it to her until it had passed all the tests and patents and approvals. She needed a cure fresh off the clinical trials that most people didn't know about.

But Aaron would.

Susannah heard Aaron's footsteps on the deck and the whoosh of the back door. She ran to greet him.

She'd been waiting impatiently since her appointment with Chu— eager to see Aaron, her husband, but even more eager to see Aaron, the research scientist. She gave him a quick kiss. "So. What did you find out about Dupuytren's?" She didn't ask whether he'd had a chance to investigate, only what he had found. If Aaron offered to look into something, he would do it.

Aaron shrugged off his coat. "I'm afraid the doctors are right, honey. The latest on Dupuytren's treatment was a few years ago, when the FDA approved the extended use of Xiaflex. But that's it." He dropped the coat and briefcase onto a chair. "So it's like Mathieson told you. All you can do is keep an eye on it."

Susannah moved the briefcase onto the floor. "That's not all I can do." She had done her own investigation. Too keyed up to practice, she had gone online again, scrolling through websites, searching for a link or citation she had missed.

"I looked on the internet," she told him, "and there are all sorts of alternative treatments. Biofeedback. Ultrasound, laser lights. Ginger. Lots of things."

Aaron arched an eyebrow. "Ginger?"

She pulled out a chair and sat down, propping her elbows on the kitchen table. "There's a ton of stuff about Vitamin E too, but I can't remember if it's pills or cream. And a bunch of people who got better from steroids and massage."

Aaron lowered himself into the seat across from hers. "Susannah," he said.

"Western medicine doesn't have a lock on treatments. There's acupuncture, herbs, Ayurveda. And didn't Rolfing help Leon Fleisher? I'm almost positive that was how he got his fingers to uncurl."

"Susannah," he repeated. "Anyone can put anything on the internet. It's not the same as scientific evidence."

"There's evidence for alternative treatments too. Maybe not ginger, but other things." She hoped he wouldn't ask her to produce it. She had looked quickly, scanning the options but not really focusing because she'd been certain that Aaron would bring her a better answer.

Aaron gave her a stern look. "I don't want you to get taken in by some quack who'll end up making things worse." He tapped out each point, finger by finger. "You have a diagnosis. Fact. There are specific, effective treatments for that diagnosis. Second fact. You're not at the stage when those treatments are possible. Third fact."

"Each person is different. That's what Leo said."

"In terms of onset, pace, severity—yes. But evidence is evidence."

"That can't be right. Not if each person is different." Susannah could hear the edge in her voice. She didn't want to argue with Aaron, but why was he being so stubborn and pompous? She didn't need a lecture. She needed a cure.

Suddenly angry, she pushed away from the table, rose, and crossed the room in two sharp strides. A vein pounded against her temple.

Don't, she told herself. She pressed her palms against the countertop, willing herself to quell the rage and frustration that was making her jaw clench and her stomach lurch. Nothing ruined music more than anger. You needed emotion to play the piano, but not those roiling personal emotions. You needed the emotions that were already there in the music, put there by the composer.

She drew in her breath and let the sonata's opening theme rise up inside her, in all its tenderness and majesty and hope. Schubert was thirty-one and dying when he wrote it. What was a stiff finger, compared to that?

All right. She could do this. Focus, find an answer.

She heard the scrape of Aaron's chair, and then she felt him standing behind her. He put his hands on her shoulders and turned her around. "Let's not fight, sweetheart."

Susannah blinked. "I wasn't fighting." She let out a sigh. "Just—disappointed, I guess. I was so sure you'd bring me a solution."

"I wish I could have."

"I know." She gave him a half-smile, acknowledging the silent pact they'd made, years ago. Aaron was the fixer. He liked solving puzzles, finding the way out of a conundrum that no one else had seen. And, of course, rescuing her. In return, she had given him the pleasure of her music.

Well, she hadn't been upholding her side of the arrangement. Her music had been dull, earthbound, ordinary. That was the point of the doctors' appointments and the rented Steinway, the justification for skipping James's basketball game and forgetting to pick him up. To restore the glory. For herself, and for them. To be the woman Aaron had fallen in love with and a mother James could admire.

"Actually," Aaron said, "let's do the opposite of fighting." He moved his hands down her arms. "We haven't been spending enough time together, too busy with our separate pursuits. But I have an idea." He pulled her close. "I have that conference in St. Pierre next week."

Susannah nodded; she knew about the conference. Researchers in Aaron's discipline gathered each year, presenting papers, sitting on panels, convening over banquets and seminars. This year the conference was being held on St. Pierre, a gorgeous island retreat known for its pristine beaches and turquoise lagoons. She had joked about the grueling working conditions, but secretly she was glad he was going. Aaron's absence would give her four days to immerse herself in the piano.

"Come with me." His eyes locked onto hers. "Get away from all this Dupuytren's stuff and relax for a few days. James can stay with Andrew; he practically lives there anyway." His hands on her skin were warm, familiar. "I can skip half the sessions. It'll be time alone, just the two of us."

She stared at him. He had to be joking. Her concert was in three weeks.

He gave her a slow, knowing smile. "I hear it's beautiful in St. Pierre."

"Aaron." How could she possibly explain all the things that shouldn't need explaining? She didn't have time for an idyllic getaway.

"I can't go to St. Pierre." Her voice caught. It wasn't because she was wavering; it was because she hated this, having to refuse an offer that someone who understood her should never have made.

"It's only for a few days, and you already know the sonata."

"Aaron," she repeated. Why was he putting her in this position? Had he forgotten who she was—who she had been, and was trying to be again?

"Think about it. That's all I'm asking."

"There's nothing to think about. It doesn't make sense. Not right now." She wanted to add, *Maybe later, after the concert.* But Aaron wouldn't have a trip to St. Pierre after the concert.

A veiled look crossed his face. She knew he was disappointed. He had offered a gift, and she had refused. But it wasn't the gift she was hoping for.

"I'm sorry," she said. "Bad timing, that's all."

He dropped his hands. Her heart began to race, as if she'd just committed a horrible crime. But she hadn't. All she'd done was turn down a proposal that made no sense.

She couldn't keep her thoughts straight; that was the problem. There was too much going on. Publicity photos and tabletop tests. Her father, James. The money she was going to have to find, somewhere. The phrase that kept echoing in her mind: a genetic disease.

Aaron's face was unreadable now. The hopeful ardor was gone, replaced by the neutral expression she'd seen him use with salesmen and bureaucrats. He picked up his briefcase and coat. "I'm going to change, check my email before dinner."

Susannah watched him leave. The kitchen felt huge and hollowed out. What else could she have done, said, explained? Had she been too quick, too certain?

She'd known at once which Steinway she wanted; the choice was clear as soon as she played the first few measures. Why was it so much harder to know how to answer her own husband?

She sent him a silent pledge. All right, I'll think about it.

She would make dinner, do some of those finger exercises she used to do when she was young—no matter what the doctors told her, it was bound to help—and tell Aaron her decision in the morning.

Chapter Fourteen

now

Susannah stretched her limbs under the blanket. Morning sun spilled from the skylight, slanted panels of silvery light that made the unlit places seem gray and insignificant.

She wanted to laugh, as if someone had whisked away a heavy cloak she hadn't even known she was wearing. Of course she would go to St. Pierre. A break would be good for her, and for them.

Awake now, she turned and propped herself on an elbow. The bathroom door was ajar and she could see Aaron toweling his face at the bathroom sink. Quietly, she slipped out of bed and went to put her arms around him. His back was warm, solid as a tree. She closed her eyes, breathed in his smell. "I'd love to come with you."

She could feel his muscles moving up and down as he dabbed at his neck. "To the lab?"

"Silly man. I mean, *I accept*. St. Pierre. Piña coladas, white beaches."

He tucked the towel back into its silver ring. "I think your first instinct was right, actually. It doesn't make sense."

Susannah's eyes flew open. He didn't get to un-invite her, now that she'd decided to come. "It'll be good. A chance to get away together, like you said."

She could sense him wanting to step away from the sink and felt the absurdity of her posture, clinging to his back like a baby monkey. She dropped her arms and moved aside to let him pass.

Aaron lifted his robe from the hook. "I wouldn't really be able to treat it like a getaway, now that I think about it. I'll be too busy with meetings and sessions."

She opened her mouth, ready to argue. He was the one who had offered to skip half the sessions. "Aaron," she began. Again, she felt idiotic. Beg your own husband to let you join him on a tropical island?

"It's the wrong timing," he repeated, "with your concert coming up. You were right."

That's not for you to decide. It was complicated, though, because he was agreeing with what she'd said the night before. She felt tricked, trapped. There ought to be words to unspool this and wind back to what she might have said, when he asked her to come, but she didn't know what they were.

She watched him tie the robe, giving the ends of the belt an extra tug. Behind him, she could hear the faucet dripping. She waited for him to say something more; when he didn't, she bit her lip and looked away. Seconds passed like the drops of water, falling from their own weight. Finally she said, "I'll take my shower now, if you're finished."

"All yours."

Susannah pushed the shower curtain aside and twisted the faucet. Water spurted out of the showerhead, then dropped to a trickle.

"Is it acting up again?" Aaron asked.

"No, it's fine." She jiggled the showerhead and the water shifted to a steady stream.

"You did call the furnace people, right?"

Shit. "They're coming next week." Well, once she called, they would be coming, so it wasn't actually a lie. She stepped into the shower. Below the rush of the water, she could hear him opening drawers in the bedroom, closing each one carefully instead of banging them shut the way she did. That was Aaron, attentive and deliberate. Maybe the invitation to St. Pierre hadn't been as impulsive as she had thought. Maybe he'd been considering the idea for a while, waiting for the right moment to offer. Then, when he did, she had said no.

Now she wanted to say yes. Why did he get to change his mind, but she didn't?

They seemed to be circling each other, instead of coming together. She thought about what you did in music, when a tone couldn't take you where you wanted to go. You needed a passing tone, a bridge. But first, you had to clear the pedal, stop the old sound.

Maybe she and Aaron needed to do that too. Clear the pedal, have some time apart, and then cross to the new key.

A few days apart, and then a new sound.

With Aaron away, Susannah decided to go to Boston to see Vera. She hadn't seen her teacher in a long while. They had spoken on the phone, but not in person. If anyone could tell her how to compensate for a stiffening finger, it was Vera.

Vera lived in the same apartment where she'd lived when Susannah was small. The same marble foyer and front door with a wrought iron grille. The same tiny elevator with black numbers etched onto brass disks, the two and the five rubbed smooth. Like the foyer and elevator, Vera's eyes and profile were unchanged, but below the aquiline nose there was a plastic cannula attached to an oxygen tank. "Less dramatic than it looks," she said, dismissing Susannah's concern. "Old lady lungs, that's all. They get squeezed when your back starts to hunch."

The plastic tube and metal cylinder looked more serious than *old lady* accessories. How long had this been going on, and why hadn't Vera told her?

"Are you sure that's all it is?" Susannah asked. "Do you have a good doctor?"

Vera gave an irritated wave. "Old age isn't for sissies. At least I'm not losing my hearing. Or my mind." She motioned Susannah inside and settled herself on the blue velvet couch, pulling an afghan around her shoulders.

Susannah looked around the familiar room. The lamp with its beaded shade, the sunlight filtering through the lace curtains, the Lladró figurines arranged on top of a Cherrywood credenza. Her gaze moved to the oxygen tank at Vera's side. Her own disease, its real threat only a future possibility, seemed too frivolous to mention.

"Tea?" Vera gestured at a small side table with cabriole legs. It was where Vera used to keep a porcelain candy dish with a pink rim. If Susannah worked hard, and she always did, she got a candy of her choice after the lesson.

She picked up the teapot and poured for both of them. "This place brings back a lot of memories."

"I'm sure it does. You spent a lot of time here."

Susannah returned the teapot to its trivet. "You know, you had this saying, when I was little. Play the notes, but listen to the music."

"Ha. I was a wise old bat, even then." Adjusting the cannula, Vera took two quick puffs of air, then reached for a china cup and saucer. She held the saucer aloft, pointing it at Susannah. "I hope you still do that."

"I try."

"Especially if you're playing the Schubert sonata."

"It's an amazing piece, isn't it?"

"As long as you don't let that second movement get sentimental."

"Never."

"People do." Vera took a sip of tea, lifting the cannula out of the way as she drank. "I just hope I don't die before Perez-Smith makes that recording of his."

"What recording?" Susannah had told Vera that Perez-Smith was coming to the concert, but she hadn't heard anything about a recording.

Vera's eyes glittered. "An insider secret. If you hang around the music world long enough, you know these things." She set down the china cup. "If you promise not to let it make you nervous, I'll tell you."

"Good Lord, Vera. How can I promise not to be nervous?"

"Eh. I'll tell you anyway." She gave Susannah an arch look. "It seems that your Mr. Perez-Smith wants to make a CD of pieces that were written right before famous composers' early deaths. What he'd really like are pieces written when the composer knew he was dying— you know, final cries from the deathbed, visions of the beyond, that sort of thing. He's got someone to play that little Chopin Mazurka and a group for the first bit of Mozart's Requiem, you know the part I mean, but he most definitely wants Schubert's last sonata. *Your* sonata. He wants a pianist who loves the sonata as much as he does, because apparently the B-flat Major is one of Mr. Carlo's absolute favorite compositions. So there." She folded her hands, gazing smugly at the shock on Susannah's face.

"You're kidding me."

"I never kid."

Susannah's head was spinning. "But Vera, how in the world do you know all this?"

Vera gave her annoyed look, as if to say: *I've been part of the music scene for sixty years, of course I know.*

"So that's why he's so interested in hearing me play."

"Indeed."

"Oh." She tried to absorb what Vera had told her. "I wonder if Libby knows."

"I'm sure she does. That woman is nobody's fool. She has eyes and ears on everything from Boston to Washington."

That sounded like Libby—yet the coincidence was too odd. Susannah furrowed her brow. She just happened to audition with the very piece Perez-Smith was looking for?

Vera had encouraged her to play the sonata at the audition. She had thought Vera was urging her to play a piece she loved, and that was true. But Vera had another reason that she'd kept to herself.

She met Vera's deadpan gaze. "You told Libby about the CD. And then you told her you knew someone who could play the exact piece that would get Perez-Smith to come to the concert."

The puzzle clicked into place. "And then, after we signed the contract, Libby made sure he found out. And once she knew he was coming, she used that to get the other power-brokers to come."

It was just what Libby would do. And it was why she'd been picked. Not for herself, her extraordinary playing. After all, the purpose of the concert was to raise money. Hook a major fish, and others would follow.

When Libby heard her audition, she had let her go on and on. It hadn't made sense, but Susannah hadn't let herself dwell on that. She'd kept playing, her attention on the music. Yet Libby must have signaled to the other judges to let her continue. All four movements, because she had to be sure Susannah could do it.

"So that's why she wanted me. Because I was useful."

Susannah thought of the conversations she'd had with Libby. Had Libby been playing with her, pretending not to remember which composition it was and calling it *your B-flat whatever*? Or had she simply lost interest in the musical details, too busy with the photo shoot and the press release, once she'd snared Perez-Smith?

Vera's eyes bored into her. "Stop it," she snapped. "It doesn't matter one iota what that woman has up her sleeve. It's still your chance. You're still the one at the keyboard."

Maybe. A sick feeling spread through Susannah's body. She'd thought she was the one chosen. Not a pretend story about a chosen baby, but a real choice, because of who she was. "Oh Vera."

"*Oh Vera*," the older woman mimicked. "Stop being such a child." Her voice was harsh. "What do you care? You had what they were looking for, and they had what you were looking for. That's how these things work." She grabbed the afghan, pulling it tightly across her shoulder. The gesture dislodged the cannula. It tilted rakishly, dangling from one nostril.

Susannah reached out her hand to adjust the tube, but Vera jerked away. Susannah got the message. *Adjust yourself.* Grow up.

She had come for a lesson. Well, she'd gotten one. The question was what she was going to do with what she had learned.

Vera gave a quick barking cough, then re-inserted the tube. "Now say a prayer of thanks and take advantage of your good fortune. Don't embarrass me." Her face softened. "That means, make me proud."

Susannah dipped her head, humbled by Vera's words. She could see that her teacher was tired; they wouldn't be working on the sonata today. If a disobedient finger was going to interfere with those top notes, she'd have to figure out how to deal with it herself.

She rose and bent to kiss Vera's cheek. "I'll do my best."

"Why would you do any less?"

Susannah gathered her sweater and purse, motioning for Vera to stay seated.

"Remember," Vera said, "you're the one playing. Not Perez-Smith, not me, not even Schubert."

Susannah's lips parted in a smile. "I won't forget."

She closed the door quietly, then hurried down the three flights of marble stairs. There were things she had to do now. With the possibility of a CD, she definitely needed a publicist. Some professional head shots, and a good dress. Most of all, she had to look at the sonata again, find a better solution.

Her thoughts circled back to her diagnosis. That was the main thing, getting around the damn Dupuytren's—because Perez-Smith wouldn't want someone for his CD who only had nine reliable fingers. A CD could take months and months to produce, time that she might not have.

There had to be another treatment, an answer they'd all missed. The doctors. Aaron. Everyone.

When she got home, Susannah went straight to her laptop: the other keyboard, as James called it, the one that might hold the answer to the first. She'd already found the natural treatments, the ones Aaron had scoffed at. Maybe there was something else to be found.

She typed *Dupuyten's contracture treatment* into her browser. Pages of hits. Needle aponeurotomy, fasciectomy, collagenase, things she already knew. She clicked through the sites. Nothing. Maybe doctors outside the U.S. had another approach? She hadn't tried that yet. More links. She opened one at random, a center in the UK. It listed treatment by stages of the disease. She remembered Evan Chu telling her that she wasn't even at Stage One. Well, she would be soon, if she did nothing. She scrolled to the paragraph about treatment at Stage One.

Stage One: nodules and cords, no contracture. All right, close enough. Maybe they defined the stages differently in Europe.

She kept reading, and a word leaped from the screen that she hadn't seen before. Radiotherapy. "Radiotherapy is only effective while nodules are growing and cords may be developing. This is often accompanied by aches, tingling, and other atypical sensations."

I can't make the top notes sing. Did that count as an atypical sensation?

She leaned closer. "Radiation can be effective for keeping straight fingers straight, but it cannot straighten a finger that is already bent.

Thus, in order for radiotherapy to be effective, it must be given in the early stages of the disease, when nodules are small and no additional symptoms have appeared. The chief obstacle to radiotherapy is that it is rare for someone to seek medical help at this early stage."

But she had. The article was talking about her.

"By the time most people seek help, the disease has progressed beyond the point where radiation can be effective. Hence, it is seldom an option that physicians consider."

Her pulse racing, Susannah skimmed through the details. When given at the pre-contracture stage, low-dose radiation was a simple, painless procedure. One minute, once a day for five days. You could even drive home afterward. No swelling and tearing, no nighttime splints.

The answer. The way to stop her traitorous DNA from sabotaging her chance to show the world what she was, or could be. And she'd found it herself.

All she had to do was find a radiologist who knew how to treat Dupuytren's and make him see her right now, while she was still a candidate. She would explain why it was so important. If she had to, she'd get Leo to pull more strings.

Suddenly, she was angry—at Leo, Aaron, all of them, for being so sure that there was nothing to do except *keep an eye on it*, wait until she got worse. She had known that couldn't be right, yet she'd listened to them because they seemed so certain, and she'd wasted precious time.

Well, no more. It was her concert. Her future.

She jumped up, eager to call Aaron and tell him what she had discovered. He'd be happy for her, glad to be wrong if it meant a chance for her to keep playing. No matter how tense things had been when he left, Aaron was her husband, her lover, her partner. They didn't hold grudges; they were on the same side.

She grabbed the phone and tapped on his number. It rang and

rang. He was probably in one of those seminars and couldn't answer. She thought of hanging up and calling later, but she let it ring. It would go to voicemail eventually, or he would—

"Susannah?"

He sounded distant, distracted. Service must be lousy in St. Pierre. "I have the most exciting news."

"Are you all right? Is James all right?"

"I said exciting, not disturbing." She laughed. "And yes, James is fine." Impatient now, she could hardly stand not to tell him. "You have a minute?"

"Hold on." She heard muffled conversation, then a long silence. "Okay," he said at last. "What's up?"

She began to tell him what she had learned. To her astonishment, he cut her off. "You aren't really considering radiation, are you?"

"Yes, that's exactly what I'm considering."

"Susannah. Radiation isn't like taking Advil. It has all kinds of latent consequences."

"But it *works*. It's the only treatment for someone like me."

"No," he countered. "It's not at all evident that it works. I looked into it when I was checking for you."

"All the websites—"

"Please. Don't be naive."

"What's that supposed to mean?"

"It means," he said, "that no matter what you read on some website, no causal relationship has ever been demonstrated between radiating a nodule and halting the progression of the disease." Susannah tried to interrupt, but he kept talking. "Obviously some people have had radiation and like to blog about it. But just because they don't develop the contracture, we don't know—because we can't—if that's due to the radiation, since fifty percent of people, statistically, are never going to progress past the nodular stage anyway. So they might have been in that fifty percent all along."

"But what if I'm in the other fifty percent?"

Aaron didn't seem to have heard her question. "In other words, there's no way to know if those people would have stopped at the pre-contracture stage anyway, radiation or no radiation."

"That's not a reason—"

"You can't prove causality without a control group," he went on, as if she hadn't spoken, "and you can't do a randomized control study when there are so many factors. So-called preventive measures, like radiation, have to be compared to the natural history of the condition, without treatment. If outcomes are similar, then the effects of radiation are non-significant."

Susannah had no idea what he was talking about. All she knew was that he was ruining her hope. "But why *not* do it? What's the harm?"

"I just told you." She could hear his annoyance. "You can't assume that radiation is benign. It can have complications down the road. There aren't enough longitudinal studies to rule that out. Put that together with the likelihood of no benefit, and you get a negative equation."

Her head was starting to hurt. Non-significant effects, negative equation—it sounded like a description of their conversation.

"There's no harm in doing anything I can," she repeated, but her voice had already weakened.

"That's my point. There might be harm. You have to weigh that against the odds that there won't ever be any contracture. That's the merit of the wait-and-see approach. Treatment's always an option later, if you need it."

Her grip tightened on the phone. There was something terribly wrong with the whole conversation. She hadn't called to hear a scientific lecture. She'd called to talk to her husband.

"Radiation is for serious conditions," Aaron continued. "This is hardly in that category. Dupuytren's is slow, not urgent. It might never be urgent. I can show you the statistics."

Anger spiked in her chest. She wasn't a statistic. She was a particular person. Herself. So what if radiation only helped one person in a zillion? She might be that one person. Why was he trying to spoil it—the miraculous discovery she'd made, with no help from anyone?

"Anyway, how are you?" he said. "Enjoying the peace and quiet?"

"I'd have enjoyed the piña coladas and sunsets a lot more."

"Is that *poor me*? You're the one who convinced me that the timing was bad."

"It's wistful me."

"Please don't do that, Susannah."

"Do what?"

"Manipulate me. Make it seem like I'm the villain."

She could hear noises in the background, louder now. Pressing the phone to her ear, she said, "I'm not making you seem like anything."

There was a long pause, and then he said, "Look, I have to get back. There's a big reception, I'm supposed to be there. I stepped outside to take the call because I thought it might be important."

And it wasn't. It was only me, saving my music. Susannah realized that she hadn't told him about the new development with Perez-Smith. The CD, Libby's cleverness. Most of all, the truth that Vera had thrust back at her. *You're still the one at the keyboard.* The one who had to make sure her finger didn't fail.

The silence stretched between them, dense and confusing. After a minute she said, "Yes, fine. Get back to your reception."

"I'll talk to you tomorrow." She was about to answer, but he'd already ended the call.

She looked at the computer screen, filled with the radiation website. She would do it, no matter what Aaron said. The dosage was low, safe. No breaking your fingers to make them well. One-minute treatments, and you could drive home afterward. She wouldn't need Aaron to give her a ride. She wouldn't even have to tell him.

The idea startled her. It was one thing not to tell Aaron about the audition because she knew she would tell him, later, if it turned out well, and she had. But to have a medical treatment and keep it a secret—a medical treatment he opposed?

The point of the concert was to be her whole self again. For James, so he would see. And for Aaron, so he would remember. But this was splitting her into new fragments.

If she'd been with Aaron in St. Pierre, this strange and confusing rift wouldn't have happened. On the other hand, if she'd been with him, she wouldn't have gone on the internet tonight and learned about radiation. Found an answer.

Whatever you did, or didn't do, had consequences. That was something she had learned long ago.

Part Four

Long, Long Time

When I had nothing else, I had my mother and the piano.
And that was enough.
Alicia Keyes

Chapter Fifteen
then

After tracking Simone to the Red Rooster and then running away once she found her, Susannah returned to New York. She pushed the sound of the autoharp out of her mind and threw herself into her own music.

She'd vowed not to squander her training on the weddings, ballet classes, and cocktail hour music that were spoiling her touch, but she needed a way to supplement her income from the girls' school. When she heard that a local college needed someone to teach an evening course on the Baroque Masters, it seemed like the perfect solution.

The college required all adjunct instructors to attend a four-hour orientation. By the end of the first hour she had met Aaron, who was teaching a course on biochemistry. By the end of the first week, they were lovers. After six weeks she brought him to meet her parents.

—

Dana greeted them at the door, fluttering with a girlish excitement that Susannah had never seen in her cool, unflappable parent. "Welcome, you two. Come, please. Dad's been pacing. You know him."

Tyler hurried across the foyer to join them. He clasped Aaron's hand. "Suzie tells me you teach science. What do you think of Thomas Kuhn?"

Susannah tried to catch Aaron's eye. *His beloved Thomas Kuhn,* she mouthed.

"Most people don't understand the relationship between scientific knowledge and cultural values," Tyler went on, ushering them into the living room. "They think it goes one way or the other, but it's recursive."

"Exactly," Aaron said. "Paradigm shifts happen at particular times, in particular places. And they alter those places."

Susannah's heart leapt. Her father was in heaven. And Aaron wasn't humoring him. He was genuinely enjoying the conversation. She could see him bending close, gesturing earnestly.

I love this man. She felt her mother looking at her. Turning, she answered the question in Dana's eyes. *Yes. He loves me too.*

Dana smiled. Then she said, "Shall we continue the conversation over lunch? I've made a quiche, and there's a beet salad plus some leftover corn chowder."

"It sounds delicious," Aaron told her.

Tyler motioned to the sun porch where Dana had arranged ladder-back chairs around a glass table. "Please."

"Let me help you," Susannah said.

"Absolutely not. It will take me two seconds to bring the platters in. You concentrate on enjoying yourself."

Dana set the quiche in front of Aaron and handed him a knife. "Would you like to cut it for us? I'll ladle out the soup."

Susannah watched as Aaron studied the quiche. "He's figuring it out mathematically," she explained. "Something with *pi* and a hypotenuse. The pieces will be perfectly proportioned."

She'd meant it as a joke, but after a minute of watching him make tiny careful marks along the crust, her impatience overrode her humor. "Oh, for goodness sakes." She grabbed the knife and made three slashes across the pie, cutting it into six more-or-less equal pieces. "There. Done."

"Susannah." Tyler sounded shocked.

"Oh well. Everyone knows I'm not good at waiting."

"She certainly didn't learn her bad manners from us," Dana apologized.

Aaron was less bothered than they were. "We all have our traits. I like to think of them as lovable quirks."

"You're a tolerant man," Tyler said.

"It's easy to be tolerant," Aaron replied, "when Susannah gives me so much."

She leaned into him, suffused with happiness. He took her hand under the table.

Tyler had tears in his eyes when they said goodbye. "You take good care of my little girl," he told Aaron. "You know how those artistic types can get."

"I'm on it," Aaron said.

It was a beginning, a promise.

They moved into the loft at Fourth Avenue and Tenth Street, with the crazy bathroom and a futon they had to roll up under the piano in the daytime and unfurl at night. Huge windows stretched from the floor to the ceiling. Susannah wanted to stay there forever.

Then Aaron talked about getting married, and Susannah was shocked by her response. Living together was one thing, but the idea of starting her own family, when she didn't know the family she had come from, filled her with terror.

She told herself that her reaction made no sense. Dana and Tyler were her parents. But they weren't her only parents. Her real mother was a druggie, and dead. Her real father had kicked open the door with his boot, hissing, "You need to leave. Now."

She had. Cowed, she had given up, without even trying. It wasn't like her.

The more committed she was to Aaron, the more Susannah knew she had to try again. If she wanted to be a parent herself, she had to go back to Texas. Give him another chance. Wayne. It wasn't too late.

She tallied her income and expenses. If she was frugal, she could make what was left from Dana and Tyler's graduation gift cover one more trip to Texas. She'd never told them about the earlier trips. She hadn't intended for it to be a secret, but somehow she hadn't found the moment to bring it up and after a while it seemed simpler not to. She wanted to tell Aaron, but that was hard too—not because it would hurt his feelings, since it wouldn't, but because there was so much about her search that he could never understand. He was the fourth child, the longed-for son, of a couple who had known each other since high school. Aaron had met her parents, seen how they loved her. He wouldn't understand why that wasn't enough.

The notion of returning to Texas changed from an appealing idea to an urgent need. Just as the earlier trip had led her to a deeper music, this one would free her for Aaron and the family they would have together.

She needed to do what she should have done the first time. Give Wayne a copy of the adoption papers. Reveal herself. Showing up, the way she had—no plan, no warning—had been colossally stupid. No wonder she had panicked, and he'd kicked her out. This time, she would write and introduce herself.

She had saved the address that Hollis gave her. She wrote a brief letter and booked a round-trip ticket to Texas.

—

"Good of you to come see us again." Jimmy Ray reached across the seat to push open the passenger door. There was a line of cars behind his at the curb marked *Arrivals Pickup Only*. Susannah slid into the green Pontiac and gave him a kiss on the cheek.

"Your grannie might not admit it, you know, but it means a lot to her, you coming to visit like this. She don't have much of Corinne left, and Simone hardly knows us anymore. But now she's got you."

Susannah gave a guilty wince as she pulled the door shut. She wasn't really there for Beryl; it was Wayne she had come to see. "You're kind to me, Jimmy Ray."

"Easy to be kind when you got no history. You know, who did what to who, back in the day. Nothing kills kindness more than history."

Was that true? Susannah wondered. Wouldn't a shared history make you feel connected? That was the whole point of the trip. She looked at him, curious. "You have any children, Jimmy Ray?"

"Nope, never happened. My first wife couldn't, and by the time I met your grannie we were too old."

"That's a shame."

"No shame in it," he said. "You get what you get in life."

Again, Susannah wondered if that was true. Weren't you supposed to work for what you wanted, instead of just accepting what you were given? Otherwise, why try anything? Why take piano lessons, or enter a competition—or come to Texas to search for the missing piece of yourself?

She hadn't said anything to Beryl or Jimmy Ray about her plan to see Wayne. If things worked out, she'd surprise them with her triumph. And it would be their triumph too. Her reunion with Wayne would bring a reunion with Simone, a family healing that no one thought was possible. It would be a hostess gift far more precious than yellow roses.

And if it didn't? No, it had to. She'd done it the right way, this time. Explained who she was and told him to expect her.

Tomorrow. She'd spend the evening with Beryl and Jimmy Ray, then borrow the car and drive to La Posada in the morning.

Susannah could tell from Wayne's expression that he'd gotten her letter but wasn't glad she had come. "Why are you doing this?" he demanded. There was a rumble of footsteps behind him, and children's voices. He moved to block the doorway. "You go on out back," he called. "Ruth Ann. Little Wayne. Go on now."

Susannah tried not to let her determination falter. "Because I'm your daughter."

Wayne turned back to her. His eyes were hard. "Not that I'm aware."

"Didn't you read the letter? I have the papers right here."

He took the papers and studied them for a minute. "I don't see anything here with my name on it." He handed them back to her. "Look, miss. I don't doubt that you're Corinne's daughter, like you say. But there's nothing here that proves you're mine too. Pardon my French, but she could've been playing musical beds with just about anyone back then. When her and me had Simone, it was different. We were engaged, we'd declared ourselves." He stepped away and gestured at the street. "I'm sorry you went to all this trouble for nothing, but I don't see as it's my responsibility."

Susannah couldn't give up, not after she'd come this far. "What if I got hold of the original birth certificate, the one with your name on it?"

"It's just a paper. She could've put anything down."

"But it would be enough to make it possible, right? And then we could find out, for certain. Do a DNA test."

"You are a stubborn one."

She was. That's what Dana always told her.

"All right," he said, finally. "You bring me a paper with my name on it, and we'll talk."

Susannah wanted to hug him, or cry, or both. "I'll do that. Thank you. I really—I mean, thank you." He gave a quick nod and shut the door.

She flew down the flagstone walkway to the car. She'd get her original birth certificate, not the amended one with Tyler and Dana's names that the court had issued. But how did a person do that? Should she go back to Sisters of Mercy or was it a government thing, something you had to write away for? No, that would take too long.

Then it occurred to her that Beryl—the person who had been with Corinne when she was born—might have an idea, or even a copy.

"Why in the world would you need such a thing?" Beryl wanted to know.

They were sitting on the screened porch after dinner. Jimmy Ray had made barbecued ribs with his special sauce and the smell of smoke lingered in the air. Bands of fuchsia and topaz streaked the sky. The buzzing of the bottle flies was loud against the screen.

Her birth certificate? Wasn't she entitled to her own birth certificate?

She hesitated. Beryl might be angry to hear that she was trying to connect with Wayne, but making up another story was too hard. Besides, she was tired of stories. She had come here for the truth.

"I need to show Wayne," she confessed. "He said we could talk if I brought the original certificate, the one with his name on it."

Beryl looked sad, not angry. She reached for her cigarettes. "It won't help you, sugar."

"Why not?"

She didn't answer. Susannah looked at Jimmy Ray. "Let your grannie tell it," he said.

Beryl snapped the lighter and inhaled as her cigarette caught the flame. "I was right there, just like you thought. It was my first grandbaby, after all. I wasn't about to miss that." She lifted a shoulder. "Might be I thought I'd get her to change her mind, who knows? Course, she didn't."

She tossed the lighter onto a chair and blew a perfect smoke ring. "Anyway, they come around and asked who to put down for the father, for the papers and all. But she was so mad at Wayne for running out on her like that, so she said, Oh, just put *father unknown*. She knew perfectly well who the father was and so did he. But she was too mad to give him anything to lay claim to. Didn't think he had the right, not if he wasn't going to stick by her."

Susannah stared at Beryl. The bottle flies flung themselves against the screen. The sky was the color of blood.

"That's what it says on my birth certificate? *Father unknown?*" Her heart was a fist in her throat. "Why would she do a thing like that?"

Beryl looked annoyed. "I just told you why she did it."

"I don't understand." Susannah's gaze darted from the grill to the plastic tablecloth with its red-and-white checks, and then back to the grill. "It makes her sound like—I don't know, some kind of stupid slut."

Beryl's face turned ashen. "Don't you dare talk like that about her."

Jimmy Ray pulled the napkin off his lap and laid it on the table. His eyebrows were a stern line below the V of his widow's peak. "Your grannie's right. You got no call to talk about someone's daughter like that, especially after how good Beryl's been to you." He put an arm around Beryl's shoulder. She laid her cigarette in the ashtray, then turned and buried her face in the hibiscus pattern of his shirt.

Susannah stared at them. "I didn't mean it that way. I just—"

"You got to watch your mouth, honey. Gonna get you in trouble one of these days."

"I'm sorry. I really am."

Beryl raised her head to glare at Susannah. "You should be."

No, Corinne was the one who should be sorry. Why would Corinne do that to her?

Because Corinne hadn't been thinking about her, that's why. She hadn't been a real person to Corinne, just a problem to be disposed of.

Susannah sagged into the chair. "Wayne will never believe me now."

"I told you to forget about Wayne." Beryl disengaged from Jimmy Ray's embrace, patted her hairdo, and retrieved her cigarette.

"Why does he keep rejecting me?" Tears pooled in her eyes.

"Because he's a coward, that's why." Beryl's voice was sharp. "Don't want to admit he did wrong by Corinne, so it's easier to say it wasn't his."

Susannah looked at Jimmy Ray, appealing to him for help. "It's not fair. No one thought how it would be for me."

He shrugged. "I wasn't there, but seems to me she was thinking of you, honey, what was best for you, when she took the trouble to find you a good home."

What was best for you. How could anyone know what was best for someone else?

"A lot of things ain't fair," he went on. "But just because something ain't fair, it don't mean life owes you something else in return."

Susannah wanted to explain that she wasn't asking for anything in return, only the acknowledgment that she'd been wronged. She opened her mouth to speak, then stopped when she saw Beryl's face.

Beryl had called Wayne a coward but she hadn't said that Susannah was right, or justified, or forgiven. She hadn't said, *It's okay, sugar.* She hadn't even smiled. The grimness on her face left no doubt: she was as mad at Susannah as Susannah was at Corinne.

The realization struck Susannah like the snap of a branch. Instead of bringing a new healing, she'd created a new rift.

Everything in Beryl's world had been opened to her. She had assumed it would always be like that, simply because of the gift of herself. But everyone had a limit, even a grandmother. Beryl was a mother before she was a grandmother. Her own child came first.

Jimmy Ray had put his arm around Beryl, taking her side and speaking sternly about courtesy and fairness. Yet there was a glimmer of compassion in his gaze.

Forgive me, Susannah begged.

The compassion deepened, but there was no absolution. Once you said a word like slut, you could never unsay it.

Susannah pushed out of her chair. No one told her to sit down, wait. She shoved past the screen door and stumbled into the yard. The grass brushed along her legs, slicing the hot Texas air.

Was her mother a stupid slut? And what was Dana, then? She remembered that day on the Cape, when she was a teenager and Dana had talked about being barren and hollow. What did that make her, the adopted child? Someone who had filled Dana with whatever Corinne didn't want?

She had thought she would come back from Texas healed and whole, but she was going to go back to New York emptier than when she left. No Wayne. No Beryl either, not the way it had been. Jimmy Ray was going to stand by Beryl; besides, they weren't related. *No history.*

Hollis didn't like her. Corinne was dead.

That left one person. The person she'd run away from.

Chapter Sixteen
then

Susannah was sitting at a round wooden table at the Red Rooster, right across from the table she'd occupied on her first visit to the club. She had left Lynette the day before, the air thick with tension as she and Beryl exchanged stiff good-byes, and rented a car to drive to Austin. The hell with the expense. She'd find another pupil, raise her fee, do something—but she had to talk to Simone, now, in person, because Simone was the only person who could help her understand who she really was.

Simone was still in Austin, booked for another engagement at the Red Rooster. Susannah had learned that from Jimmy Ray, whose sister Lorraine was a devoted fan of the group she called "my relations." She wouldn't have to search for her this time, only show up at the Red Rooster and—what? That was the part she didn't know.

From the story Hollis had told that day on the bayou, Simone didn't know she had an older sister. The news would be shocking; she might even think it was a hoax. A cover story might be smart,

Susannah decided. A reason for being in Austin, in case she needed to stall for time.

Country music, that was the way to get Simone to open up. She couldn't very well pretend to be another country singer, but she could be a journalist who wrote about them. She worked out the details as she sped down I-45 into Austin. Alexandra Fallon, with *The Dallas-Fort Worth Courier*—a made-up name and a newspaper that didn't exist, but she didn't think Simone would know that.

Susannah got to Austin in the late afternoon, found a hotel room in the music district, and washed her face. Then she headed for the Red Rooster, a few blocks away. This time she knew enough to order a beer. She wrapped her hands around the glass and waited for the lights to dim.

And then, there they were, running onto the stage in their white boots and fringed jackets, waving and flashing their wide happy smiles. The tall one, Ava, grabbed the microphone. "We're thrilled to be back at the Rooster. Hope y'all are too!"

The women set up their instruments, exchanged nods, and launched into *Wildwood Flower*. It must be their signature opening, Susannah thought, remembering her first visit to the club. Then they shifted into *Ring of Fire*, followed by Simone's show-stopping solo of *Long, Long Time*. The set ended with a haunting rendition of *You Were Always on My Mind*. Susannah had to admit it: they were good.

She went up to the club owner during the break. "Pardon me," she said. "I'm from *The Dallas-Fort Worth Courier* and I'd love to talk to the lead singer from the group that just performed. It's for a story I'm doing."

He eyed her skeptically. "You got a press pass? A business card?"

"I didn't think I needed a press pass to get into a club. Just an ID proving I'm over twenty-one."

"Ha." His features relaxed into a grin. "All the way from Dallas, huh?"

"Yep." Her mind sped through the possible traps. Her accent? She didn't sound like someone from Dallas. If he asked, she'd explain that she grew up in New England and moved to Dallas for the job. Her ignorance of how newspapers worked? Please. Anyone could fake that.

"Gonna mention the club by name, I hope?"

"You bet." Susannah couldn't believe she was pulling this off, yet he seemed to believe that she was a reporter. She never would have gotten away with such a flimsy story in New York.

"Don't forget to mention me, now. I'm Red Magee, proud owner."

"You've got a lot to be proud of."

He looked pleased. "I'll see if I can catch her backstage. Girl you want is Simone Russell." He disappeared behind a curtain, yelling, "Hope you girls are decent."

Susannah leaned against the bar to wait. Her flare of bravado was fading, anxiety taking its place. She had gone to La Posada and found a name and address. Then she had gone to Lynette and found a grandmother. Now she was in Austin, about to meet the person she both longed and feared to know.

The owner returned, gesturing at the curtain. "Give her a sec, then go on back."

"Great. Thanks."

Susannah willed herself to wait a full minute. Then she squared her shoulders, pushed the curtain aside, and went backstage.

The members of the Lone Star All-Girls Mother Plucking Band were busy packing up their instruments and switching from the boots they'd worn onstage to sneakers and sandals. Susannah tried to include everyone in her greeting, but her eyes were riveted on Simone. "Hi there," she said. "Thanks for being willing to talk to me. I hope I'm not intruding."

"There's always time for an *interview*," one of the girls drawled. The other two laughed, but Simone looked embarrassed.

"You're all terrific," Susannah said. "It's just that I'm focusing on vocalists. For my article."

"No worries," the tall girl, Ava, assured her. She gave Simone a playful smirk. "Don't forget us when you're rich and famous." Simone threw her an annoyed look. Ava laughed again and gathered up her poncho and purse. "Let's go, *hermanas*. Catch you later, 'Mone."

The others left, and Susannah was alone in the dressing room with Simone. A rectangular mirror was mounted on the far wall. Plastic crates of cleaning supplies and paper goods were shoved under the benches that lined two of the other walls. A broom was propped in the corner. There were no windows, only a fluorescent light fixture in the center of the ceiling and a row of bulbs over the mirror.

"Thanks for being willing to talk to me on, like, zero notice." She gestured from the broom to the plastic crates. "Is there somewhere we can go to sit and talk? This is a bit—"

"Small?" Simone quipped.

"Very."

"Not to mention no chairs."

Susannah couldn't help smiling. "Chairs would be good."

"Chairs are always good. Especially when you have to jump around onstage for a whole long hour."

Simone was likable, Susannah thought. She wasn't sure if she was happy about that or not. "Maybe we can go somewhere. If you have time?"

"Sure. Our second show isn't for a couple of hours. There's a cute little diner around the corner."

"You're on." Susannah shouldered her purse and followed Simone out the door. Simone waved to Red as they left, tossing her curls and calling out a cheerful, "Back soon, boss."

They settled into an empty booth in the back of the diner, and a waitress appeared with coffee. Susannah pushed the ketchup bottle against the tabletop jukebox. "So," she said, "tell me how you got started. Did you sing when you were little? Was your family musical?"

"Oh. Gosh." Simone tucked her hair behind her ears. "This is so weird. I mean, being interviewed and all. Sorry if I'm a little slow out the gate. This is a first for me."

"Nothing to be nervous about. We're just having a conversation."

Simone toyed with the metal plates of the jukebox, then picked up her coffee mug. She looked at Susannah, her eyes wide and blue. "It must be so exciting, being a reporter. Travelling around, talking to famous people. If ya'll don't mind my asking, what made you interested in country singers—or, I should say, people like me who want to be country singers?"

Susannah scrambled for what she knew about country-and-western music. "Hey, I'd love to be the first to spot the next Emmylou Harris or Wynonna Judd."

"And I'd love to *be* the next Emmylou Harris or Wynonna Judd." Simone flushed. "That must sound really conceited. But you nailed it, that's my dream. You're good, Alexandra—is it okay if I call you Alexandra?"

Alexandra? Red must have given Simone the name of the reporter who wanted to talk to her. Susannah felt herself flush too. "Allie is fine."

"Allie, then." Simone pulled the sugar bowl across the table. "Pardon me for reaching in front of you. Anyway, you were asking?"

"About your childhood, how it all started. Is your family musical?"

"My family." Simone stirred sugar into her coffee, and Susannah tried to quiet her heartbeat as she waited for Simone to continue. It was like a cannon in her chest. Surely Simone could hear it.

"Truthfully," Simone replied, "I don't remember my mother so much before she got sick, though I think maybe she played the guitar. But my stepmother liked to sing in the church choir and pretty soon I got to doing it too. Pamela and I, that's her name, we'd get these harmonies going and it was pretty great, actually, the way we could follow each other and make this whole new sound. We figured out this double warble that was really cool."

"So you don't know if your mother had any musical talent?"

"You mean my natural mother?" Simone shook her head. "Like I said, I don't really remember. I didn't see much of her, growing up."

Susannah flinched. *Well, I didn't see any of her.*

Then she said, "What about your father?"

"Ha. Poor Daddy. He couldn't carry a tune if it was made of feathers."

Susannah did her best to smile in response. How odd that Simone's stepmother was the one who had gotten her to sing, when Corinne was the source of their shared talent. "Did he encourage you, at least? Your dad?"

"Kind of. I mean, he liked that Pamela and I were in the choir together, and he liked that it got me to church on Sunday, but that was about it."

"Your dad wasn't big on nurturing your musical ability?"

"He wasn't against it, if that's what you're asking. He wasn't like— no singers around *here*, she'd better find a nice husband instead of chasing some silly dream." Simone blew on her coffee. "He liked it when Pamela and I got along, which we mostly did, especially when we were singing, and he thought it was pretty to hear me practicing. But that was all."

"And now, here you are." Susannah swept her hand in a wide arc, indicating the coffee shop but meaning more. "You're in this terrific band, playing real gigs. How did you get from a church choir to the All Girls et cetera?"

Simone grinned. "The girls pretty much scooped me up my junior year. You met Ava, right? She's the powerhouse, getting us bookings, organizing everything. Noelle and I had a lot of the same classes, and Maggie Rose was Noelle's roommate. We found out that we loved playing together, and we've been doing it ever since." Her grin faded.

"I wouldn't want to cut them out of anything, you know. Truth be told, even talking to you on my own feels a little bit wrong, without the girls." Frowning, she toyed with a curl. "I mean, I'd never have had a chance to play in a real club if it wasn't for Ava."

"You've always played in a group?"

"Oh, I get my special numbers. I'm the main vocalist, and then there's the autoharp. But yep, we're a team. I wouldn't want to push myself out there without them."

"It's just a newspaper article," Susannah said. "I'm not offering you a chance to cut an album or anything." She had tossed the comment onto the table as a joke. Then she saw the look on Simone's face. The excitement was there, suppressed as soon as Simone caught herself picturing that deliciously impossible event. Susannah understood. There were plenty of times she'd felt the same way.

Simone rested her chin on her fists. "Guess I'm like every performer. It's hard not to dream about making it big." There was a bright clink as the jukebox shifted, and Tim McGraw's twang filled the diner.

Susannah adjusted her coffee cup, watching as glints of silver swirled along the perimeter. She'd dreamed of it too, what Simone called *making it big*. Of course, playing at some country jamboree wasn't like playing at Carnegie Hall. The Grand Ole Opry wasn't a real opera, like Don Giovanni.

She shifted against the vinyl. "Well, you certainly have the potential."

A prickle of unease crept up the back of her neck. Was that true? The applause at the Red Rooster had been loud and genuine. It must feel good to have people shouting for you like that. You didn't get that kind of whooping applause when you played for a ballet class or a faculty recital.

"You really think I have talent?" Simone asked. "I mean, compared to all the stars you've interviewed?"

Susannah pulled herself out of her reverie. Stars. Oh, for god's sakes.

"I wouldn't be talking to you if I didn't believe you had talent," she said. "There are plenty of other bands out there." She had meant the remark to come from the fictitious Alexandra Fallon, yet she really did feel that way.

"Wow, thanks for saying that." Simone's face brightened. "Want some dessert? We could split a piece of blueberry pie."

"Sure. Blueberry's my favorite."

"Mine too."

The coffee cup jerked in Susannah's hand. A polite agreement, just to be friendly, or was there a blueberry pie gene? She set the cup on the table and looked at Simone. The resemblance between them was too obvious to miss. It was hard to believe that Red or Ava or the other members of the band hadn't seen it. Simone's eyes were thick with mascara, but they were the same eyes as hers, the color of sapphires. Corinne's birthstone.

A deep yearning opened in her chest. She longed to grab Simone's hand and tell her, "It's me. I came."

Simone signaled to the waitress. Then she turned back to Susannah. "Well, you might think you've tasted blueberry pie, but I can't believe that whatever they make in Dallas is a good as what we got here. You just wait."

Right. Alexandra Fallon, ace reporter. From Dallas.

She cleared her throat. "So, getting back to your history. Sounds like you didn't have any special training, but your talent must have come from somewhere. You have any brothers or sisters with musical DNA?"

"They're pretty young," Simone said, "but nope, no sign of it. Well, technically they're my half siblings. So no, it's just me."

Before Susannah could reply, the waitress reappeared with a Texas-size piece of pie, two forks, and an extra plate. "Here you go, girls." She put her hands on her hips and regarded them with an amused expression. "You two are sisters, I'm figuring?"

Simone laughed. "Hardly. She's from Dallas." Susannah watched as Simone lifted a forkful of warm blueberries and swooned in mock ecstasy. She pulled the other plate across the table but her appetite was gone.

Then Simone laid down her fork, her eyes bright. "I just had an idea. We have another set tonight. If you can stick around till midnight, you could hear us again. Maybe talk to the other girls too?" Her expression grew sheepish. "Guess it would make me feel less guilty, being singled out and all. But we'd love it, really. Can you? Can you stay?"

Go back to the Red Rooster? Well, why not? She'd been so focused on Simone that she hadn't paid attention to how the four women worked together. It had seemed so effortless but there was probably a plan, the same way there was for a chamber quartet. Not that she had a lot of experience with that. She'd done ensembles at the conservatory—you had to, it was a requirement—but solo piano was what she liked best.

"I could. I mean, sure. It might be good to talk to the other girls, flesh out the story."

"That's great. And it makes me feel so much better, truth be told." Simone touched her hand. "And then we're all going out after the show, so you can join us and talk to everyone. Ava's boyfriend is coming, and Noelle's brother, he's a guitarist too. And my parents, even though it's a long drive. We planned it a while back, to celebrate the anniversary of our band. Your timing's perfect."

A three-beer drive. Susannah's breath jammed in her chest. "Your parents."

Simone blushed. "Color me corny, but I'm proud of the band and I want them to help us celebrate."

Susannah couldn't move. Wayne and whatever-her-name-was.

She had never imagined she would see Wayne in Austin. She hadn't thought she would see him again, period. Not without the birth certificate he had asked for. Yet seeing her next to Simone, he would know.

Of course, she was supposed to be a reporter. That was who Simone thought she was. Simone would realize she'd been lying.

Why had she made up that stupid Alexandra business? Why hadn't she just told the truth?

Now. I could tell her right now.

Simone might be crushed to learn that there wasn't going to be an article about her in the *Dallas-Fort Worth Courier.* She might be angry and demand to know why Susannah had played a trick like that. Or she might think *I'm your sister* was another charade—the delusion of a psycho stalker who had fixated on her for some creepy reason and wanted to pretend they were related. Then again, Simone might be overjoyed to find out that Alexandra was her very own sister. Maybe she'd invite her to join them onstage, and Susannah would become the fifth member of the band.

Susannah's head was pounding. Everything was happening too fast. This wasn't anything like the encounter she had imagined.

Simone looked at her watch. "Actually, I have to get back. But I'll see you later, right?" She beamed at Susannah. "I can't thank you enough, Allie. This is so, so exciting!"

Susannah tried to return her smile, but it felt more like a grimace than a smile. It was hard to believe that Simone didn't notice.

"The girls and I have to tweak our last number," Simone told her, sliding out of the booth. "Not to mention tweaking our makeup. It won't do for the Mother Pluckers to be anything less than gorgeous." She gave Susannah a merry wave. "See you back at the Rooster."

"I'll be there."

It seemed like the only thing to say. Susannah watched as Simone wove through the diner and disappeared out the door. Then she rose and made her way back to the hotel.

Clearly, Simone had no clue that she had a sister. The waitress's remark had breezed right past her, not even stirring her curiosity. Not surprising. Why would it occur to someone to wonder if there was a secret sister and if the person sharing her blueberry pie might, miraculously, be that very sibling?

Susannah unlocked the door to her hotel room and flipped on the light. Her image stared back at her from the full-length mirror. The similarity to Simone was uncanny.

What was she supposed to do? Go back to the Red Rooster and face Wayne—so he could tell Simone that Alexandra Fallon was spying on her, lying to her, tricking her into sharing her hopes and dreams?

"I wasn't!" she wanted to cry. "I just wanted to talk to her."

She had made up that reporter story as a way to ease into their conversation, but she'd assumed that whatever came next would be up to her. If Wayne weren't coming to the Red Rooster, it would be. She could take her time, decide if she wanted to reveal who she was. It would be her choice.

Thank goodness Simone had mentioned that her parents were coming. If she hadn't—Susannah winced, not wanting to imagine it. At least, this way, she had a chance to think.

But her thoughts wouldn't hold still long enough to let her concentrate. *Yes. No.* Her mind leapfrogged from one thought to the next. She could go back to the club, forewarned, and offer herself. But Wayne would be angry at this second deception, and Simone would be too. She would lose them both. Or she could run away again, and that would be the end of it.

Stay. Leave.

The hotel room had a chenille bedspread and a framed print of horses in a field. A plastic tray with packets of coffee, sweetener, non-dairy creamer. The answer she needed wasn't here, in this airless little room. It was a cage, not a refuge. She had to get out again, walk, breathe. Figure out what to do.

Chapter Seventeen
then

The hotel was wedged between a sports bar and a Tex-Mex restaurant on a narrow street in the heart of the music district. Standing outside the entrance, taking in the sights she had brushed past in her eagerness to get to the Red Rooster, Susannah could see why Austin was called the Live Music Capital of the World. Venues were everywhere. She wondered if it was good for Simone to be part of such a vibrant music scene or if it just meant more competition— or if Simone even thought like that.

Susannah shoved her hands in her pockets and began to walk. The sidewalk was crowded but no one seemed to be in a hurry. Instinctively, she slowed her pace.

She tried to imagine Simone growing up in Texas, a place as different from her own New England suburb as Wynonna Judd was from Wolfgang Mozart. She pictured Simone coming home from school to the house on the treeless cul-de-sac, kicking off her sandals in the foyer, singing in the church choir with Wayne's wife. Pamela, that was her name.

Pamela, not Corinne. It struck her, suddenly, that neither of them had really had Corinne for a mother, not if *mother* meant someone who was there to love you and teach you and watch you grow. Simone had Pamela, who sang with her in the church choir. And she had Dana, who drove her to Boston for lessons with Vera.

Pamela and Dana were the same—raising someone else's child, doing their best to nurture a gift they hadn't bequeathed. Yet Susannah was certain that Pamela was nothing like Dana.

No one was like Dana. Not the mothers of her friends, who seemed happy with their carpools and bake sales and PTA projects. Not her teachers, her Girl Scout leader—not even Nana Sophie, Dana's own mother, who spent hours fretting about her azaleas and searching through cookbooks for the perfect béarnaise.

Dana was righteous, intense, fiercely committed to making the world—and her daughter—live up to its potential. If something was wrong, it had to be fixed. Even if her crusade made Susannah cringe. Even if no one else seemed to care.

Susannah could still remember Miss Campbell, her kindergarten teacher, and how her mother had made Miss Campbell cry and ruined their circle time. She could see the dust motes that speckled the green chalkboard and smell the rose petals Miss Campbell kept on her desk in a special cut-glass bowl.

Miss Campbell had been young and pretty, and she liked to read *Are You My Mother?* to the cluster of pupils sitting cross-legged on their red and blue carpet squares. She had a special high-pitched voice for the little hatchling. "I have to find my mother," she would squeak. "But where, oh where is she?"

The baby bird asked everyone, "Are *you* my mother?" But none of them was.

Susannah was only five, but she knew the baby bird would find his mother, and he did. They recognized each other right away because they looked exactly alike.

After school, Susannah and her mother went to the playground with her friend Kerry and Kerry's mother. It was fall. Orange and crimson leaves were everywhere, giant heaping piles on the seesaw and slide. Kerry's mother had a great big stomach. Kerry saw Susannah looking at it while they dug in the sand and explained proudly, "I have a little brother in there. That's where babies grow." Kerry dropped her shovel and ran to her mother, who was sitting on the bench next to Dana. She put her head on her mother's stomach. "I remember when *I* was in your tummy, Mommy."

Susannah placed her own shovel on the ground. She ran up to her mother and laid her head on Dana's stomach. "I remember when I was in your tummy, too."

Dana lifted Susannah's head and looked into her eyes. "Remember what we talked about?" she asked gently. "Not all babies grow in their mommies' tummies. Babies grow in different ways. Like the chicks we saw in the incubator? Remember how the chicks pecked their way out of the eggs? That's another way babies get born. There are a lot of ways, not just one."

Susannah watched her mother's mouth as she spoke. Her mother was very smart. "Okay, Mommy," she said. Then, all at once, she understood. She was like the baby bird in the book. She took Dana's face in her hands, one palm on each cheek. "What color was my egg?" she demanded. "Was it blue, like a robin? Or was it yellow?"

Dana looked puzzled, so she explained about *Are You My Mother?* and the little hatchling. Her mother's face turned dark. She took Susannah's hands away from her cheeks and held them between hers, her lips a grim line. "The teacher read that out loud?" she asked. Susannah nodded. Wasn't it okay? She loved that book.

The next day Dana stormed into the classroom. Susannah couldn't hear what they were saying but she could tell that her mother was furious at Miss Campbell, who was standing there, bobbing her head miserably. Her mother looked huge, like a tiger. The book disappeared from the classroom. Miss Campbell read *Green Eggs and Ham* instead. Susannah missed the little hatchling. She didn't know why it had made her mother so angry.

Later, she began to think that her mother took everything way too seriously. When they had a science unit on heredity in the third grade, she refused to answer her mother's questions about what, exactly, the teacher had said. It was just a bunch of pea plants. Nobody cared—except her mother, of course. And then, in fourth grade, when they had to find out how their ancestors came to America and create a family tree, her mother dragged out old photo albums and documents, and went on and on about the Richardsons and her own family, the Jouberts and the Fortineaux, who had immigrated to New England looking for religious freedom.

"You have a legacy to be proud of," Dana announced, smiling at the family tree they had made out of poster-board, photos, and real twigs. Susannah was confused. *The phone rang, and we rushed to the airport.* What did that have to do with Henri Joubert getting on a boat for America?

There was no baby bird looking for its missing mother. There was an airplane and a special yellow blanket and—Dana's favorite part of the story—the way tiny Susannah had fit right into the crook of her arm as she drank her very first bottle.

She got an A on the family tree, but her doubt grew. Was her mother a liar, or did she know who Susannah was better than she did, herself?

The phone rang, and we rushed to the airport.

When Susannah was small, she thought that was how all families got their babies. "Your birthmother loved you very much," Dana would explain, brushing Susannah's hair or helping her pull off her snow boots. "That's why she made the very best plan she could. She knew she couldn't give any baby all the things it needed for a good life." Susannah would listen intently, wondering why her mother always used the word *any*. She wasn't *any* baby; she was herself.

She wondered, too, why her mother always seemed to answer a different question than the one she had asked. When she asked about her birthmother's favorite ice cream, Dana told her that people were a mixture of what they were born with, like the color of their eyes, and what they learned, like how to play the *Minuet in G*. And when she asked why a baby started growing inside someone if that person wasn't going to keep it anyway, Dana told her that some babies grew in their mommy's tummy and others, like her, grew in their mommy's heart.

It didn't make any sense. Did the baby get to pick, tummy or heart? Or did the mother pick?

The questions of a child, Susannah thought, making her way down the crowded street, dimly aware of the twang of voices and a crescendo of laughter. Yet the questions lingered in their adult form. That was why she had returned to Austin, and to the Red Rooster.

But neither she nor Simone was *any* baby. Each of them was a particular baby. A particular woman. Simone's image bloomed, swelled, filled her mind. The way Simone's eyes sparkled as she savored the blueberry pie, lowered as she began the achingly beautiful refrain. *And I think I'm going to miss you for a long, long time.*

A different music. Nothing like hers.

She thought of Bach, how his music grounded her and raised her up, both at once. In Bach's perfect architecture, everything fit, even the dissonance. Everything had a place.

She crossed the street, quickening her pace, and found herself following a woman in a loose green dress who was walking a golden retriever. There was something about the woman that reminded her of Vera. The way she held her head, alert as an eagle.

Susannah was the youngest pupil Vera had ever taken on, only eight when her mother brought her to Vera's apartment for the very first time. Vera had to adjust the bench so her feet could reach the pedals, twisting the knobs until they wouldn't turn any further.

She had played the Mozart variations in A-major, all the way to the end of the Trio, when Vera rose from the blue velvet couch where she'd been sitting, like a genie rising from a bottle. Vera's proud features—the long nose, the deep-set eyes that never seemed to blink—loomed over her.

"You're playing like a typist," Vera barked, waving a hand over the keys as if flicking away the offending sounds. "Note, note, note. Why would you do that?"

"But every note matters!" Susannah's voice rose in protest. "If it's wrong, it's awful."

"Well, of course." Vera didn't try to hide her annoyance. "Obviously the notes have to be right. But they're just a path to the music." Vera glared at her. "You have to play the notes but hear the music."

Vera's words filled the room. She was a witch now, a dragon—ripping away everything Susannah had learned about the piano and replacing it, in a single glorious swipe, with a dazzling new possibility.

Vera turned to Dana, who was waiting in the matching armchair. "Can you bring her at 4:00 on Tuesdays? I can fit her in then."

Susannah looked at her mother. Dana was in charge of the academic press at the college where her father taught. Her mother's staff meetings were on Tuesday afternoons.

"Of course," Dana replied. Her eyes were on Vera, not Susannah. "Thank you, Ms. Evangelista."

"But Mom—"

"Hush," her mother told her. "This is important. You have a special gift."

The moment was carved into Susannah's memory. Her mother might not have understood music, but she understood that her daughter had to have it. And she made sure Susannah got it, the same way she made sure her father got the exact flavor of ice cream he liked, even if it meant going to three different stores.

Dana had named her gift. Susannah couldn't help wondering if Simone had a special gift too. And what if she did? There was room in the world for both of them. There was no such thing as too much music.

She was still following the woman in the green dress. The golden retriever trotted next to her, tail up, head alert. A man approached from the other direction. He had a dog too, a curly-haired terrier. Susannah saw the terrier strain at its leash as they neared the woman with the retriever. "Toby," the man scolded, pulling back on the leash. "Stop." But the dog reared up on its back legs, pawing at the air.

The golden retriever strained at his own leash. The woman in the green dress drew him back firmly. "Leave it," she said. The dog whimpered, then fell back. The woman reached down and gave him a treat. "Good boy."

Leave it. Everything in the dog wanted to lunge, but he listened instead.

Was that what she had to do? Leave it?

She pictured Simone striding onto the stage with her autoharp, herself walking in another direction. Doing nothing.

No, it wasn't nothing. *Leaving it* wasn't a failure to lunge, an action not taken. It was an action. A choice.

It hit her, then, like the blast of a hot Texas wind. So obvious, except it hadn't been, until now. Corinne hadn't looked at the two of them—weighing them, one in each hand, deciding which she liked best and throwing the other one away. Not a contest or a choice, but two different babies at two different times. Just like Beryl and Dana had told her.

And then, two different kinds of music. You played the music you heard, the sound that called to you.

And you played it all the way to the very bottom of the sound. That was something Vera had taught her long ago. The sound below the sound, below the silence.

"Oops, 'scuse me, honey." Two young women wove around her, apologizing.

Susannah realized that she'd been standing in the middle of the sidewalk. "Sorry." She waited till the women passed. Then she turned and headed back to the hotel.

She knew what she had to do. *Leave it.* She wasn't running away, the way she had before. That time, she had been afraid. This time, she wanted to be kind.

She needed to let Simone know not to expect her for the second show. Simone would worry about why Alexandra hadn't shown up as she promised, maybe imagine some calamity or try to track her down at the fictitious *Courier.* Susannah picked up the phone and called the Red Rooster. "I need to talk to Red," she said. "It's important."

"Hang on," someone replied. After a few seconds, she heard a male voice. "Yo?"

"It's Alexandra, the reporter you talked to earlier, about the girl band?"

"Right. They got another show coming up."

"I know. That's why I'm calling. I said I'd be there but something's come up and I have to get back to Dallas right away. I wanted to let them know. Can you get a message to the girl I talked to, the lead singer, Simone? Tell her I'm sorry?"

"Sure thing. Hang on a sec." Susannah heard him put down the phone and exchange a few words with someone, their voices obscured by the clink of bottles. Then he came back to the line. "You still gonna do a story on us?"

"I'll have to see. Priorities change."

"Well, you come back any time now. We got a table waiting right here for you."

"Thanks, Red. I just might take you up on that."

She replaced the phone in its cradle and sank onto the bed. Relief washed over her. She had done the right thing, she was sure of it. If she went back to the Red Rooster, she'd cause a lot of trouble, and in a public place. Distract from Simone's show, confuse and maybe even hurt her.

Why push herself into people's lives? She had a life.

She would have liked a chance to see Wayne, though, and prove she was his daughter. Maybe there would have been a way, if they had sat together listening to Simone sing. Surely he had known who she was all along. But if he hadn't wanted to admit it then, when he was looking right at her, why would he admit it now?

He had already given her his answer.

It was time to go home. Aaron would pick her up at the airport.

Susannah always meant to return to Texas to see Beryl and Jimmy Ray and set things right, but somehow she never did. With two sections of her Baroque Masters class to teach, along with private lessons and a growing roster of pre-shows and festivals, life was busy. She thought she would squeeze in a trip to Lynette during one of the school breaks. By the time the break arrived, though, she was deep in preparation for a regional competition and couldn't get away. By the time the second break arrived, the urgency was starting to fade. Besides, Aaron had booked a surprise weekend getaway. They rented a convertible and drove to the Finger Lakes wineries.

When she got home, there was a message from Hollis on her answering machine saying that Beryl had died, some sort of infection that got into her blood, nothing to do with all that smoking. They'd had the funeral right away. "I hope you get this message and can come on down," Hollis said, but it was already too late.

She didn't keep up with Hollis after that. They didn't have an argument; they just lost touch. Beryl and Corinne had been the glue. Without them, Susannah didn't know what to say to Hollis or whether Hollis would be glad to hear from her. It seemed easier not to call.

She thought about Jimmy Ray sometimes, but she didn't know where he went or what happened to him after Beryl died.

He had always liked country music. Maybe he'd gone with his sister Lorraine to hear *The All-Girl Lone Star Mother Plucking Band* do one of their shows. Susannah could picture him at a little table at the Red Rooster, leaning forward, tapping his toe, and then jumping to his feet and clapping so hard his hands turned as red as the rooster on the wall.

Part Five

The Musician

Music expresses that which cannot be said,
and on which it is impossible to be silent.
Victor Hugo

Chapter Eighteen

now

When Aaron returned from St. Pierre, Susannah greeted him at the door, accepted his hug, and commiserated about the traffic on the Van Wyck. She tried to put their last terrible conversation out of her mind, when he dismissed what she'd discovered about radiation as if it was something only an idiot would fall for. He couldn't have meant to sound so condescending; that was the problem with cell phones. And there was so much she needed to tell him—the shock of Vera's oxygen tank, the astonishing news about Perez-Smith—though she could see that he was exhausted. They'd talk in the morning.

But the morning didn't go the way she had expected. James was heaping scrambled eggs and bacon onto his plate when Aaron stormed down the stairs, icy water dripping from his arms and legs, a towel wrapped around his waist. "I thought those furnace guys checked the system. Didn't they fix whatever was making the hot water sputter like that? Because now there *isn't* any."

Susannah was glad he couldn't see her face. She'd never called the heating company. She had forgotten, just like she'd forgotten to pick up James from basketball practice.

"I'll call them again," she said, her eyes fixed on the English muffin she was prying from the toaster. "The guy they sent was new, probably missed something. I'll make sure they send one of the pros."

She didn't dare look at Aaron. He would see that she was lying or demand to know what the tech had said and done. Luckily, he was too cold and wet to linger. "They should have done it right the first time," he muttered, and charged back upstairs.

Susannah kept her eyes averted. "Here," she told James, dropping the toast onto his plate. "Like Grandpa says, looks good enough to eat." She filled her coffee cup and carried it to the table, listening for the sounds that signaled Aaron's return: footsteps descending the stairs, the slap of the newspaper along his side.

After a few minutes she heard the steps and slap of the paper, but when Aaron entered the kitchen, he gave her a curt nod instead of the smile she'd been hoping for. He eased into his chair and turned his attention to James. "So. How was the game?"

"Man, you should've seen it." James tugged his chair closer to Aaron's and launched into a detailed description of Saturday's game.

Susannah sipped her coffee, only pretending to listen. It was clear from the way Aaron angled his back—cutting her out of the conversation, out of his vision—that he was annoyed with her. Something really did happen during that phone call while he was in St. Pierre. It wasn't just poor cell service.

James described the game's final minutes and sat back with a satisfied grin. "Not bad, huh?" Then he plucked another strip of bacon from the platter. "So, Mom," he said, "did that driver safety place have any openings for next weekend? You know, the five-hour thing I have to take?" He broke the bacon in half and dropped both halves into his mouth.

Susannah's hand froze on the coffee cup. Another forgotten chore. Well, instead of being one more thing she had neglected, it could be the very thing that showed how much she valued Aaron's advice. "Actually," she said, "I wanted to wait and ask Dad." She tried to catch Aaron's eye. "What do you think? Is it okay for him to do it online, or is it important to do it in person?"

Aaron looked up from his plate. The coolness in his eyes was unmistakable. *Don't ask me for my opinion, since you obviously don't respect what I have to say.*

James looked from one parent to the other. "Hey, guys. Lighten up. I don't really care."

She sent Aaron a silent plea. *Not in front of James.*

Aaron turned to James again, peering at him over the top of his glasses. "They don't let you take the road test online, do they? Virtual driving, like a video game?"

James rolled his eyes. "Funny, Dad."

They were bantering; that was what they did, the three of them. Susannah dared to relax. "That'll be next, no doubt."

"We'll look into the options." Aaron folded the newspaper into quarters and laid it next to his plate. "Anyone else want to look at this, before I chuck it?"

James's face lit up with another grin. "Hard copies are so retro, Dad."

"True," Aaron said, opening his napkin, "but the online version doesn't make that special crinkling noise."

"How about saving trees?" James shot back. "Those tall green things?"

Susannah laughed. "Don't be sassy." Relief surged through her body. Everything was going to be all right.

"Girls like sassy," James said. "Right, Dad?"

"Better ask your mother."

"To a point," she quipped. "We also like supportive."

The remark slipped out, and she knew instantly that it was a mistake. She had meant to be clever, but she'd ruined the fragile truce.

"Supportive doesn't mean telling a person what they want to hear." Aaron's voice was flat, formal. The mirth was gone.

James threw up his hands. "Hey. Sorry I asked. Guess I just have the magic touch today." He stood, craning his neck. "Oscar?" The cat mewed from the other room. "Any pets wanting attention better get their butts over here."

"Not at the table," Susannah said.

James rolled his eyes again and went in search of the cat. She turned to Aaron. "Look," she began. "Just because I happen to think that radiation—"

"That's the problem," he interrupted. "You aren't thinking. You're reacting." He wiped his mouth with the napkin and tossed it onto the table. "I'm trying to help you, not make your situation worse. This *is* my field, after all. I looked into it, trust me."

"I do trust you." Susannah said, struggling for the fine edge between making him feel appreciated and standing up for what she needed to do. "But I can't sit around hoping the disease will go away. Not if there's something I can actually do."

"That's what I meant by reactive." He seemed to catch himself. "I just meant, slow down. Don't be in such a hurry to solve a problem that might not need to be solved."

No, she thought. Slowing down—waiting—was exactly what she could *not* do. Why was that so hard for him to understand?

She straightened her shoulders. "It's like what you said about the hot water heater. Fix it now. Be proactive. Don't wait until it's an emergency." A risky analogy, because she hadn't actually taken care of the water heater. But he had asked her to, and she would, and it really was the same logic.

"The human body isn't a piece of equipment," Aaron said. "That's my point."

Susannah felt the tendrils of despair start to dig in, take root. All this bickering was making things worse, not better. She took a deep breath, trying again. "I know you looked into all this. And I appreciate it, I really do."

Aaron dipped his chin. A gesture that might signify: *thank you.* Or maybe: *then act like you do.* She knew he assumed that he'd convinced her.

He hadn't, though. On the last day he was in St. Pierre, she had found a radiology clinic. She had an appointment for a consultation on Wednesday, and she planned to keep it.

When Aaron left for work, Susannah pulled out the yellow pad with the list of things she needed to do. Getting the hot water fixed was already on the list, as was finding a publicist. She added: defensive driving class. Then, half in jest: make Aaron happy.

She'd take care of the furnace business first, show Aaron that she was paying attention. But when she called, the dispatcher told her they were completely booked for the next two weeks. "It's an emergency," she pleaded.

"Is there a leak, a crack? Is your basement full of water?"

No, but there's a crack in my marriage.

"It's totally my fault. I put it off, and now the damn thing won't kick in. I'll pay whatever overtime rate you charge me if you can please, please, please get someone out here."

The dispatcher sighed. "Okay, lady, I'll get someone there tomorrow. It'll cost you twice the regular, though."

Determined, now, to attend to all her neglected tasks, Susannah made an appointment for James at the Right-Way Driving School and emailed three publicists who specialized in the performing arts. Then her thoughts turned to her father.

Visiting him wasn't something she could do once and check

off her list. She'd been vague about the timing of her next visit, and he'd accepted the excuse of the concert. But that wasn't good enough. Not anymore, not without her mother to make sure his clothes were fresh and he was getting himself to the dining room for meals instead of defrosting frozen meat pies and ravioli in the apartment—which, Susannah was certain, was exactly what he was doing.

She remembered how happy he had been to play the Anna Magdalena minuet. She remembered, too, how she had asked, "Why did you and Mom decide to adopt?" He hadn't quite answered. They'd gotten side-tracked by memories of Dana.

Determined, now, to do the right thing, she called her father and told him she would come by that afternoon. She arrived early, but Tyler was already waiting in the lobby of The Oaks. Framed in the big front window, he looked oddly shrunken, brown sweater bunched at the waist, neck thrust forward as he squinted into the glass. Susannah waved and hurried up the walkway. His face brightened, and he waved back.

"Hey, Dad." She waited for the pneumatic door to open and gave him a hug as she entered the building.

"My daughter," he told the young woman at the front desk, who smiled politely and returned to her computer. Susannah tucked her arm into her father's as they made their way to his apartment.

"Thanks for coming, honey. I'm glad for the company." He unlocked the door and ushered her inside. "Some men do fine without their wives but a lot of us don't. We're hopeless idiots, no idea how to relate to people." He bent to pick up the flyer that had been slipped under the door, a schedule of the day's activities, grunting as he straightened. "You'd think they'd figure out that most of us old farts have trouble bending."

Susannah peered over his shoulder at the list. "You ever try any of these?"

"Not me." He dropped the flyer onto the table. "Dana was the social one."

"Hey now, they've got all sorts of stuff. Chess, ceramics. We'll find an activity you can't resist."

He kissed her cheek. "You're a good girl, Suzie." He gestured at the couch, and she sat down. "Some iced tea? It's a mix, I'm afraid."

"That's fine."

He ambled into the kitchenette, and Susannah surveyed the living room. A copper bowl filled with shells, a stack of art books on the coffee table. That Kandinsky print her mother had liked, centered above the couch. The whole place looked like Dana. There was little of Tyler, just a shelf of history books and a paperweight shaped like the Lincoln Memorial.

She couldn't help worrying. He seemed frailer each time she saw him, his eyes cloudier, his shoulders more bent.

"Here you go, Suzie." He extended a glass. A slice of lemon was perched precariously on the rim.

"Thanks, Dad." Susannah took a sip of the too-sweet beverage, then set the glass on the coffee table, searching for a topic that would lift her father's spirits.

James, of course. Her father loved hearing about James.

She turned to him with a bright smile. "Can you believe that James is getting his actual learner's permit? Next thing you know, he'll be driving *me* around."

Tyler sank into the upholstered armchair. "I didn't know you needed a special permit to step up to a two-wheeler. I figured Aaron would just use his judgment about when to get rid of the training wheels."

Training wheels? It sounded like he was talking about a bicycle. James had gotten his first two-wheeler more than ten years ago. "Learner's permit," she said. "For a car."

Tyler blinked. "Yes, of course."

"He did have a two-wheeler, when he was young. With red and blue streamers, coming off the handlebars."

Her father's face shifted, the features rearranging themselves into an expression of delight. "He called it Big Boy."

"He did. I'd forgotten that."

Tyler chuckled, himself again, droll and alert. Susannah was relieved, yet the strange incident during her last visit flashed across her mind, when her father's face had turned vacant and slack.

She adjusted the glass of iced tea. There was a wet ring on the glass coffee table; he'd forgotten to give her a coaster, an oversight her mother never would have permitted. Her gaze shifted from the wet circle to the copper bowl and a pile of dusty oversized art books. Mark Rothko, Frida Kahlo, Paul Klee. Her mother's taste. Dana was everywhere and nowhere, the thread that connected her father to his past, to his life.

"Tell me a memory you have of Mom," she said, her voice soft. "A story I might not know."

"About Mom? What makes you ask?"

Because, Susannah thought. Because I want to know all the things that no one ever told me. I want you to let me into your memories before you can't find them yourself.

A dreadful thing to contemplate, but those moments troubled her, when he seemed to disappear. The comment about James's bike wasn't the first—or the second—time it had happened.

"Oh, I don't know. It just struck me that you must have so many stories, things I never knew, before I was born."

Tyler sat back, a pleased grin warming his features. "My gosh. I have a thousand stories."

"Tell me one."

He removed his glasses, studied them for spots, and set them back on his face, adjusting the wires behind his ears. "Well, now that you mention it, I'm remembering the time I was going to a conference in Chicago, back when I was a lowly instructor, and I mentioned a book I wanted to read on the plane but couldn't find a copy. I think it was out of print. Anyway, your mother found a copy somewhere, I never did know where she got it, and she took a cab all the way to the airport. Believe me, that was quite an extravagance. She talked the airline people into letting her go to the gate without a ticket—it was before they had all that security business, before 9/11. But they'd already finished boarding and were going to close the door to the jetway.

"Well, your mother wasn't one to be thwarted, especially after that taxi fare, so she bullied her way past the security people, talked them into letting her go down the ramp—like they do for people who push those wheelchairs, that was her argument—as long as she didn't step onto the actual plane. And there she was, running down the jetway, yelling my name and waving the book in the air. I turned around, she handed me the book, and they made her go back before I could say a word of thanks." He gave Susannah a smug look. "How many people would do a thing like that? Not many. But that was Dana."

Susannah smiled. "I can just see her."

"She was something." Tyler chuckled. "The book turned out to be terrible, but of course I never told her."

"Heavens no. No one wants their heroics to be for naught."

His expression grew sober. "She *was* heroic, you know. Not all heroes pull people out of burning buildings." He dropped his eyes, brushing the lint from his trousers. "Kept it private, but it was heroic all the same."

There was an odd look on her father's face—slyness and shame and defiance, all there at once in the angle of his chin, the crease between his brows. "No one knew what your mother did for me."

"Dad. What are you talking about?"

He touched the bowl of shells on the coffee table, then traced the rim with a quavering fingertip. Susannah remembered how they'd collected the shells, those summers on Cape Cod. There were three pairs of angel wings, a pink-and-white conch, and a round ivory shell called a baby's ear. She had always loved that name, imagining that the shell was the relic of an undersea merbaby, separated from its mermaid mother and washed up on the shore.

"Dad," she repeated. "What is it that Mom did for you?"

Tyler kept his eyes on the bowl of shells. Then he gave a tired sigh. "You might as well know the whole story. Before I'm gone too."

Susannah began to protest that he wasn't going anywhere, but her father shook his head. "Let me tell it." He placed his hands on his thighs and Susannah saw how skinny his legs were. His trousers drooped in loose brown folds on either side of his mottled wrists. The sun glinted on the whorls and ridges of the seashells.

Tyler's voice was quiet. Susannah had to lean forward to hear. "She let everyone think she was the one who was infertile," he said, "but that wasn't true. It was me."

Susannah's face turned as white as the shells. She had always assumed that her mother couldn't have children. Secretly—and not so secretly—she had viewed it as a defect, a missing capacity that belonged to women who were normal and whole. It had made her pity and hate her mother, in equal measure.

"Dad, are you sure?"

"We had all the tests. She was fine. I was the one who wasn't."

Susannah's thoughts were flying everywhere, racing across her childhood. She could remember Dana referring to herself as barren. True, she hadn't produced any offspring, so technically she was barren. But she didn't have to be.

There were so many questions she wanted to ask. She tried to organize the chaos of her thoughts. "Why didn't you just do—whatever it is, artificial insemination, donor sperm?"

"Because I was an arrogant S.O.B., that's why. Didn't want someone else's damn sperm in my wife, proving I was inadequate." Tyler looked almost angry. "I'm not proud of who I was, all that selfish macho bullshit. I should have given your mother a chance to know what it was to give birth, like she always wanted. But I couldn't do it."

"What happened?" Susannah knew what he was going to say but she had to hear it. The story she had wanted so much to know.

"She offered to adopt. Said it was nobody's business why we decided to go that route. But we both knew what people would assume. Truth be told, she'd say things to imply that she was the problem because she knew that's what I wanted. And I let her. I never corrected her." Susannah could see his chin trembling. "So now you know a story about your mother that we never told you."

"Oh, Dad."

His voice caught. "That was Dana for you. I wanted some foolish book, she made sure I got it. I wanted some fake potency crap, she made sure I got that too."

Susannah rose and put an arm around his shoulders. "It doesn't matter to me why you decided to adopt." She laid her cheek next to his. "I'm just glad you did."

She could feel the tears sliding down his cheek. "It sounds ridiculous now," he said, "but back then it seemed so important."

"It doesn't matter."

"It does. She could have had the experience she wanted. I wouldn't let her."

Susannah's arm was still around her father, her face pressed to his, as she fought not to cry too. She'd been talking about how grateful she was that they decided to adopt, but he was talking about how much he regretted not taking a different path.

What he was saying, although she was sure he didn't realize it, was that if he had done the right thing, she wouldn't have been his daughter. There would have been some other child, made with her mother's egg in her mother's body. Susannah herself would have been somewhere else, *someone* else, adopted by another family. Not the daughter he loved, the person sitting next to him. She knew he didn't mean it that way, yet the old wound pushed its way through her skin. The old question: Who was I meant to be?

"She loved you, Dad. She wanted you to be happy." Susannah turned so she could look into his eyes. "Anyway, it all worked out in the end. Here I am, right?"

She could hear the plea: a nearly-middle-aged woman who sounded like a little girl.

"Yes, here you are, dear child."

Something painful and complicated seized her in the chest. Around her, the world grew quiet. She felt the stillness, like a living presence.

Herself. Here, in that precise instant, on the edge of her father's chair. Did it matter how she had gotten there?

Tyler kissed her cheek. "You wait here, Suzie. There's something I want to give you." He stood, adjusted his sweater, and crossed the room. Susannah could hear him in the bedroom, opening a drawer.

He returned to the living room carrying a small box. Carefully, he removed the lid. Resting on the dark satin was a pair of diamond earrings.

Susannah raised her eyes. "Mom's?"

"I bought them for our last anniversary but she never really wore them. Everything hurt her too much by then." He gazed at the stones. "I wanted her to have something that would last forever. Guess it was my way of trying to keep her from dying."

"They're beautiful, Dad. I'm sure she loved them."

"Take them," he said. "She'd want you to have them." He gave Susannah a wistful smile. "Look pretty, and think of her."

"I will. I'll wear them at the concert."

His eyes clouded. "Are you going to a concert, honey?"

"Dad," she whispered. "*My* concert."

She could tell by the blank look on his face that he had no idea what she was talking about. "Very nice," he said. "I hope you and your friends have a good time."

It took all Susannah had to keep from crying. Their wonderful closeness, snatched away. "I will. I'll have a good time." She took the box from his hand. The diamonds were bright as tears. "I wish you could be there, Dad."

He patted her shoulder. "I do too, honey. But I don't drive much anymore." Then, as swiftly as it had come, the vagueness vanished. "You get James to take some pictures on that phone thing of his," he told her. "Never made sense to me, though. A phone that takes pictures."

Susannah didn't know whether to laugh or cry. "It isn't really a phone. They call it a device."

"Device." He gave her a devilish grin. "I prefer De Virtue."

"Oh, you." Having him *himself* again was almost as strange as having him absent. "You and your puns." Shaking her head, she reached across the coffee table and rearranged the shells in the copper bowl. The clam shell next to the chambered nautilus, the baby's ear on top. "C'mon, maestro. Let's play our duet before I have to leave."

As soon as she'd said it, Susannah regretted her remark. What if he had no idea what she was talking about?

To her relief, Tyler beamed. "I've been practicing, like I promised, but I might need another lesson. Can't quite remember the second part."

"No worries, Dad. We'll work on it together."

They went to the lounge, and she showed him the left hand of the minuet. She didn't bring up the concert again.

When she got home, she went to put Dana's earrings in her jewelry box. There, next to her silver watch, was the necklace she never quite let herself see. She touched the tiny sapphire. The stone was the color of her eyes, the color of the woman's eyes who had worn it first. Her birthstone. *Bought it with the money she made at the Frosty Freeze.*

Susannah picked up the necklace. A longing swept over her, a longing she had buried decades ago.

She remembered watching in the big square mirror as Dana braided her hair. "You're so pretty, Mommy."

"As are you, my darling," Dana would say.

Susannah, studying her face, would ask, "But who do I *look* like?"

And Dana would always reply, "You look exactly like you. And that's the perfect way for you to look." It was the sort of thing Dana always said, an answer that had nothing to do with her question.

The real question was still there. Where she belonged, what it meant to have a family.

She put the necklace back in the jewelry box and shut the lid.

Chapter Nineteen

now

The radiologist was surprisingly young. He looked cheerful and innocent—although, Susannah decided, it was probably just the roundness of his eyes and cheeks, reminding her of the emoji for *happy*.

Paul Angelini, M.D. A tiny angel.

"Indeed," Angelini said, after examining her hand and recording the measurements on a chart labeled *Lewis, Susannah*. "You appear to be an appropriate candidate for radiotherapy. But I have to be honest. You need to decide soon. Right now, all you have are two nodes and some minor expansion into the upper palm. But once you develop an actual cord, radiation would likely be ineffective."

"I understand. That's why I'm here."

He skimmed through the chart. "I don't see anything from Dr. Mathieson about family history. Any relatives with Dupuytren's?"

Not that again. "I don't know," she said stiffly. "I was adopted."

"Oh. Sorry."

Sorry for what? she wanted to ask. Sorry I was given away?

Stop it, she told herself. It was just the way people talked.

Angelini picked up a pen. "In any case, please fill me in. What were your initial symptoms? Most people aren't diagnosed so early."

"I'm a pianist. I notice changes that other people might not."

"Can you be more specific?"

Susannah looked at her hand. The difference was hard to explain to someone who wasn't a musician. To voice the melody line, you had to separate the top note and make it sing. For that, the fifth finger had to have a special quality, sensitive and precise.

The pun struck her. Node, note. Like cord, chord. A mean joke.

"My little finger feels weird," she told him. "Absent. Tight."

Angelini made a note on the chart. "People have different sensations. What you describe sounds like what some of them say after the treatment, not before. A bit of tightening, dryness, maybe some stiffness. But it generally goes away."

"You mean the radiation will make my hand even tighter? Worse than it is now?"

"No, no, I didn't mean to imply that. My apology. The after-effects—if there are any, which isn't always the case—are very mild. And far milder than the after-effects of the other treatments. If you wait, those will be your only options."

Susannah remembered what Aaron had said. A lot of people never progressed beyond Stage One. But a lot of them did.

"The main thing is the timing," Angelini repeated. "The sooner you decide, the better."

"Yes, I'm aware of that."

Susannah didn't know why she was hedging her answer since she already knew she would do it. And yet there was an unsettled feeling that was keeping her suspended, like a chord waiting for resolution into the next tone.

She looked at Angelini's smooth forehead and the fuzz on his pale cheeks. On the wall behind him there was a life-sized poster of the human body, the organs outlined in red and blue. Everything was labeled, explained.

Angelini was waiting patiently. Susannah bit her lip as the seconds ticked past. Why didn't she just tell him *yes, let's go ahead*?

It was because of Aaron. Because it was strange and wrong to be doing this without Aaron by her side. *On* her side, assuring her that she was doing the right thing and they were in it together.

She looked at the radiologist again. He had a high forehead above the cherubic face, the unmistakable signs of a receding hairline. Maybe he wasn't as young as she'd thought.

The office was oddly quiet, not even the humming of an air conditioner or the clicking of computer keys. She swallowed. What was she waiting for?

"Actually," she said, "I *have* decided. I want to go ahead."

Angelini dipped his head. "Very good. I'll need to get the rest of your records from your primary care doctor, do some blood work. Then we can schedule the treatment."

"All right." For better or worse, she had made her decision.

After leaving Angelini's office, Susannah stopped at the cleaners for Aaron's shirts and then, on impulse, at the bank. She wanted to talk to the branch manager about an idea she had—taking out a loan to help launch her career. A business loan, just her, even though the account was in both their names. There was no reason for Aaron to be involved. And even if he did find out, he would have to agree that it was better than borrowing from James's college fund, which was her only other choice. The manager wasn't in, so she made an appointment for the next day.

By the time she pulled into the driveway, the light was fading. A semicircle of blood-red sun hovered at the edge of the horizon, slipping out of sight as she turned off the engine. Streaks of cloud, still glittering, were stretched across the darkening sky. Susannah hoisted the plastic-covered shirts across her shoulder and closed the passenger door with her hip. Then she pushed past the overgrown zebra grass and coneflower stalks as she climbed the steps to the deck.

The gaudy blossoms, bent from their own weight, made her scowl. She really needed to cut them back—though why couldn't Aaron do it? He was busy, but so was she. Grimacing, she glanced again at the familiar view—the sheen of the Hudson, the tiered cliffs—but the vista didn't bring its usual pleasure.

She flung open the kitchen door, and dropped the shirts onto a chair. "Shoo," she told Oscar. The cat followed her as she went to the refrigerator. "Not your dinner, pal. People dinner." She bent to take the Chicken Marbella from the shelf where it had been marinating.

Still frowning, she pulled a basting brush from the drawer and peeled back the plastic wrap that was covering the chicken. Then she heard Aaron's step and the thump of his briefcase as he dropped it on the floor. "Smells good."

"That's the garlic. And the lemon."

"Am I right that it's the two of us tonight?"

"You are. James is out with Andrew and Zev." She dipped the brush in the sauce. "They're going to see an action movie. Something-man. I think it's an animal, or maybe an element."

"Ah yes. Potassium man."

"Iodine man."

"Osmium man, knocks you out with his odor." Aaron crossed the room and put a hand on her waist. "Unlike the smell of your delicious dinner." He peered over her shoulder as she spooned the liquid onto the chicken. "Dysprosium man, you'll never catch him." He picked an olive from the pan and popped it in his mouth.

"Show off."

"Just trying to impress you." He stroked her back, a single light stroke from nape to waist, then stepped away to open the refrigerator. He took a bottle of Chardonnay from the shelf and lifted it in a question.

"Please."

He reached into the cupboard and set two wine glasses on the counter. Susannah waited while he poured, aware of his signals, the opening measures of a familiar duet, and of her growing unease. The evening might not unfold the way he was expecting. Not after she told him her decision.

She rested the basting brush on the edge of the pan and took the glass from his outstretched hand. His smile, pleased and confident, made her shiver. Now, she told herself. Tell him and be done with it.

She took a careful breath. "I've made up my mind. I'm having the radiation."

Whether you approve or not. She didn't say that. She didn't have to.

Aaron's smile faded. "It's not logical. I explained that to you."

"I appreciate your point of view, but I've made my decision."

"It's really not a good idea."

"It's the only idea that works."

"Susannah—" His voice hardened.

"Don't. Please."

For nearly two decades she had listened to his advice. That was the agreement: she made a beautiful home, chose the colors, the flavors, the sounds; Aaron studied, analyzed, found solutions. It wasn't fair to break the agreement without his consent. She wasn't so wrapped up in herself that she couldn't see that.

She could tell that Aaron, like her, was struggling not to react. Impatience and frustration zigzagged across his features as his cooler side fought for restraint. Oh, she knew him so well.

Yes, she loved him. And no, she wasn't going to take back her decision.

She placed her wine glass on the counter. "I'm aware that you disagree about radiation. But it's my decision. My hand. My music."

"That's not a reason to be irrational."

Irrational, as if that was the worst insult he could think of.

"I know you've read all the studies," she said. "But it's my choice, not yours."

Aaron set his glass next to hers. "If you know I've read all the studies, then you ought to respect that I know what I'm talking about."

"The studies are about percentages. The likelihood of A instead of B, if your biological father happened to—oh, who cares?"

She could hear her father's voice, laced with regret. Someone else's damn sperm. Macho potency crap. Nothing to do with the odds of her hand turning into a claw.

Her own voice grew sharp. "I don't know if my biological father had a crooked finger because I don't know shit about him." Her heart jumped, thrusting upward. *Agitato. Accelerando.* About to push through her ribs.

"Susannah, please. That's not the only factor."

"Whatever," she snapped. "Apparently, it's all about heredity, and I don't know my heredity, so I might as well get myself the best and earliest and easiest treatment. You're not going to scare me off with vague little threats of post-radiation boogeymen who might never show up anyway."

Aaron didn't really know. Nobody knew.

She pushed past him and yanked open a drawer, pulling out a roll of aluminum foil. She tore off a section of foil and laid it over the pan, tucking in the sides with short angry pinches.

Her chance. Didn't he see that? She'd been muted for so long, like a melody line hidden inside a progression of chords. To bring out that inner voice, you had to focus your attention—and sustain it, no matter what, even within competing sounds.

"There's always a danger with radiation," Aaron said. "It's naive to—"

"So now I'm naive? Irrational and naive. Wow, a double header." She grabbed the heavy glass pan but it slid from her hands, crashing to the floor. The glass shattered. Chicken, olives, and prunes spilled across the tiles.

Susannah watched the mess as it spread across the kitchen floor. Her fingers, failing her. The fingers she'd always counted on. She couldn't even hold onto a stupid Pyrex dish.

"Fuck." She kicked at the pile of meat and glass, sending the splattered remains of the dish into the crevice between the cabinets. A chicken thigh slithered under the stove. A prune, like a clot of blood, stuck to her shoe. She let out a strangled cry. "Fuck. Just *fuck*." She kicked at it again.

"Susannah." Aaron put his hand on her arm. "Stop, you're making it worse."

She shook off his touch. "Really? You want to see worse?" With another kick, vicious and helpless at the same time, she sent a wedge of glass flying across the room.

He grabbed her shoulders. "It was an accident. It could have happened to anyone."

"Oh? Well, *anyone* doesn't need perfect control of her fingers. I do." *And I don't have it. Not anymore.*

"No one has perfect control."

She jerked away. She couldn't bear it, not one more second. "You don't understand. You don't understand a single thing."

"I understand that you're frustrated—"

It was that patronizing tone she hated, as if she were James, needing a parent to correct and cajole and guide her back to her senses.

Aaron didn't seem to notice—or care—because he kept talking. "That's part of the problem. You aren't listening to what I've been trying to say."

"And you aren't listening to *me*. You don't. You told me yourself. You tune me out." The forbidden questions tumbled across her brain.

Was he tired of her? Was her music so dull that no one, not even a man who loved her, could be drawn by its sound? And what if the lost glory she'd vowed to reclaim was simply—gone?

Aaron was babbling about longitudinal studies, subthreshold symptoms. What was wrong with him? In a burst of fury, she shoved his chest, ramming him into the counter. She heard the thud of flesh against stone. His face darkened. He grabbed her arm, nails digging into her skin. "Stop it," he hissed. He raised his other hand.

"*You* stop it."

He flinched. Then he dropped his hands.

Susannah began to tremble. Fear and shame knotted together inside. She twisted her head and saw the pool of spilled sauce, the clots of prune and olive.

Aaron was trembling too. Seconds passed, and then he flattened his mouth. "I have to get out of here." He glanced at her arm, and Susannah followed his gaze. Red marks were sprouting where his fingers had dug into her. "I'm sorry," he said. Then he was gone.

She stared at the flapping door, hardly believing what had happened.

She cleaned up the mess in the kitchen, grateful that James was out for the evening and wouldn't have to see or ask what had happened. She didn't know how long Aaron would be gone, but surely he'd return—soon—for dinner and reconciliation. She'd start over, make something to replace the ruined Marbella. They'd start over.

But then it was nine o'clock, and he still wasn't back. She grabbed the glass of wine he had poured for her, still on the counter where she had left it, and drank it quickly. Then she finished Aaron's glass too, placed the empty glasses in the sink, and went out onto the deck. Moonlight had washed the landscape in silver; it was quiet, eerily beautiful. From the corner of the deck she could see all the way to the road. There were no cars. No Aaron, turning into the driveway.

She hugged her elbows. She'd been resolute, then angry, and now she was ready for it to be over. She pulled on her sleeves, trying to get warm. After a minute she went back inside.

The damn cat wouldn't leave her alone. He rubbed across her ankle, meowing plaintively. "Stop," Susannah told him. Then she leaned against the sink, pressing her palms into its cold comfort. Where the hell was Aaron? Should she call his cell?

She twisted her neck so she could see the place on her arm where the red marks were darkening to a yellowish purple. He had looked as surprised as she was to see himself grabbing her flesh; it wasn't the kind of thing he did. Had she really pushed him that far? He'd been pompous but he hadn't deserved her wrath. *I'm sorry*, she thought. If she called, and he answered, that's what she'd say. *I didn't mean it. Come home.* Then, when he was home, she would explain—again— that she appreciated his concern but it was her hand and her decision.

She tore off another length of foil to cover the pasta and left the dish on the counter. Then she filled a glass with tap water and took it with her as she climbed the stairs to their bedroom. She'd read in bed for a while, take her mind off their argument; they would talk when he got back. He would see that he had to respect her judgment, she would apologize for taking her frustration out on him, and every-thing would be all right.

She must have fallen asleep because she jerked awake, knocking the book off her chest. She looked at the clock on the nightstand. 1:23. She knew Aaron wasn't next to her but reached across the mattress anyway.

She didn't know whether to be angry or alarmed. Had something happened to him? If he'd been injured, they would have called the home number. It was right there on his phone. *Home.* No, he wasn't injured. He was furious. Still, after six hours.

Wide awake now, she got out of bed and made her way down the hall to the narrow staircase that led to James's attic bedroom. He had forbidden her to come in without permission but she didn't care. She needed to see him. She pushed open the door and peered inside. Yes, he was there. Loud snores rose from the mound of blankets, along with the faint odor of marijuana. His big teenage self made her happy and annoyed: relief that he was there, mixed with irritation at the marijuana. Oscar opened an eye, then curled into a ball next to James's sleeping form.

Susannah closed the door and retraced her steps, pausing at the entrance to her bedroom. Go back to bed—who was she kidding? She flipped on the hall light and went downstairs. Maybe Aaron had gone to sleep on the couch, not wanting to wake her. He had done that a few times when he came home from a trip on a midnight flight. She'd told him that she didn't mind being woken, but he insisted that he wanted to be considerate.

The living room was empty. No flashing light on the answering machine, nothing on her cell phone. Her heart sank.

She picked her way across the kitchen, checking for stray bits of glass, and opened the liquor cabinet. It was past the time for Chardonnay. She pulled out a bottle of their good Scotch and col-lapsed into a chair. The clock on the stove read 1:47. As she drank, she watched the numbers morph into successive digits. Sometime between 2:19 and 3:04 she stopped watching, because it was 3:04 when she picked up her head again. The house was quiet. Too weary to feel anything, she let her head drop back onto her arms.

At 5:42 Aaron opened the back door and stepped into the kitchen. Susannah was jolted awake by the sound of the door banging shut. "Aaron," she whispered. He looked thin, depleted. "Where were you?"

His eyes were cold. "I came back. That's what matters."

Yes, of course. What was wrong with her? Of all the ways she could have greeted him. She pushed the hair off her face. It felt thick and greasy.

He waited. His penetrating look went right through her.

"I guess I over-reacted." The words caught in her throat. "Attacking you like that."

"Yes, you did."

She had hoped he would protest. *No, it's okay, honey.* Instead, his voice was grave. "You know, when your mother got cancer—a hell of a lot more serious than Dupuytren's, by the way—she didn't take it out on your father."

Of course not, Susannah wanted to say. That wasn't her mother's style. She thought of what Tyler had told her, how Dana had accepted responsibility for a deficiency that wasn't hers, lying to protect her husband's ego.

Her mother's style was to be nobler than everyone else. Susannah didn't know what her own style was, but it wasn't that. "I'm sorry," she said. "I just felt so frustrated."

Aaron slumped against the counter and pressed a hand to his eyes. "I've tried to help you with this Dupuytren business. But I can't, if you won't let me."

Help on your terms, Susannah thought, but saying that would only re-kindle the argument that had made him leave. "I know, and I'm grateful to you. But I don't want to be helped."

"That doesn't make sense. Why would you isolate yourself, like it's none of my business?"

"I'm not isolating myself. I just—" Her words trailed off. There was no good way to end the sentence.

"You make me feel irrelevant and useless. Or worse, like I'm part of the problem." She tried to interrupt, but he cut her off. "You've rejected my efforts to help —as if I don't know what I'm talking about or have some kind of diabolical ulterior motive."

"You know that's not true."

"Oh? Enlighten me, then."

Her eyes darted around the kitchen, looking for a tool, a cue, something that would tell her what to do. She had to fix this terrible thing between them, but she was too exhausted to think. Her head was throbbing from the Scotch and the hours bent over the kitchen table. "I'm sorry," she repeated, "I really am. But you don't seem to realize—"

Again, she halted in mid-sentence. She was sorry for some of the things she had said and for how he was feeling. But she wasn't sorry for her decision.

"Perhaps not," he replied icily, "if you mean that I'm not a pianist. But this isn't about the piano." He thinned his lips and pushed away from the counter. "I can't talk about this right now. I'm starting to feel angry and I don't want to do anything I might regret."

"Like hit me?"

"Jesus fucking Christ. When have I ever hit you?" He grabbed the back of a chair and shoved it, hard, into the kitchen table. Then he reached for his keys, lying in a heap in the center of the table where he'd thrown them.

Susannah jumped to her feet. "Where are you going?"

He gave her a look of disgust. "To take a shower. And maybe get a little sleep. I have a lab section to run at noon." He turned and walked out of the kitchen.

She groped for the back of the chair, trying not to feel sick. Aaron had never acted like this before. Neither had she.

She remembered the feeling she'd had in the radiologist's office— the tiny angel, with his careful measurements and cherubic face— when Aaron's absence felt so enormous and wrong. It was nothing compared to how she felt now.

She staggered to the sink and splashed water on her face, pushing back her snarled hair. Her fingers were thick, clumsy, unable to catch the water that slipped through them. It was like trying to catch sound in her palm.

Chapter Twenty

now

"Something's come up that might be a tad bit disappointing for you," Libby Kaufmann said. She tucked a strand of hair into the knot on top of her head.

"What do you mean?" Susannah asked. She was in Libby's office, summoned for a private conference. On the wall to her left, there was a framed poster of Georgia O'Keeffe's Radiator Building. On the right, a tall window framed a view of real skyscrapers. A humidifier hummed in the corner.

Libby adjusted the amber beads of her necklace and gave a philosophical sigh. "There's no predicting these people, you know. They get their ideas, and they do what they do."

Carlo Perez-Smith had decided that it would be intriguing—Libby's word—to expand his CD beyond the well-known classical composers who had died young. "Apparently a lot of composers died in their thirties," Libby said, "not just the ones everyone knows about. Guess all that brilliance wears you out."

Perez-Smith now wanted the CD to have variety: a hymn from

Henry Purcell, who died in 1695; a selection from the operas and show tunes of George Gershwin, who died in 1937; and a vocal piece from Lili Boulanger, to have a woman.

Chopin and Schubert, both from the late nineteenth century, might not offer enough contrast. "The point is to include different times and places," Libby explained.

Susannah tried to stifle her alarm. Did that mean he didn't want the Schubert sonata? Didn't want her? "What are you saying? Isn't he coming to the concert?"

"Well, that's the thing," Libby replied. "He's not sure. He knows all about your sonata. Like I told you before, he thinks it's a great piece. That's why he has to check out the other pieces, the ones he doesn't really know, to see which ones would go together."

"But the sonata is in, right? He's just seeing what *else*?"

"Please don't badger me, Susannah. It's Carlo's project. I'm only telling you what he said. It turns out there's a tribute to Gershwin the same evening as our concert."

"He wants to go to *that* instead?"

Libby shrugged. "He wouldn't commit one way or another. It's only a heads-up because they're doing Gershwin's posthumous work. Obviously he has to check it out."

No, it was not obvious. Schubert's sonata was obvious. You couldn't possibly have a collection of compositions-written-by-a-dying-genius without it.

Or without her. Not now. Not after everything she'd been through.

This wasn't a time to feign innocence. Susannah had no idea if Libby knew that she had discovered why she'd been chosen as the soloist, and she didn't care.

"But you planned the program around the sonata he specifically wanted to hear!"

Libby gave another shrug. "The money's been raised, which was the point. It doesn't really matter if Carlo's in the audience. No one's taking attendance."

It matters to me.

"Let me talk to him," she said. "Or you can talk to him."

"Really, Susannah." Libby made no attempt to mask her annoyance. "Carlo can do what he wants." Susannah leaned forward, ready to object, but Libby put up a hand. "He can go to whatever show he feels like. Put whatever pieces on his precious CD he wants to. He doesn't owe me—or you—anything. I just figured I'd give you a heads-up. Like I said."

Libby opened a drawer and pulled out her purse. She rummaged through its contents and gave Susannah a shrewd glance. "We could have had a dinner, you know. People like those dinners, but then you have the whole business of who sits with who. So we decided to have a concert."

Susannah got the message. Count your blessings.

Then she thought: why was she so upset? There hadn't been any CD in the picture when she went to the audition—only the shock of her lost magic, and the need to find it again. The vision of James in the concert hall, so proud of the artist he hadn't realized she was. Aaron, glowing with renewed enchantment. What did a CD have to do with it?

Yet a CD had been offered, and it wasn't fair to snatch it away. No one would want to forfeit a possibility like that, even if it seemed miraculous. Especially if it seemed miraculous.

"Yes, of course," she answered. Then, to her surprise, she heard herself add, "It's just that it would be a shame to showcase the sonata, and then miss the chance for Perez-Smith to write about it in his column. The concert, that is. And the Isis Project."

Good Lord. Where had that come from? It was clever and sly and exactly the way to get to Libby.

Libby raised an eyebrow. Emboldened, Susannah continued,

"Didn't you tell a lot of people that he'd be there? It might make you—and the Isis expansion—look bad if he's a no-show. They'll wonder if he was ever planning to come." She tried to match Libby's casual tone. "It's not about the CD because you're right, it'll be whatever he decides. It's about who takes the trouble to show up for the concert. Didn't you tell that Tony-winning set designer—you know, the one whose husband is a museum trustee—that Perez-Smith would be there?"

Libby's face was unreadable. Seconds passed. Then the corner of her mouth twitched. "I might have underestimated you."

"Well?"

"We'll see. But don't hold your breath. It's not as important to me as you might think."

Again, Susannah understood. No promises.

Libby pulled a big square mirror out of her purse, squinted at her reflection, and tucked another tendril of hair into place. "I saw a mock-up of the program notes, by the way, and they're gorgeous, especially the photo. You look stunning next to that white piano, just like I told you. I'll have them send you an advance copy." Libby dropped the mirror into her bag, rose, and gave her jacket a brisk tug. "You said something about wanting to do your own press release? Tell your people they can use the photo from the program if they want. Be sure they credit our photographer, that's all. He'll strangle me if they don't."

"Of course." Susannah didn't have *people*. None of the publicists had called her back. She made a mental note to follow-up when she got home.

"Well, good to see you," Libby said, "but I have to fly. I have a pod-cast thing in Tribeca." She gave Susannah air-kisses on both cheeks as she ushered her out the door.

Susannah didn't care that Libby had dismissed her. The person she needed to talk to was Vera, who knew everything about the music world and would tell her what to do. Who had told her long ago, "Don't you know who you are?"

She stifled her impatience during the elevator's slow descent to the main floor and hurried to a corner of the lobby. Three bars on her phone, thank goodness. She scrolled through her contacts and tapped on Vera's name.

But when she told Vera about the latest development, Vera was annoyed at her, not at Libby or Perez-Smith. "Stop whining. These things happen. Just play your music and forget the rest of it."

"I wasn't whining. I was trying to find a solution." She wanted to remind Vera: *You're the one who started all this, the one who was always after me to try again.*

"A solution to what?" Vera said crossly. "You're the only performer, you've got the stage to yourself. It's not like you're in a competition and have to outshine a bunch of other musicians."

It was a different kind of competition. She was competing with George Gershwin and Henry Purcell.

Susannah remembered the last competition Vera had tried to get her to enter, back when James was in first grade—a Chopin competition that Vera insisted would be the perfect vehicle for her return to the professional stage. She had nearly decided to say *yes* when James, racing down the driveway on the two-wheeler he'd just mastered, crashed the bike and broke his arm in three places. He was still healing when Aaron got the devastating news that his research grant wasn't going to be extended. The idea of entering a competition turned, overnight, into an adolescent dream.

Vera had ranted for weeks. Susannah, already torn, had been deeply resentful. She would feel guilty either way; couldn't Vera understand that? Then a newspaper clipping arrived in the mail about the young woman who had won, a twenty-one-year-old from Cincinnati named Jennifer Park. No note, but Susannah knew the clipping came from Vera. She threw the note away and resumed her summer institutes and master classes and church concerts. She hadn't looked back. Until now.

No, not back. Ahead. To a future that might still be waiting.

Vera was right that the concert would happen, with or without the CD. But even that was in jeopardy because of her damn finger.

Susannah caught her breath—because Vera didn't know about her diagnosis. She'd never told her.

"It's complicated," she said.

"It's always complicated."

"No, there's more to it."

She hunched against the marble wall of the lobby, shielding the phone as if she needed to keep passers-by from overhearing. There were only a few people in the lobby, most with thin white cords dangling from their ears. Susannah lowered her voice anyway, as she explained about Dupuytren's contracture and what happened when the fingers stiffened and curled. "Misha Dichter had it, actually. I think he had a form of Dupuytren's that didn't lend itself to some of the simpler treatments, but then he had the surgery and ended up being able to play perfectly again."

"What form do you have?" Vera asked.

"I don't know. It's in the early stage. They barely even call it Stage One."

"So how do you know you have it?"

Susannah told her about the nodules, the unpredictable tightening that kept her from separating the top voice from the rest of the notes.

"Well, that's no good," Vera said. "The sonata doesn't work if you can't voice the melody."

"I didn't say never. I said sometimes."

She was waiting for Vera to say: *In that case, it should be fine* or *Eh, no one will notice.* Instead, Vera gave a curt sniff. "Sometimes is enough to ruin the whole thing."

Susannah's fingers tightened around the phone. How could Vera say something so hopeless and absolute? She tried to stay calm, rational. Like Aaron. "Well, what do you suggest?"

"I *suggest* that you pick a different piece. One that doesn't depend on separating the top notes. Look at some of the late Beethoven, there's bound to be something you can use. Everyone likes Beethoven."

Susannah's attempt at composure fell away. She sagged against the marble, dizzy, frightened. "I can't do that." It had to be that particular sonata. Without it, Perez-Smith would have no reason to be interested in her.

She tried to tell herself that Perez-Smith didn't matter, but it wasn't true. Maybe it was because of Libby's warning that he might not come, or because she'd allowed the delicious possibility to dig its roots into her soil.

Why not let it matter? There was nothing wrong with being excited about a recording. Any musician would feel the same way.

Pick Vera's brains. Vera had been teaching for decades. She must know how to compensate for a disobedient finger.

The revolving door swung open, and the lobby filled with people. Shards of light spilled across the marble floor.

"Everything's been printed," she told Vera. "It's too late to change it."

Susannah knew, and she was sure Vera did too, that it wasn't unusual for a performer to make last-minute changes in the program. But if she told Libby she wanted to do that, it would be like shooing Carlo Perez-Smith away. "I need to play the sonata beautifully. Period. Maybe you know some—I don't know, some special technique?"

"For that contracture business? I've never even heard of those things you have—what did you call them?"

"Nodules."

"Nodules," Vera repeated. Then she sighed, "I'm no doctor, but I don't suppose you can go wrong with those Czerny exercises. They're good for loosening your fingers."

Susannah allowed herself a glimmer of hope. "You think I'll be okay, then?"

"How would I know?" Vera's tone was sharp again. She coughed, a harsh rasping sound.

"Vera!"

"It's fine. A lot of nothing." Another rattle, and the coughing stopped. "Some performers like to soak their hands in warm water," Vera added. "Personally, I've never found it made a whit of difference. It's your mental state, in my opinion."

Not if you have a disease, Susannah thought. But she didn't want to argue. Besides, Dupuytren's progressed slowly. That was what everyone told her.

Vera coughed again, and Susannah frowned. "Forget about me," she said. "What about you? I don't like the sound of that cough."

"Eh. My mouth was right up by the phone, that's what you heard."

"You've been to the doctor?"

"That's who gave me the damn tank. I have to haul the thing around in a little shopping cart. I look like a bag lady."

Susannah couldn't help laughing. "I can just see it."

They talked for a few more minutes. James's driving lessons, a French film she had seen, Vera's grandchildren. They didn't talk about Perez-Smith.

James dangled the string, twitching it right and left, as the cat followed with a tick-tock of its head. An orange paw shot out and caught the string as it arced past. "You are *such* a good boy," James crooned. "Such a mighty hunter."

Susannah was glad to see James so playful. He'd gotten moody and aloof, barricaded behind his bedroom door or out with friends.

She hadn't smelled marijuana again, although she was pretty certain she'd smelled beer. She had thought of confronting him, but decided it wasn't a battle she could win and thus not a battle worth fighting. Not right now, anyway. Later, she told herself. After the concert, like everything else.

"Ha!" James shouted as Oscar snagged the wiggling string. Watching James play with the cat, Susannah yearned to scoop him up and hold him close. Not the enormous James with his sweatshirts and ear buds, but a younger, vanished James. The one she and Aaron had swung between their joined hands. The one who had spread shaving cream on his cheeks because he thought it made hair grow on your face, a wondrous trick of his father's that he longed to master.

"Aren't you going to be late?" she said. "The bus comes in five minutes."

James rubbed Oscar's head before hoisting his backpack. "Nope, I'm getting a ride."

It still seemed inconceivable that James had friends who were old enough to drive. Everything was happening so fast—cars, music that made no sense to her, hours tapping away at his iPhone. Susannah marveled at how his thumbs flew across the screen.

It struck her, suddenly—astounding that it hadn't occurred to her before—that the Dupuytren's gene might be waiting in James too. She'd never asked how the hereditary pattern actually worked. Whenever one of the doctors mentioned heredity, she had changed the subject because she didn't know if anyone in the generation before her had the condition. She hadn't thought about the generation after.

The longing rose in her again—to wrap her arms around her son, shield him from whatever pain she might have unknowingly bequeathed. The whole point of limiting her career had been to make sure James had a perfect life, always knowing where he belonged, never doubting who he was.

She hadn't wanted any more children, once she had James. Just this one miraculous boy, flesh of her flesh. It was too cruel to think that the biological connection that had fulfilled her might hold a hidden danger for her child.

"What time are you getting home?" she asked.

He grabbed a banana from the bowl on the counter. "After practice. Whenever. Unless we hang out afterward."

"Let me know, okay? So I won't worry."

"You got it." He tossed her a grin and sauntered down the driveway, backpack slung over his shoulder. A white Honda pulled up to the curb—Patrick's car, the senior on the basketball team who had befriended James, much to James's delight and Susannah's unease—and James got in. She watched until they were out of sight, then crossed the kitchen to the alcove that served as a makeshift office.

Pensive, she opened her laptop. *Dupuytren's contracture treatment* was still at the top of her browser. She erased *treatment*. Next to the word *contracture*, she typed *heredity*. A page of links appeared, but they were all too scholarly. Genetic Correlates of Dupuytren's Disease. Inheritance Patterns by Gender and Region, the sort of thing Aaron would read. Not what she was looking for.

And what was she looking for?

She pictured James, spiking a basketball into a hoop. He might or might not have the Dupuytren's gene waiting in his future. Who else had it? Was there a way to find out, after all these years?

Her family history, Leo Mathieson had called it. The soil she'd come from, the Texas clay. The question had been building in her, ever since Leo told her she had a hereditary disease.

She had looked for them once, and found them, but hadn't found the wholeness she'd hoped the journey would bring. Did she dare to try again?

Her fingers hovered over the keys—*the other keyboard*, as James called it, not the keyboard her hands knew best. It seemed like folly, and yet—

A rapping on the back door interrupted her thoughts. "What now?" she muttered. She pushed away from the desk and went to see who it was. A man in a red shirt with *Kenny* stitched across the pocket was waiting outside the kitchen door.

"Mrs. Lewis? I'm here to install your new hot water heater?"

"Oh yes, of course. Today's the day. I nearly forgot."

Thank goodness they'd come. Aaron would be happy, and she wouldn't have to dread another no-hot-water episode. She ushered the man inside. "You'll cart the old one away?"

"Yes, ma'am. It's included. Just show me where to find it."

She led Kenny to the boiler room in the basement. "Mind your head, the ceiling's low." Then she gestured at the water tank and the maze of pipes. "All yours. You don't need me, do you?"

"Nope. I'm good. You can go back to whatever you were doing."

"I'll leave you to it then." Susannah flashed a polite smile, dusting off her hands as she returned to the kitchen. Her laptop was still open on the little desk. *Dupuytren's contracture heredity.* No, she thought. It was a rabbit hole, a distraction. The piano keyboard was the one she needed, not this one.

She didn't know how long she'd been working when she heard Kenny's voice. "Ma'am? I'm all done. I just need you to sign."

She looked up. "Already?"

"Ma'am?"

"In here," she called.

Kenny strode into the living room, a sheaf of papers in his hand. "Yep. It don't take long."

"And the old one?"

"In the truck."

"Perfect. Should I go downstairs so you can show me the new unit?"

"Not unless you want to. It's all automatic, nothing much to see.

Plus I got the warranty right here for you." He handed her a stack of papers and a clipboard with a pen on a chain. "No need for you to get up, even. I'll give you the papers, and I can let myself out."

"Do you need a check?"

"No ma'am. You're a regular customer, they'll charge it to your account. Easy as pie."

"Easy is good." She scrawled her signature, took the invoice and instruction manual, and tossed them onto the pile of music books. "Thanks again."

"You bet." Susannah returned to the sonata, dimly aware of Kenny's departing footsteps and the thud of the kitchen door. Another problem solved. If Aaron asked, she could say, truthfully, that she'd taken care of it.

She worked for another hour, glad to focus on the fine points of musical articulation instead of fretting about genetic patterns or schemes to entice Perez-Smith. Then, needing a break, she rose and went to the kitchen for a glass of water. The back door was wide open. Irritated, she pulled it shut. She hated that sort of carelessness. Would Kenny have left his own door open like that?

Setting down the glass, she walked to the alcove for the second time that afternoon. She hesitated, then thought: Just do it.

She pulled out the chair and gazed at her laptop. Beryl and Corinne were dead, and Wayne might as well be. There was one person left who might still be knowable.

Simone Russell, she typed. Then she hit *enter.*

There was a Simone Russell, chiropractor, in New Jersey. A Simone Russell who was a graphic designer, and another who was an IT consultant. Even a fictional Simone Russell, a character on a soap opera.

She typed *autoharp* next to Simone's name.

And there it was. Her website: *Country Blue Eyes.* Simone's face right in the center. Her blue eyes matched the lettering across the top of the page.

It had been more than twenty years, yet Simone looked oddly unchanged. Maybe it was the hair and the outfit, the same curls beneath a white cowboy hat. Along the side of the page, under another photo, was a list of engagements. Susannah scanned the text, the pictures, the endorsements. A notice in the same blue lettering caught her attention. "Miss Russell has taken an indefinite leave from performing. Please check back for updates."

What did that mean? Why had Simone stopped playing?

Then her eyes widened. Did Simone have Dupuytren's too?

Stunned, Susannah stared at the screen. She remembered the girl she had met in Austin all those years ago, so merry and open, fingers flying across the autoharp.

She scrolled back to the top and explored Simone's website, the newspaper clippings and testimonials. There was no address, no indication of where Simone lived, only a *Contact Me* button. She centered the mouse over the button, hovered, but didn't click.

She couldn't. She hadn't expected to find the website; she hadn't even planned to look for it. There was no room in her life for this right now. She had enough to worry about. Her hand, and Vera, and Libby, with her *tad bit disappointing* news that Perez-Smith might not even come to the concert. Aaron, so distant and angry, and her father, whose vagueness and confusion were starting to frighten her. The administrator of The Oaks had called to let her know that there had been an *incident*, that was the word he used. Tyler had appeared at the front desk at 6:00 in the morning, upset because he couldn't find his car keys and had a class to teach. They straightened it out in a few minutes, but the manager thought she should know.

Susannah closed the window on her browser. Her first instinct had been right. She needed to concentrate on her father, her husband, her son. She didn't have time to chase after a sister who didn't even know she existed.

Chapter Twenty-One

now

"Where's Oscar?" James asked.

Aaron glanced up from his journal. "Oscar? He's probably found a spot under the heater or in the back of a closet."

James stood in the doorway, arms dangling at his sides. "I looked in all those places. I looked everywhere. I can't find him."

"Let me get the can opener," Susannah said. "That always makes him come."

"I tried that. I rattled his dish. I even waved a can of food around so he could smell it."

Aaron frowned. "You called him?"

"Of *course* I called him." James sounded angry, but Susannah could hear the fear in his voice.

"We'll all look," she said quickly. "He has to be somewhere."

It wasn't like Oscar. He wasn't a cat who liked to hide. He was always there, slithering between their legs, searching for someone to pet him. "He can't have gotten out," James insisted. "I checked all the screens and they're fine."

Susannah froze. She saw the back door, wide open when she went to get a glass of water.

It wasn't her fault. It was Kenny's fault. If he'd wanted a check, she would have gotten up from the piano, opened the kitchen drawer where she kept her checkbook, and shut the door behind him when he left. But he'd been the one to say *no, we'll charge your account.*

She couldn't tell James. Anyway, it might not have happened that way, she didn't know for certain. And Oscar might turn up, the way cats did.

But she did know. It was the only explanation that made sense.

She said nothing, kept peering behind furniture and inside cupboards while James crooned, "Oscar, Oscar."

"I don't get it." James went to the back door, scowling at the deck.

Susannah's pulse quickened. "Even if he did get out, he'll come back. Cats are amazing at finding their way home."

After fifteen minutes, Aaron put his hands on his hips. "We're not going to find him this way. He'll surface when he's good and ready."

James clenched his fists, then whirled around and stormed out of the room.

Susannah shut her eyes. No one knew how she'd tossed the invoice and instruction manual aside and gone back to her music instead of walking Kenny to the door, the way she should have. No one even knew that Kenny had been there that day. No one but her.

There was still no sign of Oscar in the morning. James wanted to put flyers around the neighborhood instead of going to school, but Aaron was firm. "He has a tag on his collar. If someone finds him, they'll call. More likely, Oscar's prowling around nearby and he'll show up looking for his food dish. Go to school. He'll probably be here by the time you get home."

Susannah said nothing. What good would it do? She just had to wait, and hope. Listen for a cat mewing and scratching at the kitchen door. *Keep an eye on it.*

The phrase made her gag. She loathed hearing it from Leo and Aaron. It seemed like a coward's excuse.

Aaron reached past her to retrieve his briefcase from its spot against the wall. "I might be home late," he said. "I'll let you know. But don't feel you have to wait dinner."

Susannah turned to him, her forehead creasing. They always ate as a family. It was something they had decided—and honored, no matter what, ever since James was small. "How late will you be? We can wait."

"I don't know. It's going to be a nonstop day." He balanced the briefcase under his arm as he zipped his jacket. "Just go ahead without me. It's probably easier."

She remembered what Kenny had said. *Easy as pie.* But easy didn't mean right.

She wanted to pull Aaron into a *have-a-good-day* hug, but his arms were full and she didn't want to hug someone who couldn't hug back. "Well, let me know."

"Will do." He gave her a polite kiss on the cheek. Susannah held the door and watched him hurry to his car.

A ribbon of worry coiled itself around her. This wasn't good. Instead of dissipating, the tension between them was getting worse. She had to fix this, fast, but it wasn't going to happen today. Aaron had made that clear. Nonstop. Meaning: don't call.

Well, she had a busy day too. She had four students coming for lessons, one after another. She had put them off, but these were the serious ones who couldn't be postponed any longer. And after that, she had an appointment with Genevieve Macleod, the branch manager at the bank.

Susannah had been glad to learn that the branch manager was a woman. She knew you weren't supposed to think like that, yet she couldn't help hoping that Genevieve Macleod would be sympathetic to another woman who wanted a loan to help launch her career.

But Genevieve Macleod threaded her fingers together and regarded Susannah across the polished surface of her desk. "Well," she said, "the way a loan works is that it's secured by property that reverts to the loaner if the borrower defaults. It's like with a car loan. If you don't meet the payments, you forfeit the car." She coughed discreetly. "Or else it's secured by proof that your income is sufficient to make the payments."

Susannah stifled a dart of annoyance. Did Genevieve think she was ten years old, with no idea how the world worked?

"So, here's the issue," Genevieve continued. "If you don't want to use your joint account and you don't want your husband's name on the loan, then you need to show that you have enough income, on your own, to guarantee repayment. Do you have a tax return you can provide?"

She did, but it was a joint return. Most of the income was Aaron's.

"A credit card?" Genevieve asked. "In your name alone?"

Not that either. Their credit cards, like their bank account, were in both names.

"Oh." Genevieve looked disappointed, as if Susannah had set women's liberation back a decade or two.

Susannah willed herself not to get defensive. "I never thought about it, that's all." She'd been too busy making music. And if you were a couple, a family, why did you need to worry about having your own credit card?

Genevieve gave a brief nod. "Well, if you're committed to taking out a loan in your name only, we'll need some form of security. Is there something you own—you know, individually—that we could use as collateral?"

Only her Steinway. But that was worth far more than the amount she wanted to borrow, and even she wasn't desperate enough to wager her piano against a single performance. It would be like betting your pitching arm against a single baseball game. Unhappily, Susannah thanked Genevieve Macleod for her time and left.

When she got home, she found the credit card bill in the day's mail—with the ironic reminder that it was in both their names, which meant she had to share it with Aaron. She skimmed the itemized charges. The payment to the publicist was there, required in advance. The piano rental and the special tunings, as well as the long black dress, were still to come.

She'd wavered about the publicist but knew she had to do it. Professional pianists had managers who took care of those things. She didn't, so she needed someone—right away—who could create a press release and send it out to newspapers, magazines, radio stations, anyone who might give her a glowing review. And then send the reviews, assuming they were good, to orchestras and concert venues, together with a professional quality concert tape and a head shot. Libby wasn't going to do that. Susannah had asked, but Libby made it clear that promoting Susannah's career wasn't part of her job description.

Susannah had called the three publicists—again. Two said they were booked, but the third said he could do it. Susannah had signed the contract and clicked on PayPal. She hadn't let herself think about the price tag, but there it was, shocking her anew.

She shoved the bill in a drawer. She'd go over the expenses with Aaron later. After the concert.

The concert seemed to be galloping toward her, without time for everything she needed to do. A press release couldn't be thrown together in a day or two, and she needed to go over the distribution list with the publicist. She hadn't even started looking at dresses. For all she knew, James had a basketball game today that she was going to miss—and had she actually booked his defensive driving class or only thought about it?

Time. She needed to stretch it out, slow it down, make it hold more in each beat.

Then she thought: *rubato*. In music, when you needed extra time, you borrowed it from a nearby measure. That was what she had to do. Borrow from the time she might have spent on other things so she could give it, temporarily, to the one thing that required her urgent attention: the problem of Carlo Perez-Smith.

Perez-Smith simply couldn't do the CD without Schubert. It was offensive, unthinkable, to plan a recording of composers facing death and ignore the B-flat major sonata. Libby was an idiot. It was more than *a tad bit disappointing*. It was an insult—to Schubert, and to her.

The only way to make sure Perez-Smith included the sonata on his CD was to make sure he heard it played live, by her.

Susannah had been to enough performances to understand the power of live music. You couldn't forget music you had experienced directly, just as you couldn't forget the musician who had given you that experience. Unless Carlo Perez-Smith was right there in the concert hall, he might decide that another piece—or another pianist— would do just fine.

And that couldn't happen. Not now, when she'd let herself want it.

Aaron crinkled the newspaper and made the satisfied *hunh* that meant he had finished the Sunday crossword. Susannah, in the leather chair across from his, folded back a page of the *Style* section and gazed at his familiar profile. She wanted to tease him the way she used to about his special *I-finished-the-crossword* grunt, but a new caution held her back.

Sunday afternoons had always been a time she cherished—the hazy light filtering in through the curtains, the lingering smells of bacon and toast, James off at a game or out with friends. On Sunday afternoons she and Aaron had time alone. Sometimes they made love. Sometimes they just curled up and read the paper, passing the sections back and forth, stopping to read paragraphs aloud to each other.

They wouldn't be making love today; that was clear from the way they stepped politely around each other, careful not to touch. Aaron had gathered the sections of the paper and set them on the coffee table without offering them to her. Not that either.

Susannah tented her fingertips against her chin as she studied Aaron in the opposite chair. He had progressed from the crossword to whatever article he was reading now, rubbing a knuckle across his lip the way he did when he concentrated. She really needed to talk to him. Partly, she longed to break the horrible tension that seemed to be lasting forever. And partly, she needed someone else's perspective about Perez-Smith and the idea she'd come up with. With his keen mind, Aaron was the obvious choice. No matter how strained things were between them, she couldn't believe he would refuse to listen and offer an opinion.

She remembered the last time they'd sat like this, and she had asked for his opinion about the quality of her playing. It had led to that awful conversation, when she called him a prick and he called her a diva. But then, when she told him what she'd been keeping from him—the diagnosis, and how frightened and helpless she felt—he had responded with such care and concern.

That could happen again. All she had to do was tell him what was on her mind.

Delicately, she moved the *Style* section to the coffee table. "A problem's come up. I wonder if I could run it past you?"

Aaron lifted his head and looked at her over his reading glasses. "Your father?"

"No, not that." She had told him about the manager's call and her own concern. "I mean, there might be a problem, but that's not what I wanted to ask you about."

"James, then? I know he's been edgy lately, but he's pretty upset about the cat."

"No, not James." She didn't want to talk about the cat, who still hadn't returned. "It's that music producer, the person I told you about?"

She waited for Aaron to nod, showing that he understood how important this was. When he didn't, she cleared her throat and continued. "Now it looks like he might not come to the concert after all. In fact, he might have changed his mind about the whole CD."

Aaron put down the newspaper. "That's the big problem?"

A flicker of concern darted across her face. He made it sound so trivial.

"I didn't think this was about a CD." Aaron said CD as if it were a dirty word. "I thought it was about the concert. How you wanted to play for a big live audience. Connect with real people."

Susannah kept her eyes on his. Yes, that was right. That was her point about Perez-Smith, in fact—the reason he had to hear her play, live, in person. But she wanted the CD too. Why couldn't she have both?

"The CD business came up later." She could feel the sweat beading on her forehead. Trying to quell her anxiety, she added, "So I fig-ured—well, it's now or never. Because of the Dupuytren's."

"Dupuytren's? That takes years to develop. I don't see the connection."

She gathered her nerve. "I thought it could be a kind of hook."

That was her idea. A notion so crazy that it just might work.

"Dupuytren's is what gave me my idea, the one I wanted to tell you about. I thought maybe it would inspire him. Perez-Smith."

Aaron looked confused, and Susannah thought: Oh, what the hell. She might as well say it out loud. That had worked the last time, daring to say what was on her mind.

"Fingers beginning their inevitable decay but rising to the call of the music." She waited. "For the back of the CD. The press release."

"Brilliant pianist overcomes disability?" Aaron lowered his chin. "I believe it's been done."

True. Leon Fleisher. Byron Janis. Misha Dichter. "It has. But I thought maybe the double-disease thing could be a good angle. You know, composers with diseases, performers with diseases. Only a performer who's suffering herself can truly express music written in the face of death. That sort of thing."

Aaron stared at her. "You can't be serious."

Seeing his expression, Susannah knew what he thought of her idea. Juvenile, contrived. Deplorable, really, to use suffering as a marketing ploy. But it was the only idea she'd come up with.

"This whole thing is making you completely nuts," Aaron said. "I liked it better when you just played your music."

Just played your music—a tree falling in the forest, soundless to the rest of the world? That wasn't fair. Her double disease idea might be silly, but it wasn't silly to want to feel the glory again and to share that glory with the world. "Well, I like it better now."

"Susannah." He took off his glasses and ran a hand across his eyes. "It's a fund-raiser. Not the Van Cliburn competition. Not some kind of seismic game-changer."

She wanted to slap him. How did he know it wasn't a game-changer? It wasn't his game; it was hers. He was only a spectator.

Aaron tossed the newspaper onto the coffee table. Then he rose from the leather chair, scowling down at her. "I really don't get it, to tell you the truth. Why is this so important all of a sudden? It's not like you've been trying and trying to land a major gig, and now you've finally done it. You didn't even go looking for this. Vera handed it to you, for god's sakes."

"I was too busy raising James and making a home. For you, for us."

Susannah rose too. "I'm not complaining. It was what I wanted to do. But things are different now."

"Different." Aaron's face tightened.

"Maybe not different. Maybe I'm just letting myself want what I've always wanted. What I used to have."

What I used to give you. The reason you loved me.

The sense of being fully present, servant to the music. Knowing that, through you, something transcendent was taking place—not for yourself alone, because the audience was part of it. Their response completed the circle. Without that return, the sound dissolved and was lost.

Her words were a plea. "What I used to have," she repeated. "I want it back."

"Things change, just as you said. You can't put life in reverse, retreat to some nostalgically idyllic past."

"Not retreat. Advance." She searched his eyes. "Besides, I thought you wanted this for me. I thought you were on board. That's what you said, that day on the deck when I told you about the audition."

"I said I supported the concert. I didn't vow to endorse whatever crazy idea you came up with. Radiation. Double diseases. What's next?"

Susannah couldn't believe the harshness in his voice. It wasn't the voice of a person who cared about her.

Suddenly she couldn't stand it. She grabbed his arm. "What's going *on* with you?"

Aaron looked at her hand on his sleeve. "Me?" Seconds passed. Then she opened her hand and let it fall to her side. She remembered the way he had grabbed her, almost in the same spot. The marks were fading. Only four yellow-green ovals remained.

"Ask yourself that question, Susannah."

"It's not fair to pin this on me."

This. The coldness between them, the absence of the hundred small intimacies that made them a couple.

"No?"

"No. I'm just—"

"It's all about you, isn't it?" His face was grim, unforgiving. "You might want to look around once in a while. There are other people in this house besides you." He brushed off his arm, then turned and left the room.

She didn't run after him; she didn't think he wanted her to. Instead, she walked to the far end of the living room, to the piano. Solace. Purpose. The only way she could give voice to the emotions that were roiling inside of her.

It all began with your musical intention, the idea in your mind. Then you had to search for a way to achieve that intention—a way to bring forth music that didn't exist yet, except in the silence of your innermost ear.

Black shapes on a page. The migration of their meaning into your hands, and then out into the world. It was like creation itself. Like giving birth. That was what Aaron didn't understand.

She placed her hands on the keys, felt the sound rise through her fingertips. And then, in a mysterious counterpoint, a second melody appeared in the spaces between the notes. The sound of an autoharp.

Chapter Twenty-Two

now

The bold colors and shapes of the framed prints reminded Susannah of Paul Klee. Between the Klee-like posters, the Eames chairs, and the sleek modern curve of the reception desk, the waiting room looked more like the lobby of an art gallery or an elite airport lounge than the anteroom of a radiology clinic.

She reached across the table for a copy of *The New Yorker* and stole a glance at the others who, like her, were waiting to be called. A young man in an Iowa Hawkeyes tee-shirt, swiping furiously at his iPhone, an older and blonder version of James. The tiny woman with thin white hair who kept rummaging through a cloth pocketbook and whispering to the woman next to her.

Aaron should be there, waiting with her as she took this important step and began the treatment that would save her music. If she closed her eyes, she could almost feel him sitting beside her, caressing the blotch on her palm, assuring her that everything would be all right. Inconceivable that he wasn't.

A bitter taste rose up in her mouth. A lot of things were

inconceivable but they happened anyway. She hadn't told Aaron about the radiology appointment. She hadn't wanted to argue with him; there was enough tension between them already.

Aaron loved her; Susannah knew that. If someone were to ask him, she was certain he would say that he would do anything to support her well-being. He just didn't think that radiation or contrived appeals to an arrogant music critic were part of that *anything*. But this wasn't about him. It was about her, only her.

She brushed away a flash of tears. Brusquely, so the two women wouldn't think she was upset about the impending treatment, she flipped open *The New Yorker*. A book review, an article about the ecological threat to a remote peninsula in the Yucatan. Cartoons that didn't seem funny.

"Susannah Lewis?"

For an instant, Susannah was back at the audition, hearing her name. The same brisk tones, the same clipboard. She stood. The magazine slid to the floor as her arms dropped to her sides. The evil spot near the fifth finger of her right hand. The gold band on the fourth finger of her left. "Yes," she said. "I'm Mrs. Lewis." She still was, whether Aaron acted like it or not.

The assistant flashed an assuring smile. "This way, please."

Susannah retrieved the magazine, laid it carefully on the table, and followed the assistant past the curved reception desk and brightly colored posters. This was it. She was here, and she was going to do what she'd decided to do, with or without Aaron.

She'd get the radiation, find a dress, and send a note to Carlo Perez-Smith to say how glad she was that he was coming to the concert. Nothing about double-diseases, only her hope that he would like her interpretation of the sonata. She'd triumph at the concert, show Vera that her efforts hadn't been wasted, show James who she truly was. And then, once that was settled, she would heal this terrible broken connection with Aaron.

The assistant led her to the treatment room where Paul Angelini, the radiologist, greeted her with a beatific smile. "Good to see you again. We'll have you in and out of here in no time." He gestured at a computer monitor. "Let me show you the model for what we'll be doing. Everything is one hundred percent customized, all mapped out by our technicians, so we know exactly where to aim the treatment. You're in good hands."

Susannah flinched. Was he making a joke, a pun about *good hands*? No, there was no irony in his expression. He was happy for her, not mocking her.

Angelini led her to the computer and went over the imagery, pointing out where the affected areas were located. "We don't want to miss anything, and we don't want to radiate anything we don't have to."

Susannah leaned closer. "This is more than just two spots."

"A bit more," he admitted. "That's because we can identify emerging spots with our advanced technology that you can't feel on the surface. As I said, we want to do it properly. Precisely."

She swallowed. He was right, of course. That was why she was here.

The assistant fitted her with a lead apron and guided her to a table at waist-height. Angelini marked the spots on her hand and adjusted a lead cone over the area before pressing a button to lower the X-ray machine. The treatment itself took less than a minute, just as he had promised. Ten minutes later, Susannah was back in her car and driving home. Driving herself home—Angelini had promised that too, although he had meant it as an assurance of her comfort, not a sign of her aloneness.

There were four more treatments in the series, and probably a follow-up series eight weeks later. Was she really going to keep all that a secret from Aaron? It hardly seemed possible. And if she did keep it a secret, but he found out later—a bill from the clinic, a message on the answering machine confirming her next appointment—it would be even worse.

She drove slowly, her thoughts troubled. Maybe she'd wait and tell him after the five days were over. Then, since she had already done it, he couldn't lecture her about why she shouldn't. They'd be able to move on.

Or maybe, better yet, she could just wait and tell him after the concert. There was no reason it couldn't wait till then.

She pulled into the driveway, relieved to be home. It still felt odd to be walking into the house without having to step around Oscar as he wove a figure-eight between her legs, mewing for attention. She dropped her purse on the counter and was about to walk to the sink when she heard the jingle of her phone. For an instant she thought *Aaron. He knows.* No, not his ring, nor James's. She pulled the phone out of her purse. It was the administrative director at The Oaks.

Her father had another *incident*, a euphemism that Susannah was starting to dread. Apparently, Tyler had gotten up from the table in the dining room in the middle of lunch. He hadn't excused himself or offered an explanation to his tablemates—a behavior, they concurred, that wasn't like him. He had simply walked away. A staff member found him sitting on a bench at the bus stop around the corner. "I don't especially like buses," Tyler had told the aide. "The fumes, you know. All that braking, and those bathrooms."

"Why are you at the bus stop, Mr. Richardson?" the aide had asked.

Tyler had smiled sweetly. "Seems Dana's wandered off. Thought I might go to her parents' house, see if she was there."

The director assured Susannah that it was simply a moment of confusion. "It's when it turns into a pattern that we get concerned."

"Yes, of course." Then she added, "Anyone can get disoriented, you know. It's not that unusual."

"The Oaks is an apartment complex for seniors," the director continued, as if she hadn't spoken. "Not an assisted living facility. We aren't equipped to deal with memory issues."

"This is my *father*," she wanted to snap. "He was a history professor, so don't lecture me about *memory*."

It wasn't the director's fault, nor her father's. She had seen the puzzled look come over his face. It couldn't feel good, knowing you'd been absent, but not knowing where you'd been.

She needed to find a part-time aide. Tyler would hate that, so she would have to convince him that it was a good idea. It would delay the move that she was beginning to realize was inevitable. Assisted living facility. He would hate that even more, but she had to do something to help him. *Just not now, please.*

A wave of guilt washed over her. How could she even think about wanting her father to delay his problems until after the concert? If he needed her help now, then he needed it now. Still, the manager hadn't said it was urgent.

She steadied herself. "I appreciate your keeping me informed. Call any time, day or night."

"That's the plan, Mrs. Lewis. We stay in close communication with the family in situations like this. To keep you informed, as you say." The director coughed delicately. "Or if there are decisions to be made."

Susannah wished, though she knew it was irrational, that her mother was there to help. Dana would have known what to do. Of course, if her mother had been alive, her father might not be sinking like this. Dana wouldn't have allowed it.

She thanked the director again, ended the call, and sank into a chair. Her father. The one who yelled *Brava!* at her recitals, and insisted that she needed a better piano than the little spinet they'd had when she was small. The one who paid for her trips to Texas, even if he hadn't known he was doing that.

Her family and her music, the equation she'd never been able to solve.

Tiny James, placing his dimpled hands on top of hers. Aaron, so close she could feel the rise and fall of his breathing as she played one of the nocturnes he loved. Her father, and the minuet from the Anna Magdalena book. And little Corinne, who sure could pick out a tune.

The phrase echoed down the tunnel of years. Susannah could almost hear it—the wistful drawl of a wiry, blue-eyed woman in Texas with a pack of Marlboros tucked into the waistband of her stretch pants. Her grandmother. Beryl, that was her name. Hair spray and smoke rings.

Music was the thread that connected her across the generations. Through music, she belonged.

Susannah stood and went to the alcove where she kept her laptop. She logged on and launched the browser. The seconds passed with aching slowness until she found the site she was looking for.

A person was only given so many relatives. A shame to squander them.

There hadn't been anything on the internet about radiation when she first investigated. Someone who wasn't married to a researcher—who hadn't watched him track down information by following links within links—might never learn about it. If Simone had the same affliction, she might not know there was a way to stop it.

She clicked on Simone's website. *Country Blues.* Simone's turquoise eyes gazed back at her. The message was unchanged. "Miss Russell has taken an indefinite leave from performing. Please check back for updates."

She hesitated. Maybe she was being foolish. Presumptuous. Maybe Simone would think she was a meddling quack. Then she squared her shoulders. Even if Simone had found her own treatment and didn't need a savior, she might still want a sister.

Contact me.

Susannah thought of what you had to do to lift a piece of music off the frozen page. There was always a risk you had to take, a leap from your idea of the note to the real note, the one that hadn't yet been struck. You could never know, ahead of time, exactly what it would sound like. But you took that risk, if you loved the music. If you trusted that love to guide you.

Contact me.

What could she possibly write that would prove she wasn't some kind of stalker or scammer? *I got your name from the alumni directory. I'm a big fan of your music. A friend of a friend told me to look you up.*

Why did she think she had to lie? She had already lied to Simone once. What was the worst that could happen if she told the truth?

Would Simone believe her? There was no shared memory or special baby name that only the two of them knew, nothing to prove who she was. She had to try anyway, without proof, without guarantee.

"When I was a teenager, I wanted to meet our mother Corinne, but she said no. That felt pretty bad, as you can imagine, so it was a long time before I tried again and by then she had died. Then I wanted to meet our father Wayne, but I gave him a false name and caused a lot of trouble, and when I tried a second time he didn't want to know me. And then I wanted to meet you but I ran away because I was afraid. That was twenty years ago. My name is Susannah Lewis and I'm your sister. And we may have the same disease."

She reread the whole message. Then she gathered her courage and hit *send*.

Chapter Twenty-Three

now

James sped through dinner, assuring them that he'd finished his homework, and left to play Dungeons and Dragons at Andrew's house. Susannah wondered if she ought to use the opportunity to sit down and talk with Aaron—really talk, not just about radiation—but she didn't feel prepared for what might not turn out to be a welcome conversation. It seemed too soon, because she hadn't figured out what she wanted to say. Or maybe too late, because she'd already started down the road he had told her not to take.

Or maybe not talk. Maybe forgo the words that had gotten them so snarled and just meet, touch. Make love.

She stood in the middle of the kitchen, unable to decide. The copper kettle caught a flare of light from the setting sun, as if someone had struck it with a match. Behind her, the refrigerator hummed softly.

She let out a sigh and went to the piano, the place that would always welcome her. She pulled out a volume of late Brahms and opened to the piece that had shocked her, all those weeks ago, into realizing how lifeless her playing had become. The F-major Romanze.

Slowly, she pressed the seam with her thumb. What if she tried it again, in a different way? Different—how?

As if in answer, a word leapt out at her from the score. The very first instruction, under the very first note: *espressivo*. With expression.

Espressivo was spacious and fluid, yet exacting. It meant a search for the expression of the music, not for your personal expression. A deep listening, a way of letting the composer's intention come through your own emotions, your own gestures.

Susannah readied her hands and sounded the opening call. The pure C, an in-gathering, and then a leap to the glorious F chord that spanned three entire octaves. The unfolding of the theme, rising and falling, exactly as it had to—all the way to the celestial ending, the gradual ascension, drawing the listener ever so tenderly, with such exquisite precision, to the fulfillment of the promise in the opening measures. The final sound, the return to F, to home, holding five octaves in its embrace.

She held the last chord, six full beats. You had to give it the time that Brahms meant it to have, just as you had to remain at the keyboard for the measure and a half of silence that Schubert had written into the end of the B-flat major sonata. A mysterious secret, that extra silence—as if Schubert wanted to make sure the pianist would end the piece with silence. The ending mattered, in great music. It gave meaning to everything that had come before.

The chord faded, and she heard Aaron clear his throat. She turned, startled. She hadn't heard him enter the living room.

He was leaning against the doorway, his good leather jacket slung over his shoulder. "I'm heading over to the lab," he told her.

She dropped her hands into her lap, confused. "At this hour?"

"I have to check on the progress of the cultures. I can't leave everything to the grad students." He shook open the jacket and reached for a sleeve. "Good chance I'll be there till late, actually."

The air around them seemed to stiffen, to freeze in the space between inbreath and release. "I don't understand," she said. "You never go to the lab in the evening."

"It's a big project. I'm sure I told you about it."

Had he? She couldn't remember. "I don't understand," she repeated. "What's so special about these particular cultures? Why *can't* the grad students check on them?"

"Please don't interrogate me, Susannah." He found the other sleeve and zipped the jacket to his chin.

A shiver snaked up her spine. Since when did the department chairman have to stay late to check on a culture? And since when did her husband look at her that way, as if he didn't even know her?

Don't do this.

She wanted to fly across the room, put her arms around him, lay her head on his chest. *Stay, please. Stay, and I'll close the piano.*

No, she couldn't beg, it would be too humiliating. She had begged to go to St. Pierre and he had refused. It would be unbearable if he refused again.

"But *why?*"

"What's the problem? It's not like I'm cancelling a plan we made."

No, it wasn't. She couldn't even say, "I thought we could spend the evening together." The evening was half over, and they weren't spending it together. Yet she had thought, somehow, that they might still find each other. That she might walk quietly into his study, unbutton his shirt, and trace the line of fine black hairs she knew so well.

"Why do you need to go to the lab, at night? It doesn't make any sense."

"Excuse me?"

His unsaid words were loud in the room. *It makes sense to me. I can do what I like. That's what you're doing.*

Susannah stared at him. Had they really gotten to this ugly place? So swiftly? Or maybe it had happened step by imperceptible step. The same way a Dupuytren's cord pulled the finger into the palm.

There was no research emergency. He wanted to get out, away from her.

The hurt spilled into her voice. "Anything to avoid me, I suppose."

Aaron gave a humorless laugh. "I think we're avoiding each other pretty successfully right here. I don't need to go to the lab for that."

"That's a shitty way to put it."

"Is it?"

It was the bitterness that shocked her. She had never seen him like this.

"I'm only saying what we both know."

"What *you* know. Or think you know." Her mind was flipping madly through protests and explanations. He was feeling left out, unimportant. This was her fault, for neglecting him and keeping secrets. No, his fault. For nursing a grudge, withdrawing.

That stupid, stupid argument about radiation. He didn't know she had gone ahead with the treatment, so it was the argument itself. The chasm that had split the ground between them. How had it gotten so huge?

She searched his face, looking for the wounded pride she could talk him out of, the need to feel appreciated she could attend to, but his expression was deadly calm. Finally she said, "And what is it, the thing you're so sure you know?"

Aaron rubbed a hand across his eyes. "Please don't make this difficult. You haven't been any happier lately than I've been. It isn't getting any better."

That's not true. It's only temporary.

A bargain, a plea. *I'll close the piano. I'll make you happy right now.*

"I know I've been preoccupied," she began. She stopped; the sentence was oddly familiar. Then she remembered. That was what she had told James, as the justification for failing to pick him up from basketball.

"I'd call it obsessed."

"It's only until the concert."

His gaze locked onto hers. "Until the concert." He echoed her words. "Maybe we need some time apart. Until the concert, like you said."

Susannah thought he was mocking her, with his sing-song reiteration of the three words that had been her mantra but now felt like a threat. "You're joking."

"Not at all. It might be the best thing, right now."

"For you."

"For you as well. A chance to concentrate. To breathe."

I don't need to breathe. I need this horrible thing between us to end. Then she saw the weariness in his eyes, and awareness poured over her like ice. He wasn't doing this to get her to flatter him or turn to him for guidance. He was doing it to get away from her.

This was insane. The concert wasn't supposed to drive him away. It was supposed to bring him back, make him remember who she was and fall in love with her again. She had to turn it around, right now.

She was still sitting at the piano, the F-major Romanze open in front of her. Why hadn't she jumped up when he walked into the room and put her arms around him, the way she'd wanted to?

The silence seemed to last forever. Not the measure and a half of silence that Schubert demanded of the pianist, a way to linger in the fullness of what had been received, but a nothingness.

Finally she said, "So you're going off, and not just to the lab for a few hours? Is that the idea?"

"I suppose it is."

Susannah could hardly take it in. Her husband was going—where? Somewhere else, away from her.

She had to stop this. Argue, cajole, negotiate, scream—something to shock him out of this brutal stupidity. Yet she couldn't move. His words were boulders that had buried her in an avalanche she had never foreseen.

Aaron's expression shifted. What had been an evasive weariness hardened into something cold and dead that let her know he had made up his mind. Entreaties weren't going to change it. He had worked out his own equation, and this was the solution.

"And what am I supposed to tell James, when he asks where his father is?"

Aaron lifted a shoulder. "Tell him—I don't know, tell him I got an urgent call and have to do some last-minute fieldwork. For the grant."

Fieldwork. For the grant. Her disbelief turned to anger. Who the fuck did he think he was, asking her to lie to their son? "Tell him yourself. He'll be back in an hour or so."

"I'll call him. After I'm settled."

After he was *settled*? Settled where? She stared at him. He couldn't wait an hour? No, obviously not. Once he'd made up his mind, he couldn't stand to be here a second longer than he had to.

Aaron's face was turned to the window. In daylight, he would have been gazing out at the silvery Hudson. Now, without the sun, his expressionless image was reflected back at her. He looked neutral, blank. It could have been anyone.

He gave another shrug. "You know as well as I do that we're at an impasse. Maybe a little space will help."

Was she supposed to agree with him? Praise his wisdom? Tell him, *Yes dear, you know best*. Oh, this was bullshit, bullshit.

"Do what you like," she snapped.

She thought he might reply but he only patted his pocket, checking for his reading glasses, before heading up the stairs. She listened for the sounds that meant he was really going through with it. Bureau drawers opening and closing. The thunk of a suitcase hitting the floor.

And then it hit her, the truth she had missed about the concert. She had assumed that she understood the stakes: a new beginning as a musician, or back to *life-as-it-was*. Behind that was a second assumption: that *life-as-it-was* would be waiting for her in a kind of suspended animation, in case the concert led nowhere and there was no CD or calendar of exciting new bookings.

What she hadn't understood—until right now, as her husband was about to walk away—was that preparing for the concert had already changed her life and there was no going back. Whether her performance was stellar or mediocre, her old life wouldn't be waiting for her.

She had misunderstood the stakes. They weren't ahead of her, but all around. Right now.

She heard the scrape and click of the bedroom door, then his footstep on the landing. The bonk-bonk of the suitcase on the steps. She ran to the bottom of the staircase. Aaron waited while she stepped aside to let him pass. "I have my cell," he said. "Or you can call me at the lab if something comes up."

Susannah gazed at him, unable to speak. He gave a polite dip of his head. Then he strode across the L-shaped living room and opened the door, pulling the suitcase behind him. Slowly, as if in a daze, Susannah crossed the room and stood in the open doorway. She watched him walk to the carport, throw the suitcase into the back seat of his car. Get in the car and start the engine.

A tickling sensation made her look down. It was Oscar, rubbing against her leg, dirty and thin, but unmistakably himself.

She knelt and scooped him up, feeling the warm dry fur, the pulsing mass of his living self. She pressed him close, grateful for the mercy that had brought him back. And hollowed out by what had just happened.

Chapter Twenty-Four

now

There were four more radiation treatments, on four consecutive days. Low-energy X-rays, sixty seconds each, quick and painless. When Susannah asked Paul Angelini, the radiologist, how she could know if the treatment had been successful, he told her, "We monitor your hand. If the fingers don't bend, we're happy."

She knew what Aaron would think of that kind of logic. It was like wearing garlic around your neck to keep the vampires away. *See? No vampires. The garlic must have worked.*

Angelini urged her to have a second round of radiation in seven or eight weeks. "That's the recommended protocol. Very few people develop contracture after radiotherapy, but a second series is extra insurance."

"What about adverse effects?" Susannah asked. "Consequences down the road?"

"Side effects?" Angelini shook his head. "As I believe I explained, some people have a little chronic dryness, thickening, tightening, maybe a bit of decreased sensation. But not everyone experiences that, and it's just at the site of the radiation. Quite localized, quite mild."

"No. I mean, from the radiation itself. From getting repeated radiation on a specific place on your body."

He gave a dismissive wave. "Theoretically, there's always a risk of radiation-induced malignancy, but for Dupuytren's it's so low that it's virtually non-existent. There was a systematic review of the research a couple of years ago, and they didn't find a single documented case. They've been doing this in the UK since 2010, you know."

Susannah was confused. Had Aaron been exaggerating, or had he known less about radiotherapy than he claimed? "You're saying that radiating Dupuytren's isn't dangerous?"

"You mean, will it give you cancer? As I said, there hasn't been a single reported case. The worst thing we can say is that it's considered a quote-unquote unproven treatment because there aren't enough long-term studies."

"So, if someone was worried that the radiation could be harmful—?" She didn't finish the sentence.

Angelini finished it for her. "He would be misinformed. Or excessively cautious."

Her mind reeled. Aaron would never be misinformed, so he must have been overly cautious. But why?

She remembered when she first told him about the concert, that evening on the deck as they watched the sunset together. He'd been happy for her, assured her of his support. Then she found out about Dupuytren's, and the conversation shifted to the world of science, evidence, research. Aaron's world, where he knew best. Yet she had made her own decisions, disregarding his notion of *best* in favor of her own.

She told Angelini that she would call to schedule the next round of treatment. Not yet, though. She wanted Aaron with her when she came back.

Pensive, Susannah left the radiology clinic and crossed the parking lot to her car. She chirped open the passenger door, pulling it shut behind her. She didn't turn on the engine. Instead, she frowned at the windshield as she struggled to fit the pieces together.

Aaron might have felt hurt and ignored, but he wasn't vindictive. He was stubborn—well, so was she—but could he really be stubborn enough to abandon her a week before her concert? He had backed himself into a corner over this radiation business. But why? Why was he so dead set against it? He had to know that the risk of harm was minimal. He was being over-protective, absurd. Irrational—the worst insult he could fling at someone. Again, she thought: why?

Aaron loved her. So he must be afraid of losing her—not to an unlikely effect of radiation, because that made no sense. To whatever was happening that was altering their lives. The radiation was just a proxy.

Her hand flew to her mouth. How could she have missed what was so obvious?

Knowing and advising were the ways Aaron showed his love. If he couldn't do that, he had nothing to give her.

It was the same way she felt about her music. If she couldn't transport him with her playing, she had nothing to offer—and no reason for him to want her.

Of course. It all fit. At last, after these terrible days. Four endless days of disbelief, humiliation, and rage.

The first day had been the worst. Shock, a fear so cold and deep she could hardly breathe. Then anger. *Oh, let him pout. Serves him right.* Then a crushing numbness.

On the second day, she did what Aaron had asked her to do and told James that his father had to go on a last-minute business trip. For the grant. James shrugged *okay* and adjusted his ear buds; his father's business trips were nothing new. Susannah didn't like lying to James, but it seemed like a way to buy a little time until Aaron stopped this insanity and came home. Until he phoned her, maybe even that night, breathless and full of remorse. "I don't know what I was thinking."

On the third day, she saw that she hadn't needed to lie after all. It was clear from the tight private expression on James's face that Aaron had been in contact with him and that James knew where his father was staying. She wanted to tell him *your dad was the one who made up that story about the grant, not me.* But she bit back her comments, vowing not to put James in the middle.

By the fourth day, she had settled into a weary resignation. A chance to concentrate and breathe, that's what he'd called it. Until the concert. The concert was on Saturday, two days from now. She could last until Saturday. Unless—

Susannah stared at the windshield, wide-eyed, as a new possibility stung her with its unthinkable awfulness. *Until the concert* didn't mean until *after* the concert, did it? It didn't mean that Aaron wouldn't come to hear her play.

He had to come, no matter what impasse he thought they had reached. She was doing this for him, so he would remember who she was. And for James, so he would have a memory of his own—his mother, alone on the stage, doing something extraordinary while hundreds of people listened and marveled and burst into applause.

At first, the concert had been for Vera, to earn back her respect. Vera had shoved the truth in her face. "How many more chances like this are you going to have?"

Only this one. A chance to reclaim the power and the rapture. And then, to go forward. To vault into an elite tier that had never quite granted her admission.

The concert wasn't for Vera any more. It wasn't even for Aaron. It was for herself, Susannah. For the self she was meant to be.

Her head pounded, a relentless *ostinato* pushing through her body. *Ostinato*, a repeating pattern of notes. In Italian, it meant stubborn.

Like Aaron. Proud, hurt, claiming the only power he believed he had—the power to withhold.

She straightened her shoulders. If Aaron was going to be so stubborn and closed, then it was up to her to save her marriage, just as it had been up to her to save her hand. If she could push through and find a way to play with a stiff palm, she could push through and find a way to reach her unyielding husband.

She grabbed her purse and dug through the jumble of wallet and tissues and hairbrush until she found her phone. She called his cell number first, then his office. Both calls went to voicemail. Then she called the lab. "Hello," she told the student who answered. "I need to speak to Dr. Lewis, please. It's his wife."

"I'll look for him. Hang on." Susannah waited, tapping her fingers on the steering wheel. After a minute, the student returned to the line. "I can't find him. Did you try his office?"

"I did. No one picked up."

"Huh. Maybe he's on his way back. Anyway, he's not here. Sorry."

She hung up without thanking him. One of the numbers ought to have worked. She looked at her watch. Three o'clock. Aaron was always at the lab by now. Maybe the student was lazy, hadn't really looked? Or maybe Aaron *was* there but told the student to say he wasn't.

Why would he do that? Was the thought of talking to her so revolting? Wasn't he even curious? Didn't he want to hear her voice?

The fierce clarity she had felt only moments earlier—the certainty that all she had to do was relent, offer herself, and he would say, "Yes, yes, I was waiting for you to understand"—seeped away, like water into sand, or sound into silence. Maybe he wasn't waiting. Maybe *until the concert* was an excuse to get away from her, from the marriage, without an ugly scene. Maybe he just was pretending it was temporary. After all, he was sleeping somewhere else, and only an idiot would pretend she didn't know what that meant. He was probably fucking some graduate assistant in the back room right now—while that smirking little student told her: *Anyway, he's not here.*

Jesus. She was losing her mind. Aaron wouldn't fuck a lab assistant, and he would never ask a student to lie for him.

Susannah wiped her forehead. *Get a grip.* If the student said he wasn't there, then he wasn't there.

Still, it was cruel and wrong of him not to be there when she had done the hard part—picking up the phone, admitting that she missed him.

She had put her heart into preparing for the concert, but that didn't mean she had pushed Aaron out to make room. She hadn't stopped loving him. Did he think she had?

She sagged against the leather seat and closed her eyes. She could almost see, imprinted on her lids, the shards of glass and the splatter of Marbella sauce from that unforgettable evening. Useless, irrelevant—that was how Aaron said he felt. If there was an adoring graduate assistant, who could blame him?

She gave a frustrated cry, the kind of sound James used to make when he couldn't get a puzzle piece to fit where he was sure it ought to go. If Aaron hadn't arrived at the lab when she called, he would be there by now, or by the time she arrived. Until five, for sure. After that, she had no idea where to find him. That meant she had to drive over there right this minute.

She opened her eyes. The afternoon sun poured into the car. *The sun doesn't come out from behind the clouds,* he had told her. *The sun was there all along; it was the clouds, getting out of the way.*

Susannah looked at her watch again. Eleven minutes after three. Eleven precious minutes had slipped past.

It would take twenty-five minutes to drive to the campus if she made all the lights. Buckling her seatbelt as she shifted into reverse, she backed out of her parking slot and made a sharp U-turn, tires squealing as she swung onto the road. Every second that ticked past was a second that kept her from where she needed to be. She roared around the slower cars. Cars, trees, orange traffic cones, everything melted as she sped past. There, at last, the entrance to the highway. She shot up the ramp.

Shit. The highway was a parking lot, three lanes of traffic at a dead stop. Susannah jammed her foot on the brake. She looked over her shoulder to see if she could back down the ramp but there were two cars behind her. *Shit again.*

She craned her neck and saw the flashing lights of a police car. There must have been an accident. God knew how long she'd be stuck there. She gave the horn a frustrated shove. It was nearly four o'clock. She wanted to jump out of the car and sprint toward campus.

She forced herself to calm her furious breathing. *Adagio,* not *allegro.* Then she shifted into neutral and dropped her hands onto her lap. Against the denim of her jeans, they looked the same as they always had, as if the whole thing—Dupuytren's, the argument about radiation—had been a bad dream.

After a few minutes she rolled down the window, but there was nothing to see except the same ocean of cars. Exhaustion overcame her, crushing and abrupt. Probably just as well that the backup from the accident had delayed her. She would have looked like an idiot, barging into the lab, especially if Aaron wasn't even there.

She had been so proud of herself. Solving each problem that came up. Renting a better piano. Finding the perfect dress, the perfect photo for the press release, the perfect cure for her hand. As if life was a list, with items to be checked off.

She tasted salt and realized that tears were dripping down her cheeks and into her mouth. She rummaged in her purse again, found a rumpled tissue, and wiped her face.

If only there was a treatment that could correct the thing between Aaron and her that had gotten bent and deformed, restore it to its rightful shape, heal her family the way radiation had healed her hand.

Maybe it was like a Dupuytren's cord—a thick unnatural growth that had to be softened, then broken, so the whole could be set right again. Swelling and bruising might follow until the fingers healed, but that was the only way to restore the music. It was too late for the treatment that might have stopped the hardening while it was still forming, below the surface.

Susannah flexed her hand, opening her fingers into a fan and rolling them closed. After a while she heard the sound of engines as traffic began to move. She shifted out of neutral and inched forward. Resigning herself, she looked at the dashboard, though she already knew. She wasn't going to make it to the lab by five o'clock.

The line of cars picked up speed but she drove slowly, staying in the right lane, and got off at the first exit. She steered around the cloverleaf and back onto the highway in the other direction, heading home.

When the phone rang, Susannah thought—for a wild, joyous instant—that it was Aaron, getting back to her after he heard the student's message or calling because he had felt her reaching out to him.

But it wasn't his special ring. She didn't recognize the number, and the voice was unfamiliar. "Are you Susannah Lewis?"

"I am. Who's this?"

"My name is Felix," he said. "My mother was Vera Evangelista."

The verb tense slashed through her like a scythe. "Was?"

"Yes, I'm sorry. My mother died last night."

"Oh dear god. What happened?"

He had gone to bring her groceries and the newspaper, Felix explained, and found her sitting in the armchair with the oxygen cannula on her lap, head flopped on her chest. He told Susannah about Vera's COPD—chronic obstructive pulmonary disease, from bronchitis that had never really been cured, exacerbated by years of exposure to fumes, dust, pollution, and his father's hand-rolled cigars.

Vera had dismissed the oxygen as *old lady lungs*. Susannah had left it at that, more interested in what Vera had to tell her about Perez-Smith than in how Vera was feeling. The memory filled her with shame. "I had no idea she was so ill."

A coward's answer. Anyone with an ounce of attention would have noticed.

"There's no way to know what really happened," Felix said. "Maybe she decided she'd had enough and pulled it out. That wouldn't be out of character. Or maybe it was an accident, it fell out, she was asleep." He exhaled wearily. "They said an autopsy would tell us more, but I don't think I want to do one."

Susannah's voice caught. "Don't have one, if you don't want to." She could almost picture Vera slapping their knives away.

"Anyway," he said, "my mother had a list of people she wanted me to call in case anything happened to her. You were on it."

"She had a list?"

"She did. Right there on her bureau, so who knows, maybe she had a premonition."

"Maybe she did, if she knew she was so ill."

Susannah's voice cracked again. Vera knew she had COPD but she hadn't said anything. Even when she called to fret about a bump on her hand, Vera had talked about music. Melody lines, Czerny exercises. Susannah remembered the day she went to Boston and visited Vera in her apartment. "Make me proud," Vera had ordered. "Don't forget that you're the one playing. Not Perez-Smith, not me, not even Schubert."

No chance to say goodbye or to return with the gift of her triumph that she had planned to place in her teacher's lap. Vera couldn't have come to the concert, not with an oxygen cannula, but Susannah had pictured herself driving to Boston the next day and telling Vera how she had gathered everything Vera had taught her and given it to the sonata.

"I'm so sorry," she told Felix. "I thought the world of her."

Vera, who taught her to listen for the music that connected the notes, the great idea that needed the pianist's touch to bring it forth. Her third mother. Without Vera, there would have been no ripening, despite Corinne's gift and Dana's determination.

"She didn't want a burial," Felix said. "She was pretty insistent about that. Just a cremation, no service."

Yes, that sounded like Vera.

"We might do something anyway, I don't know."

"If you do, please let me know."

There was so much more she wanted to say, but the only language that mattered was the one she and Vera had shared. A language of melody and counterpoint, crescendo and diminuendo, dissonance and harmony.

Without the dissonance, there could be no resolution. If Vera had taught her anything, it was that.

She said goodbye to Felix, telling him again how sorry she was. When the call ended, she tapped on her contacts. Names filled the screen. Aaron, the first name on the list. There was so much she needed to tell him. About Vera, and all the expenses she had hidden from him, and the radiation. She had told herself that they weren't lies, just omissions, but the result was the same—a wall to keep him out. He wasn't the only one who had withdrawn, hidden himself.

No more desperate phone calls or crazy drives to his office. A simple message. Four days was long enough for this particular silence.

"Please come to the concert," she wrote. "I need you with me." Quickly, she changed *need* to *want*. No, that wasn't right either. She deleted the message and wrote, "Please come to the concert. It would mean so much to me."

It was like the moment when she clicked *send* on Simone's website. She had tried not to expect too much, only launch her message, because she had to. Simone hadn't answered, not that Susannah really thought she would. Why would Simone believe that an email from a self-proclaimed, long-lost sister was anything but a prank?

She reread her message to Aaron. Then she pointed her finger and tapped the little arrow. The barest touch, less than it took to strike a key on the piano.

Send.

Chapter Twenty-Five

now

Susannah didn't really expect Aaron to answer right away, and he didn't. Maybe he wouldn't answer at all. Her message had said *come*, not *reassure me that you're coming*.

Still, she couldn't stop checking her phone. The little black rectangle seemed to hold so much power—the possibility of connection and the pain of silence. She thought of her father, alone in the apartment. She knew how much her calls meant to him. How long had it been since they'd spoken?

She could almost see him, wandering from room to room in his baggy sweater, shoulders slumped, lost in a place whose every corner evoked the person who was no longer there. Linens, art books, the heavy Mexican silverware her mother liked to use. Unlike Aaron, Dana would never return.

Susannah picked up the phone again and scrolled through her contacts. *Dad*. It used to be *Mom and Dad*, but she had finally changed it. Somehow, that little switch felt like the last and worst and hardest thing, the irreversible admission that her mother was no longer someone she could contact.

Her father answered on the first ring. "Yes? Hello?"

"Hey! Hello back."

"Dana?"

"Dad. It's me." Did she have to tell him who *me* was? "Susannah."

Tyler gave an embarrassed laugh. "Egad. You sounded exactly like your mother. Have to admit you had me fooled."

"Oh Dad. I wish it could have been her calling you."

"It's hard to believe she's gone. I know she is, but I keep forgetting."

"It's okay to feel like Mom's still there. It keeps her alive."

"She'd be happy to hear you say that, Suzie. All she ever wanted was to be a good mother, you know. To do her best for you."

Susannah tried to keep her voice light. "I'm afraid I didn't make it easy for her. Let's face it. I was a miserable teenager."

"Phooey. Every teenager is miserable."

"Not James. I'm disgustingly lucky. A whiff of beer now and then, but overall a delight."

"That he is," Tyler said. "I think his birth meant almost as much to Dana as yours did. Getting to be a grandmother. Another round, as it were."

Susannah grew still, touched by her father's words and the memory they evoked, a memory that only she and her mother had shared. Her father had his own version of the event, gleaned from a retelling over the years that made it seem as if he'd been in the room too. But he hadn't. Only Susannah and her mother had been there, and now her mother was gone.

It was a particular kind of loneliness. When someone died, you lost the chance to relive memories by recalling them together. The memory was thinner when you remembered alone.

And yet, this was a memory that could never fade—the afternoon, nearly sixteen years ago, when she had placed tiny newborn James in her mother's arms, proud and humbled and wary too, because her mother had never gotten to experience the miracle whose afterglow filled the room. She couldn't help wondering if Dana, seeing James, would be wistful, jealous, sad—if his perfect little face, still so new, would reawaken an old pain.

She had watched as Dana studied the swaddled bundle, the new little being with his round red cheeks and solemn obsidian eyes. Her mother's gaze was full of tenderness and awe, a private and complicated look that seeped into Susannah's very marrow.

Dana's voice was quiet. "I'm so glad for you, my darling, that you got to have this. The chance to ferry this precious boy into the world."

Susannah's eyes moved to James, then back to her mother. "What about you, Mom? You didn't get that."

"No. But I got everything else."

"No regrets?"

Dana traced the baby's cheek. "No one gets through life without regrets. But that's not one of mine, not anymore."

James scrunched up his face, flailing his tiny fists. "I think he's figuring out what it's like to have a body." Dana smiled. "You did that too."

The memory was so clear. It was hard to believe that the baby in Dana's arms was now an enormous teenager and that Dana herself was gone.

Only a moment had passed, but when Tyler spoke again, it was clear that something had shifted. He sounded confused, petulant. "Did you want to talk to your mother, honey? I believe she's stepped out, but she ought to be right back."

Susannah shut her eyes for an excruciating instant. Talking to her father was like trying to catch the undertow at the shoreline. Everything kept moving, changing, advancing and receding; she couldn't grab hold.

"I miss her too, Dad. I wish she could be at my concert tomorrow. I wish both of you could."

She could tell by the pause that he didn't know what concert she was talking about, so she reminded him. Again, he shifted back, found his place. "A big night for you, Suzie. Regrettably, your doddering old father can't be there, but I trust those two fine men of yours will yell *bravo* loud enough for all of us."

There was no way to tell her father that Aaron might not be there, and no need for him to know that the only person she could count on to yell *bravo* was James—that tiny creature in a pale blue blanket and cap, grown so impossibly large.

She remembered how James had been that day, twitching his legs under the blanket and grabbing her mother's thumb with his fierce little fist. The person linked to her, more deeply than anyone she had ever known. Connecting her forward, even if she didn't know what it meant to be connected backward.

"I can't believe the doctors are letting me take him home," she had whispered. "Weren't you scared that you wouldn't know what to do?"

"Every mother feels that way," Dana said. "It's a question you never stop asking yourself." She gave another smile. "I remember when you were an angry adolescent, and you accused me of trying to prove to the adoption agency that I'd done a good job, earned the title of *mother*, by the way you turned out." She wiggled her finger, and James held on. "I got mad at you, but you were right."

"I said that?"

"You did. It hurt me at the time. The truth usually does."

"Still. That was pretty bitchy of me."

"Well, I *was* trying to prove that I deserved to be a mother. If I could be the perfect mother, it would mean—oh, that the universe hadn't denied me motherhood because I wasn't worthy. That it wasn't a punishment for something else."

"There aren't any perfect mothers."

"Of course not," Dana said. "But I thought that's what I had to be, when you were small. I told myself that everything I did was for you, but it was for me too."

"It doesn't mean what you did was wrong."

"No, but I wasn't honest with myself about why I did it." She gave a soft shrug. "I suppose I got so involved in what I thought of as your destiny—you know, your talent—because I didn't feel in control of my own."

Back then, in the hospital room, Susannah had assumed that her mother was talking about her infertility and how powerless it had made her feel. But now she wasn't sure. What had Dana meant about not being in control of her own destiny? Had she felt coerced into giving up the fertility she actually did have?

You couldn't ever know the whole truth about your parents. Her mother did what she did, and then she found a new story to tell—the *chosen baby* story, a tale that made their pairing as mother-and-daughter into something that met Dana's terrible and wonderful need to believe that it really was her choice, exactly the way she would have wanted. *We jumped on a plane to Texas and brought you home.*

Tyler's words cut into Susannah's reverie. "I was thinking about your big night, Suzie, and what a shame it is that your mother can't make it."

Again, Susannah cringed. He made it sound like her mother had a scheduling conflict. She had no idea, at times like this, if he understood that Dana was really gone. "It's all right, Dad."

"I wonder if you might do me a favor, though." His voice quavered. "Do you think you could wear your mother's earrings, when you get all dressed up for your concert? The ones I gave you." He cleared his throat. "She never missed one of your performances, you know."

Susannah pressed the phone to her cheek. "And she won't miss this one. She'll be right there with me."

"You're a good girl, Suzie. A good daughter."

She remembered what Dana had told her, that day in the hospital. Her mother had handed James back to her. Nestling James against her breast, Susannah had lifted her eyes to Dana's and given voice to the question she had always been afraid to ask. "Do you ever wish you'd had a chance to give birth?"

Dana had tilted her head, considering her reply. "I view it a little differently. Truth be told, I've often thought that adoptive mothers are lucky. We have the good fortune of being able to understand more readily—because we have no images to get in the way, I suppose—that our children aren't extensions of ourselves, mini-me affirmations to reflect our traits back at us. They're strange and beautiful visitors, mysterious little beings entrusted to our care." She touched the edge of the blue flannel that Susannah had folded back so James could lie against her skin. "So, to answer your question: no, I don't. You lose one thing but you get another."

It was the sort of thing Dana liked to say. *It was all for the best. I got to have lemonade.*

In the intimacy of the moment—two mothers, marveling at the miracle of James's existence—she had accepted Dana's words as the truth. But now, after her father's confession, she wasn't sure it was the whole truth.

She would never know, because her mother wasn't there to ask. Just as she would never be able to ask Corinne what her own story really was.

It had been years, forever, since she had thought about Corinne—the unknown woman who had, as Dana put it, ferried her into life. What had it been like for her, to let her child go? Oddly, Susannah had never thought of it that way. It had been herself she had mourned, the rejected baby. But what about Corinne?

A strange new feeling poured into her. Sorrow—not for herself, the baby, but for Corinne, the mother, who had lost her child.

All her mothers were gone now. Corinne, Dana, Vera. Yet their sound lingered—three tones, filling the chord, a strange and improbable harmony.

Tyler cleared his throat again, returning Susannah to the present. "You get ready for your party now," he told her, "with your fancy earrings and all. Me, I'm going to practice that piece you gave me."

"The minuet."

"The minuet," he agreed. "I want to knock your socks off the next time you come up here."

Susannah put her lips close to the phone. "I can't wait."

When she ended the call, she tapped on the email icon, just in case Aaron had emailed instead of texting. She didn't really think he had, but it was somewhere else to check, since she'd forbidden herself from checking her text messages for at least another hour.

Instead of a response from Aaron, there was a new message in her inbox. Simone@country-blue-eyes.com.

The reply she had given up expecting, had never really expected. Her pulse pounding out a frantic *agitato*, Susannah clicked on the message.

Simone's words filled the screen, a blur of squiggles and shapes. Susannah's stomach lurched. *I can't read this.* Then her eyes found their focus.

"Wow," Simone had written. "I can't tell you how jazzed I was to get your email. I am *so* sorry it took me a while to answer. I don't check the website too often these days, so I only just now saw what you wrote me."

Susannah read the sentences over and over again. They kept breaking apart, little disconnected pieces of syntax, then re-forming into the astounding fact that Simone had actually answered her.

"I don't really remember the incident you were talking about, having coffee with a reporter back when I was playing with that all-girls band in college. But I totally know who you are because my aunt on the Dumont side told me about you a few years ago. One of her boys was working security at Target, same as my brother, and we saw each other at a barbeque the store had, July fourth, I think. We hadn't seen each other in I don't know when, but she looked kind of familiar and we got to talking. She told me she'd met you, only she couldn't remember your last name, so I had no idea how to look for you. But you can imagine how curious I was."

Hollis. Susannah had nearly forgotten her. Hollis had told Simone about her?

"Anyway, in case you were wondering why I'm on a break from the country western circuit, I have to tell you that it's for the best reason there could possibly be."

Best reason couldn't mean fingers like claws, stiff and unresponsive. Susannah willed herself to keep reading.

"Can you believe it, here I am, pregnant for the very first time at the ripe old age of 38? It's a miracle baby, that's for sure. I thought I couldn't have kids and it just about tore me up, Matt too, he's my husband, but what do you know? I thought I was too old, but hey, guess not. The doctor said I have to take it easy, that's all, no jumping around on stage or bouncing around on those tour buses."

Pregnant. No Dupuytren's, then. No defective gene, no threat of being silenced.

If Simone really had Dupuytren's, Susannah could have helped her find a treatment. It was better that Simone didn't need her help, but now she had nothing to offer. Except herself.

An image filled her vision. Simone, onstage in her fringed jacket and bright green bandana, surrounded by the other members of the band. The swell of the music as their instruments joined together. Simone's voice echoed across the years. "We'd get these harmonies going and it was pretty great, the way we could follow each other and make this whole new sound."

Susannah stared at the screen, hardly daring to breathe or blink, as if the slightest movement would chase away the comprehension that was forming in her astonished mind—like an image appearing in a pond only when it was absolutely still.

The real difference between them.

Simone played with a group, happy to be part of a larger sound, while she played alone, a solo performer crying: Listen to *me*. Love *me*.

It had nothing to do with the kind of music they played or their choice of instrument. Martha Argerich, one of the world's greatest pianists, had decided at the peak of her career to play only with orchestras and chamber groups. She had been clear about her reason. The immense space around the piano made it too lonely. There was no pleasure for her in that aloneness.

Simone had never doubted where she belonged, so she could join in anywhere. Susannah couldn't imagine what that would feel like, to care as much for the harmony among the instruments as you did for your own sound.

She wiped her brow, shocked by the sweat pouring down her face. Of all days, the evening before the concert of her dreams. To feel this, now, to question the very heart of her music.

"Anyways, if you want to talk on the phone, I'd love it. Here's my number. Call any time."

Susannah gazed at the phone number. There would be a voice on the other end. A voice she remembered from years ago, at a diner in Austin.

When she ran back to New York instead of returning to the Red Rooster, she had thought that the best thing was to let it all go. No matter what she did, it wouldn't unspool the past. So she had gone on with her life. Bought new curtains for her apartment, learned the Goldberg variations, met Aaron.

It wasn't your past that you had to give up, though. Only the story you told yourself about your past. Chosen baby, discarded baby. Real daughter, real mother.

She had carved her world at the wrong joints. They were invented categories, attributes that resided in her mind but not in the things themselves. If she stopped parsing life that way, the categories dissolved.

Susannah touched the screen. *I'd love it.* Why would Simone write that if she didn't mean it? All right, then. She'd call her after the concert.

No. She'd been saying that about everything.

She would call her right now.

Her finger faltered as she tried to tap out the number. Not the Dupuytren's finger, just a quivering index finger that couldn't seem to find the right circles on the keypad. She started over. It took three tries.

She heard the click of the call being answered and knew at once that it was Simone. The same voice that had told her, "You nailed it, that's my dream." The same voice that had lifted in a bittersweet tremolo: *I Will Always Love You.*

"Hello?"

"It's me. Susannah."

Part Six

The Concert

After one has played a vast quantity of notes and more notes,
it is simplicity that emerges as the crowning reward of art.
Frederic Chopin

Chapter Twenty-Six

now

Susannah slipped the thin plastic covering off the hanger and shook out the dress she had bought for the concert. The knit was loose, flowing: a dark gray with flame-blue trim to match her eyes. Not the regulation black gown. She'd looked at those but decided to buy a dress she loved.

She laid the dress on the bed. Then she turned her wrist and gazed into the bowl of her palm, extending and retracting her fifth finger, like a little man taking a bow. The finger seemed fine, but she knew Dupuytren's was still there, waiting in her genes. Everyone had warned her: no matter what you did, the contracture might recur, the flexibility vanish. Even with radiation. You couldn't be certain the radiation had worked; you could only know it hadn't if your fingers tightened, lost their grace. The truth, hidden in the future, was that her fingers would either bend or not bend. If, when, how much—no one could tell her.

She had been relieved to learn that Simone didn't have the same condition—at least, not yet—although there had been a flash of disappointment that she wouldn't have someone to share it with, a musician who would understand. But they would share other things. She had promised to visit when Simone's baby was born. Simone told her they had an electronic keyboard; maybe the two of them could play together? Susannah started to explain that it wouldn't work—she played classical music, not electronic, and definitely not country—but caught herself in time. Why begin their relationship with a declaration of what she couldn't, or wouldn't, do? Then she told Simone about her concert, and Simone had been happy for her. "You go and knock 'em dead," Simone had declared. "I'll bet they clap their heads off."

Susannah didn't doubt that there would be applause; even if you were mediocre, people clapped. The only person who would really be able to tell if she was exceptional or merely adequate would be Carlo Perez-Smith—if he came. Another thing she didn't know.

She had talked with Libby one last time but hadn't asked about Perez-Smith. Libby had been uncharacteristically giddy, full of last-minute ideas. No, Susannah had told her, she did not think an encore was appropriate. And no, she didn't want flowers near the piano. She reminded Libby to reserve two seats in the center of the second row. One was for James. The other was for Aaron.

She tried not to think about Aaron. It was hard to imagine him not being there, yet it was just as hard to believe he would come.

Susannah dropped the dress over her head, straightened the hem, and went to the jewelry box on her dresser. She took out the diamond earrings that had belonged to Dana and put them on. Then she reached into the jewelry box again and found the necklace with the single sapphire. She raised it to her neck and fastened the clasp.

She looked at her hands one more time. The wedding ring on the left hand. The nodule, smaller but still there, on the right.

Then she closed the bedroom door and stepped into the hallway.

"James," she called. "You ready?" He'd made it clear that he didn't want to arrive ninety minutes early, as she had to, but there wasn't an alternative. If Aaron had been there, he and James could have driven in later. But Aaron wasn't there.

When James didn't answer, she called again, her tone sharper. "James. We're leaving in five minutes."

She heard the clatter of feet on the attic stairs. "Hey. Mom. You go on ahead." He swung through the doorway. "I'm gonna grab some pizza with the guys first. Andrew, Zev, Zev's cousin, he's here from Baltimore, remember I told you? There's plenty of time. Patrick can drop me at the concert hall."

"Patrick can *not* drop you at the concert hall." Sometimes James's independence was too much. She had told her father that James was easy, and he was, but this breezy shift of plans, this cavalier announcement that he was going off with his friends, was unnerving and unfair. She didn't need any surprises right now, so close to the performance. "You're coming with me. We already settled that."

"Mom. Be a pal. What does it matter how I get there?"

"The concert's all the way in Manhattan."

"Obviously. You told me, like, ten times."

She didn't like James's sarcasm any more than she liked his plan. "Patrick's driving you into Manhattan, just to be nice? I don't buy it."

"Not just to be nice. A bunch of them are going to a party. It's on the way."

"A party in the city? At sixteen years old?"

James gave her another *Mom, please* look. "Patrick's eighteen so *yes* he can drive at night, and *yes* in the city." He flashed one of his irresistible grins. "Not that *I'm* going to a party in the city. I'm going to hear you play your super-amazing sonata. So it's okay. Really. It's just a ride."

Susannah didn't know whether to be indignant or amused. Mostly, she felt outmaneuvered by her lovable and oh-so-charming son. As if sensing that she was wavering, James wrapped an arm around her shoulders. "Plus, this way I don't have to sit there for like, forever, with nothing to do. If they even let me into the auditorium, which they probably won't. I'll be in some nice safe pizza place instead of wandering around New York getting into trouble. See? It's better for everyone."

Susannah wished she knew what to insist on. "I think I'm supposed to be stricter."

"You're supposed to be nice. And you are."

She didn't have the heart to argue. Oh, why not let James go off with his friends? Otherwise, he'd slouch in the passenger seat, pouting the whole way into Manhattan, making her feel tense and guilty. She tried to find that elusive line between letting him know she cared and giving him space. If Aaron were here—well, he wasn't.

She sighed. It was better for her too, just as James had said. She could be alone and quiet before the performance instead of trying not to react to a put-upon teenager in the other seat.

"Patrick knows where the concert hall is?"

"Yup. And Google knows."

"You remember it begins at eight, right? You sure that's enough time to get pizza and still get there before the curtain?"

"Yes, Mom. Like I said."

"You have your ticket?"

James dropped his arm. "Have I ever not showed up for one of your things when I said I would?"

Unlike me. Susannah didn't know if he was clever enough to work in a guilt-inducing barb about the basketball game she had missed, or simply trying to sweet-talk her with reasons to trust him. "Fine," she conceded. "But don't forget your iPhone. I promised Grandpa you'd take pictures."

He arched an eyebrow, looking eerily like Aaron. "Me, forget my phone?"

"For Grandpa," she repeated.

"*Mom.* I said I'd do it, okay?" Then his face softened. "I'll be there for your big moment, I promise. I'll be the one with the giant Go, Mom sign."

Susannah softened too. "I'll be looking for it." She gave him a quick squeeze. "Behave yourself with Patrick and those hooligans."

"You know me. Mr. True Blue."

"The bluest."

"I'll text you when I get to the concert hall."

"Thanks, honey. I might not answer because I'll be prepping but do it anyway."

James gave one of his mock salutes. "You got it."

Susannah watched him saunter out of the room. Children were so careless with their parents' love. *Oh, this old thing?* Like an extra blanket thrown on the bed, there to be pulled up if it got cold.

She would drive in by herself, then. Aaron had never answered her text, but she'd saved a seat for him. She hoped, for James's sake as well as her own, that he wouldn't be seated next to an empty chair.

The evening she'd been preparing for. The bull's-eye she had kept in her sight as she shaped her bow, sharpened her arrow.

The rented Steinway was in place, right in the center of the stage, with two huge arrangements of gladioli and irises—even though she had told Libby she didn't want them—on either side. Susannah caught the scent of lemon from the polish they must have used on the hardwood floor.

She walked to the piano and dipped her head in acknowledgement. Not a bow. It had always seemed like bad form to do that before you played, a false humility. Then she looked out at the audience, search-ing for James's Go Mom sign, but couldn't find it. He'd probably been joking. Anyway, the rows were too dark. She couldn't see past the edge of the stage.

She seated herself on the bench, feeling the silence that came before, and included, the music. She could hear Vera's command, as if Vera were right there in the concert hall. *Play the notes but hear the music.*

Play for yourself, Vera had told her. Not for Perez-Smith, not even for Schubert.

Love the music. Only that.

She could feel the three women who had made her—circling her as she adjusted her position on the bench, smoothing the gray folds of her dress, brushing her hair. Corinne, who could sure pick out a tune. Dana, nurturing a talent she didn't share. And Vera, insisting that she could be more than a producer of notes.

She touched the keys and felt their welcoming readiness. The sonata was waiting for her, in all its purity and majesty. Waiting for her to know what it wanted of her, to understand it anew, in this very moment. To bring it to life, midwife to the music. And then, to let it go.

You didn't grab the music like a flag to hoist over the country of yourself. You simply played.

Susannah could feel her wrists, her knuckles, the arch of her fingers and the little pads. They knew every movement, every pattern and landing. She could do what she knew how to do, and the sonata would be perfect. Or she could let it all go, dare to simply be present at the birth of each sound, and the sonata would be real.

She raised her eyes. She saw the coral and peach and purple of the gladioli, the flowers she hadn't wanted. So much color, so much life.

Just play. Be Susannah, as she played. Fully alive, risking that some of the notes might be wrong. Risking that her finger might not do what her mind thought it should.

Her finger might fail, but she wouldn't. There was no failure because there was no success, nothing to achieve, nothing to get. Only something to give. Herself.

Just play.

The magic belonged to the music, not to her. It had never been absent.

Just play.

The celestial opening theme, piercing her with its yearning and hope. The octaves that used to be so easy—somehow she stretched that extra millimeter to the top note. Again and again, all the way to the exultant E-flat and the C that was entirely full, yet poised in expectation. The dark rumbling in the bass, like a call from the beyond. The return of the theme, reminding her of its hope, even as her finger slipped for the tiniest instant and then found its place.

She played. The call of the *andante sostenuto*, drawing the listener to a celestial union that could never be attained. And the answer, as the need to attain fell away. The perfection of each C-sharp. Nostalgia and regret and acceptance, all at once. Not sentimental, just as she had promised Vera.

Then the scherzo, full of delicacy and joy. And, finally, the abandon of the last movement—because after you had looked into the abyss, as Schubert had, joy was the only place to travel.

She played, listening as she played. It was an utterly new piece, different from the way she had practiced.

Forty-five minutes. The house lights went on. Everyone was standing and applauding madly, including Perez-Smith, whom Susannah recognized from his photos. He had come, he was right up front. She could see his mouth. Two syllables, over and over. *Bravo.* The applause was louder than she had thought possible.

She scanned the second row, searching for the faces she wanted to see. But there were two empty seats, right in the center.

Aaron hadn't come. Nor James.

No Aaron, that was bad enough. But no James?

She searched again, but the seats were still empty. They couldn't have missed this—her triumph, her transformation. Her mind raced. Maybe they had jumped up and squeezed past the shouting bodies so they could be the first to greet her backstage? She looked for two figures making their way along the row but saw nothing.

Everyone was looking at her now, smiling and cheering. She gave a deep bow, though the pain in her chest made it hard to breathe. Someone tossed a long-stemmed rose at the stage.

Libby ran toward her with a bouquet. More roses. Dark red, this time. Susannah took them and bowed again.

Libby leaned close and whispered, "Carlo's here, you know. And he *adores* you. I'll introduce you at the reception."

She made herself nod in agreement. Her face was wooden. Her arms, holding the flowers, were the limbs of a marionette. She walked backward, clutching the bouquet. The heavy velvet curtain gave way. She stumbled into the dressing room. It was empty.

She dropped the flowers, not caring where they fell, and reached for her purse. They had to have left word. She groped in the jumble of wallet and keys for her cell phone.

There were four text messages from Aaron. *Call me.*

Who the hell was he to tell her what to do, when he hadn't even shown up? But four messages? And where was James? Her hand shook as she tapped on Aaron's number.

"Susannah." His voice was ragged. "Have you heard from James?"

"No, I haven't. And he wasn't—"

Aaron cut her off. "Something's wrong. I got a text from him a couple of hours ago. His friend was going to drop him at my place—"

The phrase *my place* was like a knife. Susannah pushed the pain aside and made herself keep listening.

"—so we could go to the concert together. A surprise."

"You were?" The pain turned to a tentative joy.

"Were," he repeated. "But he never showed. I keep texting and calling, but he doesn't answer. It's not like him."

Susannah's heart missed a beat. James was constantly on his phone. Not calling, not answering his father's calls? Impossible—unless he was angry at Aaron and had left him waiting on purpose. Set this up to punish him.

He might be angry. *Ought* to be angry, since his father had walked out on him too. But James wouldn't have punished her as well, not this way. "No, it isn't," she said.

"Is he there? Have you seen him?"

"No. I mean, I don't know if he's here. The concert just ended."

"Any chance he left you a message?"

Not even the briefest *how did it go, your big concert?* His unsaid words hurt, but she told him, "Let me check."

She moved the phone away from her ear to look at the screen. A message or missed call from James should be there, along with the texts from Aaron, but maybe it hadn't registered in the shock of Aaron's four messages. She squinted at the screen. Nothing. Then she checked the history to be sure. "No. He didn't."

"No? Then what the hell is going on?"

Pinpricks of alarm shot up her spine, but she willed herself to stay calm. There were *please turn off your cell phone* signs all over the lobby. If James had arrived late—which he probably had, no thanks to that damn Patrick—they would have made him turn off his phone and he wouldn't have been able to text anyone, Aaron or her. And, being late, he would have had to stand in the back. That was why his seat was empty.

Now that the program was over, he was probably making his way backstage, full of elaborate stories about why he'd been delayed. Fine, he hadn't stopped to text. Why text when he'd be with her in person—just as soon as the over-stuffed, over-dressed patrons of the Isis Project stepped aside to let him through?

Susannah's concern shifted to irritation at the people who were keeping her son from reaching her. She wanted to shout *let him through, you idiots.* Instead, she told Aaron, "I'll try to call him."

She swiped the J's and tapped *James.* After six rings she heard his cheerful greeting. "Hey, it's me. Not the real me, the alternative me. But it will be the real me when I call you back, so leave a message."

Susannah frowned. He had to have turned on his phone by now. There was probably no signal in the auditorium, or else he was too busy trying to elbow his way through the crowd. She left a message anyway. "Where in the world *are* you, James?" Torn, again, between annoyance and fear, she chose annoyance. Fear would mean there was something to be afraid of. "I do expect a minimum of courtesy if you're going to miss my concert. I don't care what your story is. Call me back right now."

Her gaze swept the dressing area. She could hear Libby's voice, muted by the heavy curtains but audible as she bragged about how she had "discovered" Susannah. A few minutes, that was all she had before Libby burst backstage and dragged her off like a trophy.

She hit *redial.* "James. I'm going to keep pestering you until you pick up."

She waited, giving him a chance to answer. Maybe she hadn't stayed on the line long enough the first time. The auditorium was sure to be noisy with after-performance chatter; he probably hadn't heard the jangle of his phone or hadn't gotten to it in time. Maybe he'd forgotten to charge it.

Or maybe the ride with Patrick had fallen through. Maybe they'd lost track of time while they were having pizza, or gotten lost, and he was afraid she'd be furious at him for missing the concert. Well, she would be, once she knew he was all right.

Too many maybes. She needed James, not theories about where he was.

"Look, I'm not mad, okay? Just a little worried, so pick up, please, so I know you're okay." She waited, hoping James would come on the line, but there was no response. No click to signal that someone was there.

Damn it. What party were they going to, anyway? She should have asked. She didn't even know Patrick's phone number. What the hell was the matter with her? Shaking now, she tapped *Aaron* again. "No answer. I'm getting worried."

"You know for sure that he left the house?"

She didn't. She had left first. "No." She blinked. "You think he might still be at home?"

"It's a possibility."

No, she couldn't picture it. James wouldn't have let her down, forgotten, refused to come.

"I can't believe he's not here, in the auditorium."

"He'd be in his seat, wouldn't he? Or backstage. Or texting you."

She wanted him to be in the auditorium, but Aaron was right. Too much time had passed since the concert ended.

"The house is a logical place," Aaron said. "If James isn't answering his phone, it could mean he's asleep. Or passed out. Stoned, drunk, who knows."

"I just can't believe he would do that."

Tonight, of all nights. Her beautiful concert.

A beat passed, then another. "Still no text?" Aaron's tone was clipped. "No sign of him?"

Susannah threw a glance at the burgundy curtain that separated her from Libby, whose voice was growing more and more animated. "No."

"Then he's not in the concert hall. He's still on his way, for some bizarre reason, or he's still at home."

Home. Hearing Aaron call it *home* made her hurt and hope and rejoice. It was still Aaron's home, even if he hadn't been there.

"I'm heading there right now," he said.

"Yes. Me too."

Where else was there to look? Some unknown pizza restaurant? Some generic party in Manhattan?

Her heart cracked, split open. What kind of mother didn't even ask for the address? If you were a mother, it was what you did. Insisted. Paid attention.

"Hurry."

The word sent a bolt of fear through her body. Susannah grabbed her coat and flew down the corridor. She heard footsteps and a voice calling out to her. Turning, she saw Carlo Perez-Smith, with his big white teeth and eager wave. She felt the pull of his wave, beckoning her toward the very thing she had wanted so badly. Then she shuddered. Screw the reception. She raced down the steps, out the door, to the spot they'd reserved for her next to the back entrance. She threw open the car door. She had barely pulled it shut before slamming her foot on the gas pedal and careening out of the parking lot.

Chapter Twenty-Seven

now

Susannah tried James's number three more times during the hideously long drive from Manhattan to Abner's Landing. Each time she ordered, "Hey Siri, call James," her desperation grew. And each time the insipid voice replied, "Calling James," she wanted to scream with impatience. The third time she left another terse message. "James, call me *right now.*"

She pressed her foot on the accelerator—hard, fierce, nothing like the way she pressed the piano pedal—and shot across two lanes of the expressway. The highway unspooled in front of her, the other cars meaningless shapes in the darkness. She steered around them, daring them to get in her way, willing James to call her back.

What was the quickest route home at this hour? There was always construction, congestion. She had a vague memory of a sign warning drivers about nighttime work on the parkway; maybe she should go a different way. She scrolled through the radio stations, looking for the one that advertised up-to-the-minute updates on traffic and weather. Jabbing the button, she overshot the frequency, then found it on her second try. The weather report came on first, taking forever. Then a commercial for a new Toyota dealership. And finally, the traffic, cutting to a solemn voiceover.

"Route 26-A is still closed to traffic in both directions due to a southbound accident earlier this evening involving multiple fatalities. State police are not releasing details because occupants of one of the vehicles were minors. There were five people in the car, according to the police report. At least one is dead. A double-trailer freight truck was also involved, and the driver of the truck is believed to have suffered fatal injuries as well. We'll keep you posted, but at this time all traffic is being diverted onto alternate routes."

Susannah froze.

Foot glued to the pedal, hands like talons on the steering wheel, she sped into the black tunnel of the road ahead. Her fault. The words pounded on her temples. Her fault. For letting him go off with Patrick, pretending to be sweet but secretly relieved.

Please, she begged. A single word. *Please.*

She arrived at the house before Aaron. Barely stopping to turn off the ignition, she abandoned the car in the middle of the driveway, the door hanging open, and burst into the kitchen. The smell of grilled cheese assaulted her. James had been here, eaten a sandwich. A light was on in his room, and a wild hope shot into her chest. Maybe he was there, as Aaron thought. Asleep, stoned. She forgave him already.

"James!" she yelled. "James!" Oscar sidled into the living room, slithering across her ankles. She scanned the deserted room. Then she pried the cat away—gently, because he was James's cat—and tore up the stairs. James's bedroom was empty. His phone charger dangled from an outlet but the phone, like James, was gone.

She looked at the clothes he had tossed on the floor, jeans and a mustard yellow tee-shirt. Then she ran downstairs again and looked around, hungrily, as if she'd missed something essential. Oscar arched his back.

The screech of brakes, a car door slamming, then Aaron's step on the deck. She wheeled around when she heard him stride into the house, dropping her purse onto the floor. The cat jumped up, indignant, and ran off. Without thinking, she moved into the circle of Aaron's arms. No apology, no explanation, no checking to see if he would let her do that.

He embraced her quickly before stiffening and pulling away. *He doesn't know*, she thought. If he knew, he wouldn't pull away like that. "There was a bad accident," she whispered. "That's why 26-A is closed."

Aaron gave a curt nod. "Yes, I tried to go that way but they'd blocked it off. I had to circle around or I'd have been here sooner."

He was angry, not worried. After eighteen years, she could read his face: he thought James had fallen asleep or gotten caught up in a video game. Beneath the stony exterior, he was seething.

"26-A is the road to the parkway." Her throat was like a vice. She had to squeeze out each word. "There were five of them in the car, heading south, to the city. Five minors."

At least one is dead.

If it hadn't been for her concert, James wouldn't have been in the path of that truck.

If she'd insisted that he ride with her, he would have been safe.

If she'd been a better mother.

If. What was the pivotal moment, when something she did, or didn't do, flung him in front of that freight truck?

Aaron brushed her words aside. "Don't be ridiculous. There's no reason to imagine that some accident on a state road has anything to do with James's behavior and his unfathomable arrogance in missing your concert."

Susannah shook her head. It had everything to do with it.

"It's Saturday night," he said. "A lot of kids are driving around. The probability—"

She didn't give a crap about probability. That was all Aaron ever talked about. Logic, statistics. "When has James *not* come home without calling or texting? Not answered his phone?" She held Aaron's gaze, daring him to propose an answer she hadn't already considered and dismissed. "What else could it be? You tell me."

"I can't tell you anything, Susannah. That should be obvious." She heard the bitterness in his words. "You haven't wanted to hear anything I've had to say for quite a while."

What was he talking about? The stupid radiation? Why was he holding onto that? It had nothing to do with James.

She saw his face harden. Insane to still care about the radiation. She knew she shouldn't let herself get pulled into a debate that was already settled, but couldn't help herself. "It was my hand. My decision."

"Your hand." Aaron gave an angry snort. "That's the main thing, isn't it? You haven't really been here, ever since this business started with your hand."

"*Me*? I'm not the one who left."

"And why do you think I did?"

Susannah felt something sick and ugly rise up between them, pushing them further and further apart. This terrible thing wasn't bringing them together. It was making them hate each other.

She grabbed her purse from the floor and dug for her cell phone. "I'm trying him again." She heard the phone ring, five times, six times, knowing James wouldn't answer because the unspeakable had happened. *Hey, it's me. Not the real me.*

Everything she had been moving toward, with a single-minded devotion. The performance. Perez-Smith. Shit, all of it. Dust, spittle, nothingness.

Take everything else, only not this, not James.

The jingle of her phone cut into the silence. She felt a surge of joy, almost as unbearable as the terror. *James.* She'd been wrong. The gods were merciful after all.

But it wasn't his special ring, only that hideous marimba. She drew back, dropped the phone as if it had stung her. If the caller wasn't James, she didn't care. The marimba went on and on. Yet she had to know, just in case. Instinctively, she switched to speakerphone just as Libby's voice, loud and irritated, filled the room.

"Where in the world did you *go*? Carlo is totally dying to meet you. He has a whole new idea about how to make you the centerpiece of his project, you lucky dog. So call me back right this second."

Oh, for fuck's sake. Susannah wanted to throw the phone across the room, smash it into a million pieces. But she couldn't. James might call.

The terror hit her anew, hard as a fist. She doubled over, knuckles pressed to her mouth, and stumbled to the couch. No legs, no bones, just a useless sack of a body, like the pile of clothes James had dropped on the floor.

The phone rang again, with its cruel gaiety. It was Libby, even though it had only been a minute. "I mean it, Susannah, where the fuck *are* you? You don't get to play your little sonata and then run off. People are expecting you to show up at the reception, that's part of the deal. Not to mention poor Carlo chomping at the bit to talk to you. That's what you wanted, right?" There was a pause, and then she added, "I'm doing my best here, stalling for time. But call me ASAP. Or better yet, get your sweet little ass right back here."

Susannah couldn't stand it. She looked at Aaron, begging him to share her horror. Why wasn't he saying anything? Did he think she was upset about Libby's call, fearful that she might be missing her chance with Carlo Perez-Smith, instead of fearful about her son? Was that who he thought she'd become?

She pushed herself into a sitting position. "Aaron. Please."

He wasn't putting the pieces together. The bargain she had made, years earlier.

When James was born, she had set her professional career

aside—defying Vera, denying the very thing she'd been working so hard to attain. She hadn't known she would do that until she saw him, slick and howling and oh-so-new. Just by the fact of his birth, James was what she had never been and would never be. She had looked at him and the vow had formed itself. *You come first. You will never doubt who you are or where you belong.*

If that meant setting her career aside, then she would set it aside, with joy. Teaching, local performances, summer institutes, all that was fine because it kept her near. To aim for anything more was to break her vow. *I will do this, if James can stay safe.*

She had kept her bargain for nearly sixteen years—until now, when she had dared to reach higher. Now anything could happen, and it had.

"Aaron." Susannah made herself say the words. "I think James was in that car, the accident on 26-A. Patrick was driving them into the city, five of them. It's the road they would have taken, at that very time. It all fits."

Aaron arched an eyebrow. "That's a bit dramatic. There's no reason to assume that accident has anything to do with James."

She wanted to smack him. Why was he acting so pompous and uptight? This wasn't about who was right. It was about James.

And then she saw. He was as frightened as she was. This was what he did, when he was frightened.

Everything snapped into focus. Everything that had happened between them these past weeks—it was all there, arrayed before her. The entire score, from the opening theme to its echo in a minor key. Statement and response, crescendo and diminuendo. And the final suspension, aching for resolution.

The resolution was up to her. She was the home note. In music, it was called the tonic. The same word for something that healed and restored.

She reached across Aaron and pulled her phone out of the crevice between the cushions where it had fallen. "I think we should call the State Police instead of guessing. They'll know more than some damn radio station."

She tapped out the letters for State Police and swiped through the endless list of cities. There were too many, in places she'd never heard of, upstate or hundreds of miles away. The order made no sense. Who cared how many fucking stars they had?

Then she felt Aaron's hand on her arm. "Here," he said, extending his phone. "I've got it. This is the one we want."

Susannah turned to meet his gaze. Something had shifted in him too. He was joining her, not taking over. "Thanks." She peered at the number on his screen and tried to type it onto her own keypad. Her finger was clumsy, stupid. She kept making mistakes. Eight instead of five, an extra four.

"I can do it," Aaron offered, but she shook her head. No.

I can make my finger reach an octave. I can make it do this.

After her fourth try, the call went through. Someone answered, sounding flat and bored. Susannah tried to explain, and the person, whoever he was, transferred her to another department. She had to begin all over again, explaining who she was and why she had to know. Another transfer. She couldn't do it, not a third time.

Quietly, Aaron took the phone from her. Not because she had done it wrong, but to share the effort. Susannah watched his face while he spoke to the officer. He said a few words, asked a question. Then he said, "All right. Thank you."

His face was grim as he ended the call. "They can't release any information about an open police report. They said we could try calling a few hospitals."

"What are you saying?" Her voice sharpened. "They won't talk to us, his parents? That's insane. He's not even sixteen."

"Jesus. I can't believe I didn't tell them he's a minor." Then Aaron stopped himself. "No, that's not right. They knew the accident involved minors. They have to call the parents, if it concerns a minor child. The police, the hospital. Someone."

Her eyes grew wide. "Does that mean he wasn't in the car?"

As if in reply, the sound of an engine, roaring out of nowhere, made them jump to their feet. *James.* Susannah's heart soared. The phone call from Libby had been a false alarm—cruel but forgiven now, because this time it really was James, about to turn up the driveway.

She rushed to the front door, giddy with relief, but the sound grew fainter as the car continued down the road. She wheeled around, her eyes seeking Aaron's, glazed by the betrayal.

"You keep jumping to conclusions," he snapped. "Bad, good, bad. It just makes it harder."

His harshness, especially after the softening of the moment before, was like a slap. Their terrible apartness returned, slashing through her again.

Then, to her astonishment, Aaron crumpled into the brown chair. "This is all my fault. James should have been riding with me tonight. From our home." His shoulders jerked, and he buried his face in his hands. "I've been such an asshole."

"Aaron. No." She knelt beside him. "No. It wasn't you."

"I left you alone, for god's sakes." The words were jagged, raking the air between them. "I felt like you had no use for me, like you'd pushed me outside the circle of things you cared about. But that was just my own damn need to feel smart and important. To keep things the same, when you were growing and doing what you'd always wanted. Holding onto my pride, instead of being proud of you." The trembling spread from his shoulders, across his body. "I'm so sorry. You deserved better from me. I let you down. I let James down."

"No." Susannah wrapped her arms around him. "It was me. I hid from you—the money, Oscar, my treatment—like you would try to take something away from me, if I let you in. I was so stupid." Her eyes filled with tears. "I did push you out. That's why you felt that way."

"I couldn't seem to find my place. That wasn't your fault."

"It was. I made you feel irrelevant, just like you said. I was so focused on some imaginary future. My hand, my career." Her voice broke. "I had no idea how it would hurt to lose the people I love, right now."

He raised his head. "We haven't lost James."

"I lost you."

"You didn't lose me, you just misplaced me." He took her face in his hands. "We're not going to lose each other. And we're not going to lose James."

The very words she longed to hear. Yet they might not be true.

Oh, she would give anything to turn back the clock. To say to James, "No, I forbid you to go out for pizza and get dropped off. I forbid you to leave my sight."

You couldn't do that. You had to let your child go. At birth, or later.

She started to shake. The room blurred.

Then, all at once, the shaking stopped. Everything was still. It was like the silence at the bottom of a note, the place between. There was only the lingering smell of toasted bread and the dust motes jiggling in splinters of light.

She released her breath, its weightless substance filling her body. The shape of herself.

The trill of her cell phone shattered the quiet. She jerked, recoiling at the horrid little jingle. It couldn't be Libby, not again.

"Maybe it's the police," Aaron said. "Realizing we're his parents and calling us back."

Susannah felt for her phone again. The caller ID was Cedar Ridge Memorial Hospital. She grabbed Aaron's hand, digging her nails into his flesh. With her other hand, she pressed the green circle.

"Mom?"

James. She could hardly hear him, she was crying so hard. "Mom," he said, his voice breaking. "Mom, something awful happened."

Nothing could be awful, because he was alive. "Oh James," she breathed. "My darling boy."

"Mom. There was an accident." She could hear the agony as he struggled to form the words. "Patrick's dead." Then, again, in disbelief. "Dead."

Gently, Aaron took the phone and tapped *speaker.* "Where are you?"

James made a choking sound. "I'm still at the emergency room. I'm fine, a couple of stupid bruises. But Dad, they're such morons here."

I'm fine. Those were the only words that mattered.

"You're at Cedar Ridge? The doctors said you were okay?"

"They took all of us here." James's voice caught in another strangled sob. "Well, all of us except Patrick. They took him to another part of the hospital."

"Oh, sweetheart."

"He was drinking, Mom. Like you probably figured." That strangled sound again, tearing into her flesh. "But he didn't deserve this. Not this."

No, no child did. "My darling, I'm so sorry."

Aaron strained forward. "What did the doctors say? Why didn't anyone call us?"

Susannah held onto Aaron's hand, letting him ask the questions. She didn't care about the answers. All she cared about was the sound of James's voice.

"They were supposed to call you," James said. "I mean, like the second we got there. Like we couldn't even pee without our parents giving permission. But I knew Mom was at her concert and wouldn't have her phone on her. Anyway, I couldn't call her right before she played and mess it all up for her."

Susannah winced. His explanation, brutal and thoughtful, cut right into her soul.

"So I tried to remember your cell, Dad, only it was like I had this block. I mean, I never actually memorized either of your numbers, I just hit *Mom* or *Dad* on my phone. But I didn't have my phone any more. It flew out in the crash or something—I don't know, it was all too fast—but it was gone. I didn't have it."

Another broken sound, and then the rest of the words poured out. "I guess I was starting to freak out about how pissed you'd be, plus Patrick, everything. I must have switched one of the digits on your number, I don't know, I couldn't think straight. Anyway, they kept trying the number I gave them, but no one answered. Because it wasn't the right number."

Susannah tightened her grip on Aaron's hand. The silence of the past two hours was beginning to make sense.

James's voice rose, cracking. "They kept bugging me for another number they could try, but then things got crazy. Andrew starting freaking out for real, screaming and yelling, and everyone got all caught up with that, and I guess they kind of bumped me down their list since I wasn't hurt or anything. I was sitting there for, like, forever, and then finally this social worker came in and that's when I remembered Mom's number."

"Did anyone examine you?" Aaron asked.

"Some doctor looked me over, like the second I got here, but they won't let me leave till the neurologist sees me. That's their big thing, he's the one who has to give the all clear." His voice broke again, and he sounded like the five-year-old Susannah had been longing for, only days earlier. "I've been sitting in this stupid examination room in a fucking paper *dress* for two whole hours. I gotta get out of here, Dad."

"We'll be right there, son." Aaron pulled Susannah into the curve of his arm. "They're doing the right thing. They need to make sure you don't have a concussion."

"I don't have a concussion." James sounded petulant now. His adolescent righteousness filled Susannah with an absurd joy.

"Do the hospital people want to talk to us?"

Susannah heard the murmur of voices, and then James got back on the line. "She said if you're coming, you can bring the insurance card and all that stuff. They're not going to do anything till you get here since I'm not, like, having a heart attack."

"Just sit tight and do what they tell you," Aaron repeated. "We're on our way." Then he said, "We love you. Everything will be all right." Slowly, he disconnected the call.

Susannah stared at the phone. "Oh my god." She began to laugh and cry. Laughter, because James was alive. And then tears, because he might not have been. And because someone else's child was gone.

The mother of James's friend—a woman she didn't know, but a mother, like her—had lost her child tonight. Compassion welled up in her. The vulnerability, just from being alive, from loving, was almost too much to bear.

She turned to Aaron, her eyes wet. Then she took his hand, pressed it to her face, kissed it again and again.

"Come," he said. "Let's get our son."

Part Seven

The Music

The piano ain't got no wrong notes.
Thelonious Monk

Chapter Twenty-Eight
later

B ands of light from the open window, gold tinged with pink, spilled across the piano. Susannah could hear the trilling of birds and the hissing of insects, the whoosh of the breeze. In the distance, an airplane rumbled. She could almost hear the lapping of the Hudson.

She readied her hands and began to play. Bach, the impeccable union of passion and intention. After a few minutes she heard James come into the room, felt him stop in the doorway to listen. She kept playing, the beautiful harmonies appearing, one after another, from the movement of the separate lines.

She could feel James's hesitation. Partly, it was a new fragility, ever since the accident. The James she had known—so easy and light and certain of the world's benevolence—had become tentative and private. She understood. She had no desire to push him. Only to be there, and to play for him, because that was something she could do. Partly, she knew, it was James finding his way from the boy he had been to the man he was becoming. He was in-between, and that itself was a fragile place.

James crossed the room and sat next to her on the bench, leaning against her the way he used to when he was small. Susannah could feel the soft push of his shoulder against hers, a gift she hadn't expected but accepted with a quiet gratitude. She would be leaving on a tour in the morning. Two weeks, six cities. Perez-Smith had arranged everything—the venues, the dates, the airlines and hotels. It was more than she had dared to imagine, yet she'd hesitated when he proposed the idea. Was this really the right time to break away and put her music first? The pressure of James's arm seemed to say, "It's good, Mom. Go for it."

She shifted to Chopin's F-minor ballade, one of Aaron's favorites. The whole piece depended on those top notes. Maybe her finger would do exactly as she wanted and maybe it wouldn't, but the music could withstand her imperfection.

Then she heard other footsteps. Aaron entered the room and stood behind her, listening, the way he used to. She listened with him—this one sound, born in this very moment, and then the next sound. Like a flock of birds, each taking flight for the first time.

Aaron had urged her to accept Perez-Smith's proposal. The idea, Perez-Smith explained, was to increase her visibility before the CD came out. Later, after the CD was issued, might have made more sense, but Susannah knew that *later* was unknowable. Not only because of Dupuytren's, but also because of her father, who was going to need her. And because of life itself, which was always changing.

"Go," Aaron had told her. "Have an amazing time. We'll be here when you get back."

She let the ballade trail off and began to improvise. No written score to show her the way, only a listening for what might come next. Something unknown. A leap of faith that it would be there.

A few of the notes were muddy, flawed. But it wasn't the notes that mattered.

It was the music.

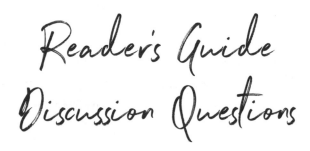

Reader's Guide
Discussion Questions

1. Susannah sees herself as someone who puts her child first. Why is that so important to her? Do you think she's actually done that? At what point (or points) is that image of herself challenged?

2. What kind of mother is Dana? What about Corinne? In what ways is Susannah like each of them, whether she realizes it or not?

3. Dana's story of the *chosen baby* is one that Susannah both treasures and resents. What role does "being chosen" play in the book?

4. *Feeling powerless* is another recurring theme. What are some of the things that make Susannah feel powerless? How does she try to claim, or reclaim, a degree of power over each of them? Do you think she is successful?

5. How do nature and nurture interact in *The Sound Between the Notes*? In what ways is Susannah shaped by nature (heredity), and in what ways is she shaped by nurture (upbringing)? Which do you think is more important for her?

6. There are many points in the book when Susannah makes a choice—for example, to walk away from The Red Rooster, to have the radiation despite Aaron's objections, to contact Simone, to ignore Perez-Smith's eager wave. Which of these decisions, for you, was the essential turning point in the story?

7. What did you think of Aaron's behavior, at various points in the story? How did the concert—the events that led up to it, and the events that followed—change him? Do you think he was the agent of his own change, or did it all come from Susannah?

8. There are many scenes in the book that depict Susannah at the keyboard. Which was your favorite? Why?

9. Picture Susannah and her relationships—with her father, son, husband, sister—five years in the future. What do you see? Do you think she has become a member of that "elite echelon" of pianists? If not, why not?

10. What does the book's title mean to you?

Acknowledgments

A s with my first book, boundless thanks to the wisdom and tough love of my two writing mentors, Kathryn Craft and Sandra Scofield, who pushed me to open and go deeper, and deeper still, so the story could grow into what it needed to be.

Kathryn and Sandra helped me to become a better writer, but I wouldn't have been able to write this particular story without understanding music far better than I did in those early drafts. For that, I'm indebted to my piano teacher Raj Bhimani, whose gifts as a teacher are matched only by his gifts as a performer. Huge thanks, as well, to Marcia Eckert and Deborah Gilwood for their loving, sensitive guidance during our summer weeks of "piano camp," known to us fortunate participants as Pianophoria.

Special thanks to world-renowned pianist Misha Dichter, who kindly and generously spoke with me about his experience with Dupuytren's contracture, and to Anthony Gilroy, director of marketing for Steinway & Sons, who patiently answered all my questions about how to rent a Steinway for a concert.

And extra-special thanks to Seymour Bernstein, piano teacher extraordinaire, whose Master Class I had the good fortune to experience. Anyone who wishes to witness the profound relationship between music and life, as embodied in Seymour, would do well to watch Ethan Hawke's outstanding documentary *Seymour: An Introduction*.

I was also helped very much by reading the words of so many extraordinary musicians in the two-volume collection by Elyse Mach (1980 and 1988), *Great Contemporary Pianists Speak for Themselves*.

My understanding of adoption and the adoption triangle comes from my own experience. Love, sisterhood, and deepest respect to all those whose lives have been touched by adoption.

A manuscript is one thing; producing a beautiful book like this one is another! How fortunate I've been to work with Brooke Warner and Lauren Wise of She Writes Press, and with Crystal Patriarche, Tabitha Bailey, and Paige Herbert of Book Sparks—what a glorious team! And another enormous thank-you to the talented Julie Metz for knocking it out of the park again with her cover.

Others who helped along the way include the savvy beta readers at *The Spun Yarn*, my writing buddy Maggie Smith, and my ever-patient and loving partner, Tom Steenburg.

Finally, my gratitude to those who read my first book and gave me the courage to offer this second one.

About the Author

© David Heald 2018

Barbara Linn Probst is a writer of both fiction and nonfiction, living on an historic dirt road in New York's Hudson Valley. Her debut novel *Queen of the Owls* (April 2020) is the powerful story of a woman's search for wholeness, framed around the art and life of iconic American painter Georgia O'Keeffe. Recipient of numerous accolades and endorsements, *Queen of the Owls* was selected as one of the 20 most anticipated books of 2020 by *Working Mother* and one of the best Spring fiction books by *Parade Magazine*. It won the bronze medal for popular fiction from the Independent Publishers Association and was short-listed for the $2500 Eric Hoffer Grand Prize.

The Sound Between the Notes is Barbara's second novel. Like *Queen of the Owls*, it shows how art can help us to be more fully human.

Barbara is also the author of the groundbreaking book on nurturing out-of-the-box children, *When the Labels Don't Fit*. She has a PhD in clinical social work, blogs for several award-winning sites for writers, and is a serious amateur pianist. To learn more about Barbara and her work, please see http://www.barbaralinnprobst.com/

SELECTED TITLES FROM SHE WRITES PRESS

She Writes Press is an independent publishing company founded to serve women writers everywhere. Visit us at www.shewritespress.com.

Lost in Oaxaca by Jessica Winters Mireles $16.95, 978-1-63152-880-4
Thirty-seven-year-old piano teacher Camille Childs is a lost soul who is seeking recognition through her star student—so when her student unexpectedly leaves California to return to her village in Oaxaca, Mexico, Camille follows her. There, Camille meets Alejandro, a Zapotec man who helps her navigate the unfamiliar culture of Oaxaca and teaches her to view the world in a different light.

Magic Flute by Patricia Minger $16.95, 978-1-63152-093-8
When a car accident puts an end to ambitious flutist Liz Morgan's dreams, she returns to her childhood hometown in Wales in an effort to reinvent her path.

The Trumpet Lesson by Dianne Romain $16.95, 978-1-63152-598-8
Fascinated by a young woman's performance of "The Lost Child" in Guanajuato's central plaza, painfully shy expat Callie Quinn asks the woman for a trumpet lesson—and ends up confronting her longing to know her own lost child, the biracial daughter she gave up for adoption more than thirty years ago.

Play for Me by Céline Keating $16.95, 978-1-63152-972-6
Middle-aged Lily impulsively joins a touring folk-rock band, leaving her job and marriage behind in an attempt to find a second chance at life, passion, and art.

Warming Up by Mary Hutchings Reed $16.95, 978-1-938314-05-6
Unemployed and depressed former musical actress Cecilia Morrison decides to start therapy, hoping it will get her out of her slump—but ultimately it's a teen who cons her out of sixty bucks, not her analyst, who changes her life.

Start With the Backbeat by Garinè B. Isassi $16.95, 978-1-63152-041-9
When post-punk rocker Jill Dodge finally gets the promotion she's been waiting for in the spring of 1989, she finds herself in the middle of a race to find a gritty urban rapper for her New York record label.